P9-CFG-178

House on Fire

Also by Denis Hamill

Stomping Ground
Machine

House on Fire

Denis Hamill

THE ATLANTIC MONTHLY PRESS
NEW YORK

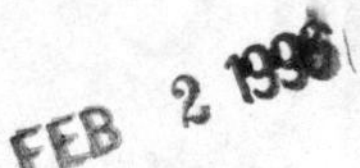

Published simultaneously in Canada
Printed in the United States of America

FIRST EDITION

Library of Congress Cataloging-in-Publication Data

Hamill, Denis.
House on fire / by Denis Hamill.—1st ed.
p. cm.
ISBN 0-87113-614-7
I. Title.
PS3558.A4217H68 1996
813′.54—dc20 95-38297

The Atlantic Monthly Press
841 Broadway
New York, NY 10003

10 9 8 7 6 5 4 3 2 1

Dedication

This book is for The Wild Kingdom, which is what I call my kids—Sean, Katie, Nell, with all my love.

Acknowledgments

I would like to thank Danny Gorman, retired FDNY firefighter, and Ray Garvey, retired NYPD cop, for their professional guidance. These two great friends and fathers also offered advice on both of those crucial elements of this book.

I'd also like to thank Dr. John Elefterakis, of Brooklyn, and Dr. Kevin Basralian, of Manhattan, for their medical guidance.

Part I

Prologue

Before he learned his wife and child were missing, Kevin Dempsey was almost a happy man.

He stood alone on the sidewalk, gazing up at his new house.

The house was almost a century old, but he thought he should give it a name. Like a castle or a country or a ship.

Or a child.

Or a family.

A house should have a name. But I'll wait until Polly and Zoe get home from Disney World, he thought. Another three hours. Let them help choose a name for the new house.

He marveled at the three-story limestone here on Langston Place in Windsor Terrace in Brooklyn, a neighborhood of drowsy, tree-lined streets sandwiched between the meadows of Prospect Park and the eternal pastures of Greenwood Cemetery. The house was his and Polly's now and would someday belong to his three-year-old daughter, Zoe. And her future brothers and sisters, as many as Kevin could convince Polly to bring into the world.

And into the new house.

Let it overflow with kids, Kevin thought. Let kids with dirty faces and untied sneakers lean from every window, sit on every stoop step, run in and out of every door, all day long, loud and boisterous, exploding with the life Kevin Dempsey would help give them.

But these days Polly was saying she wanted no more babies because Zoe had been a breech birth, requiring a C-section, leaving another unsightly scar. This scar was in addition to those left by the Halloween fire. . . .

If future children required similar surgery, as was likely, Polly said she wanted no part of them. But Kevin hoped Polly would change her mind when she returned with Zoe from a week in Disney World, to find that Kevin had bought the family a new house as her birthday surprise.

Kevin opened the wrought-iron gate that was cemented into the century-old foundation blocks of the areaway. He held the metal handle of the gate, rotating the smooth knob into his curled right palm, feeling the solid coldness next to his sweaty skin on this early September morning.

He stepped up into the areaway, clicking his leather soles on the coarse stone, and let the gate spring shut with a firm, locking clang. It sounded like swords crossing, he thought. The proud clatter of a homeowner closing his gate on the world. A sound that let everyone know that this was now Kevin Dempsey's property.

No small thing, owning a piece of the world, Kevin thought. It was like another kind of birth, another entity for which he was responsible, another dependent that relied on him and his toil for survival. A home for him and Polly to shelter and raise their children, to build their family into a vital social unit that would establish an important place in the world. This house made fatherhood, his proudest accomplishment, bona fide.

Kevin brushed past the limestone stoop that led up to a private second-story tenant's entrance and walked to the street-level door. Scrawled ornamental iron gates curlicued over the windows. He unlocked and swung open the thick oak door and inhaled the warm breath of the new house, a smell he was sure he would live with for the rest of his life.

The gray enamel vestibule had a flagstone floor and a second wooden door that led to a dank mysterious storage space under the stoop. In there, he thought, I will keep the children's sleds and bicycles and baby carriages. Little Zoe can keep her doll carriage in there too, and I can store spare tires and odds and ends for the car. When I have sons old enough to play baseball and football, their equipment will be right there for them to grab on the way to Prospect Park. They will rule the gridirons and the diamonds the same way he had when he played with his best friend, Anthony Scala, through the glorious seasons of his youth.

Today was for celebration, Kevin thought.

Even Anthony Scala, once his inseparable pal, now his family doctor, whom he usually only saw these days when he was ill, would be dropping by the party to help celebrate the new house. If anyone would understand the true value of a house it would be Anthony, Kevin thought. A second mortgage on the Scala house had sent Anthony through medical school. Zoe would have that same security now.

Kevin thought more of Zoe and the children of his future as he pushed through a third door to a second vestibule, where metal hooks for winter coats lined the wall. Here he had laid the indoor-outdoor carpeting for snow boots and umbrellas. Through this portal the kids would enter from hours of sledding on Monument and Suicide and Sugar Bowl hills in the park, their faces scoured red with cold, undressing and aching for a cup of hot chocolate and a place close to Daddy's big armchair by the roaring fireplace in the twenty-five-foot oak-trimmed living room.

Inside the third door from the street was the long hallway where the kids would slap their wet gloves on the steaming radiator to dry before running down the corridor to the country kitchen, where a Mulligan stew would bubble on the stove in winter and barbecue smoke would drift in from the back yard in summer.

A flight of steps led from the hallway to the bedrooms upstairs. A second staircase led to a future tenant's apartment on the third floor. Kevin squeezed the top of the newel post in his large left hand and rubbed his flesh on the old polished varnish. Mine! he thought.

He stepped on the first of sixteen wooden steps, the third one squeaking like a kitten as his weight lifted off it. Kevin grabbed a foot of banister at a time, and then let his hand retreat over its beveled length until he was certain he had touched every single inch of it as he ascended. He traced his right hand along the smooth plaster of the wall as he climbed.

The stairwell was like a lifeline running through the center of the new house, offering passage to its inhabitants and visitors to wander and explore and make use of every room, branching off into bedrooms that were smaller satellite worlds of their own. Each step up the stairs of the new house was like a milestone in Kevin Dempsey's life.

This is mine, he thought again.

He had not inherited it or won it or chiseled it from some poor naive widow. He had earned it with his hands and his back amid smoke and flames, and now it belonged to the family he was born to raise. And these were his stairs, the symbolic sum total of all his life's work. The steps of a house that would be a home, for his wife and child and their Dempsey children of tomorrow, on into the ages. If he was a Brit, like Polly, maybe he'd call it the House of Dempsey.

Kevin reached the first landing, and with both arms he swung wide the oak doors to the master bedroom. Light slashed through the wooden shutters across the gleaming parquet floors and the king-sized bed with the brass headboard that the moving men had set up. Kevin imagined himself and Polly making all those new babies here in this room, fucking on the bureau top and the floor and on the bed and in her rocking chair by the window. He could hear her playful laughter and her leering taunts and then her lustful moans.

And now, as Kevin walked through the twenty-five-foot-long bedroom toward the two children's rooms in the rear, he pulled open another door and looked into Zoe's room, a fantasyland of Disney characters: Mickey, Pluto, Donald, Goofy. Wallpaper, curtains, sheets, lamps. Boxes of toys and clothes were stacked on the floor and dresser top. Kevin could almost see little Zoe lying in her canopy bed staring up at him through the gauzy cover and smiling as he read her a Pippi Longstocking bedtime story, here in the quiet of the back of the house overlooking the new back yard. Someday Zoe would have a little sister to help dress and play dolls with. Zoe would do her sister's hair and read her the same stories that Kevin now read Zoe.

There was another room next to Zoe's that for now would be okay for guests but soon would be for his first son. There would be bunk beds when the second and third sons arrived. There would be boxing gloves for each of them hanging from the wall. He'd build a ring in the cellar. Like their father had, they would fight in the New York Golden Gloves, and the whole neighborhood would show up to cheer.

Kevin already had a desk arranged with a home computer and printer for the kids' homework and a set of the *Encyclopaedia Britannica* and a complete collection of Nancy Drew and the Hardy Boys in the bookcases and an illuminated globe and a big Webster's dictionary. This would serve as Kevin's office until he had a son who would live and grow in the room and make it his own, with posters of great athletes and rock stars on the walls.

And for the first two years, maybe three, they would rent out the third floor to some yuppie couple willing to pay enough rent to cover two-thirds of the mortgage. After that, when he had a lieutenant's salary and, later, chief's pay, Kevin would turn the top floor back into bedrooms for more and more children of his own. He wanted six, maybe even seven children to live with him here, top to bottom. He wanted to hear them fighting and playing and growing up all around him in this great new house in Brooklyn. The house, that no matter what he and Polly and Zoe might call it, all the neighbors on the block and in the neighborhood would come to know as the Dempsey house.

Because from this building would come, every morning, a great family of children named Dempsey who would be the best-read kids in the neighborhood and would excel at sports and at whatever they chose as a trade or a craft or a calling or an art or a dream in life. The Dempsey boys would be honor roll students and Golden Gloves champions and Zoe would be the first woman mayor of New York.

There would be no limits to what the children of Kevin Dempsey, man of the Dempsey house, could do in the world. And it would all start here, in this house, in that bed, with his wife, Polly.

And all the children to come under this roof will be blessed with a great big sister named Zoe, his firstborn, who will pass on all that Kevin Dempsey and Polly Edgeworth Dempsey can teach her, he thought.

This was going to be the Place, the house where Kevin did his most important work in life. As a husband and father. As a man. Man of the house. House that he owned. Owned from hard work.

So he couldn't wait to see Polly's face when she saw the new house—her house, of course, as much as Kevin's. Lady of the house. House she deserved.

Polly's plane would be landing in about two hours, bringing her home with his Zoe from a week in Orlando, Florida.

Zoe would go nuts, rush to Kevin with the crooked turn in the right knee, a bone condition that would require her to wear a corrective brace to bed at night until she was seven. She'd leap up and hug Daddy, the adorable little fingers locking around his thick neck, kissing his face all over, telling him in her squeaky excited voice, "I love you, Daddy!"

Kevin lived to hear those words from his baby. He had cut his hands to jerky, plastering and wallpapering her room himself. (Well, his best buddy Carmine from the firehouse helped too, between six-packs.)

Kevin had worked two extra jobs—bartending and driving car service—around his fireman's schedule to save the money for the down payment for the new house.

Now he prayed Polly would like it. Maybe a happy home would even get her to wear again the dead-tight faded blue jeans she wore for him on the night they first made love. So he could wrestle them off her on the big bed, in the new bedroom, over her perfect ass, the ass that four years ago graced thousands of magazine and billboard jeans ads. Before the fire ruined her modeling career. Before her father lost her modeling money in the BCCI banking fiasco of 1991—after losing most of his own in the stock market crash of 1987. Before the stretch marks and the C-section scars from the pregnancy and birth of Zoe added to the scars left by the burns from the fire at the Halloween party. Before Kevin Dempsey had saved her life and courted her throughout her hospitalization and convalescence. Before she had grown cold and indifferent in bed after three years of marriage. Before she had become obsessed again with talk of money and security and status.

If the house made her happy and if he could have her again the same way she was in the beginning, that would be worth it all.

He needed some happiness in his life right now.

Kevin had enough other stress. His older brother, Frank, a cop lieutenant, was facing indictment for supposedly stealing a million and a half dollars in drug money from a police evidence room. And about twenty guests were due here in the new house in three hours for Polly's surprise twenty-seventh birthday party.

The new house was Kevin's surprise birthday gift to Polly. It had cost him $289,000, and in the buyer's market of the mid-nineties he'd only needed a $40,000 down payment and managed to get a 6½ percent mortgage with three points going to the bank. Working for the Fire Department was a passport to home ownership. Banks loved city workers, especially uniformed services, because even in a fiscal crisis they were the last ones laid off.

Kevin had been trying to convince Polly to go back to modeling part-time again. She was reluctant because of her age. Twenty-seven is considered old in a racket where fourteen-year-old anorexics are considered hot. Add motherhood to the résumé, and the agencies have you doing yogurt and denture cream ads for the equivalent of half-price senior citizen discount money. She could no longer model underwear or bathing suits, due to the various scars. And close-up facial shots were out because the faint burn marks were picked up by the flood-lit fashion lens.

But Kevin knew she could still do runway and catalog work. Polly had said that was demeaning, "for over-the-hill bimbos." But Kevin had worked his ass off for the down payment on the house, and he was going to insist she go back to work. It was important for her mental health too. Kevin believed work was the food of the soul. It proved your self-worth. It gave you value and standing. Work was life.

Motherhood was a miraculous calling. But for Polly motherhood would never be enough, and it also caused some resentment. She called her stretch marks and C-section scar "war wounds." A few times, Kevin had caught her looking sideways at Zoe, as if she were partly responsible for ending her career. Her youth. Freedom. She'd throw a glance and then an icy double-take fix on the kid, as if she were a crime victim looking at a suspect in a lineup. It worried Kevin.

That's one of the reasons he'd sent them down to Disney World. He needed her out of the way to close on the house and arrange the surprise party. But, more important, Kevin wanted Polly and Zoe to be alone together, just mother and daughter, without the distractions of domestic pressures and friends calling to say how well they were doing out there on the circuit of the beautiful people from which she came: the designer parties, the tropical shoots, the film festivals, the cruises, the premieres. The places where models were always invited as party favors for the rich and powerful.

Of course Polly had been reluctant to go to Disney World at first because it was so "vulgarly American and housewifely." But when Kevin pushed it, saying Zoe deserved the break, the mother-daughter bonding, she finally gave in. Kevin meant to make the travel arrangements, but Polly had said no, adamant that she make the plans herself. She said she needed at least three thousand dollars for the trip. Kevin couldn't really afford it, but he gave her the money and told her not to put any more on the credit cards because the interest would be a killer.

Now Polly was coming home to a surprise birthday party and a new house, and Kevin was as anxious as an air traffic controller on a stormy night.

If there were three of me, we'd all be in a fucking puzzle factory, he thought.

Kevin rattled down the stairs now and moved through the living room toward the kitchen. He looked around at the furniture, all in its place. He had tipped the yarmulke-wearing men from Moishe the Movers a hundred dollars and they put everything down gently, so the newly varnished floors wouldn't get scraped. As he searched for scratches, he rubbed his eyes.

He was exhausted from all the preparations and worried sick about his jammed-up brother Frank and nervous about Polly's reaction. They'd been sparring lately, she pissed off about no money and he grumpy under the financial and emotional and physical strain of secretly closing on the house. And now he was worried whether she'd like it.

The only thing that calmed him down was writing short stories in his head, yarns that blended real life with imagination to produce a fresh concoction of how Kevin Dempsey saw the world around him. He had been writing these stories since he was a five-year-old kid, when he used to lock himself in the L-shaped bathroom of the tenement apartment with a pencil and a copybook, kneeling on the tile floor, using the toilet seat as a writing table. For Kevin, this was his chance to rearrange the furniture of the world. These "Kevin stories," as his sister Margie called them, kept him sane. Some people went out and painted graffiti on the Jersey Palisades; some ran marathons, kept bees, chanted mantras, or cared for the sick to unload stress and anxiety. Kevin Dempsey wrote stories. For him, they were reality's second draft. They made order out of chaos, gave him focus.

So before the guests arrived, Kevin enjoyed these last few minutes alone in the new house, the first he'd ever owned. Alone with the new smells and the new contours of the walls; alone to eavesdrop on the creaks and knocks and shudders; alone with the idiosyncracies of the house the Dempseys would inhabit. Kevin would have a hand in shaping the soul and personality of this house the way he shaped a story. He would craft it in the image of his own life and his new family. He would nourish it with smells and sound and laughter and the magic of kids. Great parties would rumble the floorboards and rattle the glass in the window frames. Plaster would creak and crack to fit the footfalls of the many children. Eventually the house itself would resemble a Dempsey, he thought with a smile.

He walked from the living room into the country kitchen, with the island butcher-block countertop in the center surrounded by bar stools. The copper-colored stove, refrigerator, washer, dryer, dishwasher blended in with the rural motif.

Sun spilled through the two rear barred windows. He felt the germ of one of his Kevin stories coming on.

Outside, in the back yard, a forty-foot blue spruce unfolded its fingers to a sunny September sky. Beneath the tree, a hyper stray mother cat, black and shiny as a night sea, hunched in front of an overturned wheelbarrow under which she had sheltered a litter of three kittens. The mother cat spit and hissed at a scroungy one-eyed orange tom who sat impassively on the fence dividing the yards. The tom had also lost an ear in some forgotten combat. He had a head the size of a cantaloupe and slowly winked the single cold eye as the mother cat paced back and forth in front of her young, halting her prance only to snarl and hiss at the interloper, which Kevin now named the Pirate.

First a black kitten emerged from under the wheelbarrow, goofy on unsturdy legs, meowing for food. It was followed by a black-and-white kitten, also looking for milk. Then came a third kitten, orange, with markings similar to the Pirate's. The mother, in a frenzy, nudged or carried each kitten back under the wheelbarrow, keeping an ever-blazing eye on the tom.

Drama, Kevin thought: parent, progeny, predator. The tent poles of a story. He would scribble it down tomorrow in the firehouse and later give it to Margie, who taught school, to read, edit, and hold with the other stories, a sketch to be fleshed out later.

Kevin knew the themes he wanted to explore. The Pirate was not sitting on the fence gaping at the mother cat just for sex. He had no bad intentions for her young. No, the Pirate wanted something quite different. Something more. Something crucial. With eight of his nine lives clearly squandered, he now wanted desperately to belong. Wanted something larger than the empty wicked nights of the wandering tom. He was no longer young, out trying to prove his virility. He had obviously been through the wars, losing an eye and an ear along the way in the battle for turf and sex.

At least one of those kittens might be his. (Female cats can be impregnated by different fathers in the same mating period, so there was no way to be certain.) Proof of parenthood is one of the great aching doubts of the male gender. Kevin decided the Pirate was here to see what could be his final offspring. He sat alone on the fence like a father staring at his new infant through the glass of a maternity ward.

Or perhaps the old cat was seeing in the small feline family what might have been, if his worst luck had been his best. In that light, the Pirate momentarily reminded Kevin of his older brother, Frank. Unmarried, a physical wreck, childless, middle-aged, in trouble. Searching for some final love or happiness in a ruined life.

Thinking of Frank made Kevin feel sad and grateful at the same time: sad for the brother he loved so much but grateful for his own lot in life. Grateful for Polly and Zoe and the kids to come. For this house. Without all that he would be no different from Frank, probably a lounge lizard and alone in some one-bedroom apartment where there would never be a need for a Christmas tree. No different from the Pirate sitting on the fence between lonely middle age and the grave, his war wounds all he had to show for the conquests of youth.

Whenever Kevin thought about his youth he thought of Anthony Scala, who had been with him on most of his own conquests. Anthony was no physical match for Kevin on the playing fields, but he was his partner in almost everything he'd done. Kevin would not play on any team unless Anthony was a teammate. Wouldn't go on a date with a girl unless she brought a friend for Anthony. They sat across from each other in school, went to the movies, the beach, and the library together. Fought side by side, shared their first beer, got arrested for jumping a subway turnstile together, and lost their virginity in the same week. They even got the mumps together. Both caught the germ from that stooge Bobby Bronsky, the one who married Kevin's first love, Lucy Carbone. Kevin, Anthony, and Bronsky had swigged from the same bottle of champagne together on that terrible day after the championship game. That was another particularly bad memory best left buried on this day of celebration.

As seniors in high school, Kevin and Anthony had even shared the same dream of becoming doctors. Anthony's father was normal and did not gamble, so he had managed to buy a house with the money he earned from a fruit and vegetable stand. Kevin's father, a city cop, was usually two months behind on the rent for the family apartment because he always paid Pinebox the bookmaker before Kernis the landlord. And when it came time to finance college and medical school, Anthony's father took out a second mortgage while Big Paulie invested in cold daily doubles. Anthony was awarded a stethoscope while Kevin swung a fire ax.

But fate had blessed Kevin Dempsey. He had a beautiful wife and a wonderful daughter and now he had a marvelous house, with a one-eyed cat and a family of kittens in the yard from which Zoe could take her pick of the litter. Anthony was divorced from a childless marriage and, frustrated, was moving out of New York to California, still searching for happiness despite his medical degree.

So there's a piece of Anthony in the Pirate too, Kevin decided. Had it all, and has so little now.

He stared at the kittens beneath the wheelbarrow, being nursed by the mother in full view of the Pirate. There was something sad in knowing that as soon as the kittens were able to walk and fend for themselves, the mother cat would disappear from their lives. The way Kevin's mother had gone out of his life at the age of five, when she died giving birth to his kid brother, Mike.

Mike had married at eighteen, and Kevin was certain he did so because he needed another mother figure in his life. His Irish-born wife, much like the one who had married dear old Dad, gave birth to four kids in five years. Kevin thought that for Mike they were more like little brothers and a sister than offspring.

Margie was already gone when Kevin moved out. Then Mike left, leaving Big Paulie alone. As alone as the Pirate, who now hopped down from the fence and walked slowly across the neighboring yard. After all his kids were gone, Big Paulie lived for Father's Day and Christmas visits from his kids and grandkids.

Kevin watched the Pirate strain to get over another hurricane fence, thinking of Big Paulie still working as a cop long after he should have retired. And then when the scandal with Frank broke in the papers, Big Paulie had just decided there wasn't any reason to go on and bailed out on his own terms.

A large piece of Big Paulie was in the Pirate too, Kevin thought, as he watched the old cat disappear behind a neighbor's drooping willow tree.

The story of the Pirate was about everyone who was ever terrified of being alone.

I need a title, Kevin Dempsey thought, before he learned his wife and daughter were missing. But first I have a party to host. . . .

1

The party guests were supposed to shout surprise at one o'clock. But Polly and Zoe weren't on the noon flight from Orlando at JFK airport.

Two o'clock came and Carmine Plantamura, Kevin's best firehouse buddy, called from the airport and said they hadn't come in on that flight either.

Now it was four o'clock, and the food was running out and the guests were getting antsy. Carmine was on the phone again.

"What do you mean they're still not there?" Kevin said into the telephone, and took a deep slug of his vodka and soda. He'd switched to vodka after four Beck's beers when the second call from Carmine said there was still no Polly and Zoe. This was the third call and the fourth vodka, and he was starting to feel them.

If my wife and kid are missing I might as well have my balls cut off, Kevin thought. Without my family, I am nothing. Half a man. They are my destiny.

"Carmine, calm down, talk slower, in English," Kevin said.

On the phone, Carmine was telling the same story about how he had checked with the desk, had them call Orlando and double-check other airline reservation lists, cancellation orders, and standby sheets.

As Carmine talked, Kevin stood in the archway between the kitchen and the living room, looking over the guests in the crowded living room. Jimmy Savage, Tommy Tighe, a guy named Burke, and a few other firemen friends were there. Savage and his wife were the only blacks in the room. Houlihan, Mills, Gorman—all bartenders from nearby Farrell's—were all with their wives. Sullivan the Steamfitter with his wacky wife, Irene. She never took a drink in her life until he went into AA. Now she was a drunk and he was sober. She claimed his coed AA meetings drove her to drink. And three of Polly's friends: Morton, the dickhead Brit banker; a photographer friend, another limey, forty years old with a ponytail, named Miles Barker; and Polly's best friend, a model and actress named Sarah Cross. Sarah was an air force brat and grew up all over the world. Nobody could take their eyes off Sarah, Kevin thought. Especially Frank. Poor Frank, he's gonna do time. All he does is stand by himself in the kitchen as if preparing for solitary.

"Are you sure?" Kevin said into the phone, his voice rising in frustration. He took another slug of his drink. "Sure you didn't just miss them and she went home to the old apartment?"

Carmine was certain. "I'm telling you they weren't on any of the planes," Carmine said.

"Check again with the friggin' desk, Carm? Maybe I have the wrong day?"

Carmine told him their names weren't even in the computer.

"I'm starting to worry," Kevin said, beginning to slur from booze. "I have a roomful of people here. She doesn't even know I bought this fuckin' house for her birthday. Where could she be? Go back to the desk and check again. I'll hold on. Go . . . hurry . . . please. . . ."

Kevin stood with the phone in his hand, watching his sister, Margie, move through the crowded living room, past Kevin's friends; past her eleven-year-old son, Little Paulie, who was walking around with a tray of hors d'oeuvres; past her youngest brother, Mike. Mike, also a cop, who didn't talk to the eldest Dempsey brother, Frank, because he blamed Frank for their father's suicide two months ago. Big Paulie Dempsey had hanged himself when the *Daily News* printed a Manhattan district attorney's leak that Frank was the sole suspect in the theft of one and a half million dollars in Dominican posse crack cash from the police evidence room up in Washington Heights. His father had jammed his nightstick through the sprinkler pipes in his apartment and put the rawhide from the nightstick around his neck. The squeak of the rawhide on the pipe as Big Paulie swung was a sound Kevin would never forget. . . .

"Maybe you better handle the phone, Margie," Kevin overheard Mike say, as he stood talking to Anthony Scala. Anthony was dressed in an expensive suit, French loafers, a silk tie with a palm tree print. His hair was dark and styled up over a tanned forehead. He had supple tight skin and perfect white teeth but an edgy, nervous manner that always made Kevin wonder if Anthony had been born during an IRS audit.

"Kevin's drinking pretty good since the first call come in," Mike said to Margie, loud enough for Kevin to hear. "Zooming vodka. He looks like he's taking lessons from Frank."

Mike, who was twenty-five, was the one the family called "a sensitive kid." Maybe it was because he was raised from birth without a mother. But the sensitivity had turned sour since he became a cop, Kevin thought. His "us against the world" cop complex wasn't helped by being only five foot eight, the shortest Dempsey.

"I have to speak to Frank before I leave," Anthony said to Mike. "Alone."

"Why, got the name of a good prison doctor?" Kevin heard Mike say. Mike looked to Frank and Margie, who had also heard what he said. Frank just raised his glass to Mike and drank.

"Watch your mouth," Margie said to Mike. "Frank is family. We stand together."

Mike looked abashed under Margie's scowl.

Kevin looked with sadness at Frank, who asked, "Who is the absolute goddess inside drinking beer straight from the bottle?"

"Polly's best friend, Sarah," Kevin said. "Sarah Cross. You like that? Come on, I'll introduce ya."

"Don't waste the woman's time," Frank said.

"You're forty, for Christ sakes," Kevin said, smiling. "She's almost thirty. It's okay. Us adults won't mind. Really."

Frank smiled, drank more booze, and shook his head no.

Carmine came back on the telephone line. "What's that, Carm?" Kevin said. "I know you checked the desk. Check with the airport cops. Maybe they were mugged in the ladies' room. Maybe they were kidnapped. You can't leave there without Polly and Zoe!"

Margie walked to the CD player, shut off the Beatles singing "Yesterday," and moved to the kitchen. She coaxed the phone from Kevin's hand.

"Carmine," she said into the phone, "this is Margie. Come on to the new house. I'll make some calls. We'll get to the bottom of this. No use you standing out there like a fool. The party's over."

The guests had listened.

"Sorry, folks," Margie said, cradling the phone. "Looks like a breakdown in communication. Let's call it a day, huh?"

2

Zoe Dempsey carried her Pepper Face Doll with the pushed-in face down the aisle of the big plane. She held her mommy's hand as the lady with the wings on her dress who had brought her soda and dinner on the plane said goodbye. Zoe said goodbye back.

"Is Daddy gonna pick us up, Mommy?" Zoe asked.

"I told you that you were going to get a brand-new daddy," Zoe's mommy said as they stepped into the big airport.

"I don't want a new daddy," Zoe said. "I want my Daddy daddy."

"You'll like your new daddy even better," Zoe's mommy said.

"No! No, I won't!" Zoe said and started to cry, clutching her Pepper Face Doll.

Zoe's mommy picked Zoe up into her arms and kissed her and wiped away her tears.

"Let's talk about this later," she said. "First let's get our luggage, and then we'll go see our new house on the hill."

"I want my Daddy daddy to come to the new house on the hill," Zoe Dempsey said.

3

As the guests pulled on coats and jackets, Kevin fell silent, worried about Polly and Zoe. He stared out the window at the back yard, drinking beer, listening to the ice clink in Frank's tumbler of booze a few feet away. He glanced at the wall phone, hoping Polly would call. The phone number was the same as the one in the old apartment. Then he looked over at Frank again. He wanted to say, Frank, you fucked up everything. You never got married, never had kids; you fucked up your relationship with our kid brother, Mike, over poor dad's death. And now look what you've done to yourself, you dumb bastard!

If he said what he was thinking he would have said more. Why couldn't you live a normal life, Frank? Like me, with a wife and a kid. Why couldn't you do your job legal? You were always so fond of the Law, pushing it as gospel. Why did you have to break it? Why'd you have to steal, Frank?

"Well, when Polly finally does get home, she'll love the place," Frank said, trying to brighten things up.

"The old man always said, Once you own your own back yard you're a true American," Kevin said.

"The only real estate he ever owned is the mausoleum he and Mom are lying in," Frank said. "Where we'll all wind up. I never told you, did I? He even won that in a poker game in Pinebox Pirino's saloon. Hot shit, no? He won the family tomb in a card game and later on mortgaged it twice to pay gambling debts to some of Pinebox's crew members. He probably would have done it again or sold it, except he buried Mom in it. And he's lying next to her now—at peace, I hope. She was some woman."

"I remember her death better than her life."

"You, you can find her in the mirror," Frank said. "And in your big and generous heart, Kev."

"I wish the old man could have been here today," Kevin said. "To see the house, you know? He never had one."

"Oh, he's here somewhere, all right," Frank said. "You can bet the house on it—like he would have. He never had a house because he always owed the house. But when you want him, you'll find him."

Kevin remembered again seeing his father swinging from the sprinkler pipe in the apartment on Prospect Avenue.

Frank had found him first and called Kevin, who contacted Margie, who told the kid brother, Mike. His father's shoes were freshly polished and the shoeshine box rested on the front page of the morning *Daily News,* which had a picture of Frank with the headline CRACK-CASH COP QUIZZED.

The coroner said Big Paulie Dempsey had swallowed Ex-Lax hours before his suicide so he could clean himself out before "hanging up." He didn't want to be found with shit in his pants. He was a neatnik. Even the soles of his shoes were clean.

He had gotten a shave and a haircut and donned a Chinese-laundered shirt and a freshly dry-cleaned suit with pointed hankie in the pocket. He'd made sure all his bills were paid and the lights were off, to save on the electric. Frank said he'd found no note, instead just pairs of aces and eights next to a deck of cards on the kitchen table, a dead man's hand. Frank had left the body swinging until the crime scene cops arrived, so there could be no doubt about foul play. A dead cop always had enemies.

When Kevin had arrived, Frank sat at the kitchen table with a double vodka in his right hand, staring up at Big Paulie squeaking there. Frank kept drinking, staring, refilling his glass from a vodka bottle, drinking, gaping. Frank never took his eyes off him. Kevin looked at his dad and glanced away quickly and wanted to cut him down. But Frank had told him to leave him be, it had to be done by the book. Frank was the prime suspect in the dope money rip-off and still insisted his father's suicide be clerked by the book. Before the cops came and cut him down and hauled him away in the morgue wagon, Kevin had listened for a full ten minutes to the tight squeak of the rawhide on the pipe.

In the middle of the night, when he couldn't sleep, he would think he heard the squeak again. It was a sound that only his little Zoe's breathing could make go away.

The old man was a proud bastard and he couldn't live with the shame, Kevin reasoned. His final fastidiousness was his last testament—even though his son turned out dirty, Big Paulie Dempsey died as clean as his police whistle. The press came around asking questions, but after the family agreed to stonewall them, they kept their distance. There were no reporters at the funeral when they placed Big Paulie Dempsey next to his beloved wife in the mausoleum in Greenwood Cemetery, just a few old cop friends. And Pinebox Pirino, who stood at the bottom of the hill, and a cop, Summers, from Internal Affairs.

That was almost two months ago already. He hadn't seen Frank without a drink since. I should talk, he thought. I'm half looped right now. But Frank was always a heavy boozer, as heavy as Big Paulie. And he'd taken a nosedive since the money went missing from the property room. Went into a tailspin after Big Paulie's suicide. As if the death and the cash were a pair of anvils around his neck, pulling him down into a sea of booze.

Although Mike barely talked to Frank anymore, Kevin didn't blame Frank for his father's death. But he was also pissed off at Frank, for fucking up his own life.

Margie walked into the kitchen, followed by Mike.

"Kevin, I'm going upstairs to make some more calls, try to locate Polly," Margie said. "You should say goodbye to your guests."

"Let them finish their drinks," Kevin said. She nodded and walked back inside and then into the hallway to go upstairs.

"How's the job treating you, Mike?" Frank asked, as he extended his hand to his younger brother. Mike glanced at Kevin and then reluctantly gave Frank his hand, withdrew it, looked at it, and jammed it into his pants pocket.

"You know, Frank," Mike said, looking Frank straight in the eye, "as long as there's *criminals,* I'll have work. Like the IAB mutt parked across the street. You keep him employed."

Frank nodded, said nothing. Mike was talking about Summers from NYPD Internal Affairs Bureau, who still followed Frank looking for the million and a half in cash.

"The shoeflies have been to my house twice, going through personal belongings, my wife's stuff, my kids' toy boxes, my garage, toolshed," Mike said in a low voice as he leaned closer to Frank. "In front of my wife and kids. My neighbors see them come and go. They come see me in the precinct, root through my locker like I was in high school. The other guys on the job look at me like I got HIV. No one wants to ride with me because the shoeflies tail the car, so I'm in Community Patrol, pounding a fucking beat in the second highest murder precinct in the city. So you ask how I'm doing, and I gotta say, Simply fuckin' marvelous. Okay, big brother?"

"I'm sorry about all that," Frank said. "Really I am." He sipped his drink.

"Come on, guys, huh?" Kevin said. "I got enough problems here."

Kevin took a swig of his drink and moved toward the living room. Anthony Scala now held a trench coat and was coming to say goodbye.

"Hey, doc," said Kevin, embracing his boyhood friend. "I'm gonna see you again before you leave town, right?"

"Not leaving for the coast till the end of the week," Anthony said. "Let's get together."

"Promise," Kevin said, turning to Mike and Frank. "Even if we never did get to go to med school together—"

"Hey, you probably already saved more lives as a fireman than I ever will as a doctor," Anthony said.

"—I could have done it, ya know," Kevin said, with just a trace of boozy resentment.

As Kevin finished the second part of his sentence, Anthony draped an arm over Kevin's shoulder, smiled, and joined him, mimicking him as if he'd heard the same line a thousand times. "But my old man didn't have a house to take out a second mortgage on like yours did," they said in unison. Kevin looked slightly abashed but let the booze laugh it away.

"His old man was connected, whaddaya talkin' about?" Mike said. "Of course Anthony had a house. All guineas have houses. The first English word they learn when they get off the boat is *cement*. The second is *equity*."

Anthony laughed, draping his other arm around Mike's shoulders.

"Yeah, now I'll have equity for Zoe's med school or Harvard law," Kevin said, playfully disengaging himself from Anthony, throwing an imaginary combination to Anthony's midsection. "That's what this house means to me. That my kids won't have to scrounge like I did."

"You're sounding like a guido already," Mike said.

"When I get out there," said Anthony, gasping from Kevin's shadowboxing, "I'll have to find a new house too. Pool, tennis, Jacuzzi. You gotta come visit."

"Gonna miss you, Anthony," Kevin said, patting his friend on the cheek. "But you always did want to live out there: the sun, the broads, the money. You always said, 'I'm gonna have me a Mercedes with California plates and a beautiful blonde.'"

"Sounds more like you," Anthony said, laughing.

"If my beautiful blonde ever turns back up," Kevin half joked. "But really, man, I wish you luck. I know we don't see each other that much anymore. You have your world, I have mine. But that doesn't mean I still don't love you, ya know."

"Call me," Anthony said and they shook hands, piling all four of their hands together. They each winked, the way they always had, to let each other know that, no matter what, they'd never be too far apart in case of trouble.

Anthony walked to Frank before he left. "Frank, can I have a word with you outside?"

Frank freshened his drink and followed Anthony out into the hallway. Kevin moved toward the living room and overheard Anthony say, "Frank, about your liver . . ."

Kevin didn't want to hear any more bad news. He walked into the living room and said goodbye to his firemen friends and the neighborhood guys and their wives. They all wished him luck with the new house and left.

Margie came down the stairs with worry lines creasing her forehead.

"They have no record of Polly or the baby staying at any of the Disney World hotels," Margie whispered. Kevin looked evenly at her. He swallowed hard and searched the ceiling for ideas.

"Maybe a nearby motel," he said.

"They're checking for me," Margie said, and began collecting glasses. "I have to call back in a bit."

Jesus Christ, where is my wife and kid?

Another of Kevin's fireman friends, Tommy Tighe, staggered sideways toward him from the toilet. Tighe always looked high, his eyes forever blood-rimmed.

"Your sister still looks fucking great," Tighe said in Kevin's ear.

"Tell her, not me, you married asshole," Kevin said and smiled, casting off him with his right hand. Tighe jigsawed out of the house.

Across the room, Kevin saw Clive Morton, Polly's rich and handsome friend from London who was a successful investment banker with some British firm on Wall Street. Polly had gone to university with him, he a graduate business student, she a freshman, before she dropped out to model. That was a pre-Kevin Polly. Kevin always suspected there had once been something between them. Morton and Polly's father had done business over the years, but Polly was vague about her relationship with Morton except to say he was part of the "old school crowd." Whenever Kevin asked about old boyfriends she'd say, "Kevin, don't ever worry about bumping into *my* old boyfriends. You shop in different stores."

"Kev, old chap, so good of you to invite us," Morton said. "Interesting place, this Brooklyn. Coming here, we got lost in some intergalactic place called Left Hook. Still, such a dandy of a little house."

"Red Hook," Kevin said, thinking that he'd like to introduce him to a real left hook. "*Dandy* of you to come."

"I'm sure Polly just messed up the times," said Sarah Cross, shaking her head, smiling, kissing Kevin on the cheek. "She never was any good with schedules. Maybe next time I'll get to meet your famous brother."

She nodded toward Frank, who was walking from the hallway back into the kitchen, slugging his booze.

"I'm sure he'd like that," Kevin said. "He's shy."

"It's a great house," Sarah said. "Polly is going to love it."

"I love the fireplace," said the photographer, Miles Barker. "I photographed Polly in front of a fireplace when she was seventeen. She was stunning."

How about I punch you in the fucking mouth and make you shit Chiclets for a week? Kevin thought. "Yeah, I saw those snaps," he said.

"Hot," said Miles.

"Hot," said Kevin, thinking, I'll cut off your ponytail and make you swallow it. "Yeah, really hot."

All three shook hands with Kevin and left. Kevin had squeezed Morton's hand too hard, felt the knuckles crush together, and saw the tweedy banker grimace in surprise.

The crowd was gone now. All that remained was family.

"I called the concierge at the Contemporary Hotel in Disney World back," Margie said. "He checked for me, but none of the local hotel registers have had a Polly Dempsey or Edgeworth and child."

"Jesus Christ, Margie, what do you think happened?"

"I checked the airline again, and the computer finally showed those two passengers canceled the morning of the flight down. *Down.* They say they never went. Kevin, what is going on?"

"I don't know," Kevin said.

"When did you talk to her last?" Margie asked.

"Yesterday. Morning, I think," he said, feeling stupid, the drink blurring his memory.

"Did she call collect?" Frank asked.

"No."

"Maybe she was using coins in a pay phone," Margie said.

"No, Zoe was watching *Sesame Street* on TV," Kevin said. "I could hear Big Bird in the background. I spoke to Zoe. She was learning the letter D. She was spelling Dad but Polly took the phone and said she had to go. She was in a rush. I got mad because I wanted to talk longer to Zoe and maybe I was a little drunk, but Polly hung up on me."

Kevin sat in a kitchen chair, embarrassed, thick-tongued, exhausted. While his brothers and sister stared at him, Kevin tried to balance a round-topped salt shaker on top of the matching pepper shaker. It kept falling off, granules of salt spilling through the holes in the cap onto the table.

"That's my brains," Kevin said, pointing to the scattered salt on the table. His family said nothing.

Frank sipped his drink. "Will someone please tell me everything that's going on here?"

Margie sagged a bit and sat down at the table. She seemed exhausted by the effort to remain calm.

"There's no record of Polly or Zoe Dempsey ever leaving New York on any of the airlines serving Orlando in the last week," Margie said. "I checked under Edgeworth too. Nothing. There are no records of them in any of the hotels or motels or guesthouses in the Orlando area."

"She's somewhere," Frank said.

"Very profound," said Mike. "Another case solved by Lieutenant Frank Dempsey, Missing Persons Bureau, also of missing money fame—"

"No need for that, Mike," Margie said.

Mike frowned and Frank silently took a sip of his liquor.

"Did she use the credit cards?" Margie asked.

"Don't know," Kevin said, thinking, Margie's a better cop than the real cops here. "She paid cash for the tickets and took cash with her. About three thousand. I put it aside special from driving car service."

"Did you ever see the airline tickets?" Margie asked.

"Yeah—no—well, I saw the *folder.*"

"What were you fighting about recently?" asked Frank.

"Money," Kevin said. "Always money. She wanted to move and I said we couldn't afford it. I didn't tell her about the new house. I wanted it to be a surprise. She thought I was holding out on her. Meanwhile I was working three jobs and saving money for three years."

"Why didn't you ask Frank for some money?" Mike said. "He's got a mil and a half—"

"Hey," Margie said. That was all Margie had to say. Frank didn't react at all. Mike fell silent, as his wife Bridie, with the round red Irish face, walked in from the yard with their four kids.

"We better get going," Bridie said to Mike as she took the children's Mets jackets from Margie's son, Little Paulie. "Tomorrow's a school day."

Mike nodded and got up from the table and pulled on his own matching Mets jacket and kissed his sister goodbye. He walked to Kevin and put his arm around his shoulder.

"She's probably just pissed off," Mike said. "No big deal."

"She has my baby," Kevin said.

Mike nodded. "Well, you can't call Missing Persons yet," he said. "She's only missing since last night, when you talked to her on the phone and everything was fine. Sun's just going down now. She has to be missing forty-eight hours before Missing Persons gets involved. Call me when you hear."

Kevin nodded and finished his beer and opened another one. Bridie finished dressing her kids and said goodbye to everyone with a wave, and then she and Mike and the kids were gone.

As soon as "Mike the drink counter" left, Frank poured himself a double shot of vodka. Margie was back on the phone for a long time calling the other airlines to see if Polly and Zoe might have flown into Miami and rented a car. But she was battling busy signals and put on hold several times and told the information was not available at this time. Her son Paulie was now the only person in the living room, watching TV, and the place echoed with the absence of the crowd.

"Mom, I gotta get home to finish my science report," Paulie yelled. "It's due tomorrow."

Margie nodded to Little Paulie to wait as she watched Kevin pour himself a shot of booze and throw it down, followed by a belt of his beer.

"Margie, I'm scared," Kevin said. "You think they're all right?"

"Yeah, I can feel it in my belly," Margie said. "Mom used to say she could feel when something was right or wrong. I can too. I feel they're okay."

"Ever since Zoe was born Polly's been on my case," Kevin said. "Almost always money. No other broad on my end. I don't think she fools around. But who really knows?"

"What's your feeling?" Frank asked.

"Sometimes I feel Polly wished she married money instead of me," Kevin said and then took some beer. "Her family certainly did. They call me 'The bloke who extinguishes ghetto fires.' "

"Yeah," Margie said. "I guess it didn't matter to them that one of the fires you extinguished was her."

"Listen, Kevvie, Margie, it's Sunday," Frank said, taking the helm. "Believe me, it's hard enough to find out what the hell is going on in a situation like this anytime, never mind Sunday. Like Mike said, Polly and Zoe aren't missing persons yet. So look, Margie, you go home. I'll stay with Kevin. If anything happens, I'll call."

"I can always take off work tomorrow," Margie said.

"Go to work," Frank said. "The world is too dumb for you to miss a single day of teaching."

Margie nodded and smiled sadly. Paulie walked in with his mother's jacket, and Margie donned it and went to Kevin, who drained his beer as he stood up. He was getting drunk now.

"Listen, Kev, everything will be fine," Margie said. "I'll pray. I still do that once in a while. This is worth it."

Then she and Paulie left.

Frank showed no visible effect of the booze except that his hands were now steady as he took a seat at the kitchen table opposite Kevin. "Okay, let's not get overly melodramatic," he said. "More bizarre things have happened. Back in the sixties and seventies whole families disappeared into cults. Kidnapping is possible. But this doesn't fit."

"Why?" asked Kevin.

"Because she called last night," Frank said. "If she were being held against her will, she would have said so or the kidnappers would have asked for a ransom by now."

"She wants to play mind games with me, okay?" said Kevin, who was talking with one eye closed now, as he finished his sixth shot of vodka and as many beers since Carmine's first call.

"They'll turn up," Frank said. "The world is small if you want privacy. And immense if you want attention."

"Yeah, maybe," Kevin said.

"Especially with a child," Frank said. "Kids might be small but they always make themselves heard and known. Kids are harder to hide than a building. They can't keep a secret. They're blabbermouths. They can walk and they can talk and laugh and cry. People take notice of kids, especially a beautiful little girl like Zoe. Teachers, doctors, dentists, flight attendants, bus drivers, barbers, and candy store owners notice children. Other children notice children. I should know, I had two little brothers and a sister."

"But no kids of your own, Frank," Kevin said, bleary-eyed. "How come?"

"Kevvie, I think you should go up and hit the sack," Frank said. "There's a phone up there. I'll sleep down here on the couch."

"I'm all right," the drunken Kevin said.

"You're not all right," said Frank. "Come on, I'll take you up."

Frank helped Kevin to his feet and led him through the doorway to the stairs.

"Frank, Frank . . ."

"Yeah, Kev?"

"Why'd you have to break your own fuckin' heart?"

Frank didn't answer.

They reached the top step and Frank steered him to the bedroom and dropped him on the bed.

"There's supposed to be a wife and kid here!" Kevin Dempsey shouted through the new house before sleep took him.

4

When the phone in the new house started ringing, Kevin was in that semi-zombie state where dreams and reality meld. He was reliving one of the most painful memories of his life, a patch of time he now called the Week of the Worm of Jealousy. A time when first love, perhaps the strongest of all loves, led to humiliation. When the worm entered his life, undulating and writhing, innocence died. First love takes the boy from childhood to adolescence. First betrayal takes him into manhood.

Kevin wasn't sure which part of that experience was dream and which part was memory or conscious embellishment or semiconscious imagination. It didn't matter. The essence never changed. The Week of the Worm was a milestone in his life, like the deaths of his mother and father and the birth of his child Zoe.

The sequence was often jumbled, but the details and the events were always the same. The dream started with a genderless voice, an anonymous phone call in the night: "Lucy Carbone has decided to give *it* up. If Lincoln wins, Lucy Carbone's gonna give her cherry to Bobby Bronsky. If John Jay wins, she'll give it to you. She only gives it to a *winner.*"

One telephone call, that single intrusion in the night, infected Kevin Dempsey with the worm of jealousy.

That night, in the sweaty dark, every imaginable insecurity played on Kevin. He lay awake, woozy, tossing, itchy. When he did manage to drift off into some amorphous altered state, lost between conscious angst and subconscious terror, he found himself running on an uphill gridiron, desperately trying to cling to a slippery football.

The crowds in the stands and on the sidelines are both cheering and jeering him. The ball keeps squirting out of his hands like a greased piglet. Then the pigskin even has the snouted face of a little pig, slimy with canned-ham gelatin, and the harder Kevin grips the piglet-ball, the farther it launches from his hands. When it hits the ground it sprouts legs and corkscrew tail and begins to laugh. With the football stitches laced down its back, it dashes between his legs and around his feet and races from sideline to sideline, laughing and squealing. Instead of him playing with the football, the football is playing with him.

And every time Kevin recovers the fumbled piglet-ball, he looks ahead to the distant end zone at the top of the inclined football field. Way up there, in the unattainable distance, is Lucy Carbone in her canopied bed. The bed is now smack in the middle of the end zone and Lucy is in the bed, naked and on all fours, and there is Bobby Bronsky, in full Lincoln High football regalia, his big number 68 on his helmet, his tight pants pulled down around his hips, humping Lucy Carbone doggie style. The two of them are laughing, fucking, panting as Kevin runs up the field toward them, chasing the squealing, elusive piglet.

Now the field becomes a rolling treadmill and Kevin is running in place. The piglet, back in his arms, looks up at him and, in the same genderless voice as the one on the phone, asks, "Why bother, you asshole? You already lost your girl!" The piglet laughs again and it pops from his hands. It runs in circles around Kevin, who runs in desperate place on the treadmill field.

Kevin cannot gain any ground on the treadmill as he tries to get to Lucy and Bronsky. All he can hear is the mocking laughter of the swelling crowd and the endless taunting of the piglet and the humping of Lucy and Bronsky in the end zone. And now the piglet comes running and leaps back into Kevin's hands but then transforms in his hands into a giant slimy worm, slithering through his fingers and up his jersey sleeve, along his arm, over his neck, and entering his ear, boring into his brain, the worm of jealousy claiming a warm and dark and marshy home in his pounding head.

After that long-ago anonymous phone call in the night, for the entire week before the championship Lincoln High game, Kevin rarely slept, and when he did he awakened shivering from the same dream of the piglet and Lucy and Bronsky and the worm.

He remembered uneaten meals, missed practices, aimlessly walking the night streets. He followed Lucy Carbone through the Brooklyn afternoons like a young man obsessed with his own inadequacies. Once he stood in a doorway across from her house all through the night, staring up at her window. When he should have been at football practice, he furtively shadowed Lucy to cheerleading.

One day near the end of the week, he and Anthony even followed Lucy Carbone with her cheerleader friends out to the Lincoln High field to watch their football team practice. Lucy had disguised herself with a head scarf and big sunglasses. Kevin saw Bobby Bronsky walk to the fence to chat with her, and he remembered waiting for Bronsky after practice and easily beating the larger jock in a street fight because Kevin knew how to box.

He remembered brutally punishing Bronsky, who lay on the sidewalk; he stopped only when Lucy screamed and Anthony pulled him off. He remembered how ashamed he was when Lucy mocked him for following her, telling him she had only gone to spy on the Lincoln High cheerleader routines. She called him a jealous asshole and stormed off.

By the end of the week, Kevin Dempsey had lost his girl, dropped twelve pounds, and missed all the practices, and he never slept the night before the championship game. His coach and his teammates were furious and called him a choker. The championship game, college scouts, scholarships all weighed in the balance.

He remembered how on the morning of the championship game, the phone rang and rang and rang. . . .

Now, here in the new house, Kevin finally realized the ringing phone was real and not in his dream, and he picked it up. He gazed around at the ceiling and out the shutter slats of the new master bedroom windows.

He couldn't decipher which was dream, which was memory, which was embellishment. He only knew that the Week of the Worm of Jealousy, which sounded like the title of some violent Latin novel, was a dark patch in his past that surfaced whenever his present was turbulent.

He was still fully dressed. His mouth tasted pasty and foul, and his breath bounced off the plastic receiver. It smelled like stale booze and the wrong words and what he imagined as the odor of his brains. He heard a hollow sound on the phone. The light coming through the slotted wooden shutters told him it was morning.

"Hello," Kevin said and sat up in the empty bed, suddenly remembering that Polly and Zoe were missing. "Hello?"

"Hello," came Polly's voice. "Kevin?"

Kevin's heart surged. "Polly? Where are you? How's the baby? What the hell happened? Polly?"

There was a pause. He heard the hollow texture of long distance; then Polly answered.

"Kevin, this isn't easy for me," Polly said. "Please listen. I know this is going to be painful—"

"What is this, for Christ sakes?" Kevin demanded. "Where are you?"

"Out of your life, Kevin," Polly said. "For good."

Kevin stood up, holding the phone in one hand and pacing, wiping the sticky corners of his mouth with his sleeve. He felt suddenly dizzy.

"What is *that* supposed to mean? For Christ sakes, Polly. Listen. I bought you a house. You understand? A *new house*. I'm in it right now. It was supposed to be a surprise. Ours."

There was a pause on the other end.

"I'm so sorry, Kevin," she said, her voice almost a whisper. "But even that wouldn't have mattered. It's over. The whole charade."

Kevin moved the phone away from his face and looked at it as if to make sure he wasn't hearing things or still dreaming or listening to the worm of jealousy.

"Polly, where the fuck *are* you?" Kevin shouted. "You can't do this shit to me over the phone. I'm talking about a *new house* here. For us. Me, you, and Zoe, our baby. Our home. It was supposed to be a surprise."

"Well, this might be a shock more than a surprise," she said. "My intention was never to hurt you. You did save my life, after all. So instead of hating me, try to forget me, okay? And Zoe as well, of course."

"What is this shit, Polly?" Kevin said.

"Kevin, it should be obvious to you by now that I'm in love with another man," she said softly, almost a plea for understanding. But the words came at Kevin like cold bullets. "If this hurts you, I really am sorry because you're a sweet, kind guy. But I won't come back to haunt, promise."

Kevin felt the weight of the words squeezing his temples together.

"Polly—"

"Just this one last time, will you let me finish, Kevin?" Polly said, her voice growing sharp and her volume rising, her British accent growing more pronounced, like an armor. "We'll never lay eyes on each other again. All further communication will be through a lawyer. He's in Europe now, traveling on the continent. He'll be contacting you in due time from London to work out the annulment, which I'm sure you'll want, being Roman Catholic. If not, I'll take another route. I'll simply disappear. You won't find me. I'm so sorry, Kevin—"

He heard her voice crack. Polly was sobbing. Kevin began to think this was a prank. He even managed to chuckle. So did Polly, through sobs. He envisioned her filing a fingernail, playing pretend as she often did. Now at least she'd tell him what the hell happened to her flight and he could tell her all about the new house.

"Well, at least you're taking it well," she said. "I wouldn't want it to be uglier than it already is. I'm most worried about Zoe, actually. She *is* fond of you—"

"Fond?" Kevin snapped. "My baby might be *fond* of goddam ice cream and Frosted Flakes, but she *loves* her father. Loves *me! Fond* . . . fuck *fond!"*

"I was trying to be nice," Polly said.

Kevin's skin began to itch as sweat leaked from his pores. It smelled as rancid as his socks. He stood in the middle of this new house hearing his wife tell him she was in love with another man and she never wanted to see him again and that his baby who loved him would forget him in time. He heard Polly blowing her nose and her sobbing stopped. In the background, he could hear little Zoe asking her mommy why she was crying. She heard Polly say, "Something bad happened to Daddy and he isn't coming back anymore."

"Polly, this isn't funny," Kevin shouted. "I want to talk to Zoe. Please let me talk to my little girl."

There was silence from the other end.

Then Kevin wanted Polly's neck in his fingers, wanted to let loose the murderer he knew lived inside him. Inside every man. He found himself strangling the phone instead. Several buttons bleeped and he panicked that he might have cut Polly off. The phone popped out of his hands.

Kevin frantically gathered up the phone and put the receiver back to his ear.

"Polly? Polly . . . you still there?"

"Yes, Kevin, but not for long," she said. "I have so much to do around our new place."

Those three words "our new place" buckled his knees. She was supposed to be saying that about this new house, not some other place, where "our" included a different man. She sounded so distant and young and detached. He could hear Zoe asking for Frosted Flakes in the background, and then heard her say, "Daddy always gives me Frosted Flakes."

"Look, why don't we meet?" Kevin said calmly, sensing Polly had had a breakdown. He walked to the window and, through the shutters, saw the world outside that he wanted to share with Polly: young couples walking to the subway to go to work, school kids hurrying up to Holy Name or down to P.S. 154, where he hoped Zoe would go to pre-K next year, a furniture truck delivering a new washer-dryer to newlyweds down the block. The sky was big and blue and the turning leaves fell from the stately Norway maples that stood erect at the curbsides of the limestones and brownstones on this clean and orderly block. It was one of the nicest middle-class streets in Brooklyn, filled with community and children and the employed: a place to raise a family with safety, dignity, and comfort and still call yourself a New Yorker. Kevin saw all that walking past and realized that the work he had done to become a part of it was now being destroyed over the telephone by the woman he loved.

"Polly, I have to see Zoe," Kevin said, hearing the numbness in his own voice. "You can have the house. I'll move out if you want. You can move in with Zoe. But I have to see my baby."

"I'm sorry," she said. "That's just not possible now. It wouldn't be fair to Zoe. She's growing older. It would only confuse her."

"Is it the drinking? I'll stop, if that's what it takes," Kevin said, wishing he had a drink in his hand at that moment. "What do you want?"

"Kevin, you must have known there were other men since we met," she said. "I couldn't wait for you to fulfill my desire for motherhood any longer."

Kevin's pain was now physical. His feelings weren't just hurt. Nausea built in him, as if his body were trying to turn itself inside out. His balance tilted off. The room spun. He had to sit. Silly dots floated in front of his sore eyes like little signals from another dimension. The new house whispered unfamiliar rumors.

"How many?" he asked softly, his tongue thick and dry. "How many men?"

"That's not important," she said. "It wasn't what I wanted, it was what I *needed*. The breeding. I needed the best to conceive the best."

Kevin covered the mouthpiece of the phone and vomited on the floor near the window. He heard a passing group of children laughing. His body rattled with uncontrollable shakes and he coughed deeply. He spit and tried to clear his throat.

"Are you still there, Kevin?"

"Poll—Polly," he said, catching his breath and wiping tears from his eyes, "maybe—maybe we can see a counselor, straighten this out."

"The die is cast."

She's delivering lines from acting class, he thought. Was all this rehearsed? Kevin could hear Zoe in the background again, asking if it was her daddy who was on the phone. He could hear Polly's phone fall from her grip, then some scuffling, and Polly telling Zoe to go upstairs to her room, and Zoe's reluctant voice trailing off. Footsteps echoed off what sounded like wooden floors in an empty house. Then Polly picked up the phone again.

"Forgive me, Kevin," Polly said. "I had to send *my* baby out of the room so I could finish this unpleasant business. Please don't think I relish any of this."

"Let me talk to her," Kevin said adamantly. "I want my baby to hear her father's voice."

There was a long silence, and then Polly said, "I wish there was an easier way to say this. Because you did save my life that night of the fire.

And you have been good and kind to my baby. You have tried, really you have, in your own way. But Kevin, *you are not* the biological father of my Zoe."

Kevin sat down slowly on the bed and felt himself detaching from his own body. He could see himself from a great height, looking down, sitting there small and puny, on the edge of the king-sized bed, his feet unable to touch the floor, the telephone enormous in his infant-sized hand.

"Polly, please, stop," he heard himself squeak. "Don't say that."

"I tried for a solid year and a half to get pregnant with you, luv," Polly said softly. "I didn't want to hurt your feelings. Because I know how important your manhood is to you, how badly you wanted a child too. The way I wanted one. While I was still young. One of the reasons I married you was because I dreamed of what a baby with you would look like. Because you are a beautiful-looking man."

"You're telling me I shot blanks," Kevin said, trembling, his eyes closed tight, the smell of the vomit staining the air.

There was a long silence.

"Those are your words," she said. "But there are many women who don't want babies. You can find—"

Kevin felt himself fall from above and crash to a spent, panting, sprawled position on the bed. When he spoke he was conscious of his jaw, moving as if on a puppet's hinge. Then he stood up, his body fluids in a rapid boil, sweating profusely.

"Listen to me, you fucking evil bitch, Zoe is *my baby,*" he bellowed with primal rage.

"Please, take a good look at yourself and a picture of Zoe sometime and be honest. Kevin, for heaven's sake, you're *sterile.*"

There was a long haunting pause and then Kevin heard clicking.

"Polly? Polly?" He was afraid she'd hung up.

Then she asked, "Kevin, do you know today's date?"

He told her she damn well knew the date. He repeated it, the day after her birthday.

"No, it's the date our lives start over," Polly said. "Me, you, Zoe, Zoe's real daddy."

Kevin exploded with all the emotional energy his body and mind could muster, his muscles contracting, his knees sagging, his teeth chattering, his fists balling. He wrestled the words into the phone, gasping between each word.

"I-demand-to-know-where-you-are-or-I'll-have-you-arrested-for-kidnapping," Kevin said.

"You won't find me," Polly said. "If you want to hurt and embarrass yourself further by going to court and by subjecting yourself and the child to medical tests, I suppose that's your right. If a judge thinks so. Depending on what country I happen to be in at the time. That's what attorneys are for. But Kevin, I implore you, don't cause yourself or the rest of us any more pain."

"If you were here right now I'd kill you."

"Yes," Polly said. "I thought you would say that . . . on tape. I'm sorry. It's for my child's protection. For me and Zoe and . . . and her real father. I'm not trying to be cruel."

Kevin heard her click off what sounded like a tape recorder. Then he heard a whir. Now Polly played back the tape, starting with him stating the date and proceeding to his threatening to kill her.

"Please don't make this ugly," Polly said. "Don't make me use this. Accept it. You are not Zoe's father, I promise you. But I'll say this before I go: Once, I almost did love you. Other less complicated women have and will. I'm sorry. You're still young. There will be others. I wish you only happiness."

Kevin heard Zoe's voice one last time, as she walked in sobbing, asking Polly for her daddy, before the phone clattered into silence and Kevin heard a dial tone.

He stood there staring at the receiver in his hands. His fingernails were filthy. Sweat had soaked his shirt. The room smelled of vomit. He was trembling, and he suddenly became cold and his feet ached. His body still felt oddly foreign, as if it did not belong to him. He twisted the plastic phone as powerfully as he could in his large damp hands, popping the tendons and veins in his neck, trapping his breath, grunting and groaning with uncaged fury, squeezing until his arms and shoulders and stomach muscles tightened to the point of tearing and the phone finally snapped in half.

Kevin yanked the wires out of the phone and stomped the remains with his stocking feet. He could feel no pain as he crunched the hollow plastic, the anger acting as some primitive anesthetic.

Then he opened one after another of the packed boxes until he found the gown Polly had worn at their wedding. He tore it and used it to mop up the vomit from the floor. He found the family photo album and searched until he found the baby pictures of Zoe. He removed one and walked to the mirror on the dresser and looked at himself and the baby picture next to his own face.

He wiped away tears, as he studied Zoe's eyes and the shape of her nose and the lips and the ears in the photo, thinking, Are those my features in her face? Is my little girl some other man's child? Do I adore someone else's kid? Does my blood course in Zoe's veins? Is my baby my baby? Am I losing my fucking mind?

Clutching the photos to his breast, he fell to his knees and started to cry uncontrollably, the body-racking sobs echoing off the high ceilings. He could hear the sounds of children from the street, a world he no longer inhabited.

"Kevvie," said Frank Dempsey, touching his brother's shoulder. "Kevvie, get up, kid. Come on."

Kevin's eyes were pleading for help. Frank helped him to his feet, like a cornerman tending a fighter after a humiliating knockout. He held Kevin's powerful, trembling, sweaty body in his arms.

"Frank," Kevin said, his eyes startled, his voice a low desperate whisper, "I know how to lose. I've lost Mom . . . lost Dad . . . lost friends. Seen strangers die in bad fires. I've lost fights . . . ball games . . . women, money, time. But when you lose your baby, your own flesh and blood that comes from you, your *kid,* then you lose your goddam soul. What do I do? Please tell me, Frank. What do I do?"

Kevin tried desperately to say more to his older brother, but he could not find the air to do so. He could not manage to swallow. And all he could see in his mind was Zoe, as an infant, smiling up at him from a pink crib. Her face was smaller than his fist, with little fragile bones and sparkling eyes and skin as soft as prayer. Is all that no longer mine? Was it all an evil lie?

He managed to breathe and swallow, and the words came pouring out of him again, about the phone call and Polly and some other man, who she claimed was Zoe's real father. He told Frank about the tape she had made of him threatening to kill her and how she said he would never see Zoe again. He told Frank everything she had said and wished there was more to tell but there wasn't.

"Kevin, listen to me clearly. You haven't lost anything yet except some sleep," Frank said. "Maybe a wife. That happens to the best of men. But as for little Zoe, calm down, get a grip, little brother. I might not be much else anymore. But I still have a lot of bloodhound left in me and a lot of determined Dempsey, too. I promise you, leave it to me. I'll find your baby. Then we'll see what's what and who's who. Okay?"

"It sounded like she was calling long distance," Kevin said.

"I have a few places to start looking," Frank said. "You get into the shower, clean up the mess you made here, and relax. Go see Anthony, get a sedative or something. Things could be worse."

Kevin looked up at him.

"You could be me," Frank said with a smile, poking his brother, trying to prod a smile. Kevin just blinked and watched Frank swing open the bedroom door and walk quietly out of the room.

Kevin Dempsey sat alone on the edge of the bed, in the new house that was supposed to be echoing with the sounds of his family. But all he heard was the silence and Frank's footsteps going down the stoop.

5

Kevin hit traffic near the Twenty-third Street exit of the FDR Drive, heading uptown. In his rearview mirror he saw the flashing lights of a tow truck, as it inched through traffic to clear an accident up ahead. He'd taken Frank's advice and called to make sure Anthony still had office hours in this week before he moved west. Anthony told him to come in; it was a good idea to get a complete physical before he left anyway. Anthony seemed baffled when Kevin also told him he'd like a sperm count done. Kevin said he'd explain when he got there.

Anthony was the only one outside his family whom Kevin could confide in. Carmine was a great friend, and firefighting welded its own bonds, but Carmine was older than Kevin and hadn't been there when he was young, when the foundation blocks of his life were laid. Anthony was there from the beginning. He was even there when Lucy Carbone had come and gone from his life. Anthony had seen Kevin come unraveled when those anonymous phone calls about Bobby Bronsky and Lucy Carbone, his first true love, had come in the week before the all-important championship game. He was even there when Kevin beat up Bobby Bronsky. And he was also benched on the sidelines because of him on the day of that fateful game. He'd never forget that morning. . . .

Kevin has dragged his ass up to Prospect Park to the ballfields, where a few thousand have assembled to see the championship game. He feels weak and tired and confused. He sees Bronsky on the opposite sideline, a bandage strapped over the bridge of his nose, one eye still blackened from the beating Kevin gave him a few days earlier. Bronsky points at Kevin from the sideline, pacing the cold earth like a bull ready to charge, flailing in dumb show, telling Kevin that his ass belongs to him on the field today. Here where his fancy boxing moves are useless.

Kevin's own teammates have also given him the mum freeze for missing the practices. Anthony, who only plays on the kickoff squad, is also benched. Rumors are spreading that Kevin might be on drugs. But Kevin is still eager to play ball. And then he sees her!

Lucy Carbone is dressed in the sexiest cheerleader's outfit he's ever seen her wear, designed especially for this game. The yellow sweater with the giant blue "J" dead tight around her big breasts, the short blue skirt revealing the tight bloomers harnessing the perfect bubble ass. Lucy glances disapprovingly at Kevin and turns back to her girls, leading them in a practice chant. "Hey, hey, whaddaya say? All the way with John Jay!"

Kevin looks from Lucy to Bronsky, on the opposite side of the field. Bronsky points to Kevin, then to Lucy, and then to himself and makes an obscene pumping gesture with his right hand. He is telling Kevin he's gonna fuck his girl. Telling him in dumb show in front of all these people. Ooohhhs and aaaahhhs and rolling laughter echo from the crowd. All eyes are on Kevin.

Kevin is itching to play, to show Lucy and Bronsky and the scouts and the press and the rest of the crowd that he is still the best running back in New York City. But the coach benches Kevin for most of the first half. And when he plays him in the third quarter, he uses him as a blocking back. This is not the way to win a championship football game, Kevin thinks. With spite and pettiness. But the coach is making an example of Kevin in front of his teammates and in front of Lucy Carbone, exposing him as a discipline problem to all the college scouts who are here sniffing for talent. Much to the disappointment of the crowd, he and Bronsky, who is playing middle linebacker for Lincoln, have not even made contact.

As Kevin sits through much of the grueling running game, he watches Lucy and then sees Bronsky watching her. Blowing kisses. Throwing pelvic thrusts. No one on his team talks to Kevin. Anthony just gives him a thumbs-up from the other end of the bench. Without Kevin Dempsey, the game is tied at six points each in the fourth quarter.

Up ahead, Kevin saw the tow truck finally reach a crumpled Toyota that had careened into the divider, causing a second car to back-end him. A few moronic motorists began blowing their horns, as if that would ever make the city Department of Transportation workers move faster.

Kevin hardly noticed. He was lost in the gridlock of the gridiron past, remembering the end of the championship game. . . .

In the final minute, the coach finally takes Kevin off the bench with instructions to run one of his signature plays. Now the quarterback, Cliffy Wallace, hands off to Harry Nispoli, who reverses it to Kevin on the Lincoln High thirty. It's second down and five to go, with twenty-four seconds left in the tie game. The play dazzles the Lincoln defense, opening a hole as wide as eternity. The end zone and a scholarship are gaping in front of Kevin Dempsey.

But then Kevin sees Lucy Carbone on the sidelines, in her cheerleader outfit. He makes eye contact with her. It slows him a half step—that and the toll of too many missed meals, skipped practices, sleepless nights, angst-ridden days.

The touchdown is his to blow. He holds Lucy's stare a nanosecond too long, long enough for Bobby Bronsky to slam, all two hundred and forty pounds, helmet first into his groin. Kevin staggers backward, sucking for air. All the Lucy Carbone nightmares crashing down on him at once. As Kevin backpedals, trying to maintain his footing, Bobby Bronsky lets loose an animal wail.

Another player simultaneously slams Kevin from the blind side and the football suddenly explodes recklessly into the air. Kevin watches it sail toward the sideline, where Lucy Carbone lands from a cheerleader leap. Her beautiful mouth is agape, watching the flight of the loose pigskin. It suddenly looks like the cackling, taunting piglet from the dream. As it arches, Kevin sees a pair of hands reach out, as if for his Lucy Carbone herself, but the hands snatch the ball from the air, keeping it in play. Bobby Bronsky tucks the ball into his chest and runs, right past a mesmerized Lucy Carbone, a locomotive of a man rushing for what seems an infinity.

Kevin watches Bobby Bronsky run, his eyes shifting to Lucy Carbone, who watches Bobby Bronsky sweep into the John Jay end zone for a Lincoln High championship-claiming score.

Kevin's game and championship and scholarship are lost. And Kevin is alone on the field now, his body bent in half in pain. Lucy Carbone looks at him with disgust, turns away, and leaves with the other John Jay cheerleaders. Past the mob that surrounds Bobby Bronsky, underage kids all popping champagne corks and gargling the bubbles of victory.

Anthony walks to the writhing Kevin and removes his helmet. Tells him it's okay, only a game, just a sport. Now Bobby Bronsky breaks away from the mob of fans and carries an open bottle of champagne toward Kevin and Anthony as a peace offering. Bronsky crouches, reaches out his hand to Kevin, says let's make bygones be bygones.

Kevin resists.

Anthony nudges him.

Kevin is still reluctant.

Anthony nudges him again.

The two rivals finally shake.

Bronsky even concedes the game would have been different if the coach had let Kevin play longer. Tells him he never got a beating like Kevin gave him before in his life. Kevin tells him no one ever hit him on the football field harder.

They both laugh.

Bronsky offers the champagne. Kevin shrugs, grimaces in pain, takes a swig. Passes the bottle to Anthony. Kevin asks about rumors involving Lucy and Bronsky. Bronsky tells Kevin it's bullshit. Pre-game psyche-out strategy. Bronsky, Kevin, and Anthony pass the bottle around again until it is finished, as they wait for the ambulance to take Kevin to the hospital. Bronsky even invites Anthony to the Lincoln victory party at the Knights of Columbus hall later.

But in this one week, Kevin has lost his girl, the scholarship, and the championship and wound up in the hospital with a broken pelvis and the mumps. All somehow attributable to the worm of jealousy.

"Polly was probably just blowing off some emotional steam," Anthony said, as Kevin sat in his Central Park West office in his bikini underwear, after spending almost an hour stuck in traffic on the FDR Drive.

Kevin's body was still rippling with muscles from all the years in the gym and playing sports. He continued to lift weights in the firehouse and had boxed for the Fire Department until last year, when Polly said it was embarrassing for a grown man to be fighting without getting paid. The situps between bells also had his belly looking like the bottom of an egg carton.

In the outer office, workers were packing boxes for Anthony's move to Los Angeles. In the waiting room, a bicycle messenger studied cartoons in an old *New Yorker* magazine.

"Sure, Zoe might look more like Polly than like you," Anthony said. "But she's a girl. And she's *your* daughter. Good-looking. You always were the best-looking bastard in the neighborhood."

"How do you know when a kid's yours?" Kevin asked. "How does a man ever really know? I mean, a woman always knows it's hers because she carries it. And she usually can figure out who the father really is, because she knows who she's been with. But how do I—how does *any* man—know for sure?"

Anthony checked Kevin's blood pressure. Kevin could see concern in the doctor's face.

"Your blood pressure is through the roof," Anthony said, shaking his head. "I'm going to prescribe some tranquilizers. Maybe the cumulative abuses of your old lifestyle have finally caught up with you. The old fast-lane Kevin: football star, boxing champ, drink all night, score with every babe, drag-race the fancy cars. Excuse me, I know you've been good the last few years, but you're thirty now and it's time to pay the check. Stress can kill. I'm giving you a mild trank."

"I hate drugs, you know that. I only used coke once."

"Yeah," Anthony said with a laugh. "With the nurse I brought to your party in that great pad overlooking the park."

"You brought three nurses, Anthony," Kevin said, grinning.

"Yeah, but she was the one I was after," Anthony said.

"You never told me," Kevin said. "Either did she."

"She didn't know either," Anthony said, and they both laughed. "The shy skinny guinea syndrome. Ah, history. An M.D. and a million babes ago. But I really think you should have a tranquilizer."

"Nah," Kevin said, "no drugs. I'm dopey enough."

"Hey, alcohol is the granddaddy of all drugs."

"Okay, so I'm a hypocrite," Kevin said. "Forget my blood pressure. I want to know if I'm a father. I gotta know for sure, or else I'll wind up playing dice with baby blocks in a rubber room on one of the farms the city sends you to."

"There's no reason not to think you're the father," Anthony said.

"We were married over a year before Polly got pregnant, for Christ sakes."

"For some couples it takes years and special diets and timing and new positions," Anthony said. "For some, it's automatic. Remember, her body went through unbelievable trauma in the fire. That could have temporarily altered her hormones. Then the psychological depression she went into afterward because of the scars the burns left. And the skin grafts. And losing her modeling career because of the scars on her hands, arms, and shoulders. I helped treat her, remember. She was depressed. Depression can make the body react strangely. Everything is relative, Kev. We're talking about creating life here, not painting a house."

"What about a DNA test?"

"If the baby were here, with the okay from both parents or a judge's order, sure," Anthony said. "I could only do it that way. The lab won't even process a DNA paternity test without its being authorized up the kazoo. But I have Zoe's and yours and Polly's blood types on file. I'll do a hereditary matchup. In the meantime, I'll need fresh blood from you."

"I think I might have a lock of hair from the baby packed in some box at home. Would that be enough to prove she's mine?"

"I'd have to have samples of the mother and father and the baby in order to do a complete DNA profile," Anthony said. "*And* the judge's order. It's a messy problem, all right. But the blood and sperm count should suffice. Don't forget there's an innocent in the middle here."

"I'm aware of that, Anthony," Kevin said. "I know how tricky this is. Maybe I'm being selfish. But Christ, I need to know who the fuck I am!"

"You need to know just how badly you've been used," Anthony said. "Your dignity is on the line here. That's it, isn't it?"

"If Zoe isn't mine, how do I face people? Family—they'll understand. But friends? The firehouse?"

"Well, whatever the truth is, be straight, Kevin. Talk the way you're talking to me."

"You're different," Kevin said. "We're . . . we're lifers. Best friends. Plus you're my doctor."

"Isn't it enough just to love the kid no matter what?" asked Anthony.

"That's if she comes back to me," Kevin said. "Even if she did, and Zoe isn't mine, I don't know if I could live with the deceit. If I'm not her father, that means somewhere her real father would be deprived of her. Robbed of *his* fatherhood. I couldn't live my life that way. And what if Polly disappears? What if Polly really never comes back with Zoe? What if she splits to England or Europe or somewhere?"

"Do you think that's possible?" Anthony asked. "Did she sound that final?"

"She sounded like she meant every word," Kevin said. "Her parents are in England, all her old friends. Boyfriends. She would never tell me anything about old boyfriends. Plus the courts there would protect her because she's still a British subject."

Anthony walked to a tray of medical instruments and put blood samples into various glass test tubes and marked them. Kevin had his back to Anthony, who held his blood in his gloved hands.

"Did she sound like she was really in love with this other guy?" Anthony asked.

A whirlpool of vertigo spun inside Kevin again and passed quickly. He was afraid to mention it to Anthony because he would insist on some prescription.

"I'd need to look her in the eyes," Kevin said. "It's hard to tell on the phone."

"Did she give you any clue as to who he is?"

"Nah," Kevin said.

This was hard, talking about his private life, his rocky relationship with his wife, the woman he loved, the mother of the child he thought was his until this morning. He felt like he was standing in Macy's window for all to see in X ray. Kevin thought of going to a stranger, a doctor he didn't know. Have him cup his balls, cough, say ah, leave a sperm sample, and wait for results. But that was too clinical, impersonal. This was about his wife and kid. Fuck, it was about his life. Anthony was the only one he could truly trust.

"She'll be back, Kev," Anthony said. "It's probably just a phase."

Anthony wore a white coat and a perfectly knotted blue tie with a red stripe. Since childhood, he had always been clean and well dressed, with clear, glistening skin and spotless half-moon fingernails.

The movers were banging the furniture around in the outer office. Their actions made another piece of Kevin's earth shift. The last of Kevin's childhood pals was shipping out.

"There's one other thing," Anthony said, removing a stick of litmus paper from Kevin's urine sample. "You're drinking way too much. Your liver is swollen, and there's an awful lot of yeast in your urine. I hope you don't have active enzymes; that might be early signs of cirrhosis. Your urine tells me you're not eating right, either. And your skin is dehydrated and pasty-looking. Your hands are trembling and your eyes are bloodshot and your reflexes are like a window shade wound too tight. One touch and it snaps. In short, you're a mess."

"Jesus, just what I need, the old school cheer," Kevin said.

"A mess but a strong mess," Anthony said. "You need sleep and relaxation and nourishment. You're a tough son of a bitch, but you have to unwind. Don't, for God's sake, drink. It won't soothe your nerves, it'll make them worse. Buy some magnesium tablets if you won't take tranquilizers. Eat bananas for the potassium. I'll give you a B-twelve shot. Drink lots of water for your skin, it's dying of thirst. So are your eyes; they need water, especially after crying. Emotional stress dehydrates the system. So does alcohol. You could use a few days on a saline drip. Your stool seems blood-free under the microscope, but your urine is like battery acid. The only thing you have going for you is that you're thirty, like me. Young enough to recover from most damage and old enough to know better. Thirty is the yellow caution light. Proceed with care, Kev."

Anthony motioned him onto his stomach and jabbed a syringe with the B-12 into his buttocks. The pain was minimal. He didn't feel uncomfortable being naked in front of Anthony. They'd seen each other naked since they were kids in circle jerks, locker rooms, and crash pads with broads.

"You know, I've been trying to determine exactly when you stopped calling shit shit and said stool instead. The day you get your first stethoscope do you start calling piss urine? Even when you're from Brooklyn? You call your dick a penis, too?"

Anthony laughed at Kevin's ribbing, as he pulled off his surgical gloves with a snap and Kevin sat up. Kevin needed a laugh.

"Nothing wrong with your brain," Anthony said. "Still as crazed as when you were ten."

"No, serious, how come you use all the formal terms even with me?" Kevin asked.

"If I wasn't professional all the time, I might be treating a seventy-year-old woman and say to her, 'Sorry, hon, but your piss test says you got lifelong clap.' Get serious, Kevin. Don't be a pain in my testicles."

"Speaking of testicles, should I go into the porno parlor now?"

Anthony smiled and handed Kevin a porno cassette titled *Sin Hips* and an empty glass jar. Kevin looked at the cassette and laughed. "When we were kids they said dirty pictures and masturbation would make you blind. Now my doctor prescribes them. The world changes."

"The only way we can test your sperm count," Anthony said.

"Remember when we were kids in Holy Family we used to go up to the abandoned building, me, you, and the guys, when we were first getting hair on our balls, and we used to get hot books and have contests to see who could shoot the farthest when we whacked off?" Kevin asked.

"It's called ejaculate projection," Anthony said. "I never won."

"Me neither. Vito Splendorio was the oldest, so he always won. He swore it was from his mother's homemade Sicilian clam sauce. His father told him that when he discussed the birds and the bees with him. Vito was convinced seagulls were the birds with the biggest dicks because they ate clams and oysters, remember? Who knows? He was sixteen in the eighth grade. His IQ was about the same as his age, but boy could he shoot."

"You're a sick bastard, Dempsey," Anthony said, laughing. "With you, memory is dangerous."

"Talk about youth being wasted on the young, huh?" Kevin said. "Vito the Shooter. He's probably in Congress now. Who the fuck knows what happened to all those guys from Holy Family. Even the school is gone. It's a senior center now. Christ, I wonder if I'll wind up back there in a wheelchair."

"Just go take care of business." Anthony laughed.

"You miss those days, Anthony?" Kevin asked, stalling, hefting the cassette. "I do. I miss being young, real young. I really do. I look back now and it's like visiting somebody else. I miss who I was as a kid. Before Lucy and the big game and Bobby Bronsky. Certainly before Polly and marriage. It was so much simpler then. Maybe that's why I wanted a kid of my own so bad. To live as a kid all over again."

Kevin paused, inhaled deeply, and continued.

"I miss it. I miss you being my best friend and hanging out together after school, robbing subway tokens and breaking into drugstore weighing machines for dimes and quarters and all the other crazy shit we did together."

"Yeah, sometimes I do too," Anthony said. "I miss the wonder of discovery and learning new things, ya know? Seriously. I think about it a lot. I think about what it was like, going to school every morning and learning something new. New words, new math, new science. I remember the first time I learned the word *subtle*. I walked around calling everything subtle. 'Hey, man, this is a subtle pizza, subtle beer, subtle sunset. . . .' "

Kevin laughed. "Yeah, I remember, until you told Kathy the Redhead she had beautiful subtle tits. She wasn't subtle when she smacked you across the face."

"And that was the most skin I ever got off her," Anthony said, laughing. "But of course you nailed her a few weeks later. But, yeah, those days. Christ, I used to dream about being a doctor even then. And I'm lucky because as a doctor you learn new things all the time too, like when you were a kid. I mean this life, medicine, it's been very good to me. I've won big awards and made good money, and I'm going to California. Maybe I can get in on a university research team, discover something important. I'd like to be remembered for something."

"Jesus, it must be tough giving up such a good practice," Kevin said.

"Time to move on," Anthony said. "There are sick people everywhere."

"Fires, too," Kevin said.

Anthony nodded, as Kevin pulled on a robe. So many years crowded into the room, Kevin thought. Like magic. Common experience and memory and the unbreakable cables of friendship. Yet there was an almost tangible sadness in the air that neither could touch but both could feel.

"Yesterday," Kevin said, "I thought I had everything. A job I love. A family I love. A new house for us. I was almost a happy man. And now here I am today trying to find out if I'm the father of my baby. If somebody's really driving the Big Bus, the driver must have a mean streak in him as wide as Prospect Park."

Anthony glanced at his watch, then at the moving men, who continued packing boxes in the outer office, and the messenger who waited for the lab samples.

"We better hurry before they take the desk," Anthony said. "Now go into the porno parlor there and make believe it's after school in the abandoned building. See if you can outdo Vito Splendorio."

Kevin laughed and walked into the darkened windowless room. He plugged in the video cassette and watched the mechanical images come to life in front of him on the television screen. He removed his shorts and at first nothing at all happened. The porno didn't do it for him. He was afraid that if he thought about Polly his dick would go limp.

Instead he closed his eyes.

And here comes Lucy Carbone. It's my first time. It's a month after the worm of jealousy and the fumble in the big game. A month since the fractured pelvis. A month since me and Anthony both came down with mumps.

Forget Anthony and the mumps. Here comes Lucy, down Sixteenth Street, sweaty in her cheerleader uniform, after the practice for the John Jay holiday show. Her big tits are bouncing under the white sweater. I'm waiting for her on the stoop, feeling awkward, foolish. And she asks how I'm feeling. I say I'm feeling okay now. All better. She says her parents are out at a movie in Manhattan, which means far, far away. She invites me upstairs. As soon as we step into the apartment Lucy is all over me. She puts her arms around my neck and pushes her tongue into my mouth, and she smells of perfume and hair spray and fresh sweat. Her hands are all over my ass and my arms and my balls and cock. Saying how much she missed me. That she's never been with anyone else. Not Bronsky. Not anyone. That she wants me to take her cherry. Take it now. And she's down on her knees and nibbling my balls and cock through my dungarees and breathing hot air on my dick, and now she opens the top button of my pants. Saying she's been dreaming about doing this for the whole month we've been busted up. Now I hear the magical crackle of the zipper going down. The pants are yanked down. Snap! My dick flaps out over the sticky elastic band of the Fruit of the Looms and slaps back against my hard belly. My cock is steel hard and pointing straight up and she grabs it with both hands, on her knees, in the foyer and she puts it in her mouth and starts sucking the knob, making wet slurping sounds, licking it like an ice cream and moaning, and I'm bending over to grab her big tits. She stands up and pulls off all her clothes—sweater, bra, skirt, panties. She leaves on her saddle shoes and socks and takes me by the dick and leads me to her parents' bed that smells like beer and sweat and old sex, and she sprawls flat and spreads her beautiful strong cheerleader legs, the pom-poms on her saddle shoes vibrating and little tinkles coming from the bells on the laces. I'm dying of pain, but she takes my rock-hard cock and guides it into this impossibly tight little hole between her legs and screams that she wants me to shoot it into her. I'm scared but she wraps her legs around my lower back and the little shoe bells are ringing madly now and the pom-poms are tickling my thighs and she digs her nails into my ass and pulls me deeper and she's yelling for me to fuck her harder and harder. And so I grab her by the hard white cheeks of her ass and feel the wetness in the crack. I'm ready to erupt and now I do and my body jerks crazily out of control and I'm coming so hard and so much that I can't pull it out and Lucy won't let me anyway and she's screaming for more and humping and bucking and screaming and I keep squirting and squirting and squirting. . . .

Kevin had brought the glass jar out to Anthony and was sitting on the edge of the examining table.

"And two months later I had to come up with the money for the abortion that I didn't want her to have," Kevin told Anthony.

"What? You never told me that," Anthony said.

"I didn't? Probably too ashamed. You know: an *abortion,* in that neighborhood."

"But Kevin," Anthony said, "that was Bobby Bronsky's kid, not yours."

Kevin was silent for a long moment, a dopey half smile frozen on his face.

"Fuck are you talking about?" he asked, his eyes narrowing.

"Lucy Carbone *was* seeing Bronsky on the side at the same time as you. For Christ sakes, we even saw her disguise herself when she went out to see him practice that day. Don't you remember? The day you beat the shit out of him?"

"That was just because of my paranoia, adolescent jealousy," Kevin said. "Phone calls from the other team, trying to distract me. It worked."

"No, no, no," Anthony said. "Dial up reality, Kev. Lucy and Bronsky were definitely an item back then. You didn't know that? When you went into the hospital?"

"But he told me to my face it was bullshit," Kevin said. "After the game. He shook my hand, shared his champagne, said it was a lie."

"After the beating you gave him, you expected the truth from him?" Anthony said and laughed. "They even did it that night, the night we lost the championship game. For Christ sakes, I saw them getting it on in the back of a van in the parking lot outside the Knights of Columbus where they had the victory party."

"You mean the night of the day I fumbled, don't you, Anthony?"

"The team lost the game, Kev," Anthony said, his back to Kevin, marking the sperm specimen jar and placing it into a white paper bag, which he stapled shut. "It wasn't just you. Bronsky gave you a broken pelvis. And me and you the mumps. I caught the mumps too, from sharing the champagne with Bronsky."

Kevin sat staring at Anthony, incredulous. "Now you're saying I lost the *girl* that day too?" Kevin said.

"Lot of water under the bridge," Anthony said. "You have better things to worry about now."

They were both silent a moment, as Anthony walked to the outer office and handed the bagged sperm and blood samples to the messenger in the waiting room.

"We can only wait, now," Anthony said. "Maybe the tests will be back tomorrow. The day after, the latest. The day I leave."

"Right now, I have to go to work," Kevin said.

"Why don't you take a day off?" Anthony suggested, removing his coat and hanging it on a hook on the back of the inner-office door. Kevin followed Anthony out toward the receptionist's empty desk in the outer office.

"Nah, going to work will take my mind off things," Kevin said.

"Yeah, I understand," Anthony said. "Then I'm prescribing you to read a book, something light, escape a little."

Kevin nodded and pulled on his jacket, preparing to leave. Anthony put on his suit coat.

"Are you sure Lucy was fucking Bobby Bronsky when I was going out with her?" Kevin asked.

"It was the talk of the neighborhood," Anthony said. "Remember, you were in the hospital and laid up awhile."

"Why didn't you tell me?"

"Nobody had the balls to tell you to your face. Me included. Look what it had already done to you. If you knew she gave up her cherry to him on the night he won the big game, you might have murdered them both. They were drunk. Everyone clapped as the van rocked. I just told you, I saw them."

Anthony turned out the inner office lights and pulled the locked door shut behind him.

All these years later, Kevin still felt like killing both Bobby Bronsky and Lucy Carbone. Kill them both, while fucking. He had to put the murderer within back in his cage. The worm of jealousy never goes away, Kevin thought.

"Lucy told me I was the first one," Kevin said.

"Christ, in that neighborhood all the girls said that until they were married," Anthony said. "She finally did marry Bobby Bronsky. So what does that tell you? But my guess is she went to you, after him, because he wouldn't pay for the abortion. Then went back to him."

"Then the kid she aborted might not have been mine," Kevin said.

Anthony was buttoning his coat and looked at Kevin as if he were odd. "Who cares? That's ancient history. Teenage lust. Think about now." He paused. "My opinion, nonmedical? Everything's gonna be fine between you and Polly. Believe me."

"You really think so?" Kevin asked.

"Yeah. Go see a movie. Read a book. Get your mind off it. Be good to yourself."

The outer office was empty now of nurses, receptionist, movers, messengers. Anthony turned off the lights, locked up. They passed a uniformed black doorman with white gloves who dozed on a chair in the vestibule with a *New York Post* on his lap. Outside on Central Park West they shook hands, and Anthony told Kevin he'd call with the test results as soon as they came in. There was nothing left to say. Kevin watched Anthony walk to his Mercedes, with its protective shield of M.D. license plates, entitling him to park almost anywhere at any time. The M.D. plates were an emblem of success, a dream come true. A similar dream had vanished for Kevin Dempsey, just like so many other illusions were vanishing. Some guys score. Some guys fumble.

Even Lucy lied to me, Kevin thought, as he walked downtown toward Columbus Circle, past the Mayflower Hotel where he used to hang out with friends before he was married. He'd even spent the night with Polly there once, on Valentine's Day, in a suite overlooking the park.

Near the A train subway station, a panhandler approached Kevin with a blue and white cup, one of the tens of thousands of beggars who live in the streets of New York. Kevin dipped a dollar into the cup, thinking, I could be one of these poor assholes. Cold, lousy, hungry, nuts. Three more bums rose from the subway stairs and were on him now, at the wide sweep of sidewalk outside the Gulf and Western Building. Kevin waved them off.

"Once a fool, twice a pervert," Kevin said to the crowd of bums and tried to remember where he'd read that. Was it Voltaire? Aristotle? He'd read it and made it part of his firehouse philosophy arsenal. Kevin spent most of his down time in the firehouse reading. Most guys in the firehouse were big readers. Kevin liked philosophy, metaphysical explorations of life in between encounters with real death. He especially liked Marcus Aurelius's *Meditations* in the firehouse. Sometimes, the meditations helped between bells on a tough summer night or after he'd dragged three dead kids out of a Christmas-tree fire. "Look beneath the surface: never let a thing's intrinsic quality or worth escape you." Book Six, meditation three. Kevin knew it by heart.

"Who you calling a pervert, motherfucker?" said one panhandler. He was in his twenties, tall and broad-shouldered, animated with jail muscles in a sleeveless Yankees T-shirt. He swiped through the air at Kevin with an 007 folding knife. Kevin dodged the blade and smashed the guy in the chest so hard with a right hand that the man lifted off his feet, sailed toward the entrance of the subway stairs, and landed flat on his back, scattering a flock of ratty pigeons. Kevin looked down and saw himself lying helpless on the field the day of the fumble. He kicked the knife into the middle of the traffic circle, lifted the bum off the ground, and sat him on the low marble retaining wall of the office building.

"Don't hit me no more, brother," said the young bum, trembling. "Please don't hit me no more. Ever since my bitch threw me out, I been a-hurtin' something bad. But I ain't no pervert."

As the sky cracked and a soft rain began to fall on the city, Kevin looked down at the beaten, frightened man and wondered where he'd dropped his ball.

6

Frank Dempsey walked along Wall Street looking for the building where this British banker named Clive Morton worked. If Polly had made her way back to England, Frank wanted to see what her Brit pals knew about it.

He carried the *New York Post* under his arm and a sixteen-ounce bottle of Gatorade half filled with vodka in his inside jacket pocket. He kept the jacket unzipped so the bottle wouldn't show a bulge. The vodka didn't smell as heavy as something like scotch, but all booze breath stood you apart like an identifying birthmark.

Frank felt good to be able to carry a newspaper that didn't have his name and picture in it. The *Post* had used the same shot of Frank so many times in the last two months that they could have given him a column called "On the Take" by Frank Dempsey.

He looked behind him and saw Summers, the IAB cop, tailing him at a discreet distance. Summers was in his late thirties, about six feet tall, and walked like a sentry with an erect posture. Summers had followed him earlier, as he did every Monday morning, to Greenwood Cemetery, where Frank visited the crypt that held his parents. There, Summers stood discreetly at the bottom of a knoll among the tablets of the dead, with his hands in his pockets of his suit jacket or smoking his cigarettes.

Every week, usually on Monday, Frank would go into the mausoleum, take care of business in the company of God and the dust of the family dead, and leave after fifteen minutes. Rain or shine, Summers would wait and smoke and say nothing. He always made Frank feel unclean.

On the corner of Wall and Broad streets, the religious freaks were droning on about salvation. Frank didn't worry much about his own salvation anymore. Anthony Scala, his doctor, Kevin's friend, had told him in the hallway outside Kevin's kitchen yesterday that without a liver transplant he had a year at the outside to live. The next time jaundice set in would almost certainly be the last. Dr. Scala said his liver was so badly eaten away by booze and the chronic hepatitis and cirrhosis that there was little chance of rejuvenation. Anthony had said he didn't like giving him the news at the party, or while he was under so much other strain, but he was leaving for California and wanted Frank to know how sick he was. He told him he belonged in a hospital while a nationwide search for a liver took place. Anthony had also told Frank that there was a very slim chance of getting a new liver because the Liver Foundation rarely let an available one go to an alcoholic whose problem is self-inflicted. You do not give precious livers to alcoholics who might go out and abuse the new one like the old.

He wondered what his mother thought of him, looking down from her celestial perch. Knew she would be terribly saddened about what he had done to his body and his life. He remembered the time she walked into the apartment kitchen from her bedroom, where she had been breast-feeding Margie to sleep. Frank was six and was sipping from a big quart bottle of beer that Big Paulie had left open in the refrigerator. Mom went berserk. Tore the bottle from Frank's hand and smashed it into the sink. Dragged Frank into the bathroom and held his head over the toilet, put a finger down his throat until he vomited up the beer. How much it burned coming through his nose! Frank remembered being put into bed, with no lights to read, kept from going outside to play. The commotion waked little Margie, and she began to wail. Frank felt awful, frightened and remorseful. But confused because his mother had always been such a saintly, gentle woman. And because Big Paulie had secretly been giving him his first sips of beer for more than a year now, with promises of never telling Mommy. Big Paulie told little Frank it would make him big and strong.

Years later, Frank learned that his mother's father, Frank's maternal grandfather, had died from cirrhosis when Frank's mom was just fifteen. She had never recovered from it. She was certain the dirty booze gene was in the bloodline.

Later his mother and Big Paulie had a huge fight over the open bottle of beer. She banned alcohol from the house. Big Paulie used this as an excuse to do all his drinking away from home, out in the saloons. So Frank had prayed to his mother's soul earlier in this morning, hoping she would understand and forgive him now. Things just are not going well for the Dempseys down here, Mom, he thought.

If I can stretch the trial and the appeals, I'll never have to do time on earth. If I have to, maybe I can get a medical extension in the courts. The secrets about the money can die with me, and the family can move on. I've had my run. Mike is an angry young man, but he'll be okay. Fine wife, good kids. Margie never needed help. It's Kevin who needs something now, Frank thought. He married bad. We all said that at the time, but not to Kevin. We knew Polly would never be happy married to a civil servant in Brooklyn. She was too pampered, fanciful, dreamy for the hard realities of child-rearing in a working-class neighborhood. In some ways she was too beautiful. She was resented by many of the women who never saw her shop with coupons clipped from the *Daily News* in Key Food. She traveled from Brooklyn to Dean & Deluca's in Manhattan to shop for dinner. She bought her clothes and had her hair done in Manhattan too. Of course, in the end it is none of your business, Frank thought. Besides, who was Frank Dempsey to lecture anyone on how to live a life? He wasn't at all surprised that Polly had decided to leave Kevin. But he was unwilling to allow that she had absconded with Kevin's daughter, Zoe, Frank's goddaughter. That was unacceptable.

He stood in front of Federal Hall at the feet of the statue of George Washington and watched a one-armed vendor do a juggling act with a hot dog and roll. A sign on his cart said GI JACK and he'd spring open the roll with thumb and forefinger, slap it down on a piece of waxed paper, spear a hot dog and holster it into the bun, slather it with the mustard stick, switch to tongs to heap it with onions and sauerkraut, wrap it water-tight, bag it, with one paw, so fast as to marvel, and shout, "One with everything on it!" After each one he pocketed the bills and gave change. GI Jack was like a one-armed one-man band. He wore a Korean war VFW Post hat and was working a few feet from another stainless steel wagon where a Korean was selling shish kebab. After each "One with everything on it" announcement, GI Jack would turn to the Korean and snap, "No surrender!"

The Korean ignored him and sold his beef-on-a-stick to the bundled-up lunch crowd. Old wars were being fought here on Wall Street in front of the father of the country, Frank thought. There's a war in my family too. There's a war in my body. There's a war in the courts. And there's a war in Kevin's life, and here comes somebody who might provide me some intelligence from the war zone.

Right across the street, Clive Morton stepped out of the building on the corner of Wall and Broad streets. He was wearing a long blue trench coat over a light-gray linen Armani suit and expensive black leather boots. He was with a man with platinum hair, dressed in a dark suit and an olive overcoat. The second man was younger, in his early thirties. They walked down Broad Street with Frank behind them.

A light rain began to fall. Frank put the sociably acceptable pint-sized Gatorade bottle to his lips, and took a long swallow, grimacing as it went down. He took a final slug and it was gone. He deposited the bottle in a trash can and shivered as the booze made its mysterious journey through his body and brain.

The lunch crowd began to swell on the street as Frank followed his quarry. Taxis and trucks honked for passage. Pretty women in early fall fashions worried about their hair and walked with their eyes cast downward to the rain. Frank kept his eyes squarely on the back of Morton's head. The platinum guy stopped and bought a *Daily News* at a kiosk and placed it over his head in lieu of an umbrella. Women rushed past him in the rain, umbrellas bobbing. So many women, so little time, Frank thought. All so beautiful. But none as beautiful as the one at Kevin's party, Polly's friend, Sarah Cross. Goddammit, Frank, you never had a great love in this life.

He turned, and Summers was behind him like a Xerox copy. He nodded hello, but Summers stared into a bookstore window. He felt sorry for Summers. When his kid asks him what he did all day, he'll have to tell him he followed a man around. That's if he tells the truth. Maybe he would juice it up with a few shootouts and car chases.

After Summers went home the other Internal Affairs guy, Magno, would sit outside Frank's apartment house all night listening to Lite FM. There were different shoeflies assigned to weekends all the time.

Morton and the younger man joined a small crowd filing into a restaurant called Osbourne's. Frank felt the wad in his pocket, a thousand in cash that IAB would like to have its hands on. Along with the rest of the million and a half. Give or take a few thousand. In their hiding place, the stacks of bills were piled so high he'd stopped counting them. One thing was sure: IAB would never count them either.

From the beginning he had to steal the money for the family's sake, not for himself. They didn't know that and didn't need to, never would. But he didn't feel bad using some of it to help out Kevin, who was family.

Frank paid his lawyer a twenty-thousand-dollar retainer from his legitimate meager savings account. He hired a Court Street hack because it didn't look like the lawyers were going to do him much good in court anyway, without Frank offering names or giving back the missing money. He was the only suspect they had, and they were going to hang somebody.

Right now, having something of his own to investigate again gave Frank purpose and almost made him want to go for the dry-out and try to save his life. But he had made up his mind that he would never do prison time, so he might as well go out this way, on a mission. His only fear of death was meeting someone in eternity he'd locked up and sent away wrongly. It was every decent cop's nightmare, that you put some good kid in a bad place and steal a piece of his earthly life. You should get at least purgatory for that. If a cop did that on purpose—and a lot do for brownie points or promotions or racism or personal vendettas—he should go directly to the damnation of hell, Frank thought. Frank did believe in the eternal furnace.

But his God was not a punishing God. He didn't condemn you for being a screwup, Frank thought. Only the truly wicked take the express elevator down. Frank was a believer, all right. Nothing made sense otherwise.

Frank followed as Morton and the platinum guy walked into the wood and brass gleam of Osbourne's. He had his hat pulled low. Morton didn't notice Frank as he approached the maître d'. The maître d' sat the two men at a booth near the window close to the bar. They hung up their coats on brass hooks at the booth. Osbourne's was an expensive but reliable steak and chops place.

Frank took his seat at a bar that had a half inch coating of polyurethane, which made your drink slide onto your lap if you didn't keep a cocktail napkin or a coaster under it. Frank hated that because you couldn't connect the wet ring stains on the bar or dig your nails into the unvarnished bar-top wood like you could in a regular beer-and-a-ball saloon. Ah, the mechanics of drinking. Claiming your spot, circling your stool, placing a newspaper to your right to ensure elbow room, then digging in your nails to get a grip on your bar space and making your mark with your glass. It was territorial. "That's my spot," was part of the basic vocabulary of a seasoned saloon drinker. In New York City you staked your claim by leaving your money on the bar in front of your spot, even when you went to the john. But in places like this, the bartender rang up each drink on a tab and expected you to pay at the end of your fill with a credit card.

"Will you be eating at the bar, sir?" the black-vested bartender with the red bow tie asked Frank.

"Only if you put an olive in my double Stoli rocks," Frank said.

The bartender smiled and built the drink. Vodka didn't make Frank drunk, it merely kept him from seizure. Scotch could get him drunk if he cracked the second quart after midnight. Cognac, one bottle. But he rarely did that in public.

He could hear Morton and the other guy ordering from a tall leggy waitress in a short black skirt. Frank glanced peripherally at the young girl, thinking: thoroughbred stock in a glue-factory job.

"Yes, dear," he heard Morton say to the girl. "I say, now if you were dining with me, I think I might fancy what you'd order."

"I was thinking about Chinese later actually," the waitress said, smiling.

"We could order some from my place if you'd like," Morton said, grinning lasciviously. "Say around eight?"

He's a total cretin, Frank thought. A rude, nasty, pompous ass. The way Frank liked them when he was in control. And having control, over someone who didn't know you were even there, was always so easy. You learned that on surveillance. You could force anyone to make a left turn even if they wanted to go right, if you were thinking two steps ahead. And Frank was more than two steps ahead of Morton.

"Would you like to hear the specials?" the waitress asked politely.

"No, my treasure," said Morton. "Actually, I'd like a sirloin about as rare and tender as you are. And just as juicy, if that's at all possible."

Coming from a hard hat with half a load on in a Blarney Stone at lunchtime, this might be partially excused except for the "juicy" part,

Frank thought. But Morton thinks he's pedigree. He needs a lesson in manners, Frank decided, about how to talk to a working guy's daughter.

Frank heard the platinum guy order "the same" and then each man ordered Bombay gin martinis, stirred, not shaken, and drained, twist. Frank took out his folded C-notes and peeled two off the wad. The waitress approached the bar and gave the bartender the drink order. Frank stepped beside her.

"Here's two hundred dollars," Frank said.

"Hey, pal, I test positive for HTR . . . as in Hit The Road."

"All I want you to do is wait until the Brit orders his second drink. Then drop it on his lap."

The waitress looked at Frank and then at Morton and then at the two folded C-notes Frank was pressing into her hand. Morton was staring at her but Frank was careful to keep his back to Morton. There was a remote chance, after all, that Morton had noticed him at the party.

"Mister," the waitress said, smelling his boozy breath, "maybe you had too much—"

"You could buy a comfortable pair of shoes with that deuce," Frank said. She looked back at Morton, who winked at her. She smiled.

"I'll probably get fired," she said.

"I'll trip you," Frank said, "and take the blame."

The bartender brought the two martinis. The waitress looked nervous. "You know this asshole?"

"Friend of the family," Frank assured her. "Just be sweet until the second round."

The waitress pocketed the money and shook her head and delivered the drinks to Morton's table. Frank finished his martini. The bartender fixed Frank another drink and the waitress walked back to get drinks for another table. She exchanged a grin with Frank and took the drinks for the other table and walked past Frank.

"If I wasn't going out with a guy, I'd tell you you're kinda cute," she said. "And nuts. I like that in a guy. Nuts. Not that kinda nuts. You know what I mean."

She blushed.

"You're a beautiful woman," Frank said.

"Thanks," she said. "That's nice. Especially when someone nice says it. Another time, another life maybe, huh?"

"That would be *nice,"* he said.

"Oh, well." She laughed and delivered her drinks. She was a lovely girl, Frank thought. She had legs like a dancer with long tendons in her thighs and strong bunched calves. Like Sarah Cross's legs. He hoped her guy was good to her. She seemed like a good egg. He felt a dull ache in his left side. The monster wanted fed. He sipped his martini and eavesdropped on Morton and his friend.

"You mean she just never showed up?" the platinum guy asked.

"That's my Pollyanna," said Morton, with the glass to his lips, staring at the waitress, who was bending over another table. "My God, that tea girl has an arse as high as a giraffe's."

The platinum guy turned to see and nodded and they both laughed. Frank swallowed his drink with a grimace.

"Well, you're the only one who ever seems to be able to track her down," said the platinum guy. "A few of the others have tried and so have I, but to no avail."

"Tell them that for me she's never hard to find," said Morton, as he screwed himself sideways in the booth to get comfortable. "But my God, the so-called family home is buried in the belly of the beast of *Brooklyn.* I mean *buried.* It might as well have been in Brixton! Polly would absolutely perish there. The poor fireman bought it as a surprise, but of course she knew. It was her cue to fly the coop, as they say." He took a sip of his drink and patted his lips with a linen napkin. "Too much money involved for her to be bogged down. In the end, her marriage was nothing more than a fling. Polly is still quite fond of money. Polly will never stray as far as she once did from the money she is used to."

Frank watched him nibble an olive from a toothpick. He looked like a gerbil eating lunch, Frank thought.

"Whose money?" asked the platinum guy.

"Ours," he said. "Of course. Which reminds me, I must call London right after lunch."

The waitress came over and picked up the empty martini glasses. She walked back to the bar and looked at Frank, who was on his third martini now and rubbing his palms together. The waitress took a deep inhale and let it out slowly, in preparation for her task. Frank winked and she winked back as the bartender brought the drinks to her. Frank drained his glass, left a twenty-dollar bill to pay for the drinks and a tip for the bartender. He watched as the waitress approached Morton's table, put on his Irish hat and dark glasses and got up from his stool.

Frank passed the waitress as he strode toward the men's room at the rear of Osbourne's. "On the *rocks* this time," he whispered, stumbling into her hard. She tipped forward as Frank mumbled "Excuse me" and faked a stagger toward the men's room. Then he heard the explosion behind him.

"Jesus *wept!*" Morton shouted, as glass shattered and silverware rattled on the floor. "Good God!"

"That man bumped into me," the waitress explained, pointing to Frank, who staggered toward the men's room, raising his hand like a basketball player admitting a foul.

"I know, I saw the blundering idiot! I'm not blind. God almighty! My linen Armani is fucking ruined!"

Frank waited behind the door of the single-bowl men's room. Morton was shouting as he entered. "You drunken fool!"

Frank snapped one arm around Morton's neck and sprayed NYPD-issue Mace into Morton's eyes and quickly fastened the bolt on the door. Morton tried to scream but Frank's arm was rammed against his Adam's apple, clogging the passage from the larynx. Frank took wet paper towels from the sink top and pressed them against Morton's eyes to take away the terrible burning sensation and keep him from screaming but adding to his temporary blindness.

Morton reached both hands to the cold compress, which kept Morton's hands occupied and freed one of Frank's. With the free hand, Frank unbuckled and unbuttoned and unzipped Morton's trousers and let them fall around his ankles. This immobilized Morton's legs and added to his vulnerability.

Standing behind him, Frank whispered into Morton's ear, "Where's Polly?"

Morton shook his head.

"Where's Polly?"

"Who are you?" Morton croaked. "I can't believe this."

"Where's Polly?"

"My God. Look, I don't know for sure. She could be anywhere."

"Where's Polly?"

"She's been homesick. She has family in England. . . ."

"Who's she with?"

Frank spoke directly into the ear so the hot breath would penetrate and further menace Morton. Patient whispers, hot breath, blindness. They usually bring clarity. Frank now eased slightly on his throat. Morton didn't try to fight.

"Men fall all over Polly," Morton croaked. "But I don't know who—"

"Last time. Where's Polly?"

"She'll get in touch. She said she had a proposition that would make us big money. She said we would both get rich. That's all I know. Maybe you and I can do business—whoever you are."

"How much money?"

"A lot. With Polly that could mean anything. Maybe a million. Maybe more. But she says she has a deal. She'll be in touch."

"So will I," Frank whispered. He pulled the pants over Morton's shoes. "You know I could have killed you, don't you?" he whispered.

"Yes."

"I can anytime I want," Frank whispered. "Keep that in mind."

Still wearing the walking hat and dark glasses, Frank carried the pants with him when he left the men's room. He hung them on the brass hook at Morton's booth, where the man with the platinum hair stared confused, mouth agape. Frank tipped his hat at the waitress on the way out of the restaurant.

"Tell management the men's room needs cleaning," Frank said. The waitress smiled. The platinum guy stared back toward the rest room.

Outside, Frank nodded to Summers, who did not return the greeting. Summers followed Frank in the falling rain toward the subway up on Wall Street.

7

Kevin loved the Coliseum bookstore at Fifty-seventh and Broadway. The store occupied the entire northwest corner of the intersection, its windows a constant attraction for tourists and natives in search of the best collection of contemporary and classic books in New York. New York writers, and there was no shortage of them, all envisioned their books being displayed in the windows of Coliseum Books. It was considered a great literary showcase, the equivalent of a musician playing Carnegie Hall, which was right down the block. Or a theater opening on Broadway, and it was after all Broadway. Or a Fifty-seventh Street art gallery exhibit, and the bookstore was on Fifty-seventh Street too. For a writer to be seen in the window of the Coliseum was to have made it in New York.

Kevin had some time to kill before work in the afternoon and Anthony had told him to go easy on the booze, so he was browsing through the rows of popular fiction, looking for a new thriller, man of action, code of honor, boy meets girl, falls in love with girl, loses girl, gets girl back, girl gets killed, boy deals with loss of girl with booze and sadness and impotence and then violently avenges girl's death.

Something like that.

But most of the new fiction was geared toward women.

So Kevin thought he would grab a woman's book instead, to get in a female's frame of mind, maybe better understand Polly. He hadn't read that many women writers. He liked crime stuff by P. D. James and Sue Grafton. He lifted one of Grafton's many "letter" books, *"K" is for Killer*. He liked the way she used each letter of the alphabet to trigger a title. John D. MacDonald had used colors for his books: *The Green Rip-*

per, The Girl in the Plain Brown Wrapper. Kevin thought if he ever wrote a thriller series he could use numbers: "One Is for Loneliness," "Two Is a Crowd," "Three Is a Family."

He thought immediately of Polly and Zoe. Gone. And he felt a hollow knocking in his gut.

He put back the Sue Grafton and ran a finger over some volumes by Susan Sontag. He'd read some of her stuff but found it dense, blizzard deep. He'd read a fascinating excerpt of her book on photography and never looked at photographs the same way again. That's why he'd tried to belittle Miles the photographer by calling his pictures of Polly "snaps."

Goddammit, why does everything trigger Polly?

Anne Rice was good for a chill. Her *Interview with the Vampire* was scary and smart and hip. He'd read a few short stories by that Chilean lady, Isabel Allende. She really understood men. And Dorothy Parker. She thought like a man. It was a line of hers that Kevin once thought summed up his life with Polly: "Sometimes the fucking you're getting ain't worth the fucking you're getting."

Again with Polly on the brain.

Kevin avoided the feminist diatribes because it was the nineties and men were men and women were women again. At least that was the rumor, and Kevin hoped it was true. He certainly didn't feel much like being told he was an asshole by some austere dame who wanted to blame men for cellulite, tit gravity, and menopause. At a twenty-five-dollar admission price.

He liked some other women writers. Joyce Carol Oates, especially her book on boxing. The woman at least liked men and understood the sexual/violent exhilaration of fear and combat. She considered men on their own terms. Maybe because she loved her father. She was smart. But some of her short stories that he'd read in *Playboy* were so overwhelmingly sad.

Kevin moved out of the fiction aisle, past a schoolmarmish woman browsing through calendars of male models. Kevin made her for a graduate student doing research for some paper on the new sexual exploitation of men. Where women were driven to breast implants, liposuction, and face-lifts, men were now taking steroids by the bucketful to look like the male models and strippers of the dysfunctional talk show circuit and the beefcake calendars. The woman put back the beefcake calendar and chose one by Matisse. Eclectic, Kevin thought, and smiled.

Kevin watched the schoolmarm and suddenly missed school. He'd finally gotten his Liberal Arts BA going nights for six years to Kingsborough Community and Brooklyn College. He'd read most of the normal stuff in school: Steinbeck, Fitzgerald, Faulkner. Mark Twain and Graham Greene were both great. And the micks: O'Casey, Yeats, Behan. And that Edna O'Brien was always a three hard-on read. She wrote about men fucking women better than most men did. One college professor, a woman, had said that was because she wasn't writing about women getting fucked. In her books it was the women who were doing the fucking. That always sends the mercury to the top of the old bim-bom-eter—which rhymes with thermometer, Kevin thought. James Joyce was amazingly good but he made your muscles ache. You felt punchy after reading and rereading Joyce, until, at the end, it felt like someone had beat the shit out of you. Then there was Camus, Sartre, a little Freud. Kevin called them life's literary janitors. They helped clean up the Big Mess.

His favorite entertainment writer was James M. Cain. Better, he thought, than Chandler of the down-and-dirty ilk. That's what Kevin loved about bookstores, you could walk in and argue with yourself for an hour or more and prove your points by picking a copy of each of those people's works off the shelf and paging through it.

Some people got the same tactile pleasure from roaming through hardware stores, playing with tools and gadgets. Most women Kevin had known loved boutiques and department stores that way. Kevin hated department stores. It's where men were sentenced to do community service work for emotional crimes against women.

Right now, he was looking for a good woman's book because he was trying to figure out what made them so goddamned complicated. He looked down the WOMEN'S BOOKS aisle and saw a black woman with high cheekbones and enormous eyes squatting, perusing books on a lower shelf. She chose one and stood. And seemed to keep on standing in stop action. She was tall and athletically toned, her tight dungaree jacket zipped over large breasts. She glanced at Kevin, grinned politely when she caught him watching her, revealing large white teeth. Then she turned, and a man was there in front of her. He had watched Kevin ogling her and her smiling at Kevin. The man wore a tan trench coat over a dark suit and tie. He was about forty and in good shape, a gym bag slung over his shoulder. The woman kissed him on the lips but the man stared at Kevin wordlessly as she nudged him toward the register with another glance back toward Kevin. He stood rock still, fixed on Kevin.

Don't, pal, Kevin thought. Don't make me fight you.

At the woman's quiet urging, the man grudgingly turned from Kevin and strolled toward the cash register at the front of the store. Kevin watched them go. The woman wore skin-tight jeans and Timberland boots. Jesus Christ, Kevin thought, what an ass. No wonder he's possessive, it's like Polly's. . . .

Polly is driving me totally crazy.

The man with the black woman looked back at Kevin from the front cash register but Kevin turned away. He empathized with him now. Eventually she will cheat on you, pal. She has the look in her eye, and almost every man who sees her will want her. And she knows. He always felt that way when he walked with Polly: men wanting his wife. Suddenly, the words Polly had spoken to Kevin on the phone raised welts on his heart again. She leaves for Disney World with the baby and now, from the road, she says by phone that the marriage is over and the kid is someone else's and she's never coming back. And she says she was taking other guy's dick into her body. One of those men that looked at her the way I just looked at that woman, he thought. Maybe even a man she flirted with when I was with her. Later, took his semen and made a baby and told me it was mine. And now she says Zoe is some stranger's little girl.

Christ almighty, he thought. Why is all this happening to me? Kevin had worked hard. He had his BA now, which was no small thing in his neighborhood. His job. College graduate in the fire department usually means eventual brass. He could study for the lieutenant's test. Then, later, after he got his MA, he'd become a chief, Kevin thought. End up hauling down close to a hundred large a year, with a house and car and credit cards and checkbook. More than material possessions. Talking about comfort, personal pride, accomplishment here, he thought. *Earned.*

Maybe think about getting a summer place and put some dough

away for the kids for college, in those IRAs or CDs, whatever. Still have money for a nice vacation down Key West come February, see Hemingway's house, bounce around Duval Street, get shit-faced, water-ski, ride the mopeds, fuck on the hotel balcony during sunsets. Maybe go to Hawaii. A good fucking life.

A good fucking life. That's not a small accomplishment, a good fuckin' life, Kevin thought. So why'd it all go so wrong?

"Excuse me," said a woman who looked about twenty-two. She was dark and tall, dressed in a long expensive leather coat that hung loosely from padded shoulders. Her face was angular, her eyes large and round with gold highlights. Her tanned skin was flawless. Kevin stepped to the side, startled by her beauty. She smiled and bent at the knees to get a book by Mary Gordon. "Now there's a broad who can write," Kevin said in a half whisper, suddenly conscious he was speaking. "Mary Gordon."

The girl straightened and smiled and held a corner of the book to her full lips. She touched the binding to the gleaming enamel of a front tooth.

"What do you buy a father-in-law for his birthday?" she asked. Kevin was surprised and felt awkward.

"I dunno," he said. "Does he like sports? Boxing? Football?"

"Nah," she said.

"Movies?"

"Nah."

"What does he like?"

"Me."

Kevin did a double shake of his head and smiled.

"Oh, then why don't you buy him a diary?" Kevin said. "Then he can read what he likes about you after he writes it."

"That's not a bad idea," she said. "Then I could see what he really thinks about me, when I'm not around."

"You'd read his diary?"

Kevin saw the gold band on her ring finger.

"Of course I'd read his diary," she said. "I'm having his baby, aren't I?"

Why didn't I choose a saloon instead of a fucking bookstore? Kevin thought. This is called following a doctor's advice? Another fucking flake. A literate nut into the bargain. Beautiful and young and knocked up by her father-in-law.

"Jesus Christ, does your mother-in-law know?"

"She did."

Kevin backed away from her with his hands in his pockets. He smiled and tried to turn away but she followed him.

"Buy me lunch," she said. She didn't ask. She announced.

"Nah, I don't think so," Kevin said.

"You're a fireman."

Kevin touched the FDNY patch on his jacket.

"You'll be easy to find," she said, as she chewed on some peanut brittle. "Come on, I'll let you buy me lunch. You can trust me. I'm pregnant."

"I'm married," Kevin said, showing her his gold band.

"So am I."

"Does your husband know about your father-in-law? And the baby?"

She smiled and nodded and wrinkled her nose. She was following Kevin around the aisles now. He saw her put the Mary Gordon book into her pocketbook as if she already owned it. She looked more like a bobcat than before. She had on expensive knee-high leather boots, the way Kevin liked them on girls. Pregnant, nuts, and sexy, Kevin thought. He knew why she was so sexy to him. Because she was stalking him.

"My husband is doing time."

"Sorry to hear that," Kevin said. "For what?"

"Killing his mom," she said.

"I see," Kevin said. "Then you and his father got it on after he went away."

"Yeah," she said. "Then too. I'm famished, fireman."

"Why'd he kill his mother?"

"She told him she caught me and his dad fooling around," she said. "She told my husband. Her own son. She shouldn't have interfered. But my husband is faithful and supportive. He didn't believe her. He was sticking up for me. He's loyal like that."

"So he killed her?"

"No," she said. "My father-in-law killed her in a fight afterward. My husband just took the weight for it. I told you, he's loyal like that."

"And so your husband is doing time for the murder your father-in-law committed and you're carrying the father-in-law's baby?" Kevin said, as he stopped in front of a display of greeting cards.

"My husband wanted the family name to go on," she explained.

"Of course," Kevin said.

"But there's really nothing that serious between us," she said. "Me and my father-in-law. Not yet, anyway. I just want to get him a book."

Kevin stopped in front of a row of Hemingway's Scribner's oversized paperback editions.

"You're either a pathological liar or very fuckin' weird, lady," Kevin said. "Either way, you're scary."

"And I like firemen, too," she said. "Dangerous."

"Good," Kevin said. "Find one who's single."

"Are there any?"

"Plenty, divorced anyway."

"Your wife fucks around, you know," she said, as Kevin stopped near the *New York Times* bestsellers display rack.

"What? How . . . I mean, what makes you say that?"

"Because I could see from across the store that you're this great-looking guy, alone, talking to yourself, looking at women's books. Staring at that black woman's ass like you wanted to brand it, right in front of her man. Danger! Because you weren't afraid of him but you *are* afraid of me. Dangerous and vulnerable. That's horny. And because almost all the women I know fuck around on the nice guys and wind up with assholes. In the end, you are what you lose."

This broad has X-ray vision, Kevin thought.

"Don't you worry about the baby?" Kevin asked.

She grew enraged and started to shout, sticking her belly out from under the loose coat. You couldn't tell she was pregnant until she showed it off.

"Of course I worry about the baby! Why the fuck do you think I told you to buy me lunch? If I'm hungry, the baby must be hungry! You don't look stupid, so why are you acting so fucking idiotic?"

She was flapping her arms now, and people in the store were staring.

"Look, I'm sorry."

"Sorry!" she screamed and rubbed her rotund belly. "It's a little fucking late for sorry, isn't it?"

Kevin Dempsey, firefighter, instinctively looked for an exit sign, spun around, and hurried out the front door of the bookstore onto rainy Broadway. He couldn't wait to get to work. To run into fire. He wanted to cross the street in case she followed him out, so he dodged taxis and trucks and buses and cars until he put a traffic jam between him and the pregnant woman. He looked over his shoulder, and through the falling rain he saw her standing outside Coliseum Books, pointing and shouting animatedly at him. Pedestrians took short pause and small or no notice.

It startled him how sexy she was to him. It was not just the beautiful face, the feline eyes, the high boots, or the wicked smile. It was the story. And how she relished being a part of it even if it was a lie.

Especially since his own life right now might also be one big lie.

Fucking women, Kevin thought. *Fucking* women. . . .

8

Kevin Dempsey was glad for the company of men in the firehouse. The engine company, smack in the middle of Bedford Stuyvesant, was an oasis in a neighborhood that had never recovered from the carnage of the mid-1980s caused by crack. Never recovered from the dead fathers, sons, husbands, brothers. From the shattered single mothers, teenage moms, junior high school prostitutes. All multiplied a thousandfold by that single drug. Here, in a sanctuary from that grief, Kevin would sleep and try to think. The firehouse was always spotless, the floors mopped with disinfectant, the furniture dusted, the windows gleaming. The couches were deep and comfortable, the beds firm and warm. The men were tried-and-true combat buddies. The place always smelled of food and there were always books, magazines, and newspapers spread over the tabletops. The TV was always on and the men often rented videos to play on the VCR so they could pause it to go out and fight a fire and watch the rest after they returned.

It was literally a home away from home. Kevin had decided to stay there for a while, on and off duty.

He had gone to his new house only to get some clothes and program the call-forwarding so he could get his calls at work. He couldn't bear to sleep in the new house again; it was a crypt instead of a home. He needed to hear from Polly again, talk sense to her. He needed to hear from Anthony about the sperm count. He needed to hear from Frank, who was trying to track Polly through some still friendly police contacts. He needed sleep. Or action. Distraction.

He was sitting in the living room area, doodling in a notebook. Two firemen were half-dozing on lounge chairs, watching a National Geographic show on TV about elephants. The narrator on television was saying elephants were monogamous. Being an elephant, Kevin thought, was easier than being a human being. No wonder man was slaughtering them. Not for ivory, out of jealousy.

Carmine was lying on the couch in his stocking feet, one eye open, his arm on his forehead.

"You heard from her yet, Kevvie?" Carmine asked.

"Not today," Kevin said. "Polly, maybe she needs more time to think."

"Least she thinks," Carmine said. "Most of them don't do that, ya know. They emote. Dangerous, that emoting. I like that word. Learned that in an interview with Roy Scheider about my favorite movie of all time, *All That Jazz*. Some movie. Very emotable."

"Emotional, Carmine," Kevin said.

"Right," Carmine said. "Is that where that's from? Okay, that makes sense. When a broad is emotional she is emoting. So if you're saying Polly is thinking, that's different. That's at least from the mind, not the heart. With women, the heart is a gas chamber. They kill you with it. Execute ya."

"Uplifting, Carm," Kevin said.

Kevin was going to write about the cat in the yard but he thought he should write about the crazy broad in the bookstore too. Or the bum from Columbus Circle, who had tried to tell him that his life was some woman's fault. All somehow connected. Every story with a man haunted by a woman in it. Maybe it's just me. No, it can't be just me. . . .

Tommy Tighe came out of the bathroom, looking a little high. He was going on forty and still smoked pot, and some said he did a little coke too. His half-moon eyes looked like he was on the weed right now. The lieu, which is what the firemen called a lieutenant, wouldn't like that, Kevin thought. Wouldn't like it at all. Tighe should get some sleep. He always made an asshole out of himself when he got high on the job, and he was dangerous out on a run.

Kevin was writing in his leather-bound journal when Tighe did a silly two-step and playfully snatched the notebook from Kevin's hands.

"Hey, Tighe, that's personal."

Tighe began to read. *"Girl knocked up by father-in-law."* He giggled.

Kevin grew enraged, his skin blanching, eyes slitting.

"Autobiographical, Dempsey?" Tighe asked with a sneer. "Polly eatin' somebody else's cracker?"

Tighe cracked up and looked around at the other men for a chorus. No one else laughed. Kevin sprung at him and smashed his face with a right hand. Tighe catapulted off a dividing wall and raised his fists. Carmine was dragging himself out of a deep-pillowed couch.

"You motherfucker," Kevin said, bending low as Tighe swung and missed. Kevin dug a left hook into Tighe's ribs, sending him to his knees.

The older man gasped for breath. Kevin stood over him.

"Who the fuck do you think you are, reading my words?" Kevin shouted. "Commenting on my life? My woman?"

Carmine threw his arms around Kevin, but Kevin broke away and grabbed Tighe's shirt near the neck. Then big Jimmy Savage from North Carolina pulled Kevin away.

"Man, this shit ain't worth it," Savage said. "Motherfucker is crazy as a June bug, Kev."

"Who's he to talk about my wife?"

"Hey, man, you had an old lady like his, you'd diss someone else's broad too. Just balancing the scales. He's high. Tighe's always high. You just chill, now, babes."

Lieutenant Crosby walked into the room with a copy of *Time* magazine in his hand and his glasses up on his forehead. He saw Carmine lifting Tighe into an armchair, as the beaten man wiped a trickle of blood from his nose.

Crosby rarely asked questions. He usually just stared and waited for explanations. He looked silently from one fireman to the next. No one spoke. The smell of peppers and onions and Italian sausages Carmine had made for dinner clung to the firehouse. A young probationary firefighter, wearing an apron, stood at the kitchen sink with a washing brush and a skillet in his hands.

"Broads," Carmine finally explained to Lieutenant Crosby.

"Sometimes I wish I had a company full of fire fems instead of you morons," Crosby said. "Tighe, wash up. Get some sleep. Dempsey, stop acting like your namesake. Here, you're a firefighter, not a prizefighter."

Kevin nodded, ashamed he'd lost control of himself. Carmine motioned for Kevin to sit down and relax and was helping Tighe to the bathroom when the bells started. One two three four five six—

Everything stopped. The men stuffed feet into boots, yanked on turnout coats, grabbed hats. Inside a minute, Carmine was behind the wheel of their rig with the engine roaring to life.

Carmine took the curves through the ghetto streets of Bedford Stuyvesant like an Olympic bobsledder: smooth, fluid, perfect. Heavy treads devoured the wet rainy asphalt. Carmine was the best, Kevin thought. He knew every street in this warren. The other men, too, knew each address as if they were home.

Kevin got the same inner heat from the race every time they went out on a run. Each fire was like losing your virginity, with fear and danger and excitement and conquest. The job made your blood boil, your adrenaline percolate. It was sexual. It had arousal, satisfaction, climax. Kevin's belly was a kiln. He felt as if he became a part of the very fire itself, fighting fire with fire.

Kevin had loved riding the back of the rig as a probie, which is what they called a rookie. But that was against the safety rules now. So Kevin watched from the window seat of the rig. The people on the sidewalks stand frozen, Kevin thought, mouths agape, as this big beautiful red machine of sheer power sears through the secret dirty soul of the city, lights flashing, siren blaring, horns screaming. Action. Machine of action. Man of action, Kevin thought. This was respect. This mattered. This was about life. This was about death. And all the little triumphs and defeats in between in a doomed part of town, where even the scrawny trees looked homeless. This is what I do, Kevin Dempsey thought. What I am.

The apartment building was on Macon and Fulton streets, a corner house that had been torched ten times in the past two months. There were homeless squatters living there, but mostly it was just another crack house. And the crack houses were filled with kids, teenage and even younger: dealers, addicts, prostitutes, pimps. Most times the ten-, eleven- and twelve-year-olds doubled as baby-sitters for kid sisters and brothers in prams, their single mothers at work or out hustling themselves.

The saddest part was that these kids raising babies rarely learned big-people lessons, even when an infant died. They'd just go get smashed and have another baby to replace the dead baby. And so it goes, Kevin thought. Then Zoe was in his mind again, and he tried to temporarily erase her beautiful image.

Kevin saw the crowd on the sidewalks as his rig pulled up. The corner building was a crumbling prewar six-story walkup tenement.

"Let the motherfucker burn to the ground," shouted a man in a business suit across the street. Cops pulled up to cordon off the crowd as the second rig arrived.

"Nothing but crack heads and motherfuckin' gunslingers be in that rat trap," screamed a mother with a baby carriage. "I say let it burn, man. That's what you suppose to do with hell. Let the motherfucker burn."

Kevin leaped from the rig and took the nozzle as Carmine began hooking the hose to the sidewalk hydrant. He waited for Crosby and they were first in, followed by Savage, Tighe, and three other men. More hose was being unfolded onto the sidewalk, and Kevin could hear the sirens of additional approaching fire companies.

Inside, the building baked like a giant brick pizza oven. Kevin saw on the way in that most of the windows had been punched out and knew from experience that the air was feeding the flames and allowing the smoke to escape. He yanked on a Scott mask that was attached to canisters of fresh air. The roar of the fire was deafening. He used sign language to warn the others of the stairs. Rats slithered past him. Cockroaches leaped from the blistering painted walls onto his wet turnout coat. He kicked and swatted the vermin away and felt the cheeks of his ass clamp together.

Kevin followed Crosby's signal to fan out, to locate the flames, to make a search for human life. This was the most dangerous detail because you searched on your own. With no partner, you truly learned whether you had the stuff to do battle with man's most primal enemy and dearest friend, fire.

Kevin knew the crack houses were an obstacle course of rubbish and booby-trap holes in the floors, covered with paper or rugs or cardboard, which could cause you to drop into a cauldron below. Then there was always the possibility of dead bodies—victims of drug overdose, murder, or smoke inhalation.

He barked into his walkie-talkie to Carmine.

"Carmine, don't charge the line yet, we're gonna do a search."

"Ten-four," Carmine said into his radio from the sidewalk hydrant, where, upon command, he was prepared to let the pumper rip with ninety pounds of nozzle pressure.

Kevin took in his surroundings as he crawled along the second-floor landing. The crackling of the heat was disorienting and the unseen flames above roared like a great hot wind past his ears. Loud hissing came from above and below. But under all of this, Kevin was certain he could hear the tiny whimpers of a baby. He motioned with his head and hands to Crosby that he was going to move left to search. Crosby nodded, pointed Savage right, and motioned the others behind him to follow him up the next flight. He handed Kevin an ax before climbing higher into the blaze.

Kevin moved alone, low to the floor of the second-story landing, where it was cooler. Most of the tin-covered doors to the apartments were closed. Kevin touched each one and could feel heat in the metal, meaning there was flame behind it. He banged on each door and listened for sounds of human life.

All around him the mad scratching and scurrying of rodents was audible, especially from inside the walls, where they were probably choking and trapped, looking for escape holes. But from behind one door came a full-throated scream. Wait, Kevin thought. That isn't a fucking rat. Too loud for a rat. That's a kid. The screams were loud and then suddenly stopped, as if the throat had run out of air. Then he thought he could hear the hoarse rasping sound of a scream that could not make connection with the larynx, like an engine that wouldn't kick over.

Kevin touched the door to feel for heat. Not too bad. *Yet.* He stood up and swung the ax. It smashed the door to the floor. He hurried inside and dropped to his knees again, slithered along, looking for signs of life. He saw torn and charred wallpaper, lots of smoke, and empty mattresses on the wooden floor. Little holes in the floorboards showed orange flames from below. A shower of ceiling plaster bounced off his helmet, and one chunk smashed against the nape of his neck. He lay panting, only one eye open, and then saw two giant eyes in front of him. Wide, orange, and terrified. Kevin screamed. So did the cat. A fucking cat, he thought. Son of a bitch! Kevin grabbed it and sailed it toward a closed window. The cat exploded through the glass toward the street, still screaming.

Kevin had pushed himself to all fours when the bathroom door opened and a teenage Hispanic girl, no more than thirteen and almost full term, collapsed into his arms. Her blackened tongue hung from a panting mouth. Kevin rose from his knees, cradled her, ripped his air mask from his mouth, and jammed it over hers.

A gust of wind blew through the shattered window and fire swirled around him. Kevin quickly took off his turnout coat and wrapped the pregnant girl in it, the same way he had thrown a tablecloth over Polly that Halloween night. . . .

Forget Polly, he thought now. He slung the girl, now encased like a human sausage in his fifteen-pound coat, over his left shoulder. He could smell the familiar odor of singed human hair. As he moved for the door, Kevin shifted the youngster so her head faced his and they could share the Scott mask, the way divers do in underwater emergencies. Behind him he heard the ceiling inside collapse. He reached for his walkie-talkie and realized he had lost it somewhere in the struggle with the smoke, the cat, and the girl.

In the hallway of the second floor, he could hear doors slamming and voices shouting his name and he tried to shout back to them, but the roar was too loud and the air he needed for shouting might cost him his life. A tease of fresh air came from the bottom of the stairs. It tasted sweet for a moment, and then he heard a thousand deafening sounds at once.

The landing above him gave way in a cacophony of splintering wood, falling plaster, rushing wind, shouting men, the rumble of heavy sections of flooring, thumping, high-pitched hissing. And then through the cloud of dust and flame and smoke, Kevin saw a figure spiraling down toward him. It had arms and legs and boots and a turnout coat and a helmet. Kevin moved out of the way, throwing himself onto his back on the floor, the girl falling flat on top of him, and Tommy Tighe smashed across Kevin's outstretched right arm.

Kevin didn't move for a few seconds, but remained lying on his back on the second-story landing. The teenager lay on top of him, breathing heavily, unconscious.

There was a sudden eerie silence, then the nibbling crackle of fire. Tighe was conscious next to him but almost catatonic. Both of his arms were broken, bent at crazy angles. Kevin pulled his own arm out from under Tighe. Air suddenly became life itself. And there was very little. He reached for Tighe's Scott pack.

There was more yelling from the third story above, where half the landing had collapsed under Tommy Tighe. Kevin could not hear what the firemen above him were saying. He could see that there was only half a landing above him on the third story and that the staircase leading from the second story to the third had collapsed. Only half of the second-story landing where he lay, with the pregnant girl on top of him and Tighe beside him, remained intact. And this section of landing was also swaying precariously.

Kevin knew he was marooned. The other firefighters couldn't reach him even if they knew where he was. They would be evacuating through the windows onto truck ladders. They would come in again from the street and try to make it up to the second floor, but by that time it would be too late.

Kevin had to make it on his own to the smoldering, swaying flight of stairs leading down to the ground floor. This lone flight of steps, now barely standing by itself, was the only chance. The staircase was a dozen feet ahead to his left.

"Tighe, blink if you can hear me!"

Tighe managed to blink and a tear fell over his sooty lid, carving a clean path down his blackened cheekbone. Kevin wiggled his hand down to Tighe's belt buckle and grabbed hold firmly.

"Don't do a fucking thing or we are gonna die. Blink, you motherfucker, if you hear me!"

Tighe blinked.

"Okay, let me do this. Just don't try to help or it'll fuck me up."

Tighe blinked. Kevin took a deep pull on the Scott mask and held the air in his lungs and pushed the mask to the girl's mouth. He took one of Tighe's broken arms and recracked it to position it over the mask.

"Hold that there, Tighe."

Tighe blinked again. Pain was no longer alive in him. Kevin, still on his back with the girl on top of him, fed on Tighe's air pack and then gave some to Tighe. The girl was breathing steadily.

Then Kevin made his move.

He placed one hand on the landing banister to help pull himself toward the staircase. He was flat on his back with the pregnant girl on top of him. Her weight held her in place as he moved. And he held Tighe by the belt buckle with his other hand, dragging him along. He needed a few more feet.

Then suddenly the landing banister came off in his hand and he almost went over the edge of the landing, with the girl and Tighe, into the abyss. He looked down. Flames were eating through the floorboards from the basement. Kevin sucked desperately on the air mask and began to feed some to Tighe. Tighe lay still, the weight of his hand securing the girl's mask in place. The girl's swollen belly was pressed against Kevin's belly, and he thought of the poor little critter trapped in her womb.

Kevin teetered, thought he felt the baby actually move as the girl's belly flattened slightly. Not here, kid, Kevin thought. The unconscious girl groaned. Jesus Christ! Please don't give birth right here and now! The landing shifted, and again Kevin almost went over the edge to the fifteen-foot fall. Christ almighty, this girl must eat cannon balls for breakfast, he thought. And Tighe is even heavier.

Using the heel of his left foot as a push oar, Kevin dug the heavy boot into the landing, which was starting to sag. He gained six inches with each shove of his foot. But the pushing made the landing sway more.

Finally, he reached the stairs. He knew he couldn't walk down with the girl, dragging Tighe. Direct weight would make the staircase collapse. He had to use his body as a human surfboard. He hooked his arm over the girl's back as he heard splintering and crackling as the flames found hissing pockets of sap in the wood. Kevin managed to position himself on the stairs on his back, at a 45-degree angle, headfirst. The skin on his arms tore into raw exposed burns, liquid oozing from them. But the girl remained on top of him.

He found the hose with his left hand. He looped his left arm around the hose, using it as a guide, and grabbed Tighe's belt buckle, still with his left hand. Using his left foot as a push oar again, he cast off the metal post of the stair banister and managed to shove himself down a couple of steps with the resistant force. He guided himself and the girl down along the hose, dragging Tighe along. With his right hand he took the mask, sucked air, rammed it back on the girl, and closed his eyes.

Here goes, motherfucker, he thought, this might be it.

His spine was against the edge of the third step from the top. He cast off with his leg again and began to surf down on a quick incline, skimming his weight across the metal edges of the steps. He came to an abrupt stop halfway down. He cast off again, his arm still looped around the hose and clutching Tighe, the girl lying like ballast on top of him. He was afraid that, if he lived, the damage to his back could mean he'd never walk again. His spinal column hit the edge of each step with a thud as he body-surfed down the stairs with the girl and Tommy Tighe. He kept thrusting off the wall, propelling them all down the creaking stairs, following the hose. All three of them bumped and lurched along. Their own weight picked up gravitational speed, until they arrived at the bottom in a frenzied, disjointed, jumbled heap.

Suddenly, Kevin's head bumped something cool and hard. He opened his eyes and there was light and air and voices, and God looked just like Carmine fucking Plantamura, and Saint Peter had a head like a bowling ball that resembled Jimmy Savage's.

"Carmine," Kevin said. "The girl . . ."

"Kev, I love ya, baby," Carmine said. "I'm here. I'm here, baby. You're all right, sweetheart. Come on."

Savage and the probie carried the girl to the street. Carmine was back in a flash with a fresh Scott mask. Crosby and another firefighter were working on Tighe, who was still breathing. Kevin drank the air greedily, his lungs exploding, his tongue scorched and gritty with ash. His eyes felt numb. He was lifted off his feet by many unseen hands and raced outside along the cockeyed street. He looked up and saw faces. Voices called for a gurney, oxygen, water. He saw the sky. It was polar blue. He thought he saw the face of his father briefly in the clouds, but then a gull sliced across the sun like a knife through a lemon and the image was severed.

And now suddenly there was a crowd around him on the street. Savage and the probie and Crosby and the crowd. The neighbors were actually cheering.

"Fuck are they cheering for?" Kevin asked after swallowing water, still gasping air.

"You kiddin'?" Carmine said jokingly. "The cat lived."

A paramedic ran over with another water bottle, squirting it in Kevin's mouth.

"The pregnant girl?"

"Asking for pickles and ice cream."

"Thank God," Kevin said, briefly thinking of Polly pregnant with Zoe.

Carmine nodded. "Tighe's alive but bad," he said, more somber. "He's on the way to Kings County."

Kevin heard the lieutenant say he was putting him in for a big award, called the Gordon Bennet Medal, but Kevin didn't pay any attention. He would be taken to the hospital for smoke inhalation and burns and released. There would be a hero ceremony and war stories over beers in Farrell's later and extra points in his record for promotions which eventually would mean more money. This was supposed to be the biggest day in Kevin Dempsey's life as a firefighter. He hadn't fumbled. He made the end zone, he saved three lives, counting the unborn baby, and a fourth counting his own.

But all he wanted was Polly and Zoe.

9

Frank Dempsey stood at the front desk of the Manhattan Plaza Swim and Health Club on Forty-third Street between Ninth and Tenth avenues in Manhattan. Kevin had told him that Sarah Cross, Polly's beautiful friend, worked there. Frank wanted to ask her some questions about where Polly might have taken little Zoe Dempsey.

The gym was part of the Manhattan Plaza complex, built in the 1970s for people of the performing arts—actors, directors, writers, musicians, and others in the theatrical and movie and music industries of the city. The apartments were spacious and well maintained, and a whole new industry of bars and restaurants and bakeries, cheese stores, bookshops, dry cleaners, and pizza joints had opened up around them. There was a playground and a supermarket and a parking garage in the complex.

And there was also this gym—swimming pool, saunas, exercise rooms, adjoining racquet club, and tennis courts. Frank was staring through the Plexiglas windows at the hardwood floors of the gym as he stood at the front desk. The place smelled of disinfectant and perspiration and coffee. Women and men dressed in gym clothes were moving to and from the locker rooms.

Mostly women.

On the floor of the see-through Plexiglas-enclosed gymnasium were dozens of women in skin-tight leotards hopping up and down onto Reebok exercise steps as pulsating music played. Frank hadn't seen so many tight behinds since he worked vice on the West Side as a young detective.

"Sir, can I help you?" asked the receptionist. She had a face like a blond Barbie doll.

Instinctively, Frank fished out his wallet to show his badge. Then stopped. It was a month since they took it from him.

"Yes, I'm looking for Sarah Cross," he said, feeling abashed as he slipped the wallet back in his pocket.

"Sarah is almost finished teaching her class," Barbie said. "Would you like some herbal tea while you wait?"

"Yes," Frank said, the courtesy revealing her as an out-of-towner. "I'd love half a cup. That's Sarah there, isn't it?"

"It's hard to miss Sarah," said Barbie. "Just look for the ten."

"I'm too old to count that high." Frank laughed as he looked out at Sarah, who was going through the exercises with the dispatch of a drill instructor. She had a beautiful smile on her face while the others looked like they were drowning. Barbie poured half a cup of hot water over a tea bag and put the paper cup on the counter.

"It wouldn't take long to whip you into shape," Barbie said.

"I'm not into whips," Frank said as he sipped the tea. Barbie laughed.

Frank watched Sarah. She had a back as straight as a parochial school desk. She bounced from foot to foot with the grace of a bird and appeared to enjoy every step of her work. Frank turned his back, furtively took out his pint bottle of vodka, laced the tea, and downed the entire cup in a single gulp. Then he saw Sarah walk briskly across the floor of the gym. The others behind her dropped to the floor or panted for air.

Sarah's beauty, along with the tea and vodka, made Frank break into a light sweat.

She moved through the gym door with a towel thrown over her shoulder and a beautiful sheen on her scrubbed face. She was youth and health on parade.

"Sarah, this gentleman is here to see you," Barbie said.

Sarah glanced at Frank and a vague look of recognition came over her face. She shifted the weight of her body to her left hip. Her legs were long and contoured and strong. She seemed to talk with her legs, shifting her ankles, swiveling on the balls of her feet, reaching over the counter, her hard ham muscles bunching inside the spandex. She shuffled through her pink telephone messages and turned back to Frank.

She looked into his eyes, making Frank feel shorter than she was, which he wasn't. She wasn't menacing or flirtatious. She just explored Frank's face as if looking for directions on a map.

"You'd be as good looking as your kid brother if you didn't drink so much," she said. "Even better. More rugged."

Frank shook his head and grinned.

"I'm sorry—" he said and was going to continue, but Sarah cut him off, still searching his face.

"Me too."

"No. I mean, sorry for bothering you. But I need to talk to you about Polly."

"Let me shower and throw on some jeans and we'll have lunch, okay?"

"Yeah," Frank said. "Okay."

"You look like you could use a drink," she said. "Meet me in the West Bank around the corner on Forty-second above Ninth Avenue.

Tell Steve, the owner, to sit you at my table. Start with the fried zucchini strings. Even a carnivore like you will like 'em. See ya in a sec. I always did want to meet a rogue lawman."

With that Sarah did a pirouette and sashayed away, tossing her thick mane of hair over her left shoulder like a heavy scarf. If you were a hero cop she probably would have told you to take a hike, he thought. Everybody loves an outlaw.

Except poor Summers, who was waiting downstairs.

10

Steve Olsen, owner of the West Bank, said, "You're having lunch with Sarah Cross? What hundred-million-dollar movie did you produce?"

"Friend of a friend of the family," Frank said.

"I could scalp tickets for five hundred apiece to people who would like to have lunch with Sarah," Steve said.

"I can understand why," Frank said.

"She's something, all right," Steve said. "But sweet. Usually the only one she has lunch with is Polly Dempsey. I could use an armed guard at that table."

Steve took a step back and looked at Frank and then over his shoulder at the bar. Summers made a gesture for the bartender. Steve looked back at Frank.

"For a minute there, I thought you were the guy in the papers."

"I am," Frank said.

"Polly's brother-in-law?"

"Yeah," Frank said. "I'll have a Stoli, rocks."

"Sorry."

"Not as sorry as I am." Frank laughed.

"Sarah gonna be in your life story or something?"

"Fortunately for her, no. I have no choice."

Steve walked to the bar and ordered Frank's drink. Frank sat at the table in the corner near the archway between the kitchen and the entrance to the downstairs theater. You've made it to show biz now, Frank. They're already talking about your life as a story. Wish I could get a sneak preview of the final scenes.

Steve came back and placed the drink in front of Frank.

"I made it a double," Steve said. "I'm on the wagon. Have the first one on me, the second one *for* me."

Frank chuckled and then Sarah strolled in, wearing high-heeled boots, the long strong legs imprisoned in tight denim, and a beautiful, form-fitting, burgundy glove-leather jacket that was fastened at a waist as thin as a strong neck. Her powerful hips arched out smoothly. This is making me nervous, Frank thought. Control yourself. A girl at a nearby table smacked her boyfriend on the hand with a fork as he examined Sarah.

Sarah sat down beside Frank, smiling hello. She was wearing a little bit of eye makeup and a little bit of perfume and a little bit of lipstick and two little bitty earrings. He envied her; she was one of those people who knew when to stop. Unlike me. . . .

Summers stood at the bar, ogling Sarah, sipping a Kaliber alcohol-free beer.

"Beer and a salad, please, Pete," Sarah said to the waiter, who came immediately to her table with fried zucchini strings. "No glass, Pete, okay? I like it out of the bottle, factory sterilized."

"You got it, Sarah," the waiter said.

She took a portion of the zucchini strings with her thumb and second and third fingers of the right hand. The fingers you used on the eucharist, Frank thought. She nibbled the strings with real teeth that looked like they had never had a cavity. Frank ate some zucchini strings too. They were terrific and light. The waiter brought an iced bottle of Heineken and Sarah took a swig right out of the neck.

"How much did you steal exactly?" Sarah asked.

"I wanted to ask *you* a few questions," Frank said.

"Yeah, I know," Sarah said. "But I love a thief with balls who doesn't use a fountain pen or a home computer. Especially one with facial bones and shoulders like yours. Men! It's unfair how you bastards age so well. I could sculpt you into a middle-aged hunk if you gave me a crack at it."

"A crack at it," Frank said and squirmed. He felt long dormant sparks striking to life. He couldn't help smiling. Some things die hard. Bad joke, he thought.

"You should floss more to start with," she said. "The booze builds up in the gums and gives you booze breath. Why do you drink so much?"

Frank closed his mouth and ran his tongue over his gums. Then he took a sip of his drink and stared at her clear eyes.

"Do you have any idea where Polly is?"

"Vaguely," she said.

"Where?" Frank said.

The waiter came with Sarah's salad and asked Frank if he would like to order.

"He likes red meat, Pete," Sarah said. "Forces it down half chewed for fuel, but it's killing him, so today give him the free-range chicken paillard, well done. And whatever the soup is, especially if it has beans in it for protein. And a leafy salad, as green as dirty money."

Pete laughed and walked away.

"I'm not even hungry," Frank said.

"I know, my father never was either before he drank himself to death," Sarah said. "He had the same pizza-dough skin and the same disinfected smell as you. Like a clean bum. I'm not gonna let you die on me if I can help it. Not during lunch, anyway."

Frank felt like a bunch of loose parts on a worktable. Sarah was looking at him as if she were the mechanic. She dug into her salad and chewed every crispy leaf as if her life depended on it, crunched every crouton to paste, held each cherry tomato to her lips and detonated each one with her strong front teeth and let the juice explode into her mouth. Frank was gaping at the almost slow-motion ritual Sarah made of a simple salad, with French bread and cold beer. She took the half loaf of bread in her long tapered fingers and tore slowly, methodically, to separate the crispy crust with the sesame seeds from the dough, ripping the loaf toward her breast, making the crumbs fly and spin and crackle and dot and cling to her black turtleneck sweater, daring anyone to pick them off. Then she lifted the bread to her mouth, which parted slowly, as she stared into Frank's eyes. He watched her tongue come out to meet the bread. Her lips and teeth encased it and she bit down and it crunched and she chewed ever so slowly. Her eyes closed dreamily and then opened. She put the mouth of her beer bottle to her lips, tilted back her long neck to show the outline of her jaw, and took a long swallow. He watched her drink in great long passionate gulps. . . .

Frank's penis was erect, climbing against his lower belly.

"One chicken paillard," said the waiter. He slid the chicken and soup and a salad in front of Frank. Frank drained his glass and held it up to the waiter.

"He'll have what I'm drinking this time, Pete," Sarah said.

"I will?" Frank said. "I mean, yes, I will."

The waiter nodded and Frank began eating the salad. It was delicious. He tasted the chicken and it was also very good, and the bread was fresh and crisp. He tasted some of the soup. It was too hot. He reached for the butter.

"Just a little butter," Sarah said.

"What about Polly?" he asked and tried to straighten his erection so it wouldn't be so uncomfortable. He looked around. Was he paranoid or were all those people really staring at him? He was still straightening his penis, trying not to make it noticeable.

"Want me to do that?" she asked.

"Do what?" He felt ridiculous.

"Butter your bread, honey."

She beamed with mixed signals—bright smile, sad eyes, slow grinding jaws. This woman would be the hardest interrogation in the universe. Even another woman would be distracted by her beauty and her disarming personality, Frank thought. Yet it isn't a performance. It's more like a collection of all the right ingredients thrown in together, to make a near-perfect creature.

"Like the rest of us at school, Polly always had a hard time finding the right guy," Sarah said. "Why are the good guys so goddam hard to find?"

"You shouldn't have any trouble," Frank said.

"Why not? To most, I'm just another edition of tits and ass," she said.

"Do you have to talk so loud?"

"Calm down," Sarah said. "No one's watching us."

"The whole restaurant is watching us," Frank said.

"I can't help it if you're infamous."

"Me?" Frank said and laughed. His hand hovered over his plate with a piece of chicken on the end of his fork. He stared around the restaurant, and most eyes were on their table. Sarah took the chicken off the end of his fork and popped it into her mouth. She chewed with her mouth closed, and her moist lips swiveled and rotated as she did. Then she slowly licked her thumb and index finger. Control yourself, Frank thought.

"They recognize you from the papers and TV," Sarah said. "They're not looking at me."

"You could cause a traffic jam in a ghost town," Frank said.

"Yeah, right, that's why I'm teaching aerobics," she said. "I'm just another girl trying to get a big break in show biz. I'm not moaning about it. I get a movie line here and there. A commercial once in a while. I eat, I pay my rent, I'm not selling my ass in Port Authority. I'm twenty-nine so I'm never going to be a child star. I usually lie, but I'm gonna be thirty in two months. I've never gone out with a really nice guy in my life. Good-looking guys, rich guys, powerful guys, conceited assholes, a politician, pathetic slobs, liars and cheats who swore they weren't married. Yeah. All of that. Maybe two or three decent fellas who weren't looking for more than fun. But a real nice guy? Nah. Not yet, anyway. I keep trying and what do I get? Older every day in the age of AIDS. Chicken is good, eat up."

"What about Polly, Sarah?" Frank asked.

Sarah picked the crumbs off her sweater. Frank wished he was doing it. She took a slug of beer.

"Polly is different from me," Sarah said. "We were and still are friends. Best friends. Money is important to her because she came from money. Me, I'm an air force brat. I had a rich Uncle Sam, but my daddy never made more than seventy thou a year. Polly's father was born with such a silver spoon in his mouth that he almost tarnished in the sun. Until the crash of 'eighty-seven. And Polly always said she despised money, but by the same token she always complained if she went with a guy who didn't have at least a Mercedes."

"Then she must've complained about Kevin a lot."

"Not in front of me," Sarah said. "How can you complain about a guy who saved your life? I was there that night, in the fireman's restaurant. The Halloween party?"

"Everyone knows the story," Frank said. "What's-his-face in the *Daily News* even wrote a column about it."

"No one knows it like I do," Sarah said. "I saw that moron throw a match at her. The guy dressed as the Devil, who said later he was joking, throwing fireballs from hell. . . . I knew the fireman who owned the restaurant, Terry Quinn, because he was married to an actress friend of mine. He invited his fireman buddies; I invited Polly. Not only did Kevin save Polly's life, he visited her every day at the burn center. I saw him there at her bedside, in and out of uniform. When Polly was petrified no other man would ever look at her again because of the burns, Kevin Dempsey showed up every single day with roses and books and flowers and candy and jokes and funny cards and a tape player. It was some courtship. Fairy-tale time. He stuck by her through all the operations, skin grafts, convalescence. The only reason I missed their wedding was because I was doing a slasher movie out in LA. But I watched that courtship. I know your brother's a great guy. If you're half the man he is, this'll be the best lunch date I've had in months. So, no, Polly wouldn't have the balls to ever bad-mouth Kevin in front of me. And Jesus Christ, he's so good-looking into the bargain! Like you. Your parents must have been a pair of aces."

"They were Mom and Dad," Frank said.

"Well, Polly never felt that kind of unswerving adoration for *her* mom and dad, that's for sure," Sarah said. "She despises them, actually. Mostly for sending her to boarding school. By the time I was fifteen I loved being in a boarding school, in one place. I liked being around kids my age, away from my parents and army bases and a new city every damn year. In boarding school, you could talk openly about your period, puberty, guys, rock and roll, and losing your virginity."

"I'm not that nosy," Frank said, holding up his hand to stop her as the waiter placed a bottle of beer in front of him and he took a gulp.

"My dad was a major in the air force, from Michigan originally, stationed in England," Sarah said. "My mom worked in the American Embassy in London. They met cute, as they say in Hollywood, at a July Fourth picnic in Kent, near where Polly's from. Dad was some charmer.

Mom was an only child from Washington, D.C. Her dad was a mid-level State Department lawyer, so Mom took a job with the State Department and applied for foreign service. They were actually all right. I liked them together. Mom still had a social life in London until she died two years ago from breast cancer. I don't know how my father ever got to be a major. He must have had drinking buddies in high places. I loved him and I miss him. Always will. *He* was a real *nice guy*. They sent me to a Swiss school; that's where I met Polly. She still hates her parents, especially her dad, who adores her. Polly finds forgiveness hard. Unless it's directed at her."

"Who was the love of her life before Kevin?"

"Herself," Sarah said.

"No one she would have pined for?"

"Maybe secretly her daddy," Sarah said. "But only if all the chips were down."

Frank chewed his chicken and nibbled at some zucchini strings. He gulped some beer. Beer didn't taste alcoholic to him anymore. Mostly it just bloated him. He belched, covering his mouth with his napkin, and cut more of the chicken and was surprised by his appetite. He even finished the Yankee bean soup. Maybe it was the healthy company.

"She's been missing for two days," Frank said.

"That's not unlike Polly," Sarah said.

"How so?"

"Polly has no compunction about just packing up with what's on her back and leaving, throwing caution to the wind. She used to run away from boarding school all the time. She'd be in some rich count's house when she was tracked down. She just doesn't give a rat's ass about most things, especially other people or their concern for her."

"But she has a baby with her."

"She called and said she wasn't coming back, didn't she?" asked Sarah. Her eyes narrowed and cut through his camouflage.

"I'm not at liberty to say."

"Look, I agreed to have lunch with you because I always liked Kevin and because you're a safe lunch date and single," Sarah said. "That was in the papers too and confirmed by Polly. And you seem like a decent guy who's had his share of hard knocks. And because you made your money the old-fashioned way—you stole it. Maybe because I find it refreshing to slum on my lunch break. Or maybe because with a whip and a chair I could torture you into looking as good as you must have once. And because I know Polly is a flake and I know you're watching out for family interests. But if you want to shut me out, don't expect me to play Watson. Okay, Sherlock?"

Frank put down his fork and knife and toyed with the beer bottle. "I'm sorry," he said. "Yeah, she called Kevin and said she wasn't coming back. She didn't say where she was. That's one thing. Being jilted brings wisdom. Humility can put steel in your spine. Part of life."

"Tell me about it, heartbreaker," Sarah said and smiled. "Can I use that as a motivational in my aerobics class?"

"But the kid . . ." Frank was appealing to Sarah now.

"Yeah, little Zoe. An absolute angel. I bought her one of those Pepper Face Dolls when she turned three. Waited on line half a day to get one. One of those gimmicks, where the company sends out a birthday card 'Anywhere in the World' on the date of purchase, every year for the first five years, to the owner of the dolly. Zoe adores that doll as much as I adore when she calls me 'Auntie Sarah.' I have no nieces or nephews, unfortunately. And I guess I'll never have a baby of my own."

"I've seen her with that doll," Frank said, smiling. "I didn't know who gave it to her. I shop for five, come Christmas. Zoe is my goddaughter, so she's special. . . . Look, Kevin is half crazy right now."

Sarah smiled and her eyes twinkled. Ten years ago, Frank thought, if you saw this girl you would have fallen right down on the floor, belly up, pleading for her hand in marriage.

"Yeah, Daddy's little girl."

"That's the problem," Frank said. "She said she isn't bringing Daddy's little girl back either."

Sarah nibbled a crumb and didn't respond for what seemed to Frank like a spooky amount of time.

"She's off the deep end then," Sarah said with concern.

"What do you mean?"

"I was waiting for Polly to pull a number like this. See, Polly doesn't think the law applies to her unless it works in her favor. She has total contempt for the laws of nature, never mind the laws of man and society. She's what you might call uncivil. A sociopath."

"You mean she's that nuts? Capable of deciding she's allowed to just take the baby and leave with no legal considerations?"

"Oh, yeah. To Polly, the law doesn't apply if it gets in her way. I don't think she's capable of murder or burning down a disco or shooting a rock star or anything like that. But as for, like, taking Zoe and saying, 'Okay, let's go, I'm packed, I'm outa here'? Yeah, *that's* Polly. If she was tired of Kevin and her life with him, she would just pack up Zoe as if she were an extra suitcase and split."

Frank didn't want to divulge everything Polly had told Kevin on the phone Monday morning. He wanted to get more information before his brother recovered from the minor burns and smoke inhalation received in the fire where he had made the heroic rescues. Kevin would probably be in the hospital for another night. Frank wanted information soon but was careful not to give too much away, even to this beautiful, intelligent, disarming woman. Instead he decided to probe further, risking Sarah's anger.

"Did she talk about another guy?"

"Look, Polly is my friend," Sarah said sharply. "I care about her. She helped get me a modeling agent when I was doing 'go-sees' for horny losers, scrounging around town with my portfolio. And I also think the world of Kevin, who saved her life and was so good to her. But until I talk to her, hear her side of the story, I'm neutral. I don't go around ratting on my friends."

Frank knew that was a loyal way of hinting there probably was another guy. There had to be. If Polly didn't have another guy, Sarah would have just said no. She chose to protect her friend by not saying yes. And who likes a rat? This was a stand-up lady, all right.

"Kevin is more than my friend," Frank said. "He's my blood. So is Zoe."

Sarah nodded and let the silence sit on the table like a deck of cards, awaiting Frank's deal.

"Your friend could get in big trouble," Frank said.

"You'd know what that's like."

"I do, and it isn't pleasant."

The waiter came back but Sarah didn't order this time. She left that for Frank.

"Two coffees," Frank said.

"Make mine an Irish coffee, Pete."

Frank licked his lips.

"Make it two," Sarah said, and the waiter nodded. "He's paying."

The waiter smiled and left. Sarah leaned closer to Frank across the table.

"With dirty money, I hope," she whispered.

Frank looked at her over his beer bottle and tried to stifle a smile. He couldn't.

"Sometimes cleanliness is next to hopelessness," Frank said.

"Look," Sarah said, playing her hand without bluff. "Polly is crazy but she isn't stupid. She wouldn't go to jail. Not enough hot water and clean towels. Or men. If she's gonna run, she'll be hard to find."

"They'll have pictures of that missing baby on milk containers from sea to shining sea," Frank said.

"Ah, but which seas?"

The Irish coffees came and Frank took a sip of his and nodded.

"You mean by 'Which seas?' that she might take Zoe abroad? As in England?"

Sarah shrugged. She took a sip of her Irish coffee and closed her eyes, savoring it.

"With Polly anything is possible: Europe, Australia, Hong Kong, Brazil—or America."

She took another sip of her Irish coffee and licked the cream off her upper lip with a deft dart of her tongue.

"She'd be extradited," Frank said. "Kidnapping is kidnapping, even in Britain."

"Not in a matrimonial dispute," Sarah said. "Besides, Polly always has something up her sleeve. If you find her, let me know. She borrowed a hundred thousand dollars from me."

Frank looked over his coffee in astonishment and rattled the cup into the saucer.

"A hun . . . for what?"

"She said it was an investment."

"What kind of investment?"

"Not sure," Sarah said, poking at her coffee. "She's full of surprises. But she'll pay me back. She always has in the past. Of course, never this much. But twenty-five once. Fifty last time. She came through. At least I hope she pays me back. She'd better. It's all I have. My dad gave me fifty grand when I reached twenty-five. He knew he was dying. It was half his life's savings. Mom got the other half and the insurance and her pension. The other fifty I made busting my ass doing resort-runway modeling before I 'grew up' and matured, as they say in the business. Which means too old for anything but detergent and constipation commercials, unless you're a blank-eyed waif one season or a full-bodied glamour puss the next. My look was always a season behind or ahead until I got too old to ever make the cover of *Mirabella, Allure,* or *Vogue.* But I've been frugal. I earn enough to live on from the gym. And most assholes still insist on buying dinner. I let them. It isn't always right. But neither am I."

"Why'd you lend it to her?"

"She said she could double it in two months. Polly meets people who are into those kinds of schemes. Her father took a shellacking in the crash of 'eighty-seven and they lost most of *her* money in the BCCI fiasco in 'ninety-one. But he has a name and can still muster a sizable line of credit on his reputation. I'm single, working, no family. I took a gamble. If she doubles my money, as she promised, I can get the security I've been looking for. I have an offer to go partners in a midtown gymnasium. Once-in-a-lifetime deal. Other people's sweat will fall on my floors like gold coins. I told her I'd need my money back in less than two months to close the deal. She said okay. She signed a promissory note. Polly better pay me back, because my deadline to buy into the gym is now about a month away. And I don't think she'd want it out on the circuit that she's a thief."

"What circuit?"

"Oh, there's a network, a circuit, all right. It doesn't have a name. Beautiful People is sort of a sixties name for it. I call it the Heathens' Highway. But it's different now. Good-looking women plug in and out, depending on who they meet. They usually come back after each divorce. Word goes coast to coast, across to London, Paris, Miami Beach in the winter, Palm Springs, Cannes, Aspen, the Islands. The circuit consists of money and good-looking women and men who have enough of the first to afford the second. Polly wouldn't want 'thief' attached to her name among the paranoid rich of Heathens' Highway. It would cost her money in the long run, when it was time for a really big score. The burns might keep her from modeling, but she's still gorgeous."

"If you hear from her, will you get in touch with me?"

"I'll get in touch with you even if I don't," she said. Frank swallowed, didn't know what to do with his hands. So he took the last sip of the coffee. She handed Frank her card with her work and home numbers. He wrote his number on a cocktail napkin and handed it to her.

"I have a machine," he said proudly.

"Zowie, imagine that! Did you win it?"

She smiled and shook her head in a tight little orbit and widened her eyes at his innocence. Frank realized having an answering machine in this day and age was like having a belt to hold up your pants. It showed his age to say he had one, because to him they were still "new" machines. The waiter brought a check and Frank took out some cash and paid for it, telling the waiter to keep the change. He overtipped. Maybe that would get him an extra glass of water from a waiter in purgatory.

"I like this part," Sarah said. "Eating dirty money. I've probably eaten a lot of it before but it was never mentioned. Never cash. Always credit cards."

"They canceled mine," Frank said.

"If Polly doesn't turn up with my money, I'll be in the same boat. Shipmates. I like that."

"In my case, shipwreck."

Sarah smiled, and her eyes played on his face like lights.

They stood up to leave. Steve came over to say goodbye.

"A customer at the bar wanted your autograph, but I told her you were busy," he said.

Frank smiled and looked at Sarah, nodding. "See, I told you everybody was staring at you."

Sarah smiled and Steve said, "No, she wanted yours, Mr. Dempsey. You're a hot-celeb Hancock right now, baby."

They left together. Frank felt ridiculous. He hoped it wasn't going in some ledger upstairs that he'd have to explain on his fast-approaching judgment day. Idolatry. Autographs. Celeb. Lord, believe me, he thought. That was never part of the plan. No way.

He was looking at the sky and holding the door open for Sarah when he felt her arm hook through his. The gesture made him shiver. This wasn't in the plan either.

"Walk me home?"

"Sure."

They strolled down Forty-second Street toward Tenth Avenue. Hot damp wind blew off the river. Sarah snuggled close to Frank as they walked. He realized one beer and one Irish had made her loose. Frank couldn't believe the looks he was getting as he strolled down the street with her. Guys and girls stared at them—at her anyway. He knew the guys did a turnaround to check out her butt when they passed. It felt good walking arm in arm with a beautiful woman again. It had been years since he'd done it. It made him feel . . . alive . . . as a man.

As they turned the corner onto Tenth Avenue he saw Summers from IAB following. He stopped feeling sorry for him because now he could look at Sarah's butt with a sense of duty. The wind blew in circles, and Sarah's hair lashed around like a cat-o'-nine-tails. She pressed herself to him and stared into his face. He didn't feel shorter anymore.

"I'd ask you up," she said, "but I'm not in the mood for having my heart broken. Riding the jail bus with the wives and kids."

"Don't be silly," he said. "Thanks for talking to me."

"You're a real nice guy, Frank. But I can't risk falling for a con. Or a boozer."

"That was never my intention," Frank said.

"One piece of advice for nothing," she said. "Nothing, and I mean absolutely nothing, is beyond Polly's audacity. Don't mistake it for courage either, because what you'll find is that she operates on sheer arrogance. And somehow society lets her."

"Thanks again. I'll let you know what I find out," Frank said. "You sure you don't have a name I should look up?"

"Focus on the people she knows with money. Polly won't be far away."

For the first time she looked momentarily unsure of herself. Then she shoved her hands into the back pockets of her jeans and stared at him, her head at an alluring tilt.

"I'm sorry, Frank."

"I never do it on first dates anyway."

She smiled sadly, spun on her heels, and cascaded through the revolving door.

Frank watched her go and turned to Summers, who stood down the street pretending to read a menu in a health food restaurant window. Frank smiled and shrugged. Summers looked away. He thought about buying the poor guy a drink. Then he thought better of it and walked south for the A train to Brooklyn. He was hoping the subway would make Summers weary of his task. The night-shift guy had it easier because Frank rarely went out at night. That might change soon, Frank thought.

11

Margie Dempsey stood at the bedside as the Methodist Hospital nurse removed the saline drip from Kevin's arm and put a Band-Aid over the needle hole.

"He wants to go home, we can't stop him," the nurse said in her Caribbean accent. "He's signing himself out. He could use another day's rest. But the doctor says he's okay. Big strong man. He can go back to work if he wants."

Margie placed a plastic bag with clean clothes on the bed as Kevin sat up. He removed his hospital gown. His face was raw from heat exposure, and he wore a small bandage on his right arm.

"The nurse tells me you still won't take the painkillers," Margie said. "You nuts?"

"I can't think when I take pills," Kevin said. "All I *think* about is what they're doing to my *thinking*. And I need a clear head to find Zoe. What have you heard?"

"I checked your answering machine, but there was nothing from Polly," Margie said. She stepped away from the bed area as Kevin closed the curtain to dress. "Just a message from your broker about house insurance. And a return call from the bank saying your savings account hasn't been touched since last week. And Zoe's school called to say there were a few odds and ends left behind after Polly signed her out."

"Polly actually signed Zoe out of school?"

"I guess so," Margie said.

"What kind of odds and ends did the teacher mention?" Kevin asked.

"She didn't say and I didn't call her back," Margie said.

"What about Anthony?" Kevin asked. "Did he call? I'm expecting to hear from him about some tests I took."

"Nothing," Margie said.

Kevin pulled open the curtain. He was dressed in a long-sleeved, loose-fitting Jets jersey and a pair of snug blue jeans. He fastened his belt buckle and jammed his stocking feet into a pair of soft black leather loafers. The long-sleeved jersey covered the bandage on his arm, and except for the minor redness on his face, you couldn't tell he'd been through a harrowing fire.

"You sure you're all right?" Margie asked.

"Yeah, just my back is still hurtin'," Kevin said. "Muscle and bone bruises. No big deal. But I wonder what happened to Anthony. Frank left him a message, didn't he?"

"He said he did, but Anthony is moving," Margie said. "Probably taking care of last-minute details."

"How's Mike?"

"Well . . ."

"They're still bothering him at work about Frank, aren't they?"

"Least of your worries."

"Mike was always the first of your worries," Kevin said, as he gathered the few toiletry articles into the plastic bag.

"Yeah, he still worries me. The way he blames Frank for Dad's death isn't much different than him blaming himself for Mom's death," she said. "But he doesn't need the cheap shots on the job."

"He should never have become a cop," Kevin said.

"Too much like Dad," Margie said. "Hotheaded. The 'My way or the highway' mentality."

"Yeah, but the job is different, Marge," Kevin said. "The city has changed since Dad became a cop. Today's cops eat their own when they get in trouble. Speaking of which, I have to see Frank. Thanks for bringing the clothes."

They walked to the elevator together. Margie noticed a few of the smiling nurses making comments about Kevin. Kevin always attracted glances and reactions from women, Margie thought. He intrigued most women he met. Smart, mysterious, handsome, he always seemed to meet the screwballs and sad sacks. Margie remembered one of the early girlfriends, Lucy Carbone. When Kevin got the girl pregnant, Margie had lent Kevin the money to get her an abortion.

"Tell Frank to call me," Margie said. "I'm worried about him too."

"He doesn't look well, does he?"

"Someone has to talk to him about the booze," she said.

"I can't call the kettle black," Kevin said.

The elevator arrived and they got on. An orderly was transporting an old woman on a gurney. As the lift descended, Margie looked at her and imagined herself that old, still single. A single grandmother, she thought, and smiled. It would beat winding up with some pain-in-the-ass old crank. Men were an invitation to melodrama. Her brothers and her son, who would be going through puberty soon, were enough.

"What's funny?" Kevin asked as they walked across the lobby.

"All the scrambling people do, all the hassles, pain, and trouble, just to wind up getting old," she said. "It's either terribly sad or funny. I try to find the humor in it. And this family is the theater of the absurd. Pure drama. Frank's in trouble with the law he swore to uphold. Mike is part of the law Frank's in trouble with, and he's in trouble within that law on the job because of Frank's trouble. You, you're searching for your baby in a city filled with orphans. It makes you want to cry and ultimately laugh."

She stopped near the mechanical street doors and stared into middle space.

"You seeing anyone, Margie?" Kevin asked.

"Yeah," she said. "You guys. Lots of you guys. And Little Paulie. And his life only gets more complicated now as he gets older. It's a pisser. Life just never gets easier. Until you're too old to enjoy it."

They stepped outside onto Sixth Street, where a morning wind swirled with falling leaves from the maple trees of Park Slope.

"Go home to Paulie," Kevin said.

"Don't get me wrong, Kev," Margie said. "I'm not complaining. I'm just trying to put things in perspective for you. I can't say I know exactly how you feel. But I know if anyone had ever run away with my little Paulie, my life would have gone blank. I'm not sure I would have been able to handle it as well as you are."

"It's only been a few days," Kevin said.

"But I know you're dying inside," Margie said. "I know because I read those stories of yours. Since you were a kid, I know you inside and out. And I want you to know I will do everything I can to help you. I don't know what to do, but if you need me, you call me, and I'm there. We will, all of us, together, as a family, find your baby. We might be one screwed-up litter of puppies, but we are family. And what Polly doesn't understand is she ran off with a *Dempsey.*"

Kevin nodded. She saw something unsaid in his eyes as he leaned and kissed her on the cheek.

"What do you have to see Frank about?" she asked.

"Odds and ends," Kevin said.

12

Frank Dempsey walked with his kid brother Kevin through the Eleventh Street playground in Prospect Park. He wanted to update him on what he'd learned and pick his brains some more in his pursuit of little Zoe.

Kevin said he had a few hours to kill before reporting back to the firehouse. He told Frank the other firemen thought he was nuts, going back to work so soon after the big fire, but Kevin said he was feeling okay and needed the company of the men to replace the hole left by Polly and Zoe. Frank knew right now the firehouse was as close to family life as Kevin could find.

The Eleventh Street playground was where they'd done a lot of their growing up together. It was like a time capsule, Frank thought. Fenced and safe, where ghosts of childhood, when Mom and Dad were both alive, sailed on the swings and climbed the monkey bars and ran through the children's shower pool. Where both their initials were still carved in the cement near the main entrance. Where Frank had baby-sat Kevin on afternoons when Margie was minding Baby Michael and Big Paulie was chasing bad guys.

Frank remembered Kevin's first fistfight here in the playground. It was over in the sandbox, when Kevin was five, which would have made Frank fifteen. Kevin had worked hard building a sand castle, using Dixie cups and pails to make each turret different, carving out gates and towers and windows with Popsicle sticks, carrying pails of water from the water fountain to fill the moat he had dug.

The project was almost complete. Kevin was walking back with a last pail of water, to rub on the walls of his castle to make them firm, when a tall kid with red hair and a striped polo shirt walked into the sandbox and stomped the castle flat, willfully wrecking all Kevin had created. Frank hadn't seen it coming. He watched Kevin's face as the kid destroyed his castle. He expected Kevin to come running over, crying about what the big kid had done. But Kevin took one furious look at the redhead and another at Frank, as if for permission to handle it himself. Frank had nodded. Then Kevin stormed into the sandbox and, without breaking stride, hit the big redhead with an overhand right hand square in the mouth. The astonished kid staggered backward and Kevin went after him, hitting him a second shot in the nose, and the kid went down, screaming for his mother.

Frank didn't interfere, even when Kevin picked up a handful of sand and rubbed it in the redhead's wiry hair. The kid continued to bawl. By the time the mother came running, Kevin had taken off his belt and was trying to tie the kid's hands behind his back, yelling, "Gonna tie yup! Gonna tie yup!" The mother was wild, screeching at Kevin, searching for his parent. An amused Frank walked over as the mother called Kevin a monster. The redhead, his lip bloodied, continued to sob. Frank asked the woman how old her son was. She said eight. When Frank told her that Kevin was only five, the mother looked at the sobbing redhead, smacked him on the back of his head, and dragged him by the collar out of the sandbox.

In that neighborhood, before the term political correctness existed, a fair fight was a fair fight.

Frank had known then that his little brother would never walk away from a fight. After that, he and his friends used to like to take Kevin to the playground, hoping he'd get in a scrap. It was also Frank who took Kevin to the Police Athletic League when he was eight, to learn how to box.

"You thinking about that redheaded asshole?" Kevin asked now.

Frank smiled and nodded, and they both laughed.

"Bet he never forgot it either," Frank said.

The playground was part of the neighborhood furniture. It belonged to everyone and endured as something you could touch with your hands, and pass on to your children.

With school back in session, the playground was an empty stage, mostly silent except for the sounds of athletes and cheerleaders on the playing fields, across the park drive, over a small barren knoll. Frank was wearing a dark green army jacket, the same one he'd worn during the late sixties and early seventies when the vets were coming home from Nam.

Frank had avoided the war by staying in school and joining the police department after two years at Staten Island Community College, where he received an associate of arts degree. He got his BA nights at John Jay College for Criminal Justice in Manhattan while on the force.

Frank felt no guilt about missing the conflict in Vietnam. He had been opposed to it from the beginning and even protested against it. Frank wore his army jacket to Washington moratoriums, campus rallies, and here in the park too, when everyone was smoking weed and dropping acid up on Hippie Hill at Bartel Pritchard Square. Frank skipped the drug scene; he was always a juice head. He'd even contemplated the seminary for a while. But the idea of going through life without getting laid seemed too—well, un-Godly. I wasn't given this to just pee with, Frank remembered thinking as he stood wobbly-legged at the urinal up in Farrell's on a long-ago St. Patrick's Day. I think God intended that I do something useful with it.

"You taught me how to ride a bike right there by the monkey bars," Kevin said, zipping his jacket tighter in the cold sunshine.

"I remember," Frank said. "You were wearing my Sergeant Pepper's Lonely Hearts Club Band T-shirt."

"Yeah," Kevin said. "I remember that. It was your hand-me-down big red bike, too."

"I wonder whatever happened to that bike."

"Dad gave it to the PAL for poor kids when he scored at the track," Kevin said. "Then he bought me a gold ten-speed Raleigh."

"That's right," Frank said. "But I wouldn't be surprised if that old bike is still pushing. I think it was made out of Kryptonite."

"Yeah," Kevin said. "Some things are meant to last. Like the memory, man. I remember when I finally got my balance. I thought you were still holding on to the back of the seat, guiding me, balancing me, but you decided it was time for me to go it alone. Suddenly I looked over my shoulder and you weren't there. I was all alone on that bike. And I was pedaling so fast I thought I would never stop. And my legs had a mind of their own! The freedom, the independence, the exhilaration—that's what it's like on the back of a fire rig, with all that wind and power and *life,* roaring, bubbling, exploding. Jesus Christ, Frank, I can feel that bike underneath me right now! I can't wait to teach Zoe how—"

Kevin cut himself short. Frank went into his coat pocket for a pint of vodka and swallowed a sip. Kevin reached to take the bottle but Frank pulled it away and capped it, no words spoken. Kevin watched him pocket the flask.

"A month ago, Polly borrowed a hundred grand from her friend Sarah," Frank said. "She told Sarah it was for a big business deal. Sarah hasn't heard from her yet."

Kevin turned to Frank and shook his head in disbelief. "What a fucking nightmare," he said. "You sure Sarah's telling the truth?"

"Yeah," Frank said. "No reason to lie." He paused. "She also didn't deny that maybe there was another guy."

"How could that bitch come to my party in my new house knowing that—"

"Hey, wait," Frank said, defending Sarah. "She maybe *thought* there was a guy. Who knows? She said with Polly it was a possibility."

"Did you tell Sarah everything?"

"No. But she isn't what's wrong with the Dempseys."

Kevin nodded and watched Frank take another sip of the vodka.

Kevin didn't even reach for it this time. They walked and Kevin turned toward the sounds of the John Jay football team practicing in the field across the park drive. Frank saw that Kevin was lost in reverie. They walked to the leaf-strewn drive, closed to cars, and found a clearer view of the athletic field.

"What do you think I should do, Frank?" Kevin asked.

"For starts, I think you should feel good about being Kevin Dempsey," Frank said. "You're a great brother, a loyal friend, a brave fireman, and a great father."

"But I don't even know if I *am* a father."

"Stop thinking negatively," Frank said. "Even if that's true, which I don't think it is, it isn't the worst thing in the world."

"No?"

"Well, I'm not one. Christ wasn't. A minute ago you were riding your bike for the very first time, and now you're in a funk again," Frank said. "You're a good person, Kevin. Focus on that."

Kevin shrugged. He smiled and faked a hook to Frank's midsection. The idea of the phantom punch hitting his throbbing liver pushed Frank back onto the heels of his plain polished shoes.

"I want your permission to look through Polly's stuff," Frank said. "See what I can learn, huh?"

Kevin looked abashed. "You mean *every*thing?"

"Yeah. Everything. Before the trail can get too cold, ya know? Old phone bills, see who she called long distance anyway. Zoe's health and school records. Credit card bills, to see where she eats out when she's not with you. Stuff like that."

"It seems sleazy."

"Lamming with your child is the ultimate sleaze, kid. I know this is nasty, but, Christ, there's no alternative. You can go into court but that will mean lawyers, lots of sleepless nights, cops, strangers, judges, social workers, maybe even foster care if the courts think you are both too nuts to care for the kid. We have to worry that she took Zoe out of the country. And if she did, it will be very hard to wrest a child away from a mother who is a citizen of that country. It could take months for a custody battle, maybe more than a year, and I don't have that much—"

Kevin looked at him oddly. "Go ahead, finish what you were saying, man," he said. They could hear the cheerleaders now, practicing a cheer across the way. The youthful exuberance of their voices seemed to sway the branches in the trees. Frank saw Kevin riveted by their chants.

"Well, you know I probably have an indictment and a trial coming up," Frank said. "But that's nothing compared to your problem."

"Frank, if there's something else going on with Polly, you better tell me," Kevin said, turning back from the sounds of the cheerleaders.

"Else? What else could there be?"

"I know when God threw shit at this family he was throwing it through a windmill," Kevin said. "So, you know, I can handle it. Tell me. Did Polly leave me for another *woman* or something? Is she on drugs? Is Zoe in danger? What?"

"Not for another woman, no," Frank said. "Sarah didn't mention drugs, and believe me she'd know about that because she's a health fanatic. I think what this all boils down to is a matter of class."

"Or lack of it," Kevin said.

"Well, yeah, sort of," Frank said. "Polly is British. Social status and money mean more to her than they do to you and me. Our kind, the Irish, we're happy with food on the table, school tuition for the kids, and summer down the Jersey shore. Brits with money have addresses for every month of the year. I don't think Brooklyn was ever on her social calendar."

Kevin stopped to listen to the familiar chant about his old school: "Hey, hey, whaddaya say? All the way with John Jay!"

"Frank, I'm sorry what I said to you at the party the other day. About breaking the family's heart . . . or your own heart, or whatever the hell I said."

"Don't be silly," Frank said. "We're brothers here, no? You're concerned about me. I'm concerned about you. Only maybe I can help you, not vice versa. So can I look through Polly's stuff?"

"Of course," Kevin said. "But I don't know what you'll find."

The wind shook the trees, sending a cascade of leaves to the ground as they walked toward Hippie Hill, which was now just a barren patch of faded green. A lone woman on horseback cantered past on the bridle path. Frank slugged from the vodka. Kevin gave him a set of keys to the new house, the set with the #1 WIFE key chain he'd never had the chance to give Polly.

The two brothers stopped near the entrance to the park.

"You gonna be all right?" Kevin asked.

"It's you I'm worried about, Kevvie."

Frank held his arms open. Kevin was more muscular than Frank. But Frank was still his big brother. They embraced.

"Thanks," Kevin said.

"Love ya, kid," Frank said.

Kevin held the embrace longer than Frank.

"One more thing," Kevin said.

"What?"

"So where's the fucking money?"

Frank pushed himself away from Kevin, who was smiling.

"What money?"

Frank was poker-faced. Kevin shook his head and walked away backward a few feet, amused, and then turned into the wind.

13

Kevin Dempsey spotted Dr. Anthony Scala sitting in his Mercedes, parked across the street from the firehouse. He'd just parked his own Jeep up Buffalo Avenue in the FDNY white zone when he saw his lifelong friend. Instantly, Kevin felt his gizzard tighten as if someone were wringing laundry in his belly. His throat went suddenly dry. He stopped walking as Anthony got out of the car and approached him. The world sounded abruptly louder, and the tenements and rubbish-tossed lots glared sharper and starker to the eye.

A kid about eleven, wearing a wool coat with one button over a dirty undershirt, sneakers with no socks, stood in the middle of the lot, almost protectively watching Kevin, as Anthony approached. The kid held the handle of a broken umbrella and used it to duel with the world.

"Kevin, I tried to call you," Anthony said. "I just heard about the fire, the injuries. You okay?"

"Cut to the chase, Anthony," Kevin said, with a glance at the closed firehouse door.

Anthony cleared his throat and looked both ways. The wind lifted a flap of his hair as he held the folder of lab reports in his hand. The professional wrestled with the friend in Anthony's demeanor. He looked at Kevin with resigned eyes.

"Well, as far as margin of error is concerned—"

"Is Zoe mine? Yes or no, Anthony."

"No," Anthony said, snapping a finger against the folder. "But—"

"Write when you get a phone number out there," Kevin said, and turned away from his friend toward the solace of the firehouse. The kid with the umbrella handle was lunging at an imaginary foe. Kevin moved to walk away but Anthony grabbed him firmly by the arm. Down the avenue a horn honked and people shouted, a bottle smashed, and there was the distant report of a gunshot, all part of the background sound track of the ghetto.

"Goddammit, listen to this like a man," the doctor said.

The kid with the umbrella overheard Anthony's tone and stopped and stared at the two white men.

Kevin glared at his friend. "You want me to listen like a man to evidence that I'm not?" Kevin asked. "Later, Anthony."

Anthony looked him in the eye and clutched his arm.

"Please, this isn't easy for me either, Kev," he said. "I didn't want to tell your brothers or sister, so I drove out here. I'm not enjoying this, man. It hurts me too. I'm here as your doctor and your friend."

Kevin saw that Anthony was trembling slightly.

"I'm sorry," Kevin said. He peered at the kid, who stole a glance back at him. "Go ahead. Give it to me."

"The sperm count was zero," Anthony said. "It goes back to the mumps. Bobby Bronsky. The football game."

"Mumps?" Kevin said, recoiling in horror. "Bobby Bronsky?"

"Yeah," Anthony said. "We all drank champagne from the same bottle. I caught his mumps too."

"I remember the champagne," Kevin said. "And the mumps I'll never forget. So?"

"Well, thirty percent of all males who get mumps after age ten have one testicle affected by an infection called orchitis," Anthony Scala began, right there on the bleak street. "Look, Kev, you wanna sit in my car so I can explain? Civilized like?"

Kevin watched the kid with the umbrella stick fencing with his make-believe opponent, a childhood fantasy about grown-up derring-do.

"No, here's good," Kevin said. "Right here's a good place to find out I lost more than the game and my girl on that day I fumbled. So what else did I lose? You're saying my balls, too? My manhood?"

Anthony opened up a file folder and read some statistics to Kevin.

"Of those postpuberty mumps cases, ten percent will have both testicles affected, destroying the spermatogonia, the sperm-generating mother cells. The atrophy caused by the orchitis does not affect the testosterone or the ejaculate. So you would never know you had a zero sperm count. Kevin, you were part of that ten percent."

"Talk English, Anthony," Kevin said. "You mean you still get a sex drive, a hard-on. Still come, but there are no sperm cells to make a baby? That's what you're saying, isn't it? That the mumps Bobby Bronsky gave me, when I drank from the same bottle as him, after I fumbled the ball, made me sterile for life?"

"Yes."

"So that Zoe can't be my baby?"

Anthony stared at him, at his shoes, at the sky, at the kid with the umbrella sword, then back at Kevin and whispered, "Yes."

"No doubt?" Kevin asked.

"I sent it to two labs," Anthony said. "That's why I took so long to get back to you. I had to be sure."

"I didn't just have an off day? Like Doc Gooden's fast ball being slow? Michael Jordan throwing an air ball? Mighty Casey striking out?"

"Sperm count was zero in both tests," Anthony said.

"What about the blood comparisons?" Kevin asked.

"What's the point, Kevin?" Anthony answered with a question.

"I want the whole shooting match," Kevin said. "If you'll excuse the pun."

Anthony opened another file folder. "You're sure you don't want to come have dinner with me? Talk? Maybe take some time off?" Anthony asked. "A vacation. I'll write any note you need for the job—"

"I'm off now," Kevin said. "I don't work until tonight. I've been sleeping here. What did the blood say, Anthony?"

Anthony read from the file folder, which trembled in his hands. "Okay. Polly is type O, Zoe is type O, and you are type AB."

"And?"

"And that means you can't be the father," Anthony said. "I'm sorry, Kevin. It checks every way you look at it. Look, why don't we go for a drive, talk about this?"

Kevin knew Anthony was trying to ease the pain with friendship. But the doctor had spoken and the childhood bond wasn't enough to comfort him. Kevin did an off-balance two-step, as if backing away from a predator.

"Kevin, I'm so sorry. Look, the child still loves you. Millions of people raise kids that aren't theirs. A judge might even give you some sort of visitation rights. Kev, talk to me."

"I gotta go do something," Kevin said, walking away backward, forcing a smile. "I'm just glad it was you who told me, Anthony. Please keep this between us. No one else. Please. Thank you."

The kid with the umbrella handle lunged at the universe and watched his imaginary enemy sag to the earth. He looked up, saw Kevin staring at him, and smiled, embarrassed, shrugged, and ran through the lot past a baby stroller with a missing wheel. He looked back once and laughed at Kevin and kept running with his weapon.

"Look, I still think we should go somewhere and talk," Anthony said.

"After all these years," Kevin said, "I keep fumbling. . . ."

Anthony narrowed his eyes and regarded Kevin strangely as Kevin spun around, hurried up the block, got back in his car, and pulled away.

14

Bobby Bronsky was listed in the Brooklyn White Pages under Robert Bronsky of Ditmas Avenue, in that splendid area of turn-of-the-century Protestant summer mansions called Olde Flatbush or Ditmas Park. The neighborhood was near the border of ravaged modern Flatbush but its safe splendor was still intact, thanks to an armed private security force, hired by the homeowners association, who patrolled with attack dogs. Through the middle of the century, it was a neighborhood of Brooklyn's richest doctors, lawyers, Wall Streeters, and machine politicians.

Today, nouveau riche yuppies and buppies were buying up the great old Gothic, baroque, and Tudor manors in the real estate stampede of the nineties. Kevin figured old Bobby and Lucy must have done all right for themselves in the years since they'd all fallen out of touch. Somehow he knew they were there in this neighborhood, like an itch he never bothered to scratch for fear of opening an old wound; knew they had married and that Bronsky had gone into construction. But whenever Lucy's or Bronsky's names had come up over the years, Kevin quickly changed the subject. Because mention of them always conjured images of the Week of the Worm of Jealousy. A time he didn't like to revisit. Memories better left behind.

Until now.

Now he wanted to see them both.

Bronsky had gotten lucky on the day of the big game, Kevin rationalized. That's all. Ordinarily he was at best a slow and mean player. But even with the deck stacked, it wasn't enough to just make the vicious hit.

No, the bastard was behind those anonymous phone calls all along. Making a real play for my girl behind my back and whispering to me about it. Distracting me, making me blow the game, ruining any chance for a scholarship, giving me mumps. And now it turns out there was even more treachery. The mumps left me sterile, Kevin thought. But not him. I was the one in ten who had to lose his virility, and while I lay in the hospital that night he was out banging my girl, knocking her up. And like an asshole, I got duped into thinking it was my kid and paid for the abortion. Even though I couldn't get her pregnant if I wanted to.

Big fucking laugh they must have had. Because after that abortion, Kevin never heard from Lucy Carbone again. And she wound up with Bronsky.

And I find out now, Kevin thought, that when he shared his poisoned champagne that day, spread his germs, gave me mumps, that he also ruined my marriage, robbed me of fatherhood, took Zoe from my life.

Now I'll show that motherfucker what it's like to be down, Kevin thought. I'll take the bat out of the back and hit him a short six-inch bop on the bridge of his nose. Just enough to send pinwheels into his brain, make his eyes water, disorient him. Then I'll chop him down to his knees. Take his pants off. Spread him naked on the sidewalk, so everyone can see. Pull *his* legs apart. And I'm gonna swing until he sounds like a choirboy begging for mercy. If he has kids already, he won't make any more.

Kevin was parked across the street from the massive Tudor home on Ditmas Avenue. The house was impeccably well groomed, with new thermal windows, trim lawns, and sculpted shrubbery embroidering the grounds. A flagstone walkway wound to a wide entrance that climbed up four slate steps to the big white doors. Some kind of mechanical apparatus that looked like a lone train track ran from the front gate, along the pathway, up the stoop to the front doors. The bottom of one door had been artfully cut so the track could run over the threshold and into the house.

Kevin sat staring at the big house on the majestic street that thrived under a autumn-stricken canopy of Norway maples. Fall leaves rustled along the empty sidewalks, blowing across the lawns and carpeting driveways clogged with mostly foreign cars. He imagined Bobby and Lucy's happy life inside that house: fancy meals, Fourth of July barbecues, Thanksgiving dinners, Christmas mornings, Mother's and Father's days, christenings and birthdays and the omnipresent sound of children. He envisioned Bobby and Lucy smugly making love in their big warm bed in their immense bedroom when snow fell on the cold city outside—all the things he imagined for himself and his family in his new house.

"Looking for someone?" asked the private security guard who pulled abreast in his rent-a-cop car, a German shepherd with red-rimmed eyes panting on the seat next to him.

"Bronsky," Kevin said.

"They expecting you?"

"We're old friends," Kevin said.

"Okay," the guard said. "There's a push-in gang in the area. Sorry. Carry on."

Carry on, Kevin thought. What an absurd term. How do I carry on?

He got out of the car, walked to the trunk, and opened it. He took out the Louisville Slugger and hefted it in his hands. He hurried across the leaf-strewn gutter and opened the front gate. Moving with the bat concealed behind his back, Kevin climbed the four steps to the door. He rang the bell, setting off an elaborate orchestra of gongs. He leaned against the ornate doorframe, the bat hidden behind him.

The door opened. Kevin was startled by her gaunt face. Her once red-pinched cheerleader cheeks were now sunken and hollow, the color of oatmeal, with brackets around the mouth. Her dazzling eyes were now set deeper in her head. Time had not been kind to Lucy Carbone.

"May I help you?" Lucy asked.

"I'm looking for Bobby," Kevin said.

Then almost immediately she recognized him. "Kevin," she said in a detached monotone. "Kevin Dempsey?"

"Lucy."

He nodded and heard a mechanical whine coming from deep in the house, as if someone were driving a golf cart.

"Gee, you look great, Kevin," she said flatly.

"Older," Kevin said. "A little wiser."

"I must look a wreck," she said. "I've been sick."

"I haven't been feeling so well myself," Kevin said.

"I read about your brother," Lucy said. "Hope it turns out okay. Sorry about your dad. That was in the papers too."

"What's bothering me is older news than that, Lucy," Kevin said.

Lucy stepped out onto the front step of the stoop, pulling an Aran wool cardigan tight around her, folding her arms, her hands lost inside the sleeves. Her hair was still beautiful and expensively cut to a shoulder length. She wore diamond earrings and a very large and expensive diamond wedding ring. But gone was the magic of the tight yellow sweater and short cheerleader skirt. The saddle shoes were replaced by Timberland boots with loose jeans tucked into the tops. No pom-poms or little bells.

Kevin looked over her shoulder into the big foyer and oversized living room with its Iranian rugs and chandeliers, big suede couches, glass-topped tables, and fireplace. There were no paintings on the walls, and Kevin couldn't see a single book anywhere.

"Is something wrong, Kevin?" Lucy asked, almost in a lament.

"Something ain't right," Kevin said. He heard the same mechanical whine again and saw that the same odd track that ran from the gate, and over the threshold also ran into the house, splitting off in the foyer in different directions like sophisticated toy train tracks.

"Ever have any kids, Lucy?"

"One, a girl, Roberta, named for Bobby," she said. "She's ten now, at school. We planned more, before the fall. . . ."

Kevin strained to see more of the house over Lucy's shoulder but he couldn't from where he stood, against the doorframe, concealing the baseball bat.

"Fall? Fall of what? The Berlin Wall? The dollar? You look like you did all right for yourselves. You hit the lottery? Or did Bobby fall into an inheritance? What?"

"What the hell is wrong, Kevin?" Lucy asked in a low voice as the mechanical whine drew nearer. "What's with the sneer in your voice?"

"Sneer?" Kevin said. "Me? No sneer. I just stopped by to see how my old football nemesis Bobby Bronsky was doing. Compare notes. You know, to let him know I had a daughter too. Or thought I did. Until today. When it turns out she isn't mine. Just like yours wasn't mine, Lucy. Because of him."

"What the hell are you talking about?" Lucy whispered. But the conversation was quickly interrupted by the approach of the mechanical whine, followed by a voice Kevin found vaguely familiar, only weaker.

"Lucy," Bobby Bronsky called, "who's there? You know I love company. Invite whoever it is in."

"Be patient," Lucy said to Kevin in a whisper. "He gets excitable when he refuses to take his medication. I'll spike his decaf later."

Now Bobby Bronsky turned the corner on the rail track that delivered him in a mechanized contraption that resembled a skier's chair lift, but with foot pedals and compartments for a cordless phone, coffee cup, newspaper, and hand-held remote control box. Bronsky sat in the contraption like a man at the controls of a small spacecraft and manipulated it with trained dispatch to the front door. Which he pulled open wider, showing that the track ran across the foyer and up a flight of stairs.

He had a flannel blanket over his legs and wore a Giants hat and a Giants sweatshirt over his slight torso. Kevin thought his head looked too big for his neck, and it bounced from side to side as if on a spring like one of those silly toys people used to put in the rear windows of their cars. But his eyes were still bright blue and he smiled like a man who has just received an unexpected check in the mail.

"Hi there," Bronsky said, peering out at Kevin. "What can we do for—my God, Luce, look who it is! Unless my eyes are gone now too, that's Kevin, Kevin Dempsey. Standing in my doorway. Am I right?"

Kevin couldn't stop gaping at Bobby Bronsky in astonishment. But peripherally, Kevin felt Lucy staring at him instead of her husband. Knew she saw him swallow nervously and shift his weight uneasily from one foot to the other, never taking his hand from behind him.

"Yes, it's Kevin, all right," Lucy said.

"What's he want?"

"Ask him, Bobby."

"I'll do better than that," Bronsky said. "Kevin, why don't you come on in? I'll make you a drink. I can still make a great Manhattan or a martini. Of course, since the fall, with the goddam pills, one's my limit. Wouldn't want to fall out of this ass-basket the way I fell them sixteen floors."

Kevin turned to Lucy, who now stood over the track, turning her back on Bronsky, who couldn't get any closer without running her down.

"I didn't know," Kevin said softly.

"Broke his spine doing stone and derrick work on some bank in lower Manhattan," she said in the same level tones. "Faulty scaffolding. Plywood flooring broke his fall, saved his life. We settled for three million. This place was already designed for a handicapped woman who died, so we bought it. A regular dream house."

"Bring him in, for Christ sakes," Bronsky shouted, "so I can bust his balls about the fumble. Get the hell out of the way, will ya? Give a guy a break."

She stepped aside and Bronsky moved closer on the motorized chair and held out his right hand. Kevin looked down at the bony hand, covered with translucent skin, then at this desiccated, broken man who had left Kevin crippled in a different way. Kevin's right hand was on the ball bat behind his back, and he reached behind with his left hand to free it. He saw Lucy narrow her eyes, trying to see what he was concealing. Kevin nervously wiped his damp right hand on his jeans, staring at Bobby Bronsky, the man who had made him fumble, taken his girl, made him sterile. He took Bronsky's cold hand in his. It was like touching a hand in a casket. Bronsky didn't want to let go, as if he had plugged into a time when he was still the bull of the pasture.

"I sure nailed you that day, didn't I, Kevin?"

"Let me count the ways," Kevin said.

"Count them inside, we'll get shit-faced," Bronsky said excitedly. "Fuck it, I'll have two, for the old days."

"Why are you here, Kevin?" Lucy asked, her monotone and Bronsky's icy grip and his nerves finally making Kevin shiver.

"It doesn't matter," Kevin said.

"It does to me," Lucy said, putting her back to Bronsky again, facing Kevin. "This hasn't been an easy life, the last five years with him. Can't keep a nurse. He chases them all away. I've had ulcers, a nervous breakdown, and I'm trying to raise my little girl right. So don't tell me it doesn't matter. You came for a reason. What is it? Is it money? Do you need money?"

"Money," Kevin said, feeling suddenly unclean. "As I remember, it was you who came to *me* looking for money."

Kevin heard a growl from behind him, and abruptly the rent-a-cop from the private security car appeared on foot, holding the snarling German shepherd on a short leash, his hand on his holstered pistol.

"Where's the game, fella?" the security guard asked Kevin.

"What game, Hank?" Lucy asked.

"None of my business, maybe, but a man I don't know goes knocking on a neighbor's door with a baseball bat concealed behind his back, it looks kinda odd," Hank said.

Kevin brought the bat into plain view, causing the red-eyed dog to bark and strain at the leash.

"What the hell is going on out there, Luce?" Bronsky demanded to know. "I might be crippled, but I'm not deaf. Kevin has a baseball bat? Come by for a little home-run derby there, Kev?"

Lucy nodded to the security guard. "It's okay, Hank," she said. "Kevin is an old . . . friend."

The security guard shrugged, tipped his hat, and walked back toward his car with the explosive dog. Lucy closed the door further on her husband.

"You came here to hurt my Bobby, didn't you?" she asked.

"I came to even a score," Kevin said. "There's a difference. But it looks like fate beat me to it."

"I don't know what's eating you," she said with the same lifeless intonation, "but if you ever wanna hit me, call first, make an appointment, I'll take ten more of my Prozacs, and you can come and take batting practice. But if you ever get the notion again, please don't hurt my Bobby. He's been hurt enough."

Kevin stood on the stoop feeling disjointed, shaking like a man with a palsy, the wooden bat chattering on the slate stoop. Lucy stepped into the enormous house as Bobby Bronsky shouted, "Bring him in Luce, please, so I can bust his balls," Bronsky said. "For laughs. The old days."

Kevin Dempsey watched Lucy gently close the big door.

15

Frank Dempsey popped another mint in his mouth as Mrs. Bloom, the teacher from the Jelly Beans Preschool, showed him the letter from Polly.

"It says she was taking Zoe out of school because the family was moving away," said Mrs. Bloom, a pleasant, fortyish woman who had moved to Park Slope from Manhattan in the mid-eighties to accommodate the yuppies who needed preschools for families with two working parents. She had expanded to three storefronts before the crash of 1987 sent many of the stockbrokers back to places like Cleveland to pump gas for a living.

"It doesn't say why she moved?" Frank said.

"No, she just showed up last week, collected Zoe, and announced it was time to move on," Mrs. Bloom said. "She asked for a partial refund. Zoe was a year-round student; she was in our summer program too. But of course we don't give refunds. Mrs. Dempsey was always very money-conscious. Nothing but the best for her daughter, but—well, frugal."

Frank had gotten Mrs. Bloom to talk by showing her his dead father's badge. He gave her a phony name, Detective McNamara, his mother's maiden name. He said Polly Dempsey was being investigated because of credit card fraud, which wasn't far wrong. Earlier in the morning Frank had gone through Polly's personal papers in the house. He couldn't find Polly's passport but he did find Zoe's U.S. passport, with an adorable photo of her. Kevin had taken her for it before he took Polly and the baby to Cancun, a few months after Zoe was born.

Zoe's passport had given Frank some minor relief. It meant Polly was probably still in the United States. A check of her credit cards offered further evidence of that. He'd spent two hours on the phone getting information from Visa, MasterCard, and American Express on Kevin Dempsey's cards.

Frank simply told the security people on the other end that he was Detective McNamara of the Bunko Squad and was trying to get a line on one Polly Dempsey's credit because she was thought to be burning up credit cards before leaving town without a forwarding address. This was a more than occasional problem for credit card companies, especially with cardholders involved in marital disputes.

Frank took all the information on the latest activity on the credit cards over the phone, making a detailed list of merchandise she'd purchased while finishing off the last of a half pint of Gordon's vodka for the morning shakes.

In all, Polly's tab came close to thirteen thousand dollars, most of it for jewelry and clothes. It looked like she bought four of everything for herself, as if discarding an entire wardrobe and replacing it with this one. Clothes for herself from Victoria's Secret and Macy's and Bloomingdale's. And a complete new wardrobe for little Zoe too, which showed Frank that at least she was thinking about the baby.

But in looking over the itemized list, Frank saw that there were mostly fall and winter clothes on the list. Matching women's and little girl's hooded rain-resistant Eddie Bauer gear, rain slickers and matching Timberland winter boots for herself and Zoe, a London Fog trench coat, a pair of Dan Post cowboy boots, tweed pants suits. She wasn't shopping for the islands or the south of France. No bikinis or summer dresses. No shorts or sandals. No Ray-Bans or sun hats. Frank was hoping Polly might have used the cards in another city, pointing him in some sensible direction. But all the charges were made here in New York, most during the week she was supposed to be in Florida at Disney World.

No wonder she was not on the plane from Orlando that afternoon. She hadn't left New York—at least not right away. The last charge was in Macy's, two days before she was to have walked through the door of the new house.

That charge was for a man's Tag-Heuer gold watch, including gift wrap. Frank didn't think there was any need to tell Kevin about this. Yet.

"Did Mrs. Dempsey give any indication where she might be going?" Frank asked Mrs. Bloom, as he looked out the window at Detective Summers from IAB. Summers stood under the canopy of a candy store next to the Seventh Avenue F train station.

"No," said Mrs. Bloom. "She came down here and picked Zoe up in a hurry. She wanted all her schoolwork, anything she had done. Drawings, alphabet printings, fingerpainting. She had me rushing around. There were various folders. It was as if she wanted to leave no trace. But I made her sign this letter of release. I didn't want her coming back saying I owed her money or complaining to the state licensing board. You have to keep strict records."

"What kind of mother would you say she was?"

"I think Polly loves Zoe," said Mrs. Bloom. "No signs of abuse. Physical abuse, that is. But she was obsessive about certain things."

"Like what?"

"Zoe has a turn in her leg," Mrs. Bloom said. "It was in her doctor's note. The doctor said it was enough to put a corrective foot brace on at night. But she wanted me to put it on Zoe during her one-hour naptime each day here in school. I wasn't in favor of it because it stigmatized the child in front of the others. Polly got another doctor's note that said she should wear it in school, so we gave in."

"Can I see this foot brace?" Frank asked. He already knew what it was, of course, had even learned to put it on Zoe one night when he baby-sat and Kevin and Polly had gone up to Elaine's for dinner. It was one of the few places they both actually liked, Polly for the celebrities and her friends, Kevin because it was still a saloon.

Mrs. Bloom walked across the playroom, where children played with blocks and painted with their fingers. From her desk, she lifted the shackle that looked more an instrument of punishment than medicine. It consisted of a pair of white high-topped shoes, spaced eighteen inches apart, the soles spot-welded to a flat iron bar. It looked like the equivalent of leg irons for children. Which, Frank thought, in a way it was. The brace was designed to "imprison" the child's feet in a rigid position while sleeping, to correct turns in the feet or legs.

Mrs. Bloom brought the device back to Frank.

"She must have been in some rush to leave without it," Mrs. Bloom said. "She probably thought I had packed it. Not that they're hard to replace. A lot of shoe stores order them at doctor's specifications for foot and leg curvatures."

Frank took the brace from Mrs. Bloom, realizing his hands were trembling. The shoes were so small that they looked incongruous attached to the metal bar.

"Mind if I hold on to this?"

"Not at all, detective," said Mrs. Bloom. "I hope everything is well with Zoe. She is a little doll. Precocious, a good talker. Loves her dad. Even if her mom is . . . never mind."

"What? It's okay."

"Well, I always thought Mrs. Dempsey was a bit of a child herself," Mrs. Bloom said. "Not stupid, mind you, because she's bright. Well educated, in a British sort of way. But *emotionally* . . ."

"You mean she's sort of a grown-up brat, don't you?"

"Yes," Mrs. Bloom said. "And that can't be a good role model for Zoe."

Frank thanked the teacher and walked out of Jelly Beans. He crossed Ninth Street, carrying the shoe brace. People turned to stare as he paced on unsteady legs, the soles of his feet numb with booze withdrawal. He passed Steve's diner and looked in at the normal people sipping coffee and eating lunch at the counter, and as he smelled the coffee and doughnuts wafting out the door, he envied their simple normal behavior. Eating, reading newspapers, worrying about bills. To ever be normal like them again was science fiction. His was the real world of need, peopled by those citizens who need to be connected to the hose of alcohol, the way automobiles need the fuel nozzle. Life was about a full tank, half a tank, or running on empty. The mere consideration of normal people made Frank do a cold brisk inventory: trembling hands, numb feet, hollow legs, impending vertigo, the gargoyles of DTs, facing time, being followed, searching for his brother's only child.

And lovely normal Sarah. Sarah whom he'd never have a chance to love. What a waste you are, he told himself.

So unfair, he thought, and immediately recalled an old AA slogan about alcoholic self-pity: "Poor me, poor me, pour me a drink."

He slipped into Discount Liquors. He placed the corrective shoes on the counter as he opened his coat to pull some crumpled bills from his right pants pocket. A balled used tissue was mingled with the cash. The counterman looked down at the corrective shoes.

"Pint of Absolut," Frank said.

"That'll straighten out what ails ya," the counterman joked.

"The Absolut, please."

"Absolute-ly," the counterman shot back.

Frank hated jokes about drinking. Drinking wasn't funny. It was a sad, sick, serious business. And getting more serious all the time. Of which he didn't have a whole lot left.

16

Kevin Dempsey didn't need any more medical advice, but he needed to be with a friend. He couldn't bring himself to tell Carmine the whole truth: that he was sterile, that Zoe wasn't his. Not yet.

He had until midnight to get back to the firehouse to report for duty.

So he sought out Anthony Scala again. He'd been too abrupt with Anthony after his friend confirmed his worst suspicions, every man's worst nightmare, the horror that you are not complete, that your child is not yours, that your past is a hoax, a trick, a cruel joke.

What Kevin needed now was someone who knew him *when*. When he was still a whole person, a boy budding into manhood. Someone who could remember for him that kid who was supposed to grow up to be a man and a husband and a father. The kid who wanted to be a doctor too, like his best friend.

So Kevin was barely conscious of the drive over the Brooklyn Bridge, the stop-and-go traffic of the FDR uptown again, the crosstown crawl to Central Park West. He made the trip from Bobby Bronsky's house like a homing pigeon, his need of friendship, commiseration, serving as his compass.

He wanted to apologize to Anthony for shooting the messenger. It wasn't Anthony who had caused his sterility and pain. It wasn't Anthony who deceived him. The worst Anthony had ever done was care for Polly after the fire and stand as best man at his wedding. That was Anthony's only part in Kevin's failed marriage, shattered family, neutered manhood.

Now he needed to mend that fence before Anthony left. Needed what few true friends he had left. Needed to salvage a friendship that had already been strained over the years by social and economic standing, the Manhattan-Brooklyn schism, a friendship that would now be divided by a full continent.

It was unfair to drive a deeper wedge between them by treating Anthony the way he had on the street, when he was told that the laboratory reports proved he could not be Zoe's father.

It was unfair to Anthony but it was also unfair to himself, especially now, when he needed an old-fashioned friend to lean on.

"Don't bother to be ringing the bell," said the doorman at Anthony's building. "He's gone. The doctor is out. For good. Adios, amigo."

Kevin looked at the smiling man in the uniform and gray gloves who had walked across the lobby from the elevator. The doorman brushed his epaulets proudly, making the tassels dance.

"Gone," Kevin said. Gone, he thought, everything is gone. My wife, my kid, my friend, my purpose. "Gone. . . ."

"That's right, gone," the doorman said. "His nurse says he spent too much time and money on research. Not enough time on his practice. So he moved west."

"Gone," Kevin said again, feeling suddenly sorry for Anthony. He hadn't known he'd gone broke chasing another kind of dream in a test tube. . . .

"That your car parked out front on the johnny pump?"

Kevin didn't answer as he looked out at his Jeep, parked abreast a fire hydrant. He flashed to a summer afternoon when Anthony used a hollowed tin can as a nozzle to arc a stream of water from an open hydrant, which they called johnny pumps in Brooklyn. Kevin had dragged a new girl from Anthony's biology class, Lucy Carbone, into the summer spray. She flailed and screamed that she had her "friend." Kevin didn't learn until later she meant her period. He apologized. She accepted. That night he made out with her. The next night he asked her to be his girl. She'd said yes.

"All gone . . ." Kevin said again.

"Your car gonna be all gone, you don't move it off that johnny pump," the doorman said.

Kevin swallowed and turned and walked out of the vestibule. He thought he heard the doorman say "You're gone too" but he didn't know why.

He left the car at the hydrant and walked down one block to the Conservatory Bar in the Mayflower Hotel on the corner.

"Beck's," Kevin said, as he stood amid the ferns at the bar that looked out onto Central Park West. The hotel had been a hangout of the Hollywood set in the mid-eighties, when a kid from Windsor Terrace named Bobby Clark was the night manager. With grand Brooklyn arrogance, Clark had reinvented the term "giving away the store." The place was soon nicknamed by the movie crowd as Hotel California East. Clark worked deals with dozens of big-name stars who got hotel apartments on the arm in exchange for starlet groupies, Hollywood coke, and half-price cash under the table. It lasted two years before Clark got busted by management, who preferred not to bring charges against him because he could have had a parade of show-biz bigs defending him in court. That would have put the hotel on the shit list with future Hollywood types. So they cut their losses and let Clark walk away with a pink slip instead of a yellow sheet.

Kevin and Anthony and a lot of guys from the old neighborhood used to come to the Conservatory to hang out, pick up starlets and groupies from Jersey, and bang them upstairs in the rooms Clark provided free.

Kevin had partied there with Clark and the actors and even some of the writers back then. It was where he first got inspired to write for an audience instead of just himself. He met some successful Hollywood screenwriters too dumb to jaywalk on a rainy night, who demystified the idea of writing for money.

"Pass the cheese things, will ya?" said a throaty voice from the stool next to him. Kevin turned and saw she was about forty. She was attractive, with a once-beautiful face that now was betrayed by tiny crow's-feet when she smiled and tattletale wrinkles above the upper lip, the ones that are the hardest to hide. Kevin slid the Goldfish in front of her and picked up a few.

"These things are like biting your nails," she said.

Kevin looked at her hand as she reached for the crackers. Small fingers, deep wrinkles showing her age at the backs of the knuckles, but soft and smooth on the palms. She didn't bite her nails and she didn't wear a wedding ring. Kevin would have bet she didn't wear panties either.

"Nail biting is cannibalism," Kevin said.

"For nervous cannibals."

She took a sip of a mimosa, the fresh-squeezed orange pulp dotting her plump lower lip. She smoothed her black dress, which clung around two large breasts. Kevin saw her bare legs were long and tawny and tanned. He picked up a few Goldfish and popped them in his mouth and chewed slowly, staring at her tanned face, at her pretty dark eyes that dropped to his hands.

"You have great hands," she said. "What do you wash them with, thumbtacks?"

Kevin looked at his hands, which were large and thick and calloused and covered in small healing cuts, more from work around the new house than firefighting. But Kevin knew women loved hearing him say he was a fireman. Carmine always said that in the minds of some women the fireman's hose added inches to your dick.

"From the job," he said. "Fireman."

She raised her brows and let her eyes drop down his body as he stood at the bar. He wore tight jeans, boots, waist-length leather jacket, and a simple blue sweater.

"We like firefighters where I come from," she said with a grin, revealing the work of a very good dentist.

"You from California?" Kevin asked, oddly feeling nothing stirring in answer to her obvious flirtation. Her come-on was nothing new, especially in this notorious hotel pickup bar. But it was the first time since he'd married Polly that there could be no guilt in even considering a proposition. He had never cheated on Polly, even though he'd had as many opportunities as she probably had. Well, maybe not that many.

"California's a state," she said. "I'm from LA. That's a state of mind."

"Profound," Kevin said. "You give good bumper sticker."

Their fingers met in the Goldfish bowl. She looped a pinkie over his middle finger, took his thumb between her thumb and forefinger, stroked it. Gently, slowly, never taking her eyes off his face. He admired her confidence.

"Here's another profundity," she said. "I'm clean, I'm free, I'm single, I'm as horny as a bag of cats, and I'm in Room Twelve-thirty-six."

She got up and Kevin watched her sign her check and pull his check in front of her and sign that one too. Kevin left a three-dollar cash tip for the bartender and followed her out of the Conservatory to the lobby. Her high heels left little indentations on the carpet as they walked toward the elevator. Then he suddenly felt himself walking alone and he stopped and turned. She stood staring at him, a hand on her hip, sizing him up and down.

"Great buns," she said, loud enough for a counter girl to hear and smile. Kevin felt nothing. Not embarrassment, not amusement, certainly not lust.

When they entered the suite, she told him her name.

"I'm Priscilla," she said. "Like Presley. Only not that rich. But I'm not missing any nail appointments either. Excuse me while I go to the ladies."

Kevin realized she hadn't asked for his name in return. He didn't offer it. When she closed the bathroom door in the bedroom of the suite, he walked to the window overlooking Central Park. The park was beautiful from this vantage, as night gathered over the city and the streetlamps of the walkways ignited. Joggers and strollers made for the exits, before full night consumed the greenery. Traffic rushed through its winding roadways as the smear of darkness spread north past Strawberry Fields, across from the Dakota, where John Lennon had been murdered. That was one of the first places Polly had wanted to see in New York. Kevin tried to tell her that Frank Costello, the old mob boss, had also been shot across the street from the Dakota years before Lennon. That he knew about it because his father had been a uniformed cop on duty that day. But Polly wasn't remotely interested in the history of his city. She wanted to know about John Lennon, a piece of *her* history.

Now Polly was also history and night fled farther north toward Harlem, over the meadows and past the reservoir and the ball fields.

He felt smooth hands loop around his waist, and Priscilla's body pressing against him from behind, the fingers cupping and rubbing his pectorals.

"Give me those hands," she whispered and she guided them behind her to her warm bare buttocks and she made an alarmed sound like someone who was scalded. He turned to her and she wore only an unbuttoned shirt and she was on her tiptoes as she put her arms around his neck and pushed her tongue into his mouth. It felt strange, wet and urgent, the first tongue besides Polly's in three years to be in his mouth. Her behind was contoured differently too, softer, silky-skinned instead of youthfully firm like Polly's. She sucked on his tongue, slurping, as if trying to swallow it, as she backed toward the bed and started to open his belt, her face dropping, her teeth nibbling playfully in anticipation.

But his cock would not respond. He wasn't nervous or afraid. Priscilla was attractive and game and eager, but his cock was indifferent.

"My turn to go to the bathroom," he said.

She looked abashed, as the shirt hung off her shoulders now, revealing only slightly stretch-marked breasts, the nipples large and dark and hard as rubber.

He walked into the bathroom and realized that he had not been even slightly aroused. His penis was soft and shrunken, the way it would be in the cold or when totally drunk or when he was in his early twenties and snorted cocaine that one time.

He locked the bathroom door and felt ridiculous as he stared at himself in the mirror. He opened his pants and dropped them to his knees, pulled down his underwear. He looked at himself in the large mirror. He touched his testicles and heft them in his flattened fingertips, considered their value. Useless. Like two lost golf balls. And a hose to piss with. He looked in his own eyes in the mirror and thought, Outside the door is an attractive, lonely lady, looking for human connection while there's still time left, aching to prove she can still throw you one heroic animal fuck, and all you brought to the party is a useless three-piece set.

He scanned the vanity top and saw all her creams and perfumes, brushes and shampoos, conditions, hair sprays, bath gels. And there, in the soap dish, like a corpse of another man betrayed in a circle of deceit, was her wedding band.

He lifted it and looked at it closely. Tiny, plain, simple: a lie.

He pulled up his underwear, his pants, zippered and buckled them, smoothed back his hair. He took a deep breath, opened the bathroom door, and saw Priscilla lying on her back on the bed, her legs parted only slightly, revealing the moist dark pelt.

"You said you were single," Kevin said.

"I am," she said nervously.

"Liar."

He tossed the wedding band at her. It bounced on the taut sheets of the bed. She grabbed it on the second hop.

"I might have lied about being single," she said softly. "Not about being *alone.* Something my husband never is. Don't I have a right to be human too?"

Kevin walked to the door.

"Thanks a lot," Priscilla said, her voice cracking. "You're a real prince."

With perspiration drooling down his torso under the sweater, Kevin closed the door gently behind him. He wondered whether, if he'd managed an erection, if he would have used it. He wasn't sure, wasn't sure of anything any longer.

Kevin Dempsey had an hour to get to work.

17

"You don't eat, you don't talk, you look like you don't sleep," Carmine said, waving a plate of veal and peppers under Kevin Dempsey's nose. "Christ sakes, the other guys, they know what it's like. Everybody in the world has run across a crazy nut-job broad. Even crazy nut-job broads run across crazy nut-job broads. This isn't unique. It isn't cute either that you don't eat."

Kevin sat on the Nautilus machine, a heavy sweat glistening on his body, his eyes droopy. They were upstairs in the sleeping quarters, the other men downstairs watching TV and dozing on couches. The bells had been still for the more than three hours since Kevin arrived.

"It's not just an ordinary breakup," Kevin said.

"I know, because it's yours," Carmine said, chewing a hunk of veal, smothered in the sweet gravy of bell peppers and Bermuda onion. He took a crunching bite of crusty, seeded Italian bread and slugged heavily from a bottle of ice water, cubes chinking off the cold glass. "When it's your breakup, it's different. But believe me, the kid will remember you. Blood finds blood."

That word, *blood,* made Kevin's swirl with dread. Kevin looked at Carmine, the older man's chest hairs graying now but his body strong and his thinking clear, his friendship fierce. His simplicity intricate in its precision. Clutter didn't fit in Carmine's life. You were loyal to friends. You worked hard and paid the kids' tuition on time, you were kind and generous, you rooted for life over death, and you laughed whenever you could. You made the very best out of a good and modest life.

"Carmine, you know something you're not telling me you know?"

"What the fuck am I supposed to know?"

"Frank talk to you?" Kevin asked.

"No," Carmine said. "Why, what am I supposed to know that I don't know?"

Kevin yanked the handles of the machine in the rowing motion again, grunting out five more reps.

"Zoe isn't my kid."

Carmine put the plate down and wiped his mouth, swallowed. "Fuck are you, nuts or something? 'Course she's your kid. You were a girl, she'd be you."

"She doesn't look anything like me, and you know it."

"Well, she's a girl, I hope not. But the seed is there. Your seed."

"Carmine, what would you think if I told you I'm not capable of having a child? Haven't been since I was a teenager?"

Carmine looked at him askance, held his breath, exhaled in frustration. "First I'd say bullshit," he said. "But even if it's true, so what? You can get it up, no?"

Kevin chose not to answer that. Didn't mention Priscilla.

"I heard you say any man without kids is not a full man," Kevin said. "I heard you say that once."

"I was joking," Carmine said, searching for an exit. "I was probably talking about fags or priests. Men without children are . . . men without children. Sort of sad, no? I mean, even gays adopt. Shit, you're not supposed to take these things I say to heart. They're talk, just men's talk. Stupid. I dunno, Kev. . . ."

Kevin looked at Carmine, who was growing uncomfortable, trying to laugh it off.

"You're lying, man," Kevin said. "You meant it, and you were right."

"Kevin, you're my best friend," Carmine continued. "You think, if it's true Zoe ain't yours, it matters to me? I'd die for you, kid or no kid. This isn't a baby-raising contest. We're fuckin' firemen. We save kids from fires and kittens from trees and get laid whenever we can and have a few laughs. Whoever goes first, the other one plays pallbearer. Life in a nutshell."

Kevin nodded and looked at Carmine, who meant every word he said. "Didn't you say that if anything ever happened to Carmine Junior you wouldn't want to live?" Kevin asked. "Didn't you say that a million times?"

Carmine hunched his shoulders, blinked his eyes, just stared at Kevin. "Figure a speech."

"My ass," Kevin said. "But what if you found out Carmine wasn't really your kid?"

Carmine swallowed and tried to laugh again. "Jesus Christ, he's too ugly to be anyone else's. He was even born bald, like me."

"She isn't mine, Carmine," Kevin said. "Zoe isn't mine."

Carmine fell silent as Kevin began to row to nowhere again.

"Kevin—"

He didn't finish the sentence. Lieutenant Crosby came into the room, followed by Savage, who walked to his locker.

"We need two men for the truck company detail tonight, Dempsey," Crosby said. "Savage says you and him are up."

Crosby went back out the door and Carmine quickly followed, out of Kevin's earshot.

"Lieu, let me go instead of Savage," Carmine said.

"You're a chauffeur," Crosby said. "You haven't been in a truck company detail for a while."

"Savage can chauffeur here," Carmine said. "I got a vibe. I think I should be with Kevin tonight."

Crosby looked at Kevin Dempsey, who stood by the rowing machine covered in a lather of sweat, veins protruding from his arms and legs and neck. Firefighters can be superstitious, going with instinct, following the magic needle on the metaphysical compass within.

"Okay. All I want is two bodies over to Truck One-oh-five," Crosby said. "Square-root it among yourselves."

18

Two hours after they detailed out to the truck company, Kevin and Carmine were on their way to an all-hands fire at a three-story tenement filled with squatters. The front door had been padlocked by the city and the windows of the building sealed with tin and marked with large yellow boxes with big yellow *X*s drawn through them. The *X*s were put there by firefighters during an inspection to indicate that the place was booby-trapped or structurally dangerous.

Flames shot out of the peeled-back corners of the tin covering the windows of the upper two stories.

Kevin recognized the type of job it was immediately.

The squatters gained access to the abandoned building by walking through the functional building next door to the back yard. From there they would climb the fence and enter the abandoned building from the rear, through the basement door or by scaling the fire escape to the floors above.

Kevin was sitting silently with Carmine and two other firemen in the four-seat riding compartment in the Mack rig when it pulled up to the still-safe building next to the fire. They jumped out of the rig, carrying their Halligan tools, axes, and safety ropes and wearing their Scott packs on their backs.

A lieutenant ordered Kevin and Carmine to climb onto the back of the rig, into the cherry-picker-style bucket. Kevin followed instinct, going through the motions like someone making breakfast coffee. The chauffeur was on top of the rig at the pedestal now, operating a hydraulic control panel fueled by the engine of the truck.

The pistons wheezed and extended and the crane swiveled to position. Soon Carmine and Kevin were airborne in the bucket, rising high above the busy street. Their job was to get out on the safe roof, cross over to the roof of the burning building, go down the fire escape, enter the building through a window, and do a search for life inside.

As they rose, Kevin could see neighbors beginning to clog the sidewalks, bathed in the twirling lights of the additional fire companies that were now arriving on the street. He saw Jimmy Savage and Crosby and the other men from his own engine company jump off their rig and race toward the burning building in a street-level assault. They swung axes at the front door and peeled away the tin from the windows of the ground floor.

The bucket reached the roof of the safe building adjacent to the one on fire. Carmine jumped out first and waited for the almost eerily serene Kevin to step off. Kevin walked aimlessly onto the roof, looking heavenward. Carmine hurried along the rooftop, glancing back worriedly at his buddy, who traipsed behind.

A gust of wind blew smoke across the roofs, and Kevin suddenly felt the rush of another wind inside his head: a spinning wind, accompanied by a shrill white-noise siren, quite different from the sirens of the fire engines, as if wailing on a private sound track in his inner ear. The stars above looked like white lint on a black cloak. He looked out at the dark sprawl of the Brooklyn night, imagining all the happy families in all those twinkling homes: fathers with their children, helping them with homework and reading them bedtime stories, tucking them in and kissing them goodnight. . . .

"Kevin, come on!" Carmine said, nudging him. "We have to get to that fire escape, go down and do a search. Come on!"

He took Kevin by the arm and led him across the flat tarred surface to the roof of the house on fire. But there was another, different house on fire in Kevin Dempsey's head, the ideal home of wife and children he carried in his mind like a perfect destiny. That house was burning to the ground, and Zoe was trapped inside and Kevin could not get to her. Could not save her . . .

Out of the corner of his eye he saw Carmine move across the rooftop toward the fire escape. Smoke curled out of the cornices of the building. Kevin began to follow and then stopped and stared back out at the night city, focusing on a single distant window of incandescent light. He imagined a father in a bedroom, tickling his little girl before sleep, so her dreams would echo with laughter, so that whenever she imagined Daddy he would be big and strong and happy.

You will never have any of that, Kevin thought. Because you will never be a father. You never were a father. You are only half of what you thought you were and maybe even less. You will never be a fully realized man.

Suddenly he heard a loud splintering crash and then Carmine was yelling, "Oh, shit! Kevin! Kevin, quick!"

He turned and saw Carmine falling through a booby-trapped gash in the roof of the house on fire. Carmine had plunged through tar paper that had no roof sheathing under it. He sank like a man disappearing into quicksand, up to his armpits, wedged in between roof beams. An orange hue bathed his face and smoke swirled around him.

Carmine was frantically trying to free himself from between the beams as his body dangled into the burning house.

"Kevin! Throw me a line!" Carmine shouted, his hands opening and closing in anticipation. Kevin touched the quarter-inch nylon escape rope in the pocket of his turnout coat. He rolled it nervously in his fingertips as the white siren wailed in his inner ear and he thought about how he would never see Zoe skipping rope on the sidewalk in front of the new house. She was gone along with all the other dreams, trapped in the fire of a different house.

"Kevin, the fuckin' rope! For Christ sakes, these beams are gonna give out!" Carmine shouted.

Kevin looked across the roof to where Carmine was wedged and saw most of the tar paper had melted away, exposing just the smoldering skeletal frame of the cross beams. It was like a glowing tic-tac-toe board.

Kevin suddenly felt an icy shiver run down his spine. He trembled there on the next roof, holding the escape rope in his hand. He knew his friend and best firehouse buddy was in trouble, but when he tried to move his feet they would not budge. Instead, he felt something warm running down his leg. Looking up, he saw an airplane sailing high overhead in the infinite night sky. He couldn't get to Carmine in this burning house. Just like he couldn't get to Zoe in the burning house inside his head.

"Kevin! Please, Kevin, the fuckin' rope!" Carmine shouted again. Then Kevin was knocked heavily to a seated position as Jimmy Savage ran past him, carrying a tin-covered door he'd ripped from the bulkhead of the roof entrance. As Kevin watched, Jimmy Savage laid the heavy door like a bridge across the burning roof beams. He slid out across the door and fastened his nylon escape line under Carmine's arms. Carmine clutched the rope. Then Savage yanked Carmine up out of the wedge where he was trapped and dragged him along the flattened door to safety.

Kevin still sat where he had been knocked down, his rope in his hands, as Carmine was hurried to the waiting bucket. Crosby and another firefighter helped Kevin to his feet and placed him in the bucket with Carmine and Savage.

"One's hurt, one's in shock," Crosby yelled into the intercom on the bucket. "Take 'em down and get 'em treated."

The bucket descended to the street as the other firemen ran to the fire escape of the burning house to do the search that Carmine and Kevin had failed to do.

In the bucket on the way down, Jimmy Savage held Carmine in his arms, feeding him water from a squeeze bottle.

"You okay, babes?" Savage asked Carmine.

"My back is throbbing," Carmine said. "How's Kevin?"

"I don't think even he knows," Savage said.

Kevin Dempsey crouched in the bucket as it was lowered to the pedestal on the rig. He held his rope in his hand, stared at the corrugated mesh floor of the bucket, and thought about Zoe and then about Big Paulie swinging from the sprinkler pipe.

★ ★ ★

Kevin lay there on a gurney for what seemed a prison sentence, staring at the big eye of the moon that glared down on Bedford Stuyvesant. Someone was feeding him oxygen, which he didn't need, and the swirling emergency lights zipped across the smoldering building. He heard the voices of cops and other firefighters and sat up.

"You okay, fella?" came the voice of a stranger.

Kevin nodded.

"I'll be right back," said the Emergency Medical Service worker. "I gotta help load your buddies into the ambulance. They're okay. Just smoke, some burns. One's hurt but okay. So are you. Understand?"

Kevin nodded again, and the EMS worker hurried over to lift the head of the gurney on which Carmine lay, pulling an oxygen mask from his face.

"How's Kevvie . . . what about Kevvie?" Carmine demanded.

"Okay," came Savage's voice. "Shock."

"He froze," said Crosby.

The word *froze* made Kevin sit up to find half a dozen cops holding back a small crowd, watching the ambulance workers. Most of the crowd were young men in baseball hats, some carrying bagged bottles of beer, eager for melodrama. Sometimes arson was committed to lure cops to a concentrated area, leaving the precinct more vulnerable for stickups and street-corner drug deals: decoy fires, to distract Five-O, as they called the cops. "Say the fireman froze inside," Kevin thought he heard a voice in the crowd say. He was sure he heard the word *froze* whispered half a dozen times. His eyes scanned the crowd and the taunting faces that mouthed the word.

"Like a wooden Indian," said another voice.

Savage said nothing.

Kevin sat up higher, his mind a blitz of images, scattered shards of thought like pieces of a smashed mirror. He heard it again, repeated over and over by the crowd: "Froze."

He had frozen, he knew that, remembered it clearly.

He'd let his pal down. Didn't move to save Carmine, who'd saved him so many times. Best buddies.

"Froze!"

Crosby would write him up, Kevin knew.

"Froze!"

Word would hit the tom-toms. He'd be put on light duty, sent to the shrink, dissected. In saloons from the Bronx to Bay Ridge to Staten Island, from Rosie O'Grady's to Suspenders to Farrell's to Peggy O'Neil's and Terry Quinn's, the word would be out. Dempsey froze, lost his balls.

And they'd be right. They didn't know just how right they were. Like Sampson lost his courage with his hair, Dempsey lost his courage with his balls.

"Froze!"

So now, with the wife and the baby, goes the job and the reputation and the dignity. Kevin got to his feet and could smell the reek of his own urine on his boots and pants.

He began to walk toward the corner, where there was more air, more space, into the night. He had to get away. . . .

When he turned the corner, Kevin heard someone shout, "Hey, where's that other fireman?"

"He be bookin'," came a black kid's voice.

And Kevin Dempsey started to run.

He ran down Jefferson Avenue, his heavy boots clip-clopping as he moved, the fifteen-pound turnout coat weighing him down, his eyes fixed directly ahead. He didn't see the people in the doorways looking at the crazed fireman thudding down the street, past pizza parlors, fast-food Chinese and chicken takeouts. Past a pool hall where rap music thundered onto the sidewalk, past slow-moving cars fitted with massive sound systems.

"Where's the fire?" shouted a woman walking with two kids. "I got three at home. What address, fireman?"

Kevin didn't stop. Up ahead, he saw a group of teenagers standing under a streetlight, formed into a nocturnal posse, and they watched him coming.

"Where the fuck your truck, motherfucker?"

"Silly motherfucker in the zone, man."

"Maybe he got *fired,*" said a third, and the other two slid fingers over his two outstretched palms as they all laughed.

From behind Kevin came the voice of an adult, charged with authority. "Dempsey! Stop right there!"

They're chasing me now, Kevin thought. The hunt begins. They want me. To put me under their glass and examine me like a frog in biology. They'll sit me in a circle in the postfire critique, and one by one they will take me apart. *Trauma, trauma, trauma* would be the official determination. *No balls, no balls, no balls* would be the all-important unofficial rank-and-file judgment.

He stopped and surveyed the avenue and saw a church across the street, protected by a high hurricane fence and topped with razor wire. The church was called Mount Calvary. Kevin sailed his helmet over the fence into the bushes of the simple brick structure. An alley cat hurdled over the bushes, startling Kevin and making him back up across the sidewalk.

"Yo, motherfucker, you step in my shadow," said a black guy with wild eyes. He was wearing expensive sneakers and held a bottle of Olde English 40 malt liquor. Kevin's right foot was indeed in the man's shadow on the sidewalk. From down the street, a block away, Kevin heard his name being called again. "Dempsey! Stop!"

"Suppose I light you up with my fuckin' heater, firefuckin' man?" asked the black guy. He opened his coat wide. Kevin looked at his clenched, handsome face, the nostrils flaring, the eyes like bullet holes.

Kevin just backed away, spun, and began to sprint. He heard his name called again, haunting the night like a ghoulish echo. The young black man sailed his bottle in Kevin's direction, the glass shattering just behind him. "Bad enough Five-O in my face, man," he shouted. "Now fireman jumpin' in my motherfuckin' shadow!"

They'll remove your turnout coat, Kevin thought, and draw a big yellow *X* for coward down the back, so that everyone in a fire will know not to rely on you, follow you, work with you, help you. The mark of the one with no balls. Branded. Kevin unfastened the turnout coat as he ran, folding it into a thick clumsy package. He paused, looked over his shoulder, shoved the folded coat into the mouth of a U.S. Mail box, and ran again, listening to his heavy boots kabooming on the sidewalk, the urine now searing the friction burns caused by the running.

He stopped and pulled the boots from his feet, hopping several steps with each yank. He could still hear his name being called as he ran up a one-way street where no car could follow. He placed the boots inside a cardboard refrigerator box where a homeless man slept.

The man's dog bared its teeth and growled, then nipped at Kevin's stocking feet for half a block before stopping to howl at the moon in triumph. Other stray dogs in the hood joined the nighttime chorus. Kevin thought again of the Pirate, the one-eyed cat, alone in the night.

Two blocks later, wearing only socks, jeans, and a T-shirt, Kevin Dempsey found himself on the block of his firehouse. The engine company was still and locked and the street was quiet. He patted his pants pocket and the lump of his keys was there. He gasped for air. His eyes were wide and tearing from the run. Then he saw the fire truck approaching from two blocks down. He hurried to his car and jabbed the key into the lock, opened the door, removed the Club lock from the steering wheel, and started the engine. In the rearview mirror he saw that, half a block behind him, the company engine approached the firehouse.

He spun the wheel, put the gear into drive and his damp-socked foot to the accelerator, and aimed for the new house.

19

Kevin Dempsey double-parked the Jeep outside the house on the steep incline of Langston Place. In a single flourish he turned the engine off, removed the ring of keys, yanked up the handle of the driver's door with his left hand, stepped out, and slammed the door behind him. But Kevin had failed to shift into park, so the car began to roll down the steep street in the drive gear.

Kevin watched the big machine roll, glad it was night and no children were out playing. The Jeep wheeled five-car lengths before veering to the left and smashing into a Mazda, which immediately erupted into blinking head- and taillights, yelping sirens, and insidious horn honking.

Kevin watched it all. Fuck the car. Fuck both cars. Fuck the neighbors in all the silent houses. Most of them inherited their homes. Never worked three jobs to get them the way I did, he thought. Me, I earned my new house with the sweat of my balls. Which was an ironic joke. And right now, Kevin Dempsey had housecleaning to do.

Margie had invited Frank to dinner so they could talk about Kevin and the missing Zoe. The family needed a strategy. Kevin was always high-strung, and now his innermost troubles were revealed to Margie through his stories. Margie thought it was time to share some of what she knew with Frank.

She watched her brother down another cognac and chase it with a sip of espresso. He'd left most of his pasta uneaten on the plate. Margie picked it up and carried it to her cramped, spotless kitchen, where she scraped it into the garbage, still looking at Frank.

Young Paulie was already sleeping. He had to be up early in the morning.

At the sink, she turned on the water, thinking about Frank, sensing that his spirits were buoyed in the midst of family crisis. Perhaps because he was once again investigating something, feeling useful instead of a prison-bound pariah. Frank was the firstborn, the anchor. When he was gone, the family would drift, perhaps forever. She watched the water swirl in the drain.

"I wanted Kev to come over tonight," Margie said, drying her hands on a kitchen towel as she walked back toward the dining alcove. "But he's working right now. I reached him at the firehouse. All he'd tell me on the phone was that his friend Anthony got back lab reports that proved he wasn't Zoe's real dad. That he was incapable of having children. He said he was going to tell Carmine. That's all. This has to stay in the family, Frank. He wouldn't want anyone else, and I mean *anyone* else, to know. I wish he was here to talk about it. But he said he had business to take care of. It scared me. I called you because I hope Kevin isn't getting suicidal, like Dad."

"What about the girl he got pregnant when he was a kid?" Frank asked. "He asked me for money but I wouldn't give it to him. Wouldn't be a party to abortion. Not then, anyway. I still don't know if I would."

"You know what he did. He came here, to Greenwich Village Sis," Margie said. "He admitted he had sex with her. Without protection. Today it might have killed him. Back then it got her pregnant. He said he was responsible. So I made a few calls, scheduled an appointment at Planned Parenthood, gave him the money. He was seventeen, remember. So was the girl. I went with them, too, over to Second Avenue. But it bothered me. I kept looking at this girl and wondering if it was Kevin's baby she was carrying. It might not have been his. She was a desperate kid. I brought this up to him this afternoon when he told me about the lab reports. He said the girl, Lucy Carbone, had lied to him back then too. The baby wasn't his. Just like Polly had lied about Zoe. Until now. Who knows?"

"The old man would've shot that doctor with his service revolver and said he thought he'd walked in on a burglary," Frank said.

"Shot me first," Margie said. "Would have said, because I had a baby out of wedlock, that Kevin followed my example. But Kev was only seventeen. He was scared. He had a whole life ahead of him. So I helped him out. Back then, I did what I thought was the right thing. But now I'm afraid Kevin is coming unraveled."

She walked past the dining area into the living room of her rent-controlled apartment, which looked over Washington Square Park, where drug dealers and the homeless had appropriated the heart of the Village. She took a seat on the couch amid the wall-wrapped, floor-to-ceiling bookcases and the simple but handsome knotty-pine furniture. Framed photos of the family stood on the TV and on end tables next to small Mexican sculptures she'd picked up on a United Federation of Teachers package-deal vacation with Paulie three years ago.

"Frank, I'm worried about him," she said, as Frank carried his espresso and cognac snifter in to join her. "His Kevin stories reveal so much about him. I read them and they're filled with tortured characters, torn apart by their sexuality, men at war with themselves over women, filled with deceit and betrayal and violence. It terrifies me to imagine his dreams."

"I'm glad I never took a wife," Frank said.

"Maybe a wife would have stopped you from getting into trouble too," Margie said, thinking also how lucky some woman would have been to have wed him. "I wish you'd tell me what's going on with you."

Margie was exasperated. She wished for a moment that she drank or smoked or had some other vice to dive into. She hadn't had a boyfriend in almost a year. The last one had simply announced over the phone one day that he was going to marry a woman ten years younger—this after a year and a half of going out together. It had hurt her. The way Little Paulie's father had hurt her when he lammed upon news that Margie was pregnant. Other women would have tracked him to earth for the child support, but Margie thought his never seeing Paulie grow was punishment enough. She didn't want some monthly thirty pieces of silver. She was a Dempsey. She would work.

Margie was thirty-four now, and whenever a relationship went wrong she retreated into Little Paulie's life, nurturing him, educating him, reading the same books he read so she could discuss them with him. She went to all his ball games. But she knew soon he'd be dating and then marrying. She worried what she'd do when he left her and she was still single, older and alone.

In some involved, ironic way, she was almost enjoying the family crisis. It made her feel attached. Part of something larger than single motherhood. Motherhood was a choice. Sisterhood was a duty, something you were born into. A different kind of blood oath.

Right now that duty was to Frank, who was being tailed by his beloved police force. And macho Kevin, wrestling with his manhood and his fatherhood. And Mike, the youngest, sagging under the family emotional overload. Oddly, it distracted her from her own impending midlife crisis. Being the only sister in a family of Brooklyn Irish Catholic boys was more than an occasional duty, she thought. It was a life sentence. And she was doing her time.

"My problems will all come out eventually," Frank said. "I can't discuss them now."

"I don't want to read about it in the papers," she said. "I'm Margie, your sister."

"Right now we're talking Kev here," Frank said.

"Yeah," Margie said, shaking a fist. "I'd love to get my hands on that Polly. I think I could shake her until her drawers dropped. Even if Zoe isn't his, why did she have to tell him like that? On the phone? Or at all?"

She watched Frank pour a hefty snifter of cognac, the only liquor that could still make him visibly drunk if he had enough of it. She studied him rolling the cognac around in the big sparkling glass, making it look expensive and exclusive, sniffing it, popping open his eyes, and closing them a few times.

"Frank, drink it or heave it," Margie said. "Cognac is only rotgut in a tuxedo."

"I like that line," Frank said, smiling. "Is it yours?"

Margie laughed. "I don't know. I read so much I can't be sure. Maybe it's Kevin's."

Frank took a gulp, grimaced, and took a deep breath. "I'll find Polly and Zoe, and we'll have a DNA test done on them all," he said.

"That's a fine idea," Margie said. "But who knows how long it'll take to find them? Or how much time *you* have? I worry about Kevin in the meantime."

"Maybe he should take a vacation," Frank said. "I have a few leads to follow. Her British friends are involved somehow, I know they are. She borrowed money from a girlfriend who couldn't afford to lose it, for something big. Polly has a plan. Plans always have snags. I intend to be one of them."

"You found all that out already," Margie marveled.

"Yeah, maybe I should be a cop, huh?"

The phone rang and Margie hurried into the kitchen to answer it. She heard her brother Mike's excited voice. "It looks like Kevin's flipped his friggin' lid."

20

The match stuck to Kevin's fingers.

The sulfur seared and stung the tip of his right thumb as he scratched the match to life and touched it to the crinkled *Vogue* and *Mirabella* and *Allure* magazine tear sheets bearing the ads featuring Polly in her skin-tight jeans. He'd soaked the glossy paper with hundred-proof

Jamaican rum, left over from the party. The paper was wedged into the pyramid he'd made of Polly's and Zoe's belongings: clothes, toys, furniture, books, paintings, drawings.

The blaze grew quickly, as Kevin walked to the other side of the bonfire, in the center of the back yard of the new house. He splashed rum from the bottle directly onto the fire, spilling some on his clothes. He watched the flames begin to light up the night. The blue spruce was bathed in the glow. The hysterical mother cat took her kittens from beneath the wheelbarrow, one by one, and carried them in her mouth into the next yard.

Kevin took a big slug of rum and fought it down.

The flames started to crackle as Kevin lifted a wedding album from the American Flyer red wagon he'd used to cart the belongings to the yard. He put the rum bottle between his knees and opened the wedding album and studied it, page by page, by the flickering light of the marital pyre.

Polly looked so beautiful. So clean and healthy and honest in the virginal white gown. Her long slender neck circled by pearls and her perfect hair dotted with rose petals. God, how much I loved her! Kevin thought, as the heat of the blaze began warming his back through the sweaty shirt.

He removed the eight-by-ten-inch picture of Polly and glared at it. Then he laid it on a spire of flame and watched the claws of fire encircle the photograph. One pinpoint pierced through the center of the picture, devouring Polly's waistline and slurping and consuming her breasts. Finally, the flame met other flame, her face soon becoming a grotesque, disfigured, bubbly dot of blaze. Then *pop!* she was gone, into smoke and ash and the past.

"What the hell is wrong with you, asshole?" came the shout of a man in a T-shirt leaning from a third-floor window two houses away. "You'll burn down the whole fuckin' neighborhood."

"Watch your language," came another voice. "Kids here."

"I called Nine-one-one," came another voice. "They'll fix your wagon, Dempsey. Johnny-come-lately."

"Drunk. Must have got stewed up at Farrell's!"

Kevin could hear banging on the windows, people shouting, and a car alarm still blaring. But that was outside. Outside of here. No one can bother me here. This is my back yard, my piece of America, my new house. My place. Alone.

He looked at a photo of Polly in Key West, where they'd gone on their honeymoon. She wore a long-sleeved mesh top on the beach at the Pier House, standing by a sun chair, her smiling face turned to the camera. Her thong bikini bared her amazing ass in full view. Kevin stared at that ass now, as everyone else had that day, a truly great ass, the best ass he'd ever seen.

He'd seen it first in a dozen magazine ads, encased in dead-tight denim jeans. It was an ass that Carmine said should be registered as a lethal weapon. Ex-fireman friend Terry Quinn had invited Kevin and Carmine and a few more firefighters to a Halloween party at his celebrity hangout a few years before. Quinn had told them the girl in the jeans ad would be there. Kevin had told him he was full of shit, girls like that were kept on breeding farms, surrounded by electrified fences, far away from the groping hands of mortal men.

But Quinn had bet him fifty bucks Polly Edgeworth would be there, along with Naomi Campbell, Kate Moss, Christy Turlington, and a dozen other top models. Kevin came dressed as the heavyweight champion of the world, wearing a crown and boxing shoes and trunks and a robe, his hands wrapped in protective boxer's bandages.

And Polly strode in that night dressed as Cinderella, in a gown made of a synthetic fabric that looked spray-painted onto her body, showing off the perfect figure. Three other models, including Sarah Cross, came in with her, dressed as cats and witches and elves. They made a grand entrance together and then branched out into the party. Quinn introduced Kevin to Polly Edgeworth. She smiled at his costume, checked him out admiringly from head to trunks to boxing shoes, shook his bandaged hand, and pranced off into the crowd. Kevin handed Quinn the fifty-dollar bill without ever taking his eyes off her. He watched every move she made, from the bar where she got a glass of wine, to a table where she said hello to two men dressed as penguins, one of whom turned out to be Clive Morton, a banker, and the other Miles Barker, a photographer. Then he followed her with his eyes to a crowd of other models and actresses he knew by face but not by name.

And then he watched as Polly walked to the dance floor and danced with another model. "Carmine, her ass is even better in a dress," Kevin said.

"She has an ass like a wildebeest and it has trouble written all over it," Carmine said.

Then, as "No Surrender" by Bruce Springstein came on, Kevin worked up the balls to cut in on the other man and he danced with Polly Edgeworth of the jeans-ads ass, throwing left hooks and jabs and right crosses into the air as he swirled. Other dancers moved out of their way, forming a circle around them. Kevin threw off the robe and did the Ali shuffle in his boxing shoes, laces whipping, fists flying in ten-punch combinations all around the dance floor, his body rippling with muscles. When Polly rocked her pelvis his way, he feigned a stagger. When she bumped a hip, he fell into imaginary ropes. The other hip sent him reeling into Carmine's arms.

"Go for the early kayo," Carmine said. "And ask what her mother's doing tomorrow night."

Carmine sent Kevin back to the center of the floor, where he and Polly danced into a dirty frenzy, as the crowd clapped and cheered them on. And then the Devil stalked out of the crowd and threw a lit match at Cinderella and she burst into flame.

Kevin never missed a step. He pulled a tablecloth from beneath a stand of drinks, rushed to Polly as the glasses shattered on the dance floor, and wrapped the screaming woman in the tablecloth, smothering the hideous blue flames, as the costume's synthetic fabric melted in a sizzling jelly onto her velvety skin. Women in the crowd screamed, and men shouted in horror. The animal smell of burning hair mixed with the chemical smell of the melted fabric. The man in the devil costume was beaten into the floor by masked men. Carmine rushed through the pandemonium with the champagne bucket of ice and water and doused Polly, who had lost consciousness from the pain and shock.

The courtship, mostly spent at the burn unit of New York University-Cornell Medical Center, lasted six months. The skin grafts on Polly's face were near miraculous, but the damage was still visible to the fashion photographer's lens. The scars on her hands prevented her from even doing hand commercials. And the burns on her shoulders and the tops of her breasts clinched the end of her super-modeling career.

But Polly Edgeworth's beauty never diminished in the eyes of Kevin Dempsey, who saw her every single day.

Long after the pain was gone, after her friend Sarah had helped her back into near perfect shape, Kevin asked Polly to join him for dinner one night at the Oyster Bar of the Plaza. He asked her to wear jeans like the ones from the ads. He proposed to her over dinner. Polly Edgeworth accepted. Kevin led her upstairs to the best suite he could rent in the Plaza Hotel.

And that night, after two bottles of Roederer Cristal champagne, he knelt behind her and slowly peeled off her tight faded jeans. Slid them over her rump, which was even more beautiful bare. Flawless and eggshell white, arching out from the narrow hollow of her back into two perfect rounded cheeks. He remembered tracing the contours with his lips, from the waist to the firm round mounds balancing at the top of the strong thighs, perfectly tailored into two creased tucks, as if suspended on wire, defying gravity. And he explored lightly with his fingers the deep mysterious ravine that split it in perfect halves. Kevin remembered now, in the brilliance of the flames, the way the hotel room night-light illuminated tiny platinum filaments of angel hair on her skin, and how he had held on to Polly's ass that night like the trophy of a lifetime.

That night, Polly's ass became Kevin Dempsey's obsession, especially when she told him, in the heat of passion, that her ass belonged to him and him alone.

And now another man had that ass, was touching, kneading, fondling, exploring it. Was being told it belonged to him.

He placed the honeymoon photo of her bare ass onto the flames and watched it sizzle to smoke.

Then he took another slug of rum, spitting it into the fire, stoking the flames that licked and probed the open darkness.

He looked now at another wedding picture: he and Anthony, his best man. People always teased Kevin and Anthony, said *they'd* make the perfect couple, their girlfriends always complaining that they spent so much time male-bonding they must be fags. And here was a photo of Anthony with his old girlfriend Gloria, alongside Kevin and Polly. The two couples at the wedding, all smiles for the camera, arms around each other.

A few months later, Kevin remembered, Gloria dumped Anthony

over the male-bonding fights. Another confused woman who'd never understand why men sought out the company of men without wanting to fuck them. Gloria's splitting had crushed Anthony, destroyed his plans for a family. "Go marry your fag friend, Kevin," Gloria said, and went off to marry a stockbroker. Anthony was better off. If she'd stayed long enough for talk of children, she might have strayed like Polly, to another man's bed in search of perfect genes for her child . . . a child like Zoe.

He tossed that photo onto the flame now too, on top of a panda bear that went up in pointed flame from each ear. A pair of Polly's fire-engine-red high heels sizzled on the panda's lap. Polly had five different pairs of red high heels, and she only seemed to wear them on Fridays when Kevin was working nights. When she was probably out getting humped, with the high heels on, while I was at work in the firehouse in the company of men.

Men keeping the company of men was more threatening to some women than men chasing one-night-stand bimbos. They knew male bonding could be emotional. Even love. Lifelong. And because they could never be a part of that love, women became insanely jealous. Threatened, they called it faggotry even though they knew it wasn't. They were offended that, in addition to other women, they had to compete with other men for the attention of their lovers. They couldn't grasp the simple reality that men needed solace away from women. To talk about how fucking crazy women were.

You couldn't explain to a woman what having a close man friend means to a man, Kevin thought. There was no need for performance. The men that women knew, even their fathers and brothers and husbands, were almost always half strangers. The man his closest male friend knew was closer to the whole man, the man behind the performance. And that is what women secretly suspected and sometimes violently resented.

Of course men only told the entire truth to men. Not just out of deceit but out of fear of losing their woman to another man more fascinating, someone with a better lie.

But no lie of mine to Polly was ever greater than hers to me, Kevin thought, as he took a photo of Polly, Zoe, and himself and placed it on the roaring black and orange ball of flame that had been Polly's wedding dress.

The sulfur was stinging his thumb so he put it into his mouth to soothe it. And saw a giant blazing eye staring at him.

The cat.

The Pirate.

He was sitting on the fence at a safe distance, mesmerized by Kevin's antics in the glare of the flames. Kevin gawked right back at him. The Pirate's eye was a hypnotic disk reflecting the bonfire.

As he and the Pirate held the stare, Kevin could not distinguish the voices shouting from the windows, could not separate the car-alarm from the sirens of the fire engine in the street, paid no attention to the hammering on the windows and the splintering of the door of the new house.

He stared instead at the Pirate, who was transfixed with him. You're sitting on the fence alone, like the rest of us, Kevin thought, just waiting for the fire to go out.

"I never even got to say goodbye to them," Kevin told the cat, who winked the slow lonesome eye. He sucked again at the sulfur burn on his right thumb.

Kevin Dempsey then felt a hand on his shoulder, and he turned, wide-eyed, right thumb in mouth, rum bottle in the other hand.

Frank stood there as two firefighter probies with large extinguisher "cans" moved past him to douse the flames. A third used a hook pole to rake the burning pyramid to a flattened pile, as the others "pissed" with extinguishers on the smoldering rubble, sending up puffs of smoke and steam.

The cat disappeared into the darkness, and now Kevin could hear the neighbors. "Lock the asshole up in Kings County, G building, psycho ward," came one voice. "Put him in handcuffs, the crazy bastard," said another man. "What do you expect from a goddam Dempsey?" "Lock up the whole fuckin' wacko family," shouted a whiskey-throated woman.

"It's okay, Kev," said Frank Dempsey, taking the rum bottle and hiding it under his coat.

Kevin took his thumb from his mouth and stared at Frank.

Amazed.

Frank was standing in a swirl of smoke, like someone who had stepped out of the next dimension. When Kevin looked past him, he saw Margie reaching out her arms. And then Mike, shaking his head from side to side, staring at the ground. And there were the other brothers, the firefighter brothers, walking in different directions, carrying tools and pumping water onto the flames. He saw a fireman, a lieutenant, step out of the smoke. He passed the two probies and whispered to two uniformed cops, who nodded and disappeared into the haze. The lieutenant walked over to Kevin, looked him in the eye, an inch from his nose, smelled Kevin's panting breath. Without saying a word, he turned to the family and shook his head in disgust, shrugging.

"It's all right," Frank assured Kevin again.

"Oh, no, it's not," Kevin Dempsey said.

Part II

21

"I'm not an alcoholic," Kevin assured her.

"Who said you were?" Gail Levy said, grinding out a True blue in the metal ashtray.

Kevin watched her brush the thick mane of dark hair from her face, clear her throat, and carefully rub smoke from her right eye.

"If anyone's an addict here, it's you," Kevin said. "I didn't think you were supposed to smoke in a hospital."

"This isn't a hospital," Gail Levy said.

Kevin looked around the sterile office, the only hint of color coming from some small prickly cactus plants lining the narrow window ledge. Outside the window of this main building, which was a converted farmhouse, Kevin could see prefabricated dormitories where the patients bunked. Two men raked leaves from the rolling yellow lawn. Through a stand of trees, sunlight mirrored off a small duck pond.

"Well, it's a nuthouse, isn't it?" Kevin asked. "Funny farm?"

"You could call it that," she said. "Burning Bush is where they send drunks who take their family belongings into the back yard in the dead of night and set them on fire while conversing with an alley cat. Yeah, that kind of a nuthouse. Some call it a rehab."

Kevin nodded. "You left out the thumb-sucking part," he said.

"You already explained that," Gail said. "That part makes sense. I burn myself all the time lighting cigarettes, and the first thing I do is suck my fingers, too, when it happens."

"Then they should send you here," Kevin said.

"They did," Gail said.

"I mean as a patient instead of a shrink," Kevin said.

"You're not a patient, you're a client," Gail said. "I'm not a shrink, I'm a counselor."

"Same shit," Kevin said.

"I don't have an M.D., so I'm not a doctor," she said. "I'm a substance abuse counselor—"

"—who abuses nicotine and contaminates others with her smoke," Kevin said, cutting her off.

"You're a hostile asshole, know that?"

"Isn't that what you do in a puzzle factory, get your hostility out? Why else have me here? You put me through a week of detox I didn't even need, medicate me with every goofball known to man, and then tell me I have a substance abuse problem? Somebody is fucking nuts here, but it ain't me."

Kevin felt physically weak, his muscles flaccid and atrophied from too much bed rest and too many mood-altering drugs. He wanted a cold beer, something to kick-start his blood.

"There's no bars on the windows here," Gail said. "No locks on the doors. No criminal charges to hold you."

"Yeah, but I leave here before my time is up and bang goes the job and the pension," he said. "This is the proverbial rubber room."

"Go on," Gail said. "If you're talking about your job and your pension, it must mean you intend to be with us awhile."

"Twenty-eight days."

"I meant among the living."

Kevin looked at her more closely. Late twenties, thick lustrous hair, small gold-leaf earrings, open-necked blouse showing a plank of bare collarbone under tight tanned skin. Her cheekbones were pronounced and her full lips twisted into a half smile over good teeth, except for one that was slightly uneven.

"Suicide is for pussies," Kevin said, imagining what Gail Levy looked like naked. Skin probably as tight as a golf ball.

"I've been called that and I don't think about it," Gail said.

He stared at her nose. Long and elegant, like a hood ornament on a fancy car. If she had a nose job, she'd look like a knucklehead. As it was, thin and a trifle long, it was sexy.

"I have a something on my face?" she said. "You keep staring at it."

Kevin laughed grudgingly. He watched her smile; she had a nice smile, a smile that made her eyes crinkle and her teeth gleam, the one slightly uneven front tooth like a flaw in a diamond. She got up from behind the desk when the electric kettle on her file cabinet began to boil and poured water into a cup that read WORLD'S GREATEST DAUGHTER.

Christ, she's wearing jeans, Kevin thought. He loved women in jeans. Polly in jeans . . . God, Polly and Zoe . . . it's been two, almost three weeks since I saw them.

She looked over her shoulder at him with half-closed eyes, caught him staring at her buttocks. He glanced out the window at the bucolic tranquillity of upstate New York.

"Want some?" she asked.

"Nah," Kevin said. "Don't wanna abuse caffeine either."

"You're right," Gail said, sitting down. "You're an asshole, but you're right. But let's not bullshit each other. You do have a problem with booze. That's why you're here. If you and thousands of others didn't, I wouldn't be here either. I can't make you stop drinking. I can only help you understand why you do it. It's up to you to stop. It's like forest fires. Think of me as Smokey the Bear, telling you only you can prevent it. Okay, you're gonna be here another twenty-eight days. Make the best of it instead of the worst. Then you'll probably never see me again."

Kevin was starting to like her. At least there would be no bullshit.

"I have a wife and kid," Kevin said.

"No shit, Sherlock, where'd you get your first clue?" she said. "I've read your file. Twice. I have your work report. I understand there's also some problems at home."

"Yeah. The problem is there *is* no one home," Kevin said.

"Your brother Frank told me about it," Gail said.

"The blind leading the blind," Kevin said.

"He seemed like a very concerned big brother," Gail said. "You should be thankful to have such a loyal support system."

"Support system!" Kevin said and laughed. "Was he drinking Gatorade?"

"As a matter of fact—"

"Frank's the one belongs in a fucking bed here," Kevin said. "Not me. Hey, listen: I can curse here, right? I heard you could do that in therapy."

"If that's what you think you're supposed to do," she said. "Just as long as it's coming from you. Not dialogue from one of your stories."

"You know about them too, huh?"

"That you write stories, yeah. Your sister told me. I haven't read any. I'd like to read some. But don't tell me any, okay?"

He shrugged. "So what was *your* drug of choice?" he asked her. "Counselors are ex-addicts, aren't they?"

"We're talking about you here," she said. "See, I don't wanna get outa here in twenty-eight days. I wanna stay. I like it here. They pay me money to stay here. To talk to people like you, all screwed up. Back when I had to talk to an asshole like me, about me, I answered questions like that. Now it's your turn to answer my questions. So talk to me about you. Forget me. Okay?"

"Right," Kevin said. "Your ash is gonna drop in your coffee."

Gail quickly cupped her left hand under the drooping ash and, embarrassed, tapped it and threw it in the wastebasket.

"Only you can prevent nuthouse fires," Kevin said. "Never, ever, throw hot ash into the trash like that."

He gloated as Gail snubbed out the cigarette and took a long drink of the black coffee.

"Okay, firefighter-turned-arsonist," Gail said, looking him straight in the eye. "Tell me about the conversation with your wife about your baby."

"First I have to know about my friend Carmine."

"Carmine is fine," she said. "He's out of the hospital on medical leave and he's down on your list as a visitor. But you don't get any visits until you talk to me. Think of me as God."

"God as a girl," Kevin said. "Makes sense. Female power is the ultimate."

"Think so?"

"Yeah," Kevin said. "Take Polly. She gave me a child. Then after three years, total love and devotion, she says it isn't my kid. Isn't it a God complex to giveth life and then taketh life away? She just disappears with the child I adore. That's more powerful than God. They say God is a blessed trinity. Well Polly is at least two people. I know that now. The one I loved and the one I hate."

"This make you want to drink?"

"Kill."

"Who?"

"Polly. Both of her."

"Not yourself," she asked. "Certain of that?"

"Certain. But I don't know what there is to live for, either. I see no reason to use heroic methods to prolong my life."

"How about for yourself?" Gail asked. "Don't you like Kevin Dempsey enough to live for him?"

"He was okay," he said, "until he fumbled the football."

"Huh?"

"It's a long story."

"It's a long stay."

Kevin looked up at her as she got up to make herself more coffee. Another woman in blue jeans, Kevin thought, playing with my mind.

22

For thirty-five minutes now, Sarah Cross had squirmed in the waiting room of Integrity Toys, Inc., on Twenty-third Street and Broadway in the commercial toy district of Manhattan.

She hadn't heard a peep from Polly since she pulled a no-show at her own surprise party. That was two weeks ago. In the meantime, Frank Dempsey had almost convinced Sarah that her friend was on a prolonged sojourn in parts unknown. With Sarah's one hundred thousand dollars.

Sarah needed to get her money back so she could invest in the midtown health club. That opportunity might disappear if she didn't make her move. There were a few other potential investors, and Sarah could be squeezed out of the picture if she didn't come up with her share of the seed money in a month.

So Sarah was anxious to track Polly down. She'd called Polly's parents in England and they said they had no idea where their daughter was. Maybe they were telling the truth, maybe not. None of Sarah's model friends knew where she was. Sarah had asked Clive Morton and drawn a blank, although he wouldn't tell you much anyway. None of Sarah's old friends on the Heathens' Highway had seen or heard from Polly. If she had taken off with a new guy, it was into obscurity.

And Frank Dempsey had his own agenda, which was family business. Sarah barely knew the man and couldn't rely on his word, although she knew that if she came up with some skinny on Polly on her own, the cop in Frank Dempsey might swap his information for hers. As a team. She smiled at the image . . . and then shook her head.

In her hand, Sarah held the receipt for the Pepper Face Doll she'd bought for Zoe on her last birthday. One of the doll's main attractions for kids was that for five years after the purchase date, a birthday card would be mailed "Anywhere in the World" to the doll, addressed to the doll's mommy, which would be the child. In this case Zoe Dempsey.

Sarah distinctly remembered Polly filling out the paperwork for the doll's birthday when she gave Zoe the present. The doll had been almost impossible to get. Sarah had stood in line from 10 A.M. to 2:30 P.M., at the Herald Square Toys "R" Us. She had three different arguments with women who tried to cut in. The last one had almost come to blows until Sarah pulled out the can of Mace she carried in her pocketbook at all times and threatened to use it.

Now, here in the toy company's headquarters, Sarah had read the *Daily News* twice, searching for news of Frank Dempsey. His name was nowhere to be found. She wondered how Frank was doing, how he was holding up under the combined pressures of police, district attorney, family, and press. She hoped he wasn't drinking too much from the stress. She had seen that happen to her father, and it wasn't pretty. Booze is a slow downhill stagger to the hole in the ground, she thought.

Frank Dempsey would have been a terrific catch. Great-looking in a left-out-in-the-rain kind of way. Smart and funny and brimming with love for his brother. How he must be able to love a woman! she thought. So selfless, taking the time to search for his brother's wife and kid. There was a *family* man, a disappearing breed in this age of careerists and bullshit artists. So he took a drug dealer's money. That didn't make him a bad person.

But they were going to try and put him in jail. What a terrible waste. . . .

Finally, after forty-five minutes, a man in a gray suit, dandruff, a worrier, maybe thirty-five years old, name tag HARRY HOLTON, PUBLIC RELATIONS, came out to greet her.

"We having a little problem with a birthday Pepper?" Holton asked, his voice faintly effeminate. Clearly, flirtation wasn't going to work so she opted for the sob story. All those years of acting classes better be worth at least one good tearjerk.

"Well, see, I bought this doll, gave it to a little girl on my block; then the family moved away," Sarah said. "Before they moved, one of my nieces was baby-sitting the little girl in my home, and the child must have taken her mother's wedding band to play with. And lost the damned thing. Her mother was heartbroken, tore the house apart. We searched the street and the yards, everywhere, but they moved away without it. Last week the ring turned up in my niece's toy chest. I looked at my niece's Pepper Face Doll and it gave me an idea. Maybe I could trace the distraught woman through the little girl's doll. The one I bought her."

Holton looked at Sarah in total confusion. Sarah didn't want to use the real story because it reeked of a collection agency ploy.

"You expect us to track her down for you?" Holton asked, his palms up like a customs agent. "This is a toy company, not a police station."

Sarah appealed to Holton, telling him that the woman was a widow, the wedding band her only connection to the dead husband.

"A widow? I see," Holton said. "My mom's a widow. A lot of my best friends are what you'd call widows too. You understand, I'm sure. Well, do you have the name and date of birth?"

"Of the widow?"

"No, no, no. Pepper. The doll."

"All I have is the store receipt," said Sarah. "The little girl named her Mint. Pepper Mint."

"Oh, God," said Holton. "That store could have sold thousands. It could take some time. And there's no guarantee that if they moved away they would give a forwarding address. Although you'd be surprised how many do. Pepper is very popular, a milestone doll. But I'd have to get clearance, and this is the busiest time of year, Christmas just around the corner. Actually, this does seem more like a police matter to me. How do I even know you're telling me the truth?"

Sarah smiled and leaned closer. "Think of the publicity it could bring to the company," she said into Holton's ear, gingerly brushing dandruff from his shoulder. "Human interest. *Integrity Toys reunites widow with wedding band of hero husband.*"

"Hero husband?" Holton asked, now self-consciously brushing off his other shoulder himself.

"Downed pilot in the Gulf War," Sarah said, blowing away a fallen hair from Holton's suit. "I know a reporter at the *Daily News* who'd eat that up."

"Gulf War hero's widow? Are you sure you're on the level?"

"Never got to see his baby alive," Sarah assured him.

She was milking it for every drop in the cow.

"Jesus," Holton said. "I'll do the best I can. You say you have a contact at a newspaper?"

"Oh, yeah," she said. "Might be nice to get a story like that planted before the Christmas rush. *Pepper saves Christmas for grieving widow.*"

"This could take months," Holton said. "I have to get clearance from administration, then the mail department, then the birthday archives in the computer department. . . ."

"I could get my newspaper friend to profile you in particular as the man who saved Christmas."

Holton's eyes ignited as he took the receipt and copied down Polly's and Zoe's names and previous address. He gave the receipt back to Sarah. He then gave Sarah his card.

"I'll need at least three weeks," he said. "Maybe a month. It's the best I can do in a needle-in-a-haystack situation."

Sarah thanked him and stepped out of the office into the hallway.

At the elevator, she smiled to herself, pleased with her performance. She wished Frank could have seen the act and wondered how he would have handled the same situation. She was curious as to what luck he was having in tracking Polly to earth. She had thought of calling him many times, but each time she became too frightened. He reminded her too much of her father. Not his rumpled good looks, sweet demeanor, selflessness. The other part. The hard spooky drinking. The quiet sense of doom that hung over him.

She knew that somehow, eventually, she would track Polly down on her own. She just hoped it wasn't too late for her health club deal.

Sarah walked out of the office building on busy Twenty-third Street, looked right, and saw the clock on the Met Life building was approaching noon. A slight chill was in the late September air, and the women walking by were in the first fashions of fall. She came to a restaurant named Live Bait, where she used to hang out with the model crowd. She'd go there at night, after a rabbit's lunch at the outdoor tables at Union Square's Coffee Shop. After Live Bait a lot of the girls would hit the late-night downtown dance clubs hoping to get snared by a zillionaire.

Sarah went into the crowded restaurant, where beautiful waitresses delivered Cajun lunches to horny businessmen. The girls were the struggling models of the city, most long-legged with high cheekbones, up from Miami or in from Europe or the Midwest, waiting tables while trying to get together tearsheets, scrambling for whatever Claudia, Naomi, Christy, Cindy, or the other *uber*-models turned down. Angling for appointments with photographers like Steven Meisel and Bruce Weber or Scavullo. Sarah approached the waitress station and asked a few busy girls if they'd seen Polly around lately. They all knew "poor Polly Edgeworth with the burns," of course, but none of them had seen her.

The night before, Sarah had made similar inquiries about Polly before the weekly open call at the Irene Marie agency. None of the girls there, some back from post-pregnancy starvation diets or bazillionaire-boyfriend breakups and looking for work, had seen or heard from Polly either.

Sarah had to hurry now to make her noon acting class at the Lee Strasberg Theatrical Institute on East Fifteenth Street. As she turned right on Lower Broadway, she was glad she no longer ran heavy on the high fashion circuit. It was a world of glitter and depravity and money much dirtier than Frank Dempsey's. The kind of money Polly had always chased.

23

Margie Dempsey sat across from Gail Levy in the smoking section of the back room of the Lion's Head bar and restaurant on Sheridan Square in Greenwich Village and watched the younger woman blow a swirl of smoke toward the ceiling.

"Thanks for coming," Gail said, checking the blackboard menu. "Sorry for smoking. Jesus, I'm starved. What's good here?"

"Burgers, specials, the people," Margie said.

"Good. Then I'll have a single guy, rare, straight, drug-free, gainfully employed," Gail said.

"Sounds a little like Kevin."

Gail stopped cold, let the smoke leak out of her mouth, and then she blew it to the low ceiling in a long stream.

"I think I'll change my order," she said.

Margie laughed and took a file folder from her attaché case and placed it on the table. It was marked KEVIN STORIES. Margie felt a little uneasy letting anyone read them, but Kevin had given his permission. He'd never wanted anyone but Margie to see them before, not even his brothers. Margie thought of them like entries in a foot soldier's logbook, each story representing a battle in the life war that raged inside its author.

"I've chosen half a dozen stories I think are among his best," Margie said. "I warn you, these aren't Erich Segal love stories. They're pretty graphic."

"Autobiographical?" Gail asked.

"Somewhat," Margie said. "I'm not sure he believes what his characters believe. But he obviously tries to imagine *how* they think and tries to understand them. If he does identify with them, he's torn up inside. Filled with principles but doesn't see the world as a friendly place for an honest man."

"I don't know," Gail said. "That sounds kind of heroic to me."

Margie smiled, studying Gail, who was searching for a waitress with almost frantic gestures. Margie made her for a young idealist. She'd probably seen bad times before good. Stumbled onto a yuppie career searching for answers to her own pain. Which was okay, as long as she knew her limits when dealing with Kevin. He was a very complicated fella, Margie thought. He could wind up putting *her* on a couch.

"Actually, Kevin *is* pretty heroic," Margie said. "He has medals for bravery to prove it. Except for that last day."

"He hasn't talked much about that yet," Gail said.

"It'll be hard for him to do that with you."

"Why?" Gail said. "I'm from the Bronx, he's from Brooklyn. I speak his lingo."

"Yeah," Margie said. "But you're the enemy."

"Because I stand between him and his job?"

"No," Margie said. "Because you're a woman. Read the stories. You'll see."

The waitress came with sodas. Margie ordered pasta with squid, and Gail chose a chicken with mushroom sauce, specifically asking for it to be cooked without wine. Both sipped Diet Cokes. As she perused the menu, Margie moved the ashtray to the windowsill without asking permission. Gail followed the shift with hooded eyes and then slowly brought her attention back to Margie. Both moves were subtle, like positioning on a chessboard.

"What about Polly?" Gail said. "What should I know? You're the only woman I can ask about her. Is she nuts or is she telling him the truth about his daughter not being his?"

"Polly's a little flaky, for sure," said Margie. "Self-absorbed. Not exactly conceited, although she knows how to use her looks. She is beautiful. Fashion-model gorgeous."

She had promised Kevin that she wouldn't mention his sterility to anyone outside the family, and that included Gail Levy.

"He's not exactly the Elephant Man," Gail said.

"You noticed that, huh?"

"I might be a counselor, a so-called detached pro," Gail said, "but I'm not *dead.*"

"I'm not sure if she's telling the truth about Zoe not being his," Margie said. "She's an adorable kid, but she doesn't really favor either one of them in looks. I do see a stubborn streak in her that could be Kevin's."

When the food came, Gail seized the ashtray and stubbed her butt and left it on the table, smoldering. Margie thought that was like leaving someone's water running, or a refrigerator door open. She wordlessly moved what she called the "cigarette graveyard" to the windowsill again, as Gail watched in silence. Both women dug into the food. Through the eye-level window, they could see an endless parade of feet passing them on the sidewalk of Christopher Street.

Margie spied Gail peeking at the top page of the first Kevin story, one called "Tomboy," written two years earlier. It was about a doctor who kidnaps the man who raped and killed his adored wife; imprisons the rapist in the basement of his house for a full year; gives him hormone shots that make him grow breasts; surgically turns him into a woman; then sets him loose amid the rapists of New York.

When Gail flipped instinctively to the last page, Margie dramatically cleared her throat. "Don't insult the author," Margie said. "With Kevin, you always have to start at square one."

Gail smiled but looked abashed. "I'd like to take these home to read, without an audience," she said. "Study them."

"As long as you don't show them around," Margie said.

Gail nodded.

This young woman has no idea how full her hands are, Margie thought.

"You don't drink either?" Gail asked.

"Not much," Margie said, knowing the "either" was a reference to being a nonsmoker. "Maybe a glass of champagne at weddings, New Year's Eve, Christmas eggnog. Like my mom."

"Oh," she said. "Your mom didn't drink?"

"The boys take after Dad, who drank pretty heavy," she said. "Kevin has had more in the last year than ever before. I think it was the stress: three jobs, buying the new house, keeping Polly happy, our brother Frank's problems. Kevin isn't a wake-up drinker that I know of. But in the last year, I'd call him and he'd be out for a few with the guys from work. Not all-nighters, but a few hours. There's always beer in his fridge. At parties, family dinners, holidays, he usually drinks until he's high. I don't think he's the type to drink alone, though."

"How could you know that? He did that night in the yard."

"Good point."

"I gather Frank likes a cocktail as well," Gail said. "I'm trying to put together a family history."

"Frank fell into a hole," Margie said. "From a roof. You're familiar with his legal problems."

"Yeah," Gail said. "I read the newspapers. Kevin told me some more."

"Mike? He doesn't drink more than three beers at a time," Margie said.

"He's afraid of the family trap," Gail said. "But he's a high-risk candidate if he's that self-conscious."

Margie watched Gail fiddle with her cigarettes, flipping them over, biting her lower lip.

"You have something to ask that's giving you trouble?"

"Can you talk about your dad's suicide?" Gail asked softly. "How bad did it affect Kevin?"

Margie put her fork down, looked the younger woman in the eye, and took a sip of soda. "Gail," she said, "I like you. So far. But I have to know if you're qualified to delve this deep into Kevin's psyche. You're not a shrink or even a clinical psychologist. I really wouldn't want you to get points with the state licensing board on my father's grave or at Kevin's expense. I think you're smart and sweet and that you want to help. But I warn you, *know* where you're going here. Because I'm family. I'm blood. I'm involved all the way. And I fight for my family."

To Margie's eye, this counselor woman looked nervous for the first time, her confidence demoted a notch.

Gail put down her fork, took a sip of soda, and wiped her lips with the cloth napkin. Margie studied her long ringless fingers as they fumbled for props. Gail held on to the napkin, wrung it.

"Okay, let me tell you where I'm coming from," Gail said, leaning back in her chair, as if needing distance to make room for the words. "Most of my early experience was training for this job." She unfurled the napkin, smoothed it. "My mom killed herself."

"I'm sorry to hear that," Margie said. "I didn't mean to probe that way."

"It's okay," Gail said, reaching for the ashtray. "As long as this is between us."

Margie nodded. Gail leaned closer.

"I was thirteen," Gail said softly. "My dad was a nice Jewish businessman. He adored my mom, who had expensive tastes. He never cheated on her, that I know of. But he fell behind in his textile business and cheated the Feds. He got arrested for tax evasion. We were gonna lose the house. So my mom took a job."

"Oh, God," Margie said. "To save the house and pay the lawyers."

"Uh-huh." Gail removed a cigarette from the pack with her thumb and index finger. "She told my father she was waitressing at a swanky restaurant in Manhattan. She never said she was one of the main courses. It was okay for a few months. Until—"

"—she was discovered," Margie filled in.

"By a customer. My uncle. My dad's brother."

"Jesus Christ," Margie said as she watched Gail yank the match from a book advertising a legal firm with the phone number 1-800-LAW-SUIT. "He told your dad."

Gail nodded blankly. "Mom went down to the IRS office," she said, striking the match, "and blew her brains out across the caseworker's desk." She puffed the cigarette to life, blew the match out. "I took my first drink at her funeral. My first goofball that night. The day after that I lost my virginity to the undertaker's seventeen-year-old son."

"And your dad?"

"The Feds showed no mercy. He did twenty-seven months," Gail said. "I stayed with my uncle, the one who blew the whistle on my mom. I hated him. He treated me like my mother's daughter, until I ran away. Boston, Lauderdale, New Orleans, Key West. A dealer boyfriend in every town. I was sixteen when my dad got out, but I never moved back home. He works for his wonderful brother now. So I only see him on Thanksgivings."

"Look, Gail, you didn't—"

"I've been clean and sober eight years now," she said. "So if you think I'm scrounging for a case history, believe me, I got a Santa's sack of them I wish I could unload come Hanukkah. In fact, I just *did* unload—on you."

"I don't know if I'm full or buried," Margie said, watching the waitress remove the plates from the table, "but I feel better. I think you'll understand Kevin. And vice versa."

"We're supposed to treat each client the same," Gail said, moving the ashtray to the windowsill herself now and gently tapping off an ash. "But forgive me for being human if I think Kevin is really worth a second shot."

"I like you," Margie said, placing the ashtray back in front of Gail on the table the two women shared.

"Give it time," Gail said. "You won't."

They both laughed and looked each other directly in the eyes with pleasure for the first time.

"Jesus, I wish I could see Kevin laugh like this again," Margie said.

"He will," Gail said. "But only if he wants to."

Margie Dempsey looked at Gail Levy and put her brother's future into the smoke between them.

"I hope so, because after what Polly did to him," Margie said, as she rattled the ice in her glass, "I don't know if Kevin can ever love or trust another woman again."

24

The sticker for Gutter's Shoes was on the bottom of the corrective shoes. Frank Dempsey handed the brace to the salesman in the store on Fifth Avenue and Thirteenth Street in Brooklyn. Frank made the little short-armed salesman as a nervous Nellie, so he palmed his father's shield to him and explained he was looking for a mother and daughter who had disappeared. Which was true.

"So she's a little one, maybe three years old," Gutter, the salesman, said, examining the shoes. "That's the time to catch the problem."

"How many of these you sell?"

"God, could be two hundred pairs a year," Gutter said. "I mean, maybe more. Kids with knock knees, pigeon toes, deformities, accidents."

"They come from different doctors?"

"Well, yeah, they do," he said. "But there's one guy who seems to have the whole Park Slope area locked up. Money. His name is Lopez, a bone specialist on the parkside. He's very good. Arrogant but rich."

"These his shoes?"

The salesman pushed his bifocals onto the tip of his nose and studied the markings on the bottom of the flat metal bar of the brace.

"Yeah," he said. "See the letter L? He sends customers to me all the time."

"And he brings his kids here for free regular shoes come Easter, Christmas, back-to-school," Frank said.

The salesman looked up at him and smiled. "How'd you know that?"

"That's how the rich stay rich," Frank said. "You'll never walk in a poor man's shoes if you don't pay for them."

"Between you and me," Gutter said, "after the first year of freebies, I figure I'll just give him a break on the tax. Know what he did? He sent his patients all the way to Flatbush to get the corrective shoes made. Where, these days, if you go in one piece, you might come out with broken legs. Oy! It cost me. He has a south-of-the-border name, this bum, but he wouldn't go south for a quarter. So I delivered four pairs of the best sneakers, his kids' sizes, to his office. The next day . . . the *very* next day . . . two customers come in for corrective shoes from Lopez the doctor. That's NAFTA for you."

Frank smiled and nodded and took out his Gatorade bottle and washed down two vitamin C tablets and a Dristan for the hay fever that was starting to set in like a plague. Late September swirled with pollen. The red rims of his eyes were itching and he looked out onto the sidewalk at Summers, who leaned on a parking meter, browsing through the *Post*. Nothing ever seemed to bother Summers. He didn't drink, he rarely ate, he was never cranky, never late, never friendly or unfriendly, never sneezed.

He must be a ball at a party, Frank figured.

The taste of the tablets mixed with the vodka and Gatorade made Frank gag.

"You okay?" the salesman asked, as Frank held his breath and did a groping two-step to the side of the store. With one hand, Frank clutched the display counter full of loafers. With the other hand he waved at the shoe salesman.

"Oy," said the salesman. "Is this a Nine-one-one-er?"

Frank waved no at Gutter.

"If you're gonna vomit, please, make it the sneakers," he said in a panic. "They're washable."

Frank saw Gutter through a prism of tears, brought on by the retching dry heaves, a state alkies call "the bubble." The salesman's short little arms lifted and dangled at his sides like a bird ready to take flight, his eyes bugging over the top of the bifocals.

"All . . . right . . ." Frank said, straightening, wiping his eyes with a tissue. "I'm . . . o-kay. . . ."

He managed to belch, and the trapped air pocket cleared and a wave of relief washed through him. The bubble passed. He took another gulp of the Gatorade to wash down the sour saliva.

"Can you look up in the book to see if the lady who brought this to you had a replacement made?" he said, taking short little breaths.

The little salesman shook his head. "No, she didn't," he said.

"How can you be sure?"

"Because I remember this one now by the initials next to the doctor's initial," the salesman said. "P.D. Polly Dempsey might be the most beautiful woman who ever came in my store. A beautiful baby too. But Christ almighty, what a pain in the ass that woman is!"

"What do you mean?"

"She wanted to know if I could make the shoes interchangeable to color-coordinate with the baby's outfits," he said. "You ever heard such a pain-in-the-ass idea? The kid wears it to bed. What color coordination? What?"

"She had her wear it in school."

"See?" the salesman said. "She's nuts too. You don't do that to a kid. You straighten the legs, but the kid grows up and shoots a president and the nation blames my shoes."

Frank nodded. It wasn't that far-fetched. A madman a few years back on the Long Island Rail Road killed five people because he didn't like his workman's compensation settlement. Post office workers turn mass murderers over coffee-break times. A president was shot to impress a movie actress. Shoes were as good a reason as any to blast your way into American history.

"How many places sell these shoes?"

"In New York? Maybe ten."

"In the country?"

"For that you have to ask the manufacturer," Gutter said. "You get a franchise from the Achilles Heels Company. They're nationwide. It's a good product, but it's a racket at the retail level. We get a percentage. Medicaid pays too. That guy I told you, down Flatbush, he makes out like a stagecoach bandit because the local Medicaid mills send him ghetto kids who have absolutely nothing wrong with their bones, just to get a kickback on the Medicaid money from the shoe store. They collect both ends. Who checks on corrective shoes? When you're finished looking for missing persons, you should look for missing taxpayer money."

Frank smiled ironically. There was a swindle in every walk of life, he thought. Even for every bowlegged step a kid takes, there's a crooked adult picking up dollar bills from his twisted footprints. It revolted Frank that he was regarded as a runner in that same corrupt rat race.

Frank turned his back on the front door so Summers couldn't see him take the wad of cash from his pocket. Gutter looked down at the thick rolls of hundred-dollar bills that Frank held close to his belly.

"How much you make a week here, Mr. Gutter?"

"I gross maybe three thousand," Gutter said, moistening his lips with his tongue. "Maybe four on a good week. Six, back-to-school and Easter. That's gross. My average net, maybe twelve hundred a week. Why?"

"You must know someone at Achilles Heels who could get you a printout of every pair of corrective shoes sold in the last month, no?"

"This wouldn't even be in a main computer yet," Gutter said, taking out a hankie and wiping his brow.

Frank counted twenty-five one-hundred-dollar bills. He folded them and stuffed them in Gutter's shirt pocket. The little man followed the delivery of the money, gulped, and ran his tongue over his lips.

"You don't want me to hurt nobody, do you?" he asked. "I don't make cement shoes."

"No, no, you'll be helping out that little girl," Frank said. "You get me that printout, and I'll match what I just gave you."

"This is scary," he said. "You sure I'm not breaking any laws?"

"Would I let you walk a crooked mile?" Frank asked.

"So, how do I get in touch?" Gutter said. "I'll see what I can do."

Frank gave him his phone number. He told Gutter not to leave any detailed message. Just his name and number and time and he'd get back to him for more information.

"Best sale of the year," Gutter said.

"Thanks for your time," Frank said, as he stepped out of the shoe store.

The hay fever pill was making him drowsy and Frank Dempsey needed sleep.

25

Kevin Dempsey lay in bed and listened to the snoring of his roommate, Walter. He was a forty-one-year-old crack addict from North Carolina who was here on his third relapse. His snore was a roar in the country night, intermingled with the incessant rasp of the crickets and the institutional smell of the industrial detergent used on the stiff sheets. Kevin missed the fragrant fabric softener Polly used, and the smell of her perfume on the pillow. He ached for the soft breathing of her next to him, the body heat under the sheets like the womb itself, the nearness of her naked body, the long legs and the bare shoulders and the unbridled breasts and the exposed behind. . . .

He missed being a husband sleeping with his wife, as the gentle breathing and murmurs of his child came from the baby's darkened bedroom. Kevin had often purposefully stayed awake after wife and child were sleeping, just to listen to them, to assess his lucky lot in life.

Now, he recalled Zoe's tiny naked feet padding through the darkness, making her crooked-legged way to Mommy and Daddy's bed in the terrifying night, her doll-sized hands rubbing the nightmares out of her bewildered eyes. And then her arms outstretched as she ran toward Daddy's big welcoming arms and the vast bed where she could snuggle between the two large people who loved her more than anybody else in the world. She would hug the pillow as Kevin rubbed her small back, until he heard her breathing deepen once again into sound and protected sleep.

On those amazing nights, nights when life as a father, husband, provider were all in the same bed together, all warm and fed and safe, Kevin Dempsey was certain he had become a successful man. A full man. A pillar of worth and caliber. A *doer* whose life was meant for living. A life that would continue long after he had passed on, in the lives of his children and theirs after them. Kevin Dempsey saw himself as an ancestor, one his clan could someday proudly embrace and emulate. The work he did and the seeds he planted and the children he left would make him a citizen of eternity.

Kevin was certain that that achievement was as near to importance, fulfillment, and immortality as any man of any money, any religion, or any standing could or would ever know in life.

And now, as he lay here in a bed in a nuthouse, listening to the snores of a recovering drug addict, to crickets from a tank-town area code, smelling the harsh disinfectant of the sheets, as his wife lay in the arms of another man, suddenly for the first time in the twenty years since he had left the altar boys and the Catholic Church for good, Kevin Dempsey felt the urge to pray. For his dead father, who died in a state of shame. For his brother Frank, who was in deep trouble but still trying to help Kevin with his. For Mike, who was almost never happy. For Margie, who gave all her strength and wisdom to others. But mostly for little Zoe, maybe even more confused and hurting.

But Kevin could not get the words through his dry and parted lips. He decided to pray silently. But then he thought, Pray to whom? A spirit in the sky? An icon in a church? A stranger in the soul?

Instead, the events of the day flashed through his mind.

The long hours had been filled with lectures from a quack doctor about the physiological effects of alcohol on the brain. Followed by a lecture from a shrink on what it does to the metaphysical mind. Followed by group therapy, filled with people so dysfunctional as to make daytime television talk shows seem like Norman Rockwell settings.

He kept remembering one big black guy named Carter, who said he tried to kill his three-year-old son by shoving roof gravel down his throat because the court had awarded the mother an increase in child support. The mother had offered him a choice: go to rehab or call the cops. He said he was doing her a favor by going to rehab, because if he went to jail he would lose his job and she would lose her child support and have to go on welfare.

That group had almost dissolved into a brawl when Kevin suggested the man "belonged chained naked to the bars of a cage where they toss you red meat on alternate Mondays instead of here in some bucolic rehab."

"Who the fuck you think you callin' bucolic?" the man had ranted. "You wanna jump up, motherfucker? Ain't you the one who punked out on your own brothers in a fuckin' fire, you coward motherfucker? Took a nigger fireman to save your white ass. Jump up or shut the fuck up. You ain't shit to be callin' me no bucolic!"

And Kevin found himself sitting in his chair and just staring at the man, who ranted for a good twelve minutes before mealtime ended the group. Dinner was meatloaf surprise, with five different kinds of beans and peas that kept the nuthouse smelling like one gargantuan collective fart.

This is what all the years of his life had brought him to, Kevin realized, as he listened to Walter's snoring. His life as a man was in the hands of madmen.

Tomorrow he would hear another dissertation from Gail Levy, the counselor in blue jeans. She would bust ten million balls about his tendency toward violence.

Bust balls he no longer even had.

If sleep would ever come, he was certain it would not be friendly. One image stayed in his mind and that was of the face of Zoe, a face he was now certain he would never see again.

26

Gail Levy sat propped up on her down pillows, naked, suddenly conscious that she was smoking in bed while reading the stories of a firefighter.

Especially the one called "Mutual Butt," in which a fireman agrees to fill in for a buddy who needs to take a night off. It was a standard firehouse practice called "pulling a mutual," where one fireman filled in for another, who would later reciprocate. In the story, while battling a blaze, the working firefighter finds his wife in the bed of the firefighter for whom he pulled the mutual. Both dead. She had been smoking in bed.

Gail immediately stabbed her lit butt toward the ashtray on her lap without taking her eyes off another story called "The Soldier," about a soldier who comes home on leave and suspects his girl has been unfaithful.

But Gail missed the ashtray as she read, and the cigarette landed on her naked thigh. She howled and jumped from the bed. "Son of a bitch!" she shouted in the apartment, empty except for a terrified parlor cat named Mimi who screeched from the bedroom.

He got me, she thought. That son of a bitch got me! She was certain Kevin had gotten even with her. She half believed in karma, and she wondered if Kevin had sicced bad karma on her when she took his words and feelings into her empty bed. Burned her, not just for smoking in bed but for keeping him in the rehab upstate.

She padded across the deep pile carpet of the bedroom and out into the living room, which was decorated with overstuffed couches and a lounge chair. Most of the framed prints on the wall were bought in the museums around town: Monet, Picasso, Miró, Matisse, Van Gogh. Each frame cost her about seventy-five dollars and the prints no more than forty. They made the place look colorful and full of life and tasteful but it also showed she had to live on the cheap on her forty-three thousand a year, because eleven hundred a month went for rent.

But not cheap the way her old life had been cheap, when the value she placed on her pride ended at the dope dealer's stash.

Today, Gail Levy, of West Fifty-sixth Street near Eighth Avenue, inhabitant of rent-stabilized Apartment 12-L, found her value in convincing people as messed up as she once was that they still had vital human worth.

When she succeeded, it was good work, bordering on important. When she failed, she sometimes took the senseless guilt with her on the long trip back to the city. She was thankful that she only had to visit the rehab three times a week for one-on-ones with clients. The rest of her working time was spent visiting those remanded on criminal rehab to halfway houses here in the city.

She walked into the kitchenette, popped an ice cube from a tray, and held it against the burned place on her leg. Relief was instant, so she grabbed more ice and folded it into a dish towel and carried it with her across the living room to the bedroom. Her living room windows looked out on a downtown cityscape, but night had turned the bare panes into mirrors. She caught her naked body in the reflection and paused to consider it.

She posed and wondered if she looked at all like the dark-haired beauty in Kevin Dempsey's story.

Ludicrous.

She was halfway through "The Soldier," a paranoid male fantasy about a woman whose beauty drives a man half crazy. She broke her pose but stole a last glance, then hurried back to bed and slipped under the top sheet with the ice fastened to her burning thigh.

She wanted to finish "The Soldier." Another story, called "Tomboy," had made her get up from bed to check the chain latch. Twice. The second story had already caused her to burn herself. This one made her compare herself to the woman in the story.

He can spin a yarn, she thought.

She eagerly picked up the pages and continued to read "The Soldier." She had already gotten past the part about the soldier coming home from airborne jump school on leave to see his girl before leaving for Vietnam. The soldier stayed with his father for two weeks but found the girlfriend icy and indifferent. He and his dad had long talks about the girlfriend and how the soldier wanted to marry her when he got home from the war.

Everyone agreed she was the most beautiful girl in the neighborhood, a total knockout but with a reputation as wholesome as Betsy Ross's. He would have loved to have taken her home to show her off to his mother. Only the soldier had no mom. She'd died giving birth to the soldier, the way Kevin's mother had died giving birth to Mike. Margie had told Gail about that. The events of Kevin's real life were obviously grist for the mill of his life as a writer.

The soldier's two-week leave was unfulfilling. The girlfriend complained of having her period, said she was terrified of pregnancy, afraid she'd never see him alive again. She would not sleep with the soldier.

But on the morning he left, she and the father did escort the soldier to the Port Authority Terminal, where he'd begin his journey to the war. The farewell at the bus depot was emotional and poignant.

And now, as the father and the girlfriend were waving goodbye to the soldier, Gail's phone rang.

She jumped with a start but let it ring. There was no one she wanted to talk to more than she wanted to finish reading the Kevin story.

In the background she heard a familiar male voice speaking to the tape machine but could not hear the specifics.

Instead, as the caller spoke, Gail neared the end of the story, where the father and the girlfriend arrive back at the father's Brooklyn apartment. They talk about how the subway journey home has been almost unbearable, as is the cautious walk through the neighborhood streets.

Gail felt as if she were in that lurid room with them, listening and watching, as she read:

> They are laughing and giggling and now they are moaning as they kiss and embrace. A bra and a man's shirt hit the linoleum floor in the father's bedroom. And now a man's trousers and a girl's blue jeans crumple there too and men's underwear and women's panties.

And now the soldier hears the father and the girlfriend climb onto the mattress where he was conceived, as the soldier, after taking a taxi home ahead of them, lies in the dark beneath the bed of betrayal. His eyes stare at springs that begin to go up and down. In a frenzy now. Moaning and yelping.

And the soldier gets up from under the bed with a baseball bat, the Louisville Slugger that the father had bought him for Little League. And as the terrified girlfriend begs for forgiveness and the astonished father shouts that the son had stolen his wife by killing her at birth, the soldier proceeds to—

Gail held the pages over her breasts, crossed her legs, quickly leaned over the edge of her mattress, and looked under the bed.

Two huge eyes glared at her from the darkness. Gail screamed and vaulted from the bed, barely bending her knees, forgetting the burn on her thigh.

Mimi the cat screamed out from under the bed and dashed into the living room.

"You son of a bitch!" Gail shouted, her heart pounding, wondering if she was yelling at the cat or at Kevin Dempsey. She stood a breathless minute, trembling in the bedroom, still holding the story over her breasts.

She walked out to listen to her phone message and saw herself naked again in the blackened window. She self-consciously backstepped into the bedroom, took a terry-cloth robe from behind the bedroom door and pulled it around her, tying a double knot in the belt.

She pressed the PLAY button on her answering machine. It was Richard Smith, a painter she'd met at a gallery opening, a rising star in the art world, a guy she'd twice gone out with to dinner. He was asking her to dinner a third time. She knew if she went this time the poor guy would expect her to jump into bed. She wasn't remotely interested.

She liked him; he was smart and handsome and talented. If only he was as interesting as his work. His work was not her cup of tea, but others, especially critics, raved about it. So how could someone who could paint with passion exhibit none at all over dinner? Other artists? "They all suck." Politics? "It bores me." Music? "It's too easy." Writing? "It's all been done."

Two dinners, and all he wanted to talk about was how depressed he was and how badly he needed a woman to bring him to life. Gail had wanted to tell him, Don't look at me, pal. I'm not a dry-cell battery.

Plus, Richard was one of those guys who wouldn't let a woman pay for dinner, which was nice but was also a pain in the ass. That always led to the same asshole come-on, "Why don't you cook me a dinner?"

Men, the foolish bastards, always thought that was the ticket to a night at your place. But she had gotten the last guy good. Marvin, an ad executive she'd met at a musician friend's Fourth of July party, after wining and dining her in three swanky French restaurants had guilt-tripped her into cooking a meal for him. She finally gave in, told him the address, and when Marvin showed up at the homeless soup kitchen in the synagogue basement on Seventy-ninth Street, Gail met him at the door in her chef's hat and apron. She sat him down with the bums and gave him soup and bologna sandwiches.

Marvin never called again.

Too bad. Marvin was at least passionate—about French food.

Gail didn't bother to call Richard Smith back but walked instead into the bedroom and picked up another Kevin story. Mimi hopped up on the bed this time, and as Gail stroked her soft and housebound fur, she realized the story she was reading, "Pussycats," was about a one-eyed orange cat named the Pirate.

Was this the cat they found him talking to the night they took him away? she wondered.

27

Zoe finished drawing the second ear on the head with the blue crayon. Then she drew one red eye. Then a green eye. Then she drew a round brown nose. Then she drew a pink mouth on the face. Then a big happy smile.

She took the drawing to her mommy, who sat across the big room in a giant chair looking out at the pretty birds that flew over the house on the hill.

"That's a nice picture," Zoe's mommy said.

"It's Daddy," Zoe said, thinking of all the times her daddy tickled her to make her laugh.

"Your new daddy?"

"No," Zoe said. "Daddy-daddy."

"I think it's time for bed," Zoe's mother said.

"Daddy is smiling."

"Why?"

"Because Daddy is coming home soon. From work."

"Your new daddy is coming home," Zoe's mommy said.

"No, Daddy-daddy is coming home."

"Your new daddy."

"No, Daddy-daddy."

"It's time for you to go to bed, little girl."

"When my daddy comes home from work."

Zoe's mommy took Zoe by the hand and led her to her new bedroom, and Zoe began to cry.

28

Frank Dempsey awoke in the harrowing darkness.

He had so much to do in so little time. Find Zoe, get her back to Kevin, clear up his own money mess, make peace with his family, and prepare himself for judgment day, his toughest day in court.

Better get up, he thought.

He had not slept all the way through to daybreak in over two years. Yet every time he came to consciousness in the predawn night, dread consumed him like a curse. The first thing he always did was listen for the sound of his own heart to be certain he was alive.

Then he listened for the sounds of mice in the traps in his apartment on McDonald Avenue, in Kensington, in Brooklyn. If he did not hear frantic flapping or the squealing of the doomed, he knew it was safe to hobble on numb feet from his single bed to the kitchen for the first drink of the day, which was still the middle of the night.

Morning for ordinary people was filled with daylight and coffee and cornflakes, Francis Xavier Dempsey had long ago concluded. Morning for the slave of the grape and barley was ruled by the laughter of the monster in the moon.

The glass was in the freezer, tall and fresh and frosted, already packed with ice. And so was the bottle of Absolut vodka, which poured thick and syrupy when served so cold. Frank filled the ten-ounce glass an inch from the top and then added plain water from a refrigerated jug. The noisy chill of the opened refrigerator brought on an involuntary shiver, adding to Frank's trembling middle-aged hands. Alkies like him referred to this as the trembalinas or the jimjams.

He lifted the icy glass with both hands, lowered his sleep-sticky mouth to the bulging rim, and drank. The open refrigerator threw an angle of yellow light onto a corner of the kitchen, where he saw a one-inch baby mouse caught by the tail in a spring-snap trap. Its eyes glared up at him, tiny dots of terror waiting for the end. The mouse tried to scream but no audible noise would come.

Frank identified with the pathetic creature. He often felt in middle age as cornered and hopeless as the mouse now was in infancy. The baby brought to mind young Zoe, who was also trapped somewhere.

Frank had represented the Holy Ghost, the most underrated of the Blessed Trinity, as Zoe's earthly godfather, when he stood in Holy Name Church at her christening, vowing at the font to care for the spiritual well-being of the child should anything happen to her parents.

Now, with both parents unable to attend properly to her care, Frank shouldered not only the duty of the blood of family, as Kevin Dempsey's brother, but the promise he had made to God, to find and save young Zoe.

Half of this spiritual duty might be bullshit, Frank knew. But in his precarious state, one as ephemeral as that of the half-gone mouse, he was not going to play liar's poker with a dealer known to stack the deck.

He left the mouse where it was for now and carried his drink to the bathroom. The one good thing about rising in the dead of night was that no one in the apartment building was up flushing or showering, throwing off the calibration of hot and cold. He turned on the faucets.

The hot roar of the running shower caused his kidneys to relax and he urinated darkly as he sipped his translucent drink. He placed the half-gone glass on the windowsill just outside the shower curtain and climbed into the spray. The water was hot and forceful, and he let it needle and wash over him, like absolution. He brought his body to a rolling lather and shampooed and rinsed it. He put conditioner in his hair, which was thinning from the Dilantin, the pills Anthony had prescribed after his last grand mal seizure.

As the conditioner set for a full minute, he adjusted the nozzle away and took a gulp of his drink and agitated it around his mouth and swallowed, preparing himself for the ghastliest task of morning.

Brushing one's teeth, for an alcoholic with a herniated esophagus, was an ordeal of self-imposed misery that stripped away all remaining dignity.

Once the trembling hand brought the sickeningly sweet taste of the toothpaste to Frank's mouth, his stomach began to churn and buckle. The Dilantin that caused hair loss also promoted tooth decay. So brushing was important to kill the rancid odor and to preserve what teeth were left. But the toothbrush in the morning mouth always made him retch, and when he scoured the coated tongue and the bleeding gums, Frank knew he would let loose with his daily wake-up purge.

It was all right to do it in the shower because only yellow-greenish bile was produced; no solid substance would still be left in the sour stomach. There in the private baptism of the waters, the nose would run and tears would pour and Frank would cough and gag, clear his nasal and bronchial passages, until the elimination of yesterday's sins was complete.

A second brushing of the teeth vanquished the taste of bile brought on by the first.

Once that process was over, Frank would gargle with Listerine, rinse the conditioner from his hair, take the glass from the windowsill and finish the four ounces of vodka that were left, and stand under the hot stream with closed eyes until the involuntary shaking finally ceased.

When Frank stepped out of the shower, he was externally glistening, fragrant, and spotless. He held his hands out straight and the shaking was almost gone.

He was ready for a Dilantin, two vitamin C tablets, and a Dristan, all of which he'd wash down with his second drink.

Three maintenance drinks later, Frank Dempsey was ready for the beginning of the day.

Now it was 5:30 A.M. on Saturday, so he turned on Ten Ten WINS and learned there was a threat of afternoon rain. On a weekday he'd have tuned in *Imus in the Morning,* an ex-addict who knew the other forecast, the one that charts the storm within. Imus managed to mine humor from his self-inflicted horror. Frank envied him that alchemy, wished he could find the magic to laugh at himself. But when he looked in the mirror he grimaced.

Frank was just satisfied that he was now steady enough to shave. And standing there naked, he shaved as close as he could without drawing blood.

He embalmed his face with aftershave, then splashed it between his legs and under his arms and rolled a stick of scented deodorant behind it. He dried his thinning hair on the gentle cycle of the hair dryer, and as daybreak leaked through his windows he crossed his living room and dressed in dry-cleaned corduroys, polished low-cut brown leather boots, and a blue pullover sweater over a short-sleeved collared shirt.

Mutton dressed as lamb is what his father would have called him.

He opened the blinds to a view of Greenwood Cemetery, where birds chirped and squirrels foraged for food in the fulvous leaves amid the markers of the dead, a pair of whom were his parents.

Standing on the sidewalk, smoking a cigarette, leaves swaying to the sidewalk around him, was Summers from IAB. He glanced up at Frank's window and then watched a young couple wearing fall sweaters walk by holding hands. Frank lifted a glass in salute to Summers but Summers looked away, pretending not to see.

Frank's living room was furnished like the waiting room up in Smith's, where his parents had been waked, except for the framed eight-by-ten photos of his mom and dad and brothers and sister and nieces and nephews arranged neatly on his mantel. He loved each one as if the kid were his own, knowing he'd never have a child himself.

What woman would carry a child of his, especially now, when his life was reduced to a dossier? When he carried his illness around with him in a Gatorade bottle like a self-pitying cross? What woman could ever understand or tolerate his morning masquerade or how he wrestled with the scary night? It had been so long since he luxuriated in the touch of a woman that the idea of sex was as alien to him as sobriety or freedom from legal pursuit. Sex, like cornflakes in the morning and noneventful toothbrushing, was for normal people. People who shared beds at night with naked companions and cared about more than getting a double order from the liquor store on Saturday night because no take-out hard liquor was sold in New York on Sundays.

So Frank rarely thought about sex anymore because it made him miss too many other normal things.

But for some desperate reason, one he could not comprehend, since he had met her he could not shake the smiling face of Sarah Cross from his mind's bloodshot eye. If only he had encountered her a year ago, he thought, when he was still healthy and vital, his professional life still something to be proud of, his dignity intact and redeemable. Before he found out his father's secrets, before he started to drink so heavily.

He would have made a decent husband then, honest and clean and still ascending. He could have asked a lovely woman like Sarah to be his wife. Making a baby with a woman like Sarah Cross would be as heavenly as the child it might have produced.

But that was a drunk's sentimental dream. The cold reality was different. It was puking in the shower and a liver that was going to kill him.

He paused at each child's picture on the mantel until he came to focus on young Zoe.

He finished his drink, swallowed it as he looked out at Summers, who was starting to annoy him. He walked to the kitchen, replenished his Gatorade bottle with nine ounces of vodka and two ounces of orange flavoring, pulled on his jacket, sunglasses, and an Irish walking hat, and shoved the Gatorade bottle in his inside pocket. He also pocketed bottles of Dilantin, Dristan, vitamin C, and Valium, which he rarely took. He took his passport in case he got suddenly detoured and because he couldn't be sure Polly and Zoe were in this country. Once he was indicted, the court would seize the American passport, he thought. But the law didn't know he also had an Irish passport stashed with the money, in case he needed a quick exit. Big Paulie's being born in Belfast entitled all his children and grandchildren to Irish passports. Frank had had his for five years now, always thinking it would come in handy if ever skyjacked by anti-American terrorists. Who kills Irish nationals? Big Paulie would have answered, "Brits."

In an afterthought, Frank took a can of NYPD-issue Mace from a bedside table drawer and pocketed it. Just in case things get rougher than me, he thought.

He bent and picked up the trap from which the baby mouse dangled by the tail. He looked at the pointed, panicked face as it wiggled there before him, squirming for its life.

"You're lucky I'm allergic to cats," Frank said aloud, averting his liquored breath and hearing his own deep voice for the first time that day. He opened the kitchen window, pulled back the spring-snap bar, and watched the mouse fall almost weightlessly to the lawn two stories below, where it hopped away. As he shut the window, he saw the tail was left behind in the trap. He banged it off the trap into the plastic-lined trash barrel.

He would reset the trap with peanut butter when he returned, but right now he left on a different mission.

As he locked the door behind him, he felt thankful for being godfather to young Zoe. For the task of finding her had given Frank Dempsey back his worth in life for one final run.

29

Gail Levy noticed Kevin Dempsey staring at her bare legs. For the first time in his company, she was wearing a dress. Two-thirds of the way through their one-on-one hour, she rose from behind her desk to pour boiling water into her coffee cup and caught Kevin sizing her up. She hoped he hadn't noticed she was favoring one leg.

"You should wear stockings around cloistered men," Kevin said.

"I'll thank you not to comment on my anatomy," Gail said.

"I never mentioned any part of your anatomy," Kevin said. "But if I did, you'd be guilty of a double standard. As I recall, and I'm good at this, the last time we were together you called me an asshole. Twice."

Gail figured he was trying to rewrite the session, most of it about the traumatic fumble in his high school championship football game and freezing at the fire. He was trying to turn it into one of his stories, and she was determined not to let that happen.

"Yeah, well, I'm in charge here," she said. "Remember that. Here, there's my way or the highway."

"In charge of what, my drinking? My sanity? My job and future and my life? My manhood? Okay, here I am. Let's look under the hood."

He leaned over half mockingly, pretending to look up her dress. Gail instinctively crossed her legs, forgetting the desk was not open-fronted, and stopped herself in pain.

"Ow . . . shit."

She groaned, stood, and took half a step toward the window.

"Cut yourself shaving," Kevin asked snidely, "using your boyfriend's razor?"

"I don't have a boy—never mind."

She lit a cigarette and paced, trying to walk off the pain.

"You didn't happen to burn yourself smoking in bed by any chance, did you?" Kevin asked with a grin.

Gail wanted to call him an asshole again but he'd only twist the anatomical reference. As Kevin scoffed, Gail blew smoke toward the window and, noticing it was closed, opened it a crack. Wind lashed in and lifted some papers off her desk. Kevin bent and picked up a pile of stapled typed sheets and saw it was one of his own stories, "The Soldier."

"You met Margie?" Kevin asked.

"You have a sister who really loves you," she said, sitting down on the edge of the chair.

"She's the best," Kevin said.

"You're lucky to have a support system like her," she said. "Is there anyone else?"

"Frank, Mike, Carmine," he said. "Anthony. But he just moved out west. He's my oldest, closest friend. A doctor."

"I know," Gail said. "Did you discuss your problems with him?"

"Yeah."

"As a friend or a doctor?"

"Both."

"What did he say?"

"That it was confidential. That's the way I want it to stay."

"You sure you can trust him?"

"He's my best friend," Kevin said defensively. "If I can't trust him, who do I trust? You?"

"When you do your Fifth AA Step you'll have to 'fess up and trust me," she said, "or the program won't work for you. Right now, tell me again about the fire."

"I froze," Kevin said. "What more is there to say? There's schizophrenia for you—freezing at a fire."

"Ever happen before?"

"No, and my mom and dad never locked me in closets."

"Don't be a pain in the ass."

"You're gettin' anatomical again," Kevin said.

Gail glared at him, studying his naughty adolescent manner, and took a puff of her cigarette.

"Okay," she said. "Why do you always stare at my butt? You an *ass* man?"

"I never thought about it."

"Yes, you have," she said.

"How does this ass-backwards tract relate to my drinking?"

"I don't know," Gail said. "You have a way with words, and you know it. Your stories are intriguing, compelling, disturbing, well done. But I think you hide behind your facility with words the way you might behind a beer. You defend yourself with them."

"Is that what you think my writing is? Defensive?"

Gail sat back down and looked him in the eye and tried to appear as serious as possible.

"I think it might be good if you started writing your autobiography," she said. "Everyone here has to do it. The truth in plain straightforward English, going back as far as you can remember, up to your first drink, sexual experiences, your mom, dad, brothers, sister, girlfriends, pals, sports—"

"Was it Margie who told you about the fumble?" he asked anxiously.

"No, you did, our last visit," she said. "Don't you remember? You remembered me calling you an asshole. Twice."

"What did I tell you? I was still coming off the dope."

"That the day you fumbled the football in the championship game was the most humiliating day of your life."

"That's all?"

"Until the fire," Gail said. "Maybe fumbling the ball and freezing at the fire are connected."

She watched Kevin staring straight at her, his confident eyes suddenly reflective, introspective, and sad. What a man would never understand, Gail thought, is that when he looks vulnerable a woman desires him even more. The chink in his macho armor makes him all the more mysterious. All the more a man that a woman wants. Gives him dimension, depth, complexity. A boy to raise, a man to hold. It means there is an engine in his belly, cooking, boiling, ready to erupt. . . .

"Knock, knock," Kevin said.

"Huh?" Gail said, and realized she had drifted ever so slightly away from focus, yet was gaping straight at him. "Sorry. Just wondering. If you are ready . . . ready yet to tell the truth. Let me give you the Fifth Step book and you can work on your autobiography. We can go over it next time. You're supposed to read it to someone you can trust. Preferably a stranger from the program. Like me. Meanwhile, time is up."

"I see," Kevin said. "Who else reads it?"

"Oh, we publish it in the *National Enquirer* . . . just kidding. No one else sees it. You keep it. The purpose is for you to come clean with yourself and learn to confide in someone, instead of burying your secrets with booze. It's the ultimate catharsis. I call it the bullshit broom."

"It sounds like what we Catholics call confession."

"Only here we don't call your secrets sins," Gail said. "We call them symptoms of a disease. You should be taking a Fifth Step class today, your second Saturday."

"Yeah, it's on the schedule," Kevin said. "It sounds interesting." The room grew darker as storm clouds gathered in the sky outside the window. "I'll need notebooks for the autobiography. A few of them. Pens."

Gail slowly pushed herself up, biting her lip in discomfort, walked to the file cabinet, and took out two spiral notebooks, two Bic pens, and a work booklet titled *Guide to Steps 4 and 5 for Men.* Kevin pointed to the word *Men* on the booklet cover and glanced sideways at Gail with skepticism.

"These steps are different for women?"

"Just the secrets," Gail said. "Women's are darker."

Kevin grimaced and nodded. "If I tell you mine," he asked, "do you tell me yours?"

"Nope."

"That's another double standard?"

"Yup."

"Because you're in charge," Kevin said.

"You certainly are making progress," Gail said and checked her watch. "I have another client waiting."

Gail thought she detected a pinprick of jealousy in Kevin's eyes. I'm being silly, she thought.

Kevin picked up the booklet and the two spiral notebooks and the two Bic pens. He turned to leave and Gail watched him go, dressed in his jeans and FDNY sweatshirt and white sneakers. The pain of the burn on her bare leg throbbed as she regarded him.

"Kevin."

He turned.

"That cat, the Pirate, in the story called 'Pussycats'—"

"What about him?"

"Is he supposed to be you?"

"I look like a pussy to you?" he asked, slowly closing a single eye.

"I mean do you feel that alone, detached, alienated?" she asked.

She watched him leave her office, and even with his back to her she knew he was smirking as he gently closed the door. If he meows I'll kill him, she thought.

"Me-oooow," she heard Kevin intone from the other side of the door.

Son of a bitch, Gail Levy thought, and reached for a True blue cigarette. She turned to the window and watched the storm clouds rumble south.

30

Frank Dempsey stepped out of his family's mausoleum and slammed the big door, which locked behind him. Standing discreetly at the bottom of the hill was Summers, smoking a cigarette.

Frank had just finished his weekly visit to the tomb of his parents, where he prayed for Zoe and asked for his mother and father's grace-filled guidance from beyond. He hoped they had found each other and that someday he would meet them again to give it all another try.

As he made for the gate, he saw a man in a tan summer suit walking his way. He was wearing a straw hat with a bright yellow band, and he was flanked on one side by a man in a dark suit and sunglasses and on the other by a younger man, in a tight muscle shirt, with the physique of a steroid-abusing weight lifter.

Frank instantly recognized the oldest of the three as Pinebox Pirino, a powerful local bookmaker and loan shark with whom his father used to gamble and lose heavily. In fact, the family mausoleum Frank had just visited was won many years ago by Big Paulie in a card game in the back room of Pinebox Pirino's saloon, The Fifth Amendment, on Fifth Avenue in Brooklyn. Big Paulie beat a straight with a full house and said someday the mausoleum would be a full house of Dempseys. Big Paulie was a degenerate gambler from the beginning.

Pinebox had won a lot of money from Big Paulie over the years. But one thing Frank's father never lost to the hood was his badge. He could have wiped out many a debt by "tinning" for the Pinebox crew. But Big Paulie, hardly an angel, would never shit in his own back yard. If you were going to "break bread," as the cops called splitting dirty money, you didn't do it in your own neighborhood. In fact you didn't do it where anyone in the neighborhood on either side of the law would know about it.

In your own stomping ground, you polished your badge. It let you stand proudly on a moral high ground.

Frank had no good feelings toward Pinebox. He disliked the mob, with all their phony romantic bullshit about honor and wisdom and vision. The people who were attracted to the mob were the same as the ones who became dirty cops—greedy, lazy, violent people who didn't know how to do anything else. If they did know how to do something else they became plumbers, airplane pilots, composers, carpenters, zoologists, or Wall Street brokers. But the ones with no vision or wisdom or true honor either became corrupt cops or made mobsters. Whether they took their money with the power of the badge or the "made-man button" was of little consequence. It was really the power of the gun. And so, in Frank's eyes, Pinebox was simply another conniving hood who robbed the working stiff of his hard-earned pay. The way corrupt cops extorted money from bodega-owning dope dealers and took payoffs from hoods like Pinebox.

It was one of the great horrors of his life that he would probably go to his grave labeled as one of them.

As Pinebox approached, the two crew members stood back and allowed Pinebox to approach Frank alone.

"No hello, Frank?"

"You're better known for your long goodbyes, Pinebox," Frank said, with a half smile.

"I'm here visiting all my family and old friends," Pinebox said. "So many of them, gone before their time. Most for silly reasons. Violence—"

"You play, you pay," Frank said. "Isn't that the gambler's creed?"

"Some win," Pinebox said. "Me, I'm here today to pay. Pay respects to good people. And you're here paying your respects to your father. He was good people."

"And my mother. Let's not forget my mother, who put up with him," Frank said, as they passed briefly on the road. "If anyone breaks him out of purgatory, it'll be her."

"I see you have company," Pinebox said, nodding to Summers, who watched from below the small hill, making notes in a small notebook.

"So do you," Frank said, nodding to the two torpedoes who stood back at a discreet distance.

"Your father was a good man," Pinebox said.

"No eulogies, please."

"Maybe you should stop by my place some night," Pinebox said. "We'll talk. There's lots to talk about. A million things."

"Million and a half," Frank said, stepping around Pinebox and then past his men. Pinebox blessed himself and half genuflected in front of the crucifix on the Dempsey mausoleum. Frank strode toward the main gates of the cemetery, past Summers, who took up his obvious tail.

Frank needed to get rid of Summers for a while so he could get some work done without added baggage.

Work.

He reveled in the thought of the word.

Work.

It was hard enough following someone's trail without having a tail yourself. He needed to check with Gutter, the shoe salesman, to see if he'd had any luck in getting him the printout from Achilles Heels corrective shoes. But he had waited for today, a Saturday, to pay a visit to Miles Barker, the British photographer.

Being a divorced father of small children, Barker would almost certainly be compelled to join the weekend throng of men dating their estranged children. Frank had found Barker's Manhattan address on one of Polly's old Christmas card lists. But he didn't want to knock on a door that could be closed in his face. He wanted to confront Barker outdoors, with his kids, where he would be the least mobile and most vulnerable. Frank needed to do this without Summers on his heels.

But there was someone else he wanted—no, needed—to see first.

Frank pulled on his Irish walking hat and a pair of sunglasses as he exited the graveyard onto McDonald Avenue. As Summers trailed him on foot, another IAB cop snaked behind in an unmarked car.

Frank did not need a lot of time, just a minute to slip away. He walked along McDonald for two blocks toward the intersection with Church, taking a swig from the Gatorade bottle as he walked and thinking about how a clever bunco artist named Fabulous Murphy he once tailed had given him the slip. It was a mortifying experience but one he later cherished and retold.

As he neared the intersection, he saw a police patrol car parked outside of the diner on the corner. There was always a cop car in front of that diner because the Greek who owned it gave grub to cops for free.

Whenever a diner has cops parked outside with regularity, it's a fair bet that the place is on a "touch" list, a place for free cop handouts in exchange for not ticketing the double-parked customers, who more than made up the difference.

Frank looked behind him and saw that Summers was following at a steady pace. Frank almost thought of waving but did not want to be disrespectful to any man who worked for a living.

Instead, he hurried directly to the parked patrol car, where two uniformed cops were sipping coffee and chewing buttered rolls. The driver's window was open and Frank approached the car at a frantic trot.

"Officer! Officer!" Frank shouted at the wary policewoman, panting and clutching his heart.

"Slow down, pal," said the woman driver, wiping butter from her mouth.

"What . . . ?" said the policeman partner.

Frank pointed to Summers across the street, gaping at him.

"That man . . . he has a gun . . . he pulled it on me . . . as I was leaving Greenwood Cemetery . . . demanded my money . . . I ran. . . ."

The policewoman was out of the car, her hand on her gun. The other cop jumped out his door.

"The guy in the suit and tie?" the driver asked.

"He followed me down here . . . he has a gun. . . ."

The two uniformed cops dodged through the two-way traffic toward a startled Summers, who Frank knew was desperately fumbling for his badge in his pocket. But to the uniforms, Summers was a skell going for a gun. The tail car following Summers screeched to a halt and the driver leaped out.

The two uniformed cops drew their service revolvers and the policeman trained his on the driver getting out of the unmarked car. The policewoman shouted at Summers, as she held her gun on him with two hands.

"Down on the motherfuckin' ground, asshole—hands where I can see 'em!"

"I'm on the job!" was the last thing Frank heard Summers shouting from the sidewalk as he hurried down the subway stairs, flashed his father's police shield at the bored token-booth clerk, and walked through the exit gate into the subway station.

Five minutes later, as the F train moved through the dark tunnel, Frank smiled, thinking of the two uniforms tossing the two cops, only to find they were from the dreaded IAB.

At Jay Street and Borough Hall, Frank got off the F train to switch to the A train. He bought a *New York Post* at a newsstand and began thumbing through it. An item on page fourteen made his stomach waffle.

> A family of five, including an infant in his crib, was found murdered by automatic gunfire in a Washington Heights apartment late yesterday. Police say the multiple slaying had all the earmarks of a drug-related hit. Neighbors said the parents, illegal Colombian nationals, were known drug traffickers in the area. A police spokesman said the husband was a suspected member of the infamous Botero cocaine posse, with connections to the Cali drug cartel.
>
> "This hit reeks of a Botero retaliation for a double cross," said one NYPD detective connected to the case.

That's what five dead bodies got today. If it was drug related and especially if it involved illegals, it registered a news brief on page fourteen. Frank closed the newspaper as dread moved through him. He wiped his damp palms on his pants legs. The A train roared into the station, and he climbed on board and headed for Manhattan.

31

"So the way I look at it, you bailed me out and don't even know it," Carmine said, as Kevin looked from the dark sky back to his best firehouse buddy, whom he'd almost let die. Carmine held a cane in one hand, one he needed now because of double-herniated disks in his lower back. "I was getting too old for the fucking job anyways, and now they're giving me three-quarters."

"Jeez, Carm, that's great."

Three-quarters was the equivalent of winning the civil service lottery. If you had a job-related injury, you could retire on three-quarters of your salary for life, tax free because of the medical disability.

The two of them were in the dayroom of the rehab main house, a huge parlor filled with plain uncomfortable couches and stiff-backed sitting-room chairs supplemented with dozens of metal folding chairs for visitors.

Kevin and Carmine had staked claim to a pair of chairs closest to the large bay windows, overlooking the front lawn and the gravel-covered traffic roundabout leading to the main road that unspooled to the world outside.

"I'll never be able to look any of the guys in the eye again," Kevin said. "I don't know what happened. I remember thinking of Zoe. I couldn't focus."

"You had a lot on your mind," Carmine said. "Believe me, Kev. I can only thank you. What you did was get me thirty-three hunrid a month for life. The operative word there is *life*. Meaning, I still got one and they are gonna pay me for living it. Alls I gotta do is show up in Farrell's bar every morning. Oh, jeez."

Carmine looked around the visiting area of the big old converted farmhouse, at the booze-savaged men, ranging in ages from twenty-five to sixty, and their visitors, all sitting in conspiratorial clumps on folding chairs, facing each other.

"It won't ever be the same," Kevin said.

"Sure it will," Carmine said.

"Even if I go back to work, you'll be gone," Kevin said.

"Yeah, but we'll still hang out."

"Where? Coffee shops that sell beer, or bars that sell coffee? The job will watch me now. I'm a loose cannon. They can't let me get other people hurt."

"They might give you three-quarters," Carmine said.

"Psycho."

"We'd all qualify for that," Carmine said and laughed, a loud demonstrative outburst. Then he dropped to a hushed tone. "But you'll be back, Kev. It's still the best job on earth. Me, I have no regrets that I gave it twenty-eight of my best."

Kevin knew then that Carmine was here as much out of a need to do a rescue as he was to check up on a buddy. Carmine needed to be needed in a time of crisis. It was what he *did*.

"Yeah," Kevin said. "The best. And I don't know if I'm good enough anymore. God almighty, I *froze*. On the brothers, Carmine. On you. I don't deserve to be on that job. I should be replaced by some kid with balls."

"You're talking ridiculous," Carmine said. "You're the best and ballsiest fireman I ever worked with. You had a ton of shit on your mind that night, Kev."

Kevin shook his head, his mind a flicker book of fires and rescues they'd done together over the years, followed by a thousand nights in saloons, ski trips to the mountains, summers down the shore. . . .

"Who else you know buys a family home without a family to put in it?" Kevin said.

"Yeah," Carmine said, walking to the window and staring out, speaking softly. "Well, the only anniversary I ever celebrate is the day I graduated fire school. I haven't celebrated my wedding anniversary in ten, fifteen years either, ya know. Carmine Junior, he's gone, married, up there in Connecticut. And Barbara's still there, out in our house in Shirley. I still have a key, but she hates when I come home out there to the Island. She says I leave hair in the drain after a shower. It must be coming offa my chest because I ain't got none left on my fuckin' head, like when we got married. She knows I'm out there among them, Kev, drinkin' beers, talkin' to broads, OTB, Atlantic City, the track, hanging with the guys. But Barbara, she just don't *care* no more. It bothers me, but there's no way to make her care."

"She cares, Carmine. Barbara was always solid, good, caring—"

"Nah, these things happen," Carmine said. "Marriage is not a very stable institution, there, Kev. It's like—well, it's like it wasn't meant for *people*. Swans, they choose a lifelong mate, and elephants too. Even fuckin' penguins pick one bride, and don't ask me how the fuck they can tell each other apart. But *people,* if we were in a cage in a zoo, they'd have a little plaque that reads HOMO SAPIENS—MATING HABITS: FUCK AROUND. We're the animals who *live* to die fucking around. Life is one big day and night of fucking around, and then all a sudden it's over and you either had a good time or you didn't. Me, I had twenty-eight of the best. And . . . and—well, they retired me, Kev. Three-quarters, baby, they retired me."

Kevin looked up and saw that Carmine was trying hard to keep a grin plastered on his face. But his eyes belonged to a pallbearer. He kept nodding and looking for more words. Finally he turned his back on Kevin and took out his always starched and ironed handkerchief and blew his nose, as loud as he'd laughed.

Then Carmine grew excited. "Chee-sus Christ!" he shouted, loud enough to turn the heads of most in the dayroom, as he pointed out the big window at Gail Levy, walking to her car, her strong calf muscles bunching as she went. "Who the hell is that piece of fine art?"

Now Kevin saw Carmine dab at the corner of an eye.

"My counselor," Kevin said, watching Carmine shove the handkerchief into his pocket in a crumpled ball, something he'd never seen him do before. "Gail Levy."

"Your counselor? Levy? A Jew broad? Oh, I love Jewish girls. They want you for more than your body. Very caring people, Jewish girls. And I'm here feeling sorry for you? Where do you sign for a room here? What do they call this place, Club Bed? She have a big sister my age, a grieving widow mother maybe?"

Kevin thought about Gail's coffee cup that read WORLD'S GREATEST DAUGHTER. He made a mental note to ask about her mother in the next session. But he also thought about Carmine's wife, Barbara, sitting home, not caring whether he showed up anymore or not. Now that there was no firehouse to live in, where would Carmine go when the bars closed at night?

"I'll ask her," Kevin said, watching Carmine ogle Gail Levy.

"Chee-sus Christ! Those legs! What an ass-kicking she could give ya with them for coming home late, huh, Kev?"

Carmine hadn't had anyone get mad at him for coming home late in so long that half the fun had gone out of staying out.

Gail drove on the gravel roundabout and glanced up from the wheel and nodded as she crunched past the front windows of the dayroom. Kevin nodded back and Carmine histrionically threw his arms against the window as if in surrender, the cane dangling from the crook of his left arm. Gail shook her head and drove off.

They both sat a while longer, rehashing tales of yesteryear, of afternoons in Monahan's Pub in downtown Brooklyn where the married owner got his jollies by only hiring beautiful single waitresses. Of probie initiations and dopey bachelor parties and christenings, weddings, funerals, even a couple of bar mitzvahs. Kevin realized that every single story had alcohol in it.

Then Carmine told Kevin that Lieutenant Crosby had not been too harsh on him in his report. He said Jimmy Savage's wife was pregnant, and one of the probies was getting married, and another old guy named McCarthy was having a retirement party.

"Great," Kevin said and remarked no further. He imagined champagne he'd never taste. Two weeks go by and people out there were expecting brand-new babies and marrying loving brides and he was in here trying to forget both. And here was Carmine, who had fought one fire too many, and who suddenly was a man who would never get in trouble for going home late again.

"Well, I better get going," Carmine said. "I got a million things to do. Paperwork, doctor's appointment, Social Security."

Kevin nodded. A true hero chasing busywork, he thought. "Carmine," he said, throwing an arm around his neck and kissing his cheek, "I'm so, so sorry!"

Carmine swallowed, shrugged, and threw his arms around Kevin. "Hey, we're both still kickin', ain't we?" Carmine said. "So what's the point in kickin'?" He looked at his watch again, as if he had somewhere to go. "Chee-sus, I better hurry. Maybe I can beat the storm."

They shook hands and Kevin walked Carmine to the front door and watched him leave with the cane, in a rush, as if racing to a fire. Kevin Dempsey wondered where he would go.

32

Frank watched Sarah come out through the health club door with a flourish, walking briskly, checking her watch, her hair taking flight behind her. Men took instant notice of her. So did women.

Frank was tailing her to see if she would lead him to Polly and Zoe.

Sarah wore new white sneakers, a form-fitting white leotard, and a long loose blouse over that, drawn at the waist by a rope belt. She carried a large canvas bag slung over her right shoulder.

She boasted a just-toned vibrancy, endorphins exploding in every step, her face flushed with vitality, as she searched for a cab, checking her watch again.

Spotting her, Frank's heart rose and fell. His hands trembled and his mouth went dry and he took a deep inhale and held it before a slow exhale. He was sitting at a sidewalk table outside the Paradise Coffee Shop on West Forty-third Street, with an Orangina drink in front of him. He moistened his lips with the Orangina and tugged the brim of the hat lower over his face, the sunglasses obscuring the bloodshot eyes.

When Sarah hurried by he caught a blossoming whiff of her on the humid air, an aromatic riot of soap and water and clean hair, new sweat and powder and health. She smells like she was born without original sin, Frank thought.

Sarah gave up looking for a taxi and picked up an already hurried stride. She cuts through the street like she has sirens and lights, Frank thought, getting up from his seat and trying to keep pace.

He followed her along Forty-third Street, across Ninth Avenue, and uptown to Forty-fifth Street, where she turned right with a graceful pivot. He wanted to see where Sarah went, who she saw. If Polly had her money, Sarah would be on her trail. Frank thought it a good idea to be on Sarah's. But mostly he just wanted to see her. To see lovely Sarah Cross.

The walk was a performance all its own, Sarah's arms swinging and long legs striding, bag swaying and horns honking, men whistling, women elbowing their captivated men, cops smiling. Two men walked from inside a saloon out onto the sidewalk to gape.

Today, Frank enjoyed every moment of Sarah's walk, because he feared perhaps he might never see her again. A day passes, these days, and it could be the last one.

But he also wanted to see if he had the nerve to approach her. He had approached her the first time because he was on business, on a mission, on an investigation, on *duty*. That was the only way he could break the barriers with women.

That is why he was still single in his fifth decade of life. He had been too shy to speak to women most of his adult life, unless they were victims of crime or wives and mothers and sisters of crime victims.

Terminal shyness, off duty, was Frank Dempsey's bane in life. And when they took away his badge, his shield from the shyness, they took away his lifeline to women. Without that badge, he had no conduit to the female gender. No right or reason to ask the first question to a woman if he was not on duty. And now that he was never to be on duty again, there would never be one last fling to go with the one last run.

That was true punishment.

If only I could love and be loved by one woman before I go, he thought.

So he followed Sarah, to fill his mind with images of her, enough details to fill every corner of a dark bedroom ceiling in the empty night.

On Forty-fifth Street between Ninth and Eighth avenues, Frank saw Sarah join the end of a long line of girls who were filing through a stage door of a music house theater, each of them flashing Actors Equity cards to a uniformed security guard. Frank assessed the other women—mostly attractive, some stunning, and all under thirty, long-legged and thin. He knew Sarah was an actress so he guessed all these women were actresses. Dancers too, judging by their splayed feet. The hoofers of the Big Apple arriving for an open audition. A cattle call.

Frank felt indignation. How could anyone expect a woman like

Sarah Cross, in all her exquisite beauty, her radiant natural stardom, to be expected to answer an open call?

"Sorry, guy," the security guard said. "Just dames. Cards. Ya gotta have an Equity card. Else, can't letcha in dere. Lotsa friggin' freaks folly the dames around these days."

"I haven't danced since before Ebbets Field was a housing project," Frank said, detecting a long-vanished Brooklyn in the old-timer's grainy voice. It was an endangered Brooklyn accent that would be gone by the early twenty-first century, replaced by a new one slowly evolving from the children of new immigrants.

"You amemba Ebbets Fiel'?" the security guard asked. "Jeez, don't get me started on that sonuvabitch O'Malley. The city started goin' sout' the day that dick took da Bums west. Now ya need an armed guard to go to a Yankee game, and you gotta admit to your friends you went to Queens—Queens!—if ya wanna see da Mets. And alla sudden, you got lotsa friggin' freaks follying the dames around."

"Stalkers," Frank said, flashing his father's badge. "There's a girl in there who's being followed by a guy who has a mad crush on her."

"One a dem dames just went inside?"

Frank nodded. "The guy has a booze problem, obsessed like. I'm tailing her to see who's tailing *her,* get it?"

"Yeah, whadda I look like, a friggin' chimp?"

Frank stood there waiting for the security guard to give him clearance.

"Well?"

"Well, what?" Frank asked.

"Well, what the hell ya waitin' fuh? Go in dere and keep an eye on da dame afore this friggin' freak takes her sout' too."

"Right," Frank said. As he passed, the doorman took a piece of Frank's sleeve between thumb and index finger and whispered conspiratorially from the corner of his mouth.

"I used to sit down the turd base line," the security guard said. "I amemba a few years ago, a reporter, in one a the papers, interviewed a woman whose kid was killed in the housing project bedroom right where Ebbets Fiel' turd base usta be. Dat's what Walter O'Malley did ta Brooklyn."

Frank remembered how much his father hated Walter O'Malley and, like the old-timer here, used to call him Sonuvabitch O'Malley so often that Frank thought it had been the Dodger owner's first name.

Frank nodded to the security guard, slapped his shoulder, and entered the great theater.

Waiting for Sarah, he watched the girls go through auditions for a dance choreographer for over forty-five minutes. Frank stood in the back of the darkened theater, alone, and watched the women walk to the stage when their names were called by a male assistant with a deep voice.

The choreographer onstage was tall and thin, well toned, dressed in a leotard, occasionally walking to a dancer and embracing her to walk her through one of his steps.

But he was an unpleasant and rude man and treated the women like schoolchildren, scolding them, haranguing them, sometimes even ridiculing them.

"Miss, miss, miss!" he'd snapped at one dancer who couldn't get the steps perfect.

He was quickly corrected by the frustrated woman. "Mrs."

"Even worse! As I was saying, miss, stay home with the rug rats and *miss* my next call and the one after that, will you? Next!"

He'd insulted her sexual preference, her marital status, motherhood, and her professionalism all in one crass outburst, Frank thought. He'd been no kinder to half a dozen more women he said were too chubby, too dumpy, too runty, too slow, too plain, too dumb, too ethnic. The choreographer was casting a big show for big bucks, and Frank understood there was a need to eliminate people rather quickly, because time was money. But he could remember treating people in police lineups with more common decency than this fellow, whose name eluded him, even though it was a name he'd read a hundred times in the gossip columns.

Frank was doing a mental dragnet for the choreographer when the assistant called another name: "Cross, Sarah."

Frank now felt personally involved.

He watched Sarah get up from a seat in the audience, dressed only in the white skin-tight leotard, her body a strong, slender, pliable spear of bamboo as she glided down the aisle and bounded up the steps to the stage, placing her bag by the left wing. The choreographer walked to her, took her arms, and instructed her ever so perfunctorily.

Frank swallowed hard and touched the tips of each finger with his thumbs, as the music rose.

Sarah sailed into her audition, bounding and gliding and leaping through the steps, her hair flying, her tapered body like a precision instrument, touching the floor like a bird when alighting from midair.

This is what they do on street corners in heaven, Frank thought.

"Miss, miss, this is Broadway, not *Bored*-way," the choreographer said, with nasal contempt and a backhanded dismissive gesture.

Frank was appalled.

But Sarah simply shrugged and padded to her bag, donned her loose blouse, tied her rope belt, bounded down the stairs, and made her way up the aisle, checking her watch as carefree as if she'd just missed a city bus.

Frank melted back into the shadows by the far aisle and watched Sarah until she was safely past. Then he began a measured stroll down the aisle of the theater. He felt the vodka sloshing in the bottle as he moved toward the stage. Many of the girls turned to look at him as he approached.

"May I help you?" asked the choreographer's assistant.

"No, thank you," Frank said.

He kept striding along, as the choreographer took a sip from a Perrier bottle and shook his head in disgust, oblivious to Frank's approach.

"Next!" he shouted as Frank climbed the six steps to the stage. Finally the choreographer looked up and grinned.

"Don't tell me," he said. "Your real name is Norma Jean."

Frank was a foot in front of the choreographer now, and all eyes in the theater were on both of them.

Frank looked in the choreographer's hot little eyes, at this man who shook his head back and forth, waiting for an explanation, and jabbed four flashing fingers of his right hand into the choreographer's throat. The simple blinding assault caused the choreographer to collapse instantly into a clutching, gagging ball. His eyes bulged as he gasped for air. Cautious laughter came from the audience.

"Your manners are bad," Frank said. He turned and walked down the steps from the stage and then slowly up the aisle in Sarah's footsteps. The hoofers of Broadway could barely contain their approval.

Frank stepped back onto Forty-fifth Street, shook hands with the security guard, and turned toward Eighth Avenue. He was annoyed with himself for being violent but he knew he would not lose any sleep over assaulting such a miserable man.

"I saw what you did," Sarah said, stepping out of the doorway of an Irish bar called Molly Bloom's. "What an asshole."

All the moisture in Frank's mouth suddenly evaporated. "I'm sorry . . . I *was* an asshole."

Sarah laughed, a good throaty honest laugh, as she moved across the sidewalk toward him.

"Not you," she said. "Not you. Him! *He's* an asshole. You were absolutely Galahad." Frank stood watching her laugh under the cloudy city sky. Then watched her moist lips form his name. "Frank."

"Yeah."

"Why are you following me?"

He wanted to tell her, Because I can't keep you out of my mind. He didn't want to tell her he wanted her to lead him to Polly and Zoe.

He said, "I wanted to see you dance."

"Bullshit."

"Right, bullshit."

"You think I know where Polly is, don't you?"

"I'm not sure," he said.

"Well, I don't," she said. "But I do need to find her. And soon. If *you* find her, let me know, will you? I need my money."

He wanted to ask her how much she needed, wanted to give her all she wanted. But she wanted her own money back from a disappointing friend. He didn't want to insult her with a handout.

"I promise," he said.

"Why didn't you say hello when I came out of the gym and you were sitting there at the café?"

God, she knows my every move, Frank thought.

"I don't know."

"I could have taken your arm and kept the assholes from mouthing off at me," she said. "I would have liked that."

"Well, I . . ."

"Another time, maybe?"

"I . . . absolutely."

Sarah Cross stepped in front of Frank Dempsey and put her fingers behind his neck and got on her toes and leaned into his face and softly kissed him on the lips. She let her lush mouth remain pressed against his for several seconds. A wave of euphoria cascaded through him. He felt that every step of every day of his life had been predestined to take him to this moment when Sarah kissed him.

"Thank you," she said and dashed away from him and frantically hailed a taxi and climbed in, all in one motion. She rolled down the window. "Call me if you hear about Polly. And Frank?"

"Yes," he said, statue still.

"We really must do something about your drinking."

"Yes," he said, still thinking of her kiss as the taxi pulled away. "We must."

He watched the taxi disappear around the corner and he quickly took out his bottle and was about to put it to his lips. Then he remembered they were the lips that Sarah Cross had kissed, and he screwed the cap back on without drinking.

Then he opened it again. He was only fooling himself, trying to act normal.

33

Gail Levy hurried through the rain toward the parking area of the rehab. She felt half-dollar-sized drops soak her blouse and pants legs as she ran. The exertion aroused the healing burn on her leg. The keys for the seven-year-old Volvo were ready in her right hand when suddenly great gales of rain lashed into the swampy lawns of the sprawling estate. The pounding of the cloudburst created a swirling silver mist, and the great deafening *whoosh* of the driving mountain storm overwhelmed all other sounds.

Gail was pushing the key into her car door lock when she saw a ghostly figure disappear into the big empty A-frame gymnasium, two hundred yards up the knoll. Through the roaring haze, she could make out the white initials emblazoned on the back of the man's navy-blue T-shirt: FDNY.

She withdrew the key and started running toward the gym in the downpour. She wanted to see what Kevin was doing. He should be in his room, working on his autobiography, unloading the secrets and the guilt, the horrors of his past, all those things he'd tried to drown with the bottle.

She made her way to a spot beneath the overhang of the gym. She knew this place well, used it, with its full-length basketball court, climbing ropes, gym horse, chin bars, free weights, Nautilus and rowing machines, stationary bikes, StairMasters, treadmills. She'd spent many a sweaty, agonizing afternoon in here trying to hold back the approaching thirties.

Gail stood in the shelter of the overhang, her hair a spongy hank, staring through a side window of the gym in such a way that she could not be seen. She felt her nipples harden in the slight chill of the teeming tempest, and as thunder cracked and lightning scribbled in the dangerous sky, she folded her arms in a self-protective clasp, her flesh pebbling.

She watched as Kevin walked slowly through the half-darkened gym, his clothes dripping wet, lost in thought. He was silent and alone as he began to remove his T-shirt, pulling it up over the broad muscled shoulders, his biceps bunching into tight jumping balls, his triceps bulging like iron hand grips, his back a riot of movable knots. He hung the shirt on the gym horse and turned, revealing glistening pectorals and a flat plank of a belly, where his body tapered to a narrow waist.

His collarbones protruded across the top of his chest and he took a deep breath as he stood on his right leg and yanked off his left sneaker, dozens of muscles all collaborating in the simple motion. Then he switched legs and pulled off the other sneaker.

Stop there, Gail thought.

He did not.

Neither did she.

Lightning flashed, backlighting Kevin, and she could not stop watching him, as the rain pounded around her, seething off the mountain in slanting sheets. She knew she should either run away or confront him. Instead, she rationalized her obsession as "observation" of a client. She hugged herself tighter, as Kevin walked in stocking feet to lean against the gym horse, leaving damp footprints on the sparkling wooden floor. Then, with his back to her, he began to unbuckle his pants as Gail watched.

He's just a client, Gail kept reminding herself. A man in trouble. Like you were in trouble. Confused and lost and misguided. And you are here to help him.

She watched the dark wet denim pants yanked down over his behind, dragging his white underwear with them, revealing tan lines and the dark crevice that split his symmetrical body in half. He turned to step out of the pants, one leg at a time, and pulled the elastic band of the underwear back up above his hips and let it snap against his waist. He removed the pants and shook them briskly before dangling them from the gym horse.

He walked on muscular legs farther across the polished wood floor, the wet underwear revealing a dark mound at the crotch and the pink translucent outline of his buttocks.

He grabbed the chin bar and did ten quick pull-ups, all the muscles of his upper body bunching under his drawn skin.

Gail tried to pretend her own gulping swallow was commonplace. She barely heard the rain surging down the drainpipe next to her and the lashing of the trees. But aside from that, there was no other sound. There were no other people, just her, watching him, counselor observing client, him nearly naked as he walked to a full-length mirror and stood doing an inventory of himself.

His position in front of the mirror made Gail flatten herself even more to the edge of the window, against the wall. She saw raindrops climbing down a spiderweb like steps on a ladder.

And through the web she spied Kevin slowly slide the wet underpants down around his ankles and regard himself as he stepped out of them, wearing only his soaking socks.

She watched as he slowly cupped his genitals, as if weighing them, checking them for worth, estimating their value. He held and flipped and caught them as the muscles in his right arm rippled.

She had never watched a man examine himself like this before and it made her feel thirteen, indulging in some new sexual naughtiness.

As lightning flared again in the sky, she watched Kevin stand erect, his head tilted up high, all the muscles in his body tensing.

And then he spun, making her heart leap, and she witnessed him, in a blinding fury, attack the heavy bag she had barely noticed hanging there. His knuckles landed bare on the heavy leather bag, ripping off a ferocious series of punches. Left, right, left, right; left-left-left, right! Bang, wham, bang, wham, bang-bang-bang, wham!

And as he punched the bag, even over the pouring rain she heard warrior wails that came from some dark and private jungle inside him: grunts and echoes and howls and screams. All in counterpoint to bone and flesh on leather and sand. The rattle of the bag chains was like the music of the dead, and the punches came quicker and more wickedly, as if Kevin were hitting to the body and the head and heart and soul of every enemy in the world that had ever hurt him first.

His testicles and penis bounced and his ass muscles tightened and his feet fought for traction on the slippery floor.

Gail exhaled with almost every blow, as if on the receiving end. She could feel each vicious bang and wham go through her.

The murderer who lived in Kevin Dempsey resounded off the A-frame ceiling, mixing with the rattle of the rain and the long elaborate rolls of thunder. Gail devoured his every sight and sound: his hands, now skinned and bloody, a crimson blur; his body, a whirring machine of violence. She was frozen, terrified. Afraid he would discover her. Afraid he would not.

A spider rappeled down the web through which she spied on her client. And as Kevin finished the beating of the heavy bag with one final gentle tap and hug, she watched him melt naked to the wet and polished floor and roll into a fetal ball, his hands all raw and red, his face drained and blank.

And now Gail Levy began to run.

She ran through the teeming rain for the safety of her car, the burn on her leg rubbing raw against her tight wet jeans.

As she sat soaked and panting inside the car at last, with rain peppering the metal roof, Gail realized she had not been this frightened since her mother's funeral when she was thirteen.

34

Frank had been sitting at the window booth of the diner on Spring Street for two hours, watching the loft building where photographer Miles Barker lived in his studio. Frank had been trying to catch up with Barker, to ask him what he might know about Polly's whereabouts.

He was still thinking of Sarah's kiss. He'd forced down a grilled cheddar cheese on rye with mustard and extra pickle. He knew the pickle could hardly be considered greens, but it gave him the optical illusion of eating something healthful. He grinned, thinking of a heavy-set policewoman he once worked with in a sector car, who said her doctor told her she had to start eating lots of fruits and vegetables if she wanted to lose weight. So every day she littered the cop car with Raisinettes wrappers and Burger King french fries bags.

But Frank felt a different monster craving to be fed and the diner served booze, so he ordered himself a double screwdriver, took two thousand-milligram vitamin C tablets to help fight the pollen, but opted against the Dristan, which would make him drowsy. Vitamin C worked great against the hay fever, as it was nature's most powerful antihistamine. He'd also picked up a half pint of Smirnoff from a liquor store on Broadway, and he positioned himself against the wall of the booth below the window in such a way that he could pour the booze into the Gatorade bottle undetected. He topped it off with some of the mixed screwdriver for color.

Then he ordered his third screwdriver from the sixtyish waitress with elastic stockings and white shoes and sat watching the front of the dirty brick loft building. He'd telephoned there at eleven and heard

Barker answer and kids in the background and the sound of loud Saturday morning cartoons.

"Hello . . . hello . . . hello," Barker had said, annoyed. "Hello . . . hello . . . goodbye."

It was now one thirty in the afternoon and Frank got up and telephoned again. The phone rang three times and the answering machine picked up: "Hello, you have reached Miles Barker Studios. Please leave a message after the beep—"

Frank's heart sank, thinking he'd missed them when his eyes were on the vodka decanting. But then he heard the phone snap off.

"Hello . . . hello . . . Hell with you, bastard," he heard Barker say, puffing as if he'd run to get the phone. "Hold that elevator, Charles."

Frank heard the phone cradled and realized that Barker was now leaving on his weekend-father outing with the kids. All over New York, decent men who worked all week would be having dates with their children, gearing up for hours spent in movie theaters, forking over bundles to the rip-off candy counters, watching mindless Hollywood schlock packaged for gross laughs from American kids who thought snot and farts and food fights were the most hilarious social topics of the day.

But the men would spend every last buck just to be with their kids, from whom they'd never wanted a divorce. The entire social phenomenon of the weekend father was one of the saddest and most exploited of society's rituals. Because it went straight for the wallet, which no loving dad ever let stand in the way of his brokenhearted kids of divorce.

Frank knew the time to approach and exploit Miles Barker was on Saturday when he would be with the kids, when his defenses were down, when he could not run, when he would be anchored physically and emotionally to the topic Frank would broach.

Frank reached into his front pants pocket and pulled out a wad of bills, five thousand dollars in cash by his count, all fifties and hundreds. He had a similar wad in each of his other three pants pockets, and ten thousand in cash in his jacket pocket: a total of thirty thousand dollars.

Carrying that much cash did not worry him in the least, should it be lost or stolen. He did not want to get hurt by a mugger, but he also did not dread the loss. He certainly wouldn't fight or risk bodily harm for money. Especially dirty money. He couldn't spend too much of the million and a half dollars, or else later when he unloaded the money—

the money that had ruined his career, led to his father's suicide, and divided the family—there could be even more terrible trouble. But he figured he could spend anywhere up to fifty thousand and explain it as operating costs.

That it might now finance his finding young Zoe also posed no moral dilemma for Frank. He would never have the chance to explain to anyone that he originally took the money for the sake of the family. To preserve the family, not to destroy it. His predicament was so cockeyed he wished he had someone outside the family he could explain it to, someone he could trust, who would understand. Someone even to help him count it.

He left thirty dollars on the table to cover a nineteen-dollar tab. The change was for the waitress. She looked down at it as he walked toward the door.

"Hey, don't you want change?" the waitress asked.

"If I could, hon," Frank said with a half grin, "I'd change a lot of things."

"Me too," the waitress said. "My shoes, to start. Thanks, big guy."

Frank put on his sunglasses and the Irish walking hat. As he stepped outside onto the street from the diner, Frank saw Miles Barker, a grown man with a ponytail, walk out the door of his building holding a child by each hand.

He saw Barker look immediately for a taxi. Frank quickly crossed the street to where Barker stood and rudely placed himself directly in front of him and started to whistle and wave for a taxi himself.

"Here, now, man," Barker snapped. "You can see I was looking for a taxi here first."

Frank half turned. "Oh, sorry," he said. "Where ya goin'?"

"I don't see where that's any business of yours," Barker said.

"Merry-go-round," said his elder son, who was about five.

"And zoo," said the other one, who was about three.

Frank looked amusedly at the elder and then at the little boy, who stared up at Frank, sucking his thumb the way Kevin had that night in the yard. Then Frank looked at an annoyed Miles Barker.

"I bet your dad buys you anything you want," Frank said.

"Listen, mate, I'm trying to have a day out with me kids," Barker said.

"I'm sorry," Frank said and let the first taxi roll up. He opened the back door and bowed to Miles Barker and waved him inside. "Your taxi, sir."

"Thanks," Barker said, nodding, embarrassed, confused, awkwardly loading the two kids into the back seat.

The taxi pulled away and Frank hailed a second one. He was tempted to say "Follow that cab!" like in the movies.

"The zoo," Frank said.

"Where this is?" asked the taxi driver. Frank looked at his hack ID card, which bore an unpronounceable Pakistani name. Another struggling immigrant, Frank thought, like Big Paulie had been.

"It's in Central Park," Frank said. "It's uptown. It's green. Like dirty money."

Frank remembered that Sarah had ordered him a salad using that same description. The taxi driver started laughing.

"Green like dirty money, green like dirty money," he said over and over as he drove uptown.

You're looking for a missing kid, Frank thought, in a city where cabbies can't even find an elephant.

35

Mike Dempsey threw the punch with all his might, in an upward lunge, coming off the bench in the precinct locker room. It caught the cop named Melbourne under the tip of his nose, and he heard a bone or cartilage pop. It sent the bigger man reeling back across the aisle, a whine singing out of his lungs as he crashed into a row of lockers. Melbourne was wearing just an undershirt and Jockey briefs and had his gun belt loosely tied around his waist.

He sank to the stone floor, blood pouring from both nostrils.

"You hit like a pussy," Melbourne said, getting to his feet, throwing a punch back at Mike. Mike ducked under it and came back with three more clubbing overhand rights, badly thrown, but with enough arm power to knock several of Melbourne's front teeth onto the locker room floor. His jaw hung to the side of his face, clearly broken. His eyes rolled back in his head.

"Anyone else?" Mike shouted, jumping up on the changing bench, challenging the four other men in the locker room. "Anyone fuckin' else have any fuckin' thing to say about me or my brothers or my family?"

The men remained silent. One, a big square-headed patrolman named Lauderbach, attended to Melbourne, who was gagging on his own blood now and moaning and babbling what sounded like "Ma."

Fuck him, Mike thought, rubbing his knuckles. I hope he's out for a month, cost him a fortune in lost overtime. He talks like that about the Dempseys, leave him for the fuckin' sweeper, as the old man used to say.

A sergeant named Rampling walked into the locker room, at twenty-seven one of the youngest sergeants on the job. Mike always thought Rampling's confirmation name should have been Scumbag. Rampling said he'd heard the argument and then the commotion.

"I want an ambulance and every detail," Rampling said to all of them, focusing on Mike, who wiped the blood off his hand as he stepped down from the bench.

"We had a difference of opinion," Mike said, breathing hard.

"It started as a joke, Sarge," Lauderbach said, shrugging. "Ya know, Melbourne ranking on Mike's family. The usual. He said Mike had a father who hung himself. His brother Frank was a thief on the way to the joint, his brother Kevin is in the rubber-room farm for freezing at a fire. That kinda shit. But then he wouldn't stop. He asked Mike what Dempsey family plans *he* had in store for the taxpayer."

"Did Officer Melbourne strike Officer Dempsey?" Rampling asked, emotionless, staring straight at Mike Dempsey.

"Well, no, but he provoked it," Lauderbach said.

"Dempsey, do you have anything to add?"

"I don't have to take this shit," Mike said. "I'd put either of my brothers up against anybody—"

"Did Melbourne strike you?" Rampling asked in a flat even voice.

Mike said, "He couldn't strike a match on his wife's ass."

"You're suspended without pay pending a hearing on a charge of assault on a fellow officer," Rampling said. He held out both hands, palms up. "Gun, badge, ID card, please."

As he handed over the tools of his trade, Mike's first thought was where he would get the money for this month's mortgage.

Mike walked through the precinct, feeling naked and vulnerable without the gun and badge. He strode past the silent men who watched him go. Past the wanted posters on the wall, past the muster room where the new shift was gathering to go out on patrol, past the faces of men he'd pounded the beat with on dark terrifying streets.

He walked out to the parking lot to the family Chevrolet station wagon. There was a payment due on the car, too. And Bridie was saying the kids needed more back-to-school clothes and winter coats. She'd have to cash in the Christmas Club early for some of that.

Frank's greed led Dad to hang up, and now if Melbourne chose to press charges he could have me terminated from the job, Mike thought. The pension, the medical insurance, life insurance, the credit line—gone. With no skills, where do I work? No college, no connections, no seed money.

Where do I go after civil service is out of the picture? Who pays the tuition, summer camp, mortgage, car payments, insurance, medical bills? I'll have to go work for the wife's arrogant mother-fuckin' mick old man. Him, ingrate import, reminding me, Mike Dempsey, American citizen, every day, in that sickening Kerryman brogue he refuses to lose, that it's his fuckin' "shillin' " feeding and clothing my American kids.

Refuse his fuckin' donkey "shillin' " and the kids will suffer.

Then Mike Dempsey thought it could be worse. He could be like poor Kevin, with no kid to send back to school at all.

36

Frank watched Miles Barker leaning on a hurricane fence, waving to his children as they spun around on the Central Park carousel. Rain clouds darkened the sky. Parents and maids began leading their children from the park. The weekend father was eating his children's Crackerjacks and occasionally snapping a photo with a Canon Sure Shot. Frank walked up to him, still wearing the hat and sunglasses.

"Imagine life without them," Frank said, leaning on the fence next to Barker.

Barker dropped the few loose Crackerjacks he had in his hands and looked at Frank in astonishment. Two rat-colored pigeons fluttered instantly to retrieve the candied popcorn.

"Hey, what the fuck gives here, mate?" Miles Barker said. "This some sort of gimmick? If it is, it isn't fucking funny."

"Calm down, Miles," Frank said as the carousel music lofted through the empty overcast afternoon. "No gimmick. I'm just appealing to your fatherhood here."

"You know my name? Look, are you following me for my ex-wife? My support is paid up-to-date, for Christ sakes. I never miss a bloody week, I don't."

"I'm not here about *your* wife or kids," Frank said. "I'm here about the child of a friend of yours who happens to be married to my brother."

Frank took off the shades and hat and looked at Miles, directly in the eye. Distant thunder bellowed.

"You're Kevin Dempsey's brother," Miles said. "The cop from the newspapers. Christ, why didn't you come out and say so?"

"I needed to know if you were meeting her," Frank said.

"You mean Polly hasn't shown up yet?" Barker asked. "Since the party? Bloody 'ell, that's almost three weeks ago, isn't it?"

"Yeah," Frank said. "But we know she's alive, and I'm still looking for her. She took off with my brother's kid, Zoe, my goddaughter. She says she isn't coming back."

"Sounds like she's left orbit this time," Barker said.

"This time?"

"She's a bit of a space walker," he said. "You know: disappears and then turns up, lost somewhere. On a magazine swimsuit shoot on Montserrat once, she set sail with a rock-and-roll drummer right on deadline. She turned up without airfare on Paradise Island, no passport, no ID. The drummer was busted by their coast guard for poaching historical artifacts. She's a nutter. That was years ago. . . . But stealing a man's kid? Jesus Christ. If anyone ever—"

The carousel was ready to stop. The kids were screaming for more and Miles Barker ran over and handed the ticket taker two more tickets, kissed both sons, handed the younger his Crackerjacks, and the merry-go-round started up again, playing a waltz by Strauss.

He walked back to Frank, who gulped from the Gatorade bottle and put a Tic Tac in his mouth for his breath. Frank's eyes were ablaze with pollen and the tip of his nose itched. He rubbed it briskly.

"Where would she go?" Frank asked, offering a Tic Tac which Barker declined. "She doesn't have the baby's passport, so she has to be in the U.S."

"Don't be too sure," Miles Barker said. "Jesus, I hate to get involved in any of this. It sounds like such a mess. I have enough problems with my own ex-wife. Polly has always been so close . . . but just because she doesn't have the baby's U.S. passport doesn't mean she couldn't have gone back home to England. Or anywhere else, for that matter."

"How so?" Frank was intrigued.

"Polly is still a British subject," Miles Barker said. "Never became a U.S. citizen. So, as her daughter, Zoe is entitled to a British passport too. You have absolutely no idea how fucking insane it is to try to fight an international custody battle."

Frank quickly made a mental note to contact someone he knew, an old friend of Big Paulie's, to find out if Polly got Zoe a British passport.

"Polly an old girlfriend?" Frank asked.

Barker was silent a moment as he stared at his two kids. "No," he said. "But I wish she were. I'd like those memories instead of the fantasy. I was in love with her for a long time. But we never did get it on. I was still in love with her when I married my wife, who was up the pole at the time. Maybe that's why the marriage didn't last, I don't know. But I've long since gotten over it. . . . Still, I *like* Polly, she's a *friend,* as bonkers as she is. I didn't know her to mess with any particular bloke either, since she married your brother. She just attracts them. You know."

Frank nodded and looked at Barker's kids.

"See those little guys?" Frank said. "What if your wife just up and disappeared with them tomorrow? Decided she didn't want you to see them anymore? Vanished. Wouldn't you want someone like me to help you find them?"

Barker swallowed, his eyes reflecting the spinning carousel on which two enormous elements of his life howled in youthful ecstasy.

"I live for these weekends with my boys," Barker said. "No one knows the pain a man feels when he can't see his kids. Even though we're divorced, I have to be *nice* to my loathsome ex-wife on top of paying her more money than she deserves, or else—"

"Else what?"

"Or else she'll just not give me the kids," he said. "Simple as that. Just says, 'No, can't have 'em this week, pal.' Then I have to go back to court. I have to prove I am current with my support. Prove I don't abuse my kids. Prove she didn't give me the kids, when she doesn't. All she has to do is say I threatened her, and they'll give her and the kids an order of protection. She doesn't need *proof* that I threatened her! I have to prove I *didn't,* because in America the man is always the asshole in family court."

"I can tell you from experience, a lot of them are," Frank said. "Deadbeats and woman beaters."

"Or she can say they had a cold," Barker said, lost in his rage. "Or kept them home for a special school project. Or say she had to take them to a doctor, dentist, shopping. Or that I was drunk or late or never showed up. She can, and has, made up any lie she feels like. She rips up the child support check and says she never received it. If she does that often enough, they'll put me in a cage. The judge will always rule in her favor. Because she's the mother and I'm the fucking low-bred man. It's so fucking unfair!"

He sounded like a dozen divorced guys Frank had heard over the years, reduced to tears in precinct locker rooms, some of whom ended up swallowing their guns rather than be ruled by judges and lawyers and bitter women. There was, of course, an even larger group of victims of divorce, those women who were ripped off by divorce lawyers and stiffed by deadbeat fathers. But it seemed grossly unfair to Frank that decent fathers paid the price for the sins of the mutts.

"How'd you like it if she claimed they weren't yours?" Frank asked.

Barker's eyes popped open in horror, and veins rose in his neck. He hesitated a moment, staring at Frank, considering the possibility. "No! She didn't say that to Kevin, did she?"

Frank nodded. Yes.

Barker gazed back at his kids. Without turning to Frank, he said, "Morton, Polly's arsehole banker friend, is meeting her father in Boston on Monday. Maybe Polly'll be there to see him. Morton is involved in some sort of deal with her dad. Some damn biotech research project. Get-rich-quick scheme. His specialty. There are other investors. Morton wanted to know if I could round up a few models to meet the investors in Bean Town."

"How friendly are you with Morton?" Frank asked.

"He puts together investment groups and takes a cut off the top," he said. "He dabbles in high finance. In Boston it's medical research. His rich friends like to meet the top models. And I know all of them. I'm not a pimp. But some of his clients have big ad budgets and they use top models to promote their products. I get the photo gigs in return for getting gorgeous single ladies to go to big parties. It's business. Sometimes they marry these so-called investors. Sometimes they marry firefighters from Brooklyn."

"And take off with their kids," Frank said.

"That's beyond outrage," Barker said, balling two fists. "If that's what Polly did, thank God I never married her. Because for that I know I could kill someone. I love my kids. I mean, I really, really love them."

"I can see that," Frank said.

"Thanks," Barker said, smiling proudly.

"Where does Morton stay in Boston?" Frank asked.

"Always the same place: the Bostonian, right in the center of Quincy Market. The conventions are usually at the Sheraton. But he doesn't like to sleep where he steals. I like Boston, but the Brit accent doesn't go over big up there outside of Yankee circles."

Frank hadn't been to Boston in twelve years, since he picked up a pedophile fugitive on a vice warrant. Boston was a city he remembered, even from back then, when he only drank on weekends, for its great saloons.

The carousel stopped again and the attendant unstrapped Barker's kids and they ran to him, the little guy scaling his father's leg like a climbing pole, his arms going around Barker's neck. The older boy took Barker by the hand.

Frank wordlessly took the Sure Shot camera from Barker's wrist, backed away, and snapped several frames of the father with his sons. Smiling. They made a hell of a nice family, Frank thought, as he handed the camera back to Barker, the whole gesture solidifying their masculine bond.

"I like your brother," Barker said to Frank. "We don't move in the same circles but there's no pretense in him. He must be insane about his baby."

"Can I trust you to avoid telling Morton I'll be watching him?" Frank asked.

"Mum's the word," Barker said. "If Polly stole your brother's kid and Morton's involved, I'd help you do surveillance. Believe me, I know about being a man without his kids. Steals your very soul."

Frank liked him. He shook his hand and walked through Central Park and pulled on his hat and shades as thunder banged and the first raindrops began to fall. He was grateful; the rain would wash the pollen out of the air. He wondered about the pollen count this time of year in Boston.

But first he had some financial business to take care of in New York.

37

Kevin Dempsey searched for his life.

Demanding his autobiography, in longhand, in a weekend, had to be Gail Levy's idea of solitary confinement.

His life, the road he'd traveled—with all its detours and dead ends, stalls and starts, some great mileage and near-death crashes—was so complicated. And yet when Kevin was compelled to commit the journey to paper, it also seemed so aimlessly simple. Kevin thought of it as just a series of joy rides and getaways, a series of fuckups that were somehow hung together by a string of accidents that led to this human junkyard.

He had picked up only one worthwhile passenger along the way, and that was Zoe. Now Zoe had also departed.

That was the best he could assemble in his head.

He read some of the guidebook introduction for ideas:

> We require a "fresh" autobiography at the beginning of each new treatment episode or return to AA following a relapse. The autobiography is the best tool to disclose hurts, deep dark secrets, and self-destructive patterns in a man's life that continually lead to relapse. It helps him to see, clearly and in his own writing, many things in his life that require his accepting or changing them in order for him to stay sober.

"The best tool against relapse around here is the fucking food," Kevin said to his roommate, Walter, who was reading a newspaper. Outside their window, early evening rain beat a drum roll into the trees.

"Most people I know come back here *for* the food," Walter said. "It's the best rehab food in New York, believe me. I tried 'em all. Twice."

Kevin thought, I must be making progress. That's the longest conversation I've had with Walter since I got here.

The guidebook asked for earliest childhood memories up to adolescence, a description of home environment, first drug or alcohol usage, first sexual affair ("Were you drinking?," "With male or female?") Then it asked for more specifics: "Chemical dependency history and progression, to include why you are here; employment history; children, stepchildren, wives, marriages, affairs."

Kevin opened the notebook and spread his raw, swollen hands over the blank prairie of the first page. It was smooth and unblemished, like little Zoe's skin. He knew he had to get Zoe out of his mind. She was gone; she was someone else's child. He would have to get used to that, the way he had come to terms with his father's death. The pain would be there, palpable and physical, like his damaged hands, but it would someday find a peaceful resting place in the heart.

Sitting there now, propped up in the stiff bed in the room with a laconic stranger, Kevin knew that when he left here his life would be as blank again as the page spread before him.

He did not feel the remotest desire for a drink. He knew this didn't mean his drinking problem had suddenly disappeared. He was certain now he did have a problem with alcohol, perhaps one that came with the family genes. Some genetic link that magnetized his father to drink, like his father before him, and his grandmother's father, who drank himself into an early grave, and so on back into the moody Celtic centuries, evolving into a lasting and hereditary boozy Dempsey gene pool. Frank drank like a big-mouth trout. Mike watched his beer as closely as a diabetic watches his sugar intake, always aware the killer spark was there, ready to ignite. Margie, thankfully, was like Mom and rarely drank. She was obviously blessed with their mother's mother's gene pool, which thankfully didn't resemble the Dempsey side.

But Kevin's mind was clear now, unclouded. In here you did not worry about the job, bills, the IRS, the car, brothers, sister, friends, enemies, neighbors, the bank. You were told to think only of yourself. Get yourself straight, and the rest will follow.

And when he did focus on himself, on this man named Kevin Dempsey, clear-eyed and with mental clarity, he did a self-inventory. Your lifelong friend Anthony Scala, a noted doctor, has shown you scientific evidence proving you are not Zoe's father. If you are not her father, then Polly has been unfaithful and a liar from the beginning. You cannot blame an innocent child because she too has been duped. And Polly is such a sick and diabolical bitch she is not worthy of your revenge.

So wipe the innocent young child and the wicked woman from your life. Do that at least in here. Leave Polly in flames on the dance floor where you met her five years ago and move on. Consider her another pile of ash from a roaring blaze now gutted. Find another life for Kevin Dempsey, one with limits but one that at least will be the truth.

Still, when it came time to write the conventional autobiography, Kevin was in a bog. The pen would not produce the events of his life. The first person would not flow through the nib. The "I" in his past life belonged to someone else. He needed to find a new "I."

He was now a man without wife or child, forever judged as a man incapable of having children. That made him immensely different from the man who would have written an autobiography just three weeks before.

How do I write the truth about a life that was make-believe? Kevin asked himself. I never knocked up Lucy. So how can I retell the pain that event caused in the other Kevin Dempsey's life? It was bogus. I've been duped into soul-searching and guilt for something for which I was never responsible.

And, likewise, the new Kevin Dempsey had never seen his own child born as he thought he had. Never held his tiny newborn baby in his hands. Had never changed his child's diaper or soothed his blood baby in the terrifying night. Kevin Dempsey had been called Daddy, but by a little child who was not *his*.

There is no *real* life to write as *my* autobiography, he thought.

His life had been a fiction, a colossal practical joke, a stroll through Let's-pretend.

But here I am, Kevin thought. And here I don't wanna be. So fuck it. Play the game. Do it. Give Gail what she wants. I'll write my life as the fiction it's been.

As his pen touched the blank enormity of the page that was supposed to chronicle his life, Kevin Dempsey felt the ink flow out in curlicues he could not control. Like the wedge on a Ouija board, it took him where his fate desired, uncharted and unguided, the words coming one after the other, like increments of hope trying to bury the deceit.

He wrote as the rain fell outside his window. He never heard Walter say "dinner." He wrote until he fell asleep.

38

Frank Dempsey stepped into the bar called the Fifth Amendment on Fifth Avenue and Twentieth Street in Brooklyn a few minutes before ten at night. It was located by Greenwood Cemetery, across the street from Pirino and Brothers Moving and Storage.

Pinebox Pirino sat in a reclining chair in the back room of the bar, where he always was these days, watching a big-screen TV tuned to

CNN, until dinnertime, when he went down the block to eat half a pound of macaroni, a green salad with squeezed lemon, and a small piece of broiled fish. Then he'd return to look at more CNN.

The doctors had told him he couldn't eat meat anymore because of the cholesterol.

"A gangster who can't eat meat is like a Chink without chopsticks," Frank heard Pinebox saying on hidden tape to his goombah stooges after his first heart attack ten years before. So, starting in the hospital room, Pinebox had kept eating veal marsala and pork and meatballs and tripe and salami and steak until the triple bypass. But even then, Pinebox wouldn't admit he was following doctor's orders when he finally gave up the flesh.

"Meat is now bad luck," he said. "After Joey Gallo got killed in a clam house, I gave up shellfish. And after Paul Castellano got it outside Sparks Steakhouse, I put down my steak knife for good. No more meat. Strictly a loaves-and-fishes man now."

Pinebox also claimed he didn't like violence and only got his nickname because of the proximity of his territory to Greenwood Cemetery. Others in the neighborhood believed that the origin of his moniker had more to do with his sending so many enemies and disrespectful deadbeats there in plain pine boxes as permanent residents. Or maybe it was because he also had Pirino's Funeral Home down the street, a limousine service, and a headstone showroom, next door to a florist he secretly owned. Pinebox would have you whacked and then he'd get paid for the funeral and the marker and the flowers. It was common knowledge that he was so cheap that after a wake he had his workers disassemble the funeral wreaths and resell the flowers as Valentine's Day or Mother's Day bouquets.

He claimed that, as a bookmaker and loan shark, he helped people in financial need. Only when people refused to pay him back would he resort to violence, to save face. That was his boast.

But Frank did not like Pinebox. He found no glamour or humor in the mob: wise guys who were for the most part dumb lazy bastards who loaned illegally gotten money at exorbitant rates to poor saps who couldn't pay their mortgages after they lost their money gambling to people like Pinebox. You bet with him. You lost. Then you went to him for a loan before you lost the house and the wife and the kids and your dignity.

He would then extort half your check and make you run numbers for him until you paid him off, which usually was a lifelong indentureship.

There was no glamour there, Frank thought, just avarice.

But here Frank was, seeking out Pinebox, who was back from dinner, sitting in his recliner in the back room of the Fifth Amendment eating Ben and Jerry's Cherry Garcia low-fat yogurt and watching Larry King on CNN.

"Dempsey, have a seat. Want some yogurt?"

"I'll have a double vodka with water," Frank said.

"Shit'll kill ya," Pinebox said, nodding to a muscle-bound kid with tattoos.

"So will gambling," Frank said. "Ask my old man's ghost."

"Yo, on the Erie Lackawanna," Pinebox said, tugging his earlobe to indicate the place was bugged, narrowing his eyes as if to say, You crazy?

"Let's do a walk-and-talk," Frank said. "I don't have much time."

Pinebox nodded and got up and walked with Frank toward the front door, taking his pint of Cherry Garcia and a bone-handled spoon with him. The muscle-bound kid walked toward them with the drink. Frank took it from the kid without saying thanks. He knew that manners in front of these people would be misconstrued as deference.

More than anything else, Frank loathed the idea that in the eyes of the law he was now no better than these bums. Even lower, since he was a lawman who had crossed the line.

Frank remembered, as he strolled through this so-called den of honor, that more mobsters had broken *omerta,* their bullshit code of silence, in the last decade than in the previous century. Just like most young suburban-bred cops now broke the blue wall of silence whenever they faced jail time and life with blacks, of whom they were terrified without badge, baton, and gun.

But Frank had come to Pinebox because this is where people from the neighborhood went when they couldn't go to Dime Savings for financial help. This was the Dirty Money Store. This was where Frank's father always went: to gamble, borrow, pay back. This is where Big Paulie Dempsey learned to tie the knot in his noose, Frank thought. The only thing he'd ever won here was the mausoleum he lay in next to Mom.

"Un gots," Frank cursed to the half-filled bar as he left. When he

was around these people, his speech patterns changed, as if there were still enough proud cop in him that he had to climb down three flights of stairs to be on their level. He also had to prove to Pinebox that he wasn't frightened of him.

"You losing what few marbles you got left or what?" Pinebox said when they stepped outside, eating a half spoonful of the yogurt. "You don't talk open in my joint. Even out here, talk so only me and you understand, *capice*? They use directional microphones from the graveyard, the rooftops. And these video cameras film you talking, and they get deaf and dummies to lip-read what you say. So talk like this was a fuckin' IRS audit."

"How you know I'm not wired?" Frank asked and took a sip of booze.

"Because I know you're in trouble," Pinebox said, chewing a Bing cherry with his front teeth. "But you didn't come here looking for a loan."

Frank allowed himself a smile as the gangster took another heaping spoonful of yogurt, this one laden with chocolate slivers.

"You're in the moving business," Frank said. "I want you to move something for me."

"You, I never liked," Pinebox said, as he chewed. "Not when Big Paulie was alive; less, now he's dead. But I'll listen because I liked your father. So this piano you want moved, how big is it?"

"A grand piano."

"The famous one? Plays spic music?"

"Yes."

"Who does it need to be delivered to?"

"Its original owner."

"I see," Pinebox said. "That's one and a half pianos then?"

Frank smiled, thinking of the absurdity of some Fed listening on a directional microphone as they discussed one and a half pianos.

"You *are* as dumb as you look," Frank said, shaking his head. "And you didn't like my father, you liked his money. You used him. He was a sick man, and you used him."

They strolled down Brooklyn's Fifth Avenue. There were no museums here like on Manhattan's Fifth Avenue. No ice-skaters, skyscrapers, or tourists. Frank sipped his vodka from the glass as they passed a pork store, a bakery, a candy store, and a liquor store, all of which Pinebox secretly owned. And the Pirino Brothers Moving and Storage across the street, serving as Pinebox's front and money laundry.

"Way I hear it, this piano of yours, it has no serial number. It's clean," Pinebox said, scraping the bottom of the yogurt container. "So why can't you could move it yourself?"

"I need a moving company that can offer me insurance," Frank said. "Insurance that the deal ends with the delivery, *capice*? Your name is gold on the street as a moving man of his word."

"Yeah," Pinebox said, licking the spoon. "So, what's my commission?"

"I gotta move it fast and I gotta know I can trust you," Frank said. "They're waiting for it. Time is running out."

"Why me?" Pinebox asked. "There's other moving companies. Hungry ones. You don't like me. You never did. I don't like you neither. Maybe you don't think so, but I did like your old man. He had fucking heart. For a donkey. I know what a sick heart is. He was sick over you and this piano that only plays sad spic songs."

"Don't give me that horseshit dago routine about family and friends and a code of honor," Frank said, waving his hand as they strolled. "I'm offering you a business deal. You want to move the piano or not?"

"I could see to it that you play a fucking eternal harp, ya know," Pinebox said.

"Pinebox, you're a greedy half-dead old man who wouldn't die happy if you thought you passed up a quarter you could've had. And we're probably talking fifteen percent vig here."

Pinebox stopped on the sidewalk in front of the fence overlooking the Prospect Expressway and began to laugh.

"Now you sound like your father," Pinebox said. Frank was surprised, sipped his drink. "He got away with talking to me like that because he was a cop. Because he was from the neighborhood. Because I also happen to believe half the customers are always half right—as long as they lose. Which he made a habit of. But I did like him. And he talked the same way to me, only he had the Irish lilt in his voice. How come they don't make immigrants like me and him no more?"

Pinebox took out a wrinkled handkerchief and blew his nose. Without being asked, the kid with the muscle shirt hurried over and took the empty yogurt carton from his hand and carried it back into the bar.

Frank took a sip of the drink and watched the headlights booming in from the Gowanus Expressway onto the Prospect, working people and shoppers heading home from downtown Brooklyn and Manhattan, rolling out into the heartland of Brooklyn, into Flatbush and Canarsie and Sheepshead Bay.

"I don't like doing business with the spics," Pinebox said.

"If the piano is too heavy for you . . ." Frank shrugged.

"I didn't say that," Pinebox said.

Pinebox looked up at Frank, his hands in his pants pockets. Frank saw the muscle-bound kid watching from the doorway of the Fifth Amendment on the corner.

Frank was silent for a few moments, and the two men watched the headlights disappear under the overpass. Frank drained his drink and nibbled at an ice cube. His tongue was cold.

"Okay. But I ain't moving it for *you,*" Pinebox said. "Get that straight. I'm moving it for Big Paulie Dempsey's son, *capice*?"

"Fine," Frank said.

The two men listened to the automobiles rumbling underneath them for several more moments, as shoppers passed on the sidewalk and Pinebox nodded hello to the elderly Italian widows in black who remained in the changing neighborhood that once resembled an Old World hamlet.

"I wanted to go to the wake but how would it look?" said Pinebox. "Me at a cop's wake with the Feds watching?"

Frank ignored the remark as empty sentiment.

"And the law?" Pinebox asked.

"I'll deal with that."

Pinebox shrugged. "So you want me to contact this guy who wants his piano back? These people, their idea of a sit-down is chair float in a shark tank. We don't speak the same lingo."

"The dollar is fluent in all languages," Frank said. "My bet is they'll talk to you. I need you to get a promise from them that the deal is squashed, final."

"I can broker my own deal for my end with the spics?"

"Yeah," Frank said. "But if you cross me, remember, I have absolutely nothing to lose. I don't care who's listening or filming. I have never killed another human being in my life. The idea repulses me. But if you cross me, you won't have to worry about the Fifth *Amendment* anymore. I will break the Fifth *Commandment.* I'll kill ya."

Pinebox looked down at the cars, hundreds of them rolling into the sprawling, changing, violent borough of two and a half million people with over a thousand murders a year. "You couldn't kill time," Pinebox said. "I'll see what I can do."

"Thanks," Frank said. "But forgive me if I keep in mind you won't be doing it as some benevolent tax write-off."

"What the fuck you want, egg in your beer?"

"My old man used to say that," Frank said, and drained the melted ice from the glass.

"Where is this piano anyhow?"

Frank smiled. "I'll let you know, when you say it's time to move it."

Pinebox tapped Frank's empty glass, took it from him. "You better watch how much of this shit you put in your body, kid," he said. "You don't look so hot. I don't want you dying before we get to move this piano back."

Frank nodded and said he'd be in touch. He walked down Prospect Avenue to the subway. Even with thirty grand in your pocket, you could not get a yellow cab in Brooklyn.

It was Saturday night, and he would have to find a liquor store in Manhattan to buy a double order. He still wanted to duck Summers, and he needed a place to spend the night.

39

Zoe watched the bird flying over Mommy's new house. The man that Zoe's mommy called Zoe's new daddy watched too.

"What kind of bird is that?" Zoe asked him.

"A seagull," the man said.

"Is he the one that brings babies?"

"No, a stork brings babies, Zoe," the man said.

"Does a seagull bring back daddies?" Zoe asked.

The man did not answer. Zoe's mommy came into the room and heard what Zoe said.

"Don't ask so many questions, Zoe," Zoe's mommy said.

"I want to know when Daddy is coming," Zoe said.

"He isn't coming back," Zoe's mommy said.

"Oh, yes, he is," Zoe said, abruptly sobbing, then running into her new bedroom. She ran away from Zoe's mommy and the man mommy said was her new daddy.

40

Kevin Dempsey put the spiral notebook on Gail Levy's desk. He saw her glance at it and then stare at his raw and bandaged hands. Kevin noticed she had on the blue jeans again. That meant her burn was healing.

"Want to talk about your hands?"

"Not really," he said. "It's nothing."

"I watched you in the gym," she said.

He shifted his head, regarding her from a cocked angle, saw her distractedly looping her fingers around a ballpoint pen.

"In the rain?"

"Yeah."

"Did you get wet?"

Gail stopped twirling the pen. Their eyes locked, glistened, probed, dared, penetrated. Gail broke the stare. Lit a quick cigarette.

"I think that heavy bag you were beating was you," Gail said, exhaling.

"How do you know it wasn't you?"

Gail filled her electric kettle and reached for the jar of instant coffee. It was empty. "Why are you afraid of me?"

"You have power over me," Kevin said.

"Woman power?" She looked in the top drawer of the filing cabinet for more coffee but came up empty.

"No, not that," he said. "But you control a lot of what's left of my future."

"I have to go get some coffee," Gail said, moving for the door. "But hold that thought. Think about what you'd like that future to be."

He turned to watch her go, in the faded dungarees. She glanced back and caught him looking. Neither said anything.

After Gail left, Kevin picked up the postcard she had been fingering. It was a photograph of a contemporary painting, splashed with color and filled with phallic symbols. Kevin thought it looked like a man trying to turn Georgia O'Keeffe inside out. He suddenly had an image of Frank marking off time on one of those O'Keeffe calendars in a jail cell, and a shiver rattled through him.

He turned the card over and saw that Gail had been invited to a Fifty-seventh Street gallery opening in three weeks, of a new artist named Richard Smith. A blurb from *Art News* said, "Smith might have picked the lock to the twenty-first century with these new paintings."

Kevin was looking at the painting on the card again when Gail walked in carrying a jar of instant coffee. She saw him fingering the postcard.

"You always read other people's mail?"

"You always spy on people in the rain?"

"When I get paid for it."

"You know the artist?"

"Yeah," Gail said. "What do you think of the painting?"

"Looks like a bunch of dicks in a crayon box," Kevin said bluntly.

Gail stifled a laugh as she spooned coffee into a cup and poured water from the steaming kettle. She took it and sat down at the desk.

"I'll have to tell him that."

"You like his work?"

"Let's talk about you," Gail said. "Your future, remember?"

"We finished with my past already?"

"That's for your autobiography," she said. "Ordinarily, I'd have you read it to me. But I see yours is a bit too long for that. I'll take it home."

"Will you read it in bed?"

"I beg your pardon?"

"If you do, think of me and—"

"Kevin, get a grip."

"—and don't smoke."

"Oh," Gail said, momentarily flustered. "Right."

She picked up the ashtray and snubbed out her cigarette for want of something better to do with her hands.

"Why don't you just quit altogether?" Kevin said, sarcastically mimicking the jargon of a rehab counselor. "Cold turkey. You're much too vital a person to violate your face with an ugly butt. You must have low esteem. Admit you are helpless in the face of tobacco and caffeine."

Gail placed the ashtray back on the desktop and leaned in closer to Kevin, who sat on his chair facing her, his right foot resting on his left knee.

"My esteem is not in question here," she assured him. "Yours is. The focus is supposed to be on you, not my bad habits, whatever they may be."

"Sweets is your other one, I bet," Kevin said.

Gail dropped her mouth open in disbelief. "Hey, Dempsey, pal, *client,* get it straight," she said slowly. "You are the fly in the bottle here. Not me. Hear me?"

"Okay," Kevin said.

"So, you want to talk again about why a guy with hero medals freezes at this particular fire?"

Kevin was suddenly subdued, her painful words derailing him. She was talking about *him* again, about the Kevin Dempsey who didn't exist. She still didn't get it.

"I'm not who or what I was," Kevin said.

"The old brown cow, she ain't what she used to be either," Gail said, riffling the pages of the spiral notebook without looking at them. "That's why you're here. Tell me why you've changed."

"Look, it's one thing to be a sap, to be cuckolded by another man," Kevin said. "But to find out your kid is someone else's, that changes everything."

He didn't tell her about Lucy Carbone or about what Anthony said about his sterility. He didn't want to let anyone outside the family besides Carmine know that.

"That's how it affects your past," Gail said. "But *what* does it change about today? Tomorrow?"

"My place on the world map," Kevin said. "I'm no longer a father. Never was. You don't get it, do you?"

"No," Gail said. "I'm not a progenitor either. Yet. That make me take a back seat to the human race too? Do only mothers and fathers count?"

"If that's how you planned and lived your life, yes," Kevin said. "I never imagined myself without imagining myself as a father. Fatherhood is more important to me than money, my job, women, great literature, music, or art."

"Macho-babble," she said.

"It's how we differ," Kevin said. "You AA people believe in a traditional God. Some amorphous vapor. I believe in children."

"Right now, right here, I'm interested in *you,* one day at a time, sober, baby," Gail said. "In here, I don't deal with aftercare or afterlife. No matter what abracadabra gets you through the night."

Gail lifted the autobiography and opened it.

"Why don't you read me some of this?"

Kevin abruptly slammed the cover closed. "No," he said, realizing his movement had startled her.

"Okay, easy."

"Sorry," Kevin said. "But I'd rather you read it alone. I don't want your Richard Smith to see it."

"No one else will read this," Gail said. "That's not a promise, it's a strict professional vow. And what the hell makes you think Richard Smith is anything but a casual acquaintance?"

"He sent the invitation to your home address," Kevin said.

Gail just looked at Kevin and blinked several times, as if she needed incremental pauses to soak in what he was saying.

"I think you're too concerned about my personal business and not enough about your own," Gail said.

"I'm sorry," Kevin said. "I'm just not used to being suddenly single."

"Do you always try to corner women when you meet them?"

"Maybe it comes from the ring," Kevin said.

"Wedding ring?" she asked, confused.

"Boxing," he said. "Same thing."

"Oh," Gail said. "Then you see women as opponents?"

"Aren't they? Aren't men and women in opposite corners? Waiting to see who falls first?"

Gail picked up a cigarette, then thought better of it and slipped it back in the pack. Kevin watched her every move as she walked around the desk, over to the front door. Wearing the blue jeans.

"This round is over," Gail said. "Go to a neutral corner. Your family is here to see you."

Kevin hesitated as he stood in front of her. The two looked in each other's eyes again.

"You only go to a neutral corner after you've knocked somebody down," Kevin said as he stepped out into the hallway. He watched her close the door behind him with a click. He thought he heard the strike of a match.

41

Frank Dempsey had spent Saturday night in the Days Inn on Fifty-seventh Street. After seeing Miles Barker, he'd stopped in a Chinese restaurant named China Moon on the Upper East Side, two blocks from the British embassy. He went to see a bartender named Buzzy Furie, a guy Big Paulie had grown up with in Belfast. Buzzy Furie was an understated character of very few words who had been plugged into the local IRA fund-raising operations before the Northern Ireland cease-fire. Buzzy Furie, Frank knew from his father, had a contact inside the British embassy. Many a time when a Provo was on the run and targeted by a joint FBI-MI6 task force, Buzzy Furie would receive word and the wanted man would soon be back underground before an arrest could be made.

Frank wanted no such classified information. He only wanted to know if his sister-in-law Polly Dempsey, maiden name Edgeworth, had applied for a British passport for his niece Zoe Dempsey.

Frank had swallowed two double vodkas and nibbled some rice noodles at the bar, and Buzzy Furie told him to call Monday to see what he'd learned.

Before falling asleep later in the night, he'd called Margie to ask her to pick him up for the drive upstate to visit Kevin and then drop him at La Guardia. It was Sunday, so Margie wasn't working. Mike drove up separately in his own car from Staten Island after a big argument with Bridie about getting suspended and then refusing to work for her father.

The storm had given way to sunny skies as Kevin walked from the main house to where the Dempsey family sat at a picnic table near the duck pond. Without drink on the table, conversation was stagnant.

"You look well," Margie said to Kevin.

"Rested," Mike said.

"I want you to know I'm doing everything possible to find Zoe," Frank said.

"I want you to stop looking," Kevin said, shaking hands with his brothers. He kissed Margie on the cheek. "I want everyone to stop looking. Polly and Zoe are history. They're part of a past that was a lie and will not be part of my future."

He picked up a stone and skimmed it across the pond, dispersing half a dozen ducks and separating a pair of cygnets from two adult swans. Mike nudged Margie, and she shrugged and looked to Frank for a reaction. Frank shook his head as panic swirled in his head. Kevin was asking him to give up the search. The investigation. The case. Asking him to come off duty. End the last run.

"You're kidding, right?" Frank asked, still sitting.

"No. No, I'm not," Kevin said, searching for another stone. "The baby isn't mine. I have to learn to live with that."

"Is this place run by Moonies?" Mike asked rhetorically. "Swamis? Hasidic fanatics or something? You find Jesus in your cornflakes? You losing your marbles?"

"Kevin, you have to be sure," Margie said.

"I know," Kevin said, finding a thin smooth piece of slate. "I'm asking you all to just leave it lay. Don't prolong this. I need to get on with my life. I've wasted enough time in the only life I'll ever have."

Frank got up from the bench along with Margie. They walked to Kevin, who stood by the pond bank, watching the cygnets swim back to their parents through the concentric ripples caused by the first stone.

"Kevin, I have good leads," Frank said. "It might take a little while, but I'll find them."

"How about finding the fucking money you took?" Mike said, getting up and pulling up his dungarees. "The money that made Dad hang up and got me suspended and has this family torn apart."

"Ever think there might be a problem here in this family?" Kevin asked. "It doesn't do any good bad-mouthing each other. If Frank's in trouble, we gotta stand by him."

Mike nodded, ran his hands through his hair. "Maybe I spoke out of turn here," he said. "Sorry."

"Your counselor says you're making progress," Margie said, trying to change the subject. "She thinks it might be a good idea for the whole family to go to counseling together. She asked me to have lunch with her."

"Yeah?" Kevin said. "What did you say? What did you tell her about me?"

"I said I'd meet her," Margie said. "This family could use a fresh set of eyes."

They all fell silent for a moment in awkward unison. Frank felt the family was splayed, split, and splintered. He and Margie and Mike sat back at the table again, listening to the sounds of birds in the trees as other clients moved to and from the big house.

"Kevin," Frank said, wetting his lips. "About Zoe. I have a moral obligation to find her."

"Frank's right about that," Mike said quietly. "She's family too."

"And I'm her godfather," Frank said to Kevin.

"Hey, guys," Margie said. "We're here to visit, not to form a search party. Kevin can decide what he wants to do about his marriage when he gets out of here. How much longer do you have anyway, Kev?"

"Less than two weeks," Kevin said. "And I want to get out, sell the house, get on with my life. My new life."

He skimmed the second rock and the birds squawked away in different directions, leaving tremors on the still water.

There was silence again. Frank wanted to press the issue about finding Polly and Zoe, but now was a bad time to confront Kevin about it. He knew Kevin was here doing what he should be doing himself: drying out, getting help for the disease.

My life is simpler, Frank thought. I have to move the money and find the baby. He refused to believe the baby wasn't Kevin's. Some nagging piece of the cop in him kept telling him something was wrong here. Polly stuck around too long to announce the kid wasn't Kevin's. The kid acted too much like Kevin, had too much Dempsey in her not to be from this family. But no matter whose kid it was, he thought, I stood and swore before God that I would look after her welfare in times of trouble. And the present has trouble written all over it.

That's why Frank knew he needed to find Zoe, regardless of what Kevin asked. Eventually Kevin would also need to know answers to questions about her he wasn't even asking yet.

"You have to promise to call off the search," Kevin said to all of them.

"Suit yourself, but I think you're nuts," Mike said. "If it was my kid—"

"She's not yours," Kevin said quickly. "Or mine. Get it straight."

"It's your marriage," Margie said.

"Whatever you want," Frank said, avoiding a full-blown promise and knowing a vow to God supersedes all else.

"Good," Kevin said. "I'll need to get an annulment. Ask Father Flynn. I'll sell the house. Give him money from me for the Indians in New Mexico. Whatever it takes."

"I'll look into it," Margie said.

"Don't sell the house yet," Mike said. "Wait a few months. I'll put in new thermal windows, lay a new roof, repoint the backyard wall, paint the cornice, noodle around. It'll make it worth ten grand more. I got the time."

"Thanks," Kevin said. "Do that and I'll split the difference with you."

"That's a deal," Mike said. "Beats working for the mick."

"I want everyone to stop worrying about me," Kevin said. "Seems to me Frank has a bigger problem. When do you expect the indictment to come down?"

"Few weeks," he said. "Month at the outside."

"Why don't you just turn in the money and make a deal with the DA?" Mike asked. "They came to me three times to say they could swing a deal. Where is all this money anyway?"

"I'm trying to work something out," Frank said.

"Maybe when I get out we can all sit down and have a civilized conversation about it," Kevin said.

"Perhaps," Frank said.

"I hate that word," Mike said. "Who says 'perhaps'?"

"Time to go, anyway," Margie said. "At least you're looking better."

Frank rose first, itchy for a drink. He watched Margie and Mike get up. Mike shook Kevin's hand, squeezing harder than necessary, and they all walked toward the parking lot. Mike went to his car. Frank shook Kevin's hand, and Margie kissed him on the cheek, and Kevin led her off to the side. Frank could hear them behind him.

"Thanks for coming, sis," Kevin said to Margie. Frank kept watching Mike, feeling bad for his youngest brother, who was suffering because of him.

"My pleasure," Margie said. "I typed up all your stories on disks."

"You really like Gail?" he asked eagerly.

"I think she's nice, smart," Margie said.

"What does she say about me?"

"I don't know," Margie said. "She likes you, professionally. I think . . ."

"Think what?"

"Just get better," Margie said. "I'll see you when you get out."

Kevin took some folded notepaper sheets from his pocket and handed them to Margie. Margie looked at them.

"A new story?" she said.

"Called 'The Week of the Worm of Jealousy,' " Kevin said.

"I look forward to it," Margie said.

They all said final goodbyes. Mike drove off alone. Frank climbed into the car with Margie for the ride back to the city.

* * *

Frank and Margie were silent until they got on the thruway south. Margie drove as if she were landing a plane in a fog, hunched over the steering wheel, her movements tentative. It was one of the few things she didn't do with confidence, and Frank always thought it was because it was Little Paulie's father who had taught her how to drive. She'd never believed anything else he told her, so why would she believe his driving instructions?

Frank reached into a plastic airline bag at his feet, where he had stashed the shirt, underwear, and socks he'd worn the day before, and pulled out the Gatorade bottle. It was half orange Gatorade and half vodka. He had been dying for a drink the whole time at the rehab. He took a deep slug and noticed Margie quickly glance over. If she knew what it was she said nothing. The booze moved in him quickly, filling a hollow, screaming craving in his chest cavity. He took two more big gulps and it was gone.

He put the bottle in the bag, against another full one.

"You're going to keep looking for Zoe, aren't you," Margie said.

"Yes," Frank said. "I'm sorry, but—"

"Don't apologize," she said. "I'm with you. And it gives you something to do. Besides drink."

42

Frank Dempsey thought the Boston Shuttle was one of the most civilized air hops in the continental United States. There was a bar at each gate and time for one double Finlandia vodka during the forty-minute flight.

He'd come to Boston to tail Morton, to see if he was in contact with Polly, who would lead him to his goddaughter, Zoe.

The trip from Logan Airport through the Sumner Tunnel to the Bostonian Hotel was quick and traffic free. He left a two-thousand-dollar cash advance at the front desk in lieu of credit. His room had a marvelous view of Quincy Market, and he made himself a fresh drink from the minibar and stood looking out at the great walking festival of food and drink that was the pacemaker of Boston's tourist trade.

Young couples walked hand in hand over cobblestones in the early evening, some eating ice cream or pizza, others sipping piña coladas from plastic cups or swigging beers. A steady stream of humanity moved in and out of the bars and the arcades of fast food and the stands of fresh fruits and vegetables, flowers and seafood. Handicrafts of wool, stained glass, and wicker were sold from small stalls.

Frank thought it was a wonderful bazaar, an Irish American casbah of merriment in a city where quality of life was as big a tourist attraction as history. It was filled with mostly young people from the numerous universities in the greater Boston area. They were out seeking new mates or rekindling old college romances as aging hippies strummed guitars and the ever-present mimes distracted tourists.

A private security force was backed by the real Boston cops, who had little to do in this part of town except write parking tickets.

Frank called the front desk to find out if Clive Morton had checked in yet. As the clerk checked, he imagined the suave Morton, plying his polished British charm on investors eager to get in on a once-in-a-lifetime deal.

The hotel operator came back on and said Morton was expected late, which meant he was catching the last shuttle at nine, getting him into Boston at nine-forty and to the hotel by about ten-thirty.

Frank knew his business would start in the morning as this was an early town, with a 2 A.M. last call for alcohol; on a Sunday night most places put the lock on the door at 12:30 A.M.

So Frank had some time to go wander through the city. He finished his vodka and left the hotel, his pockets bulging with cash. He headed for an Irish pub called the Black Rose, with a live music stage and great big foamy pints of Guinness and polished brass and gleaming wood, dense with smoke and intelligent chatter. It had been twelve years, but Frank was delighted when he came to the end of the market to find the Black Rose was still there on State Street. On the way from the hotel, he had turned once, instinctively, half expecting to see Summers tailing him. When he looked over his shoulder, just as he passed a sweeper cleaning the cobblestones, he had a sensation of being followed.

All he saw was a woman with an attractive figure, wearing a Red Sox hat, gazing into a store window. In profile, she didn't look anything like Summers.

He shrugged and smiled, imagining Summers explaining how Frank had called the cops on him.

Inside the Black Rose, a live band called Barleycorn played traditional Irish music from the stage. The barroom hung heavy with the smell of Guinness and cigarette, cigar, and pipe tobacco smoke. Young people were crushed against the bar in animated conversation, stewed with strong drink, involved in steamy liaisons and dirty laughter.

The song was "Peggy Gordon," a haunting ballad that Frank knew was written by the Scottish poet Robert Burns, a song Big Paulie had sung many times in Brooklyn saloons late at night:

"Oh, Peggy Gor-don,
You are my dar-lin';
Come sit ye down
Upon my knee.
And tell to me
The very reason
Why I am slighted
So-o-o-o by thee."

The song with its melancholy melody went through Frank like an X ray as he lifted a pint of Guinness. He had ordered the stout just to do as they do in Rome. He had also ordered a shot of John Jameson Irish Whisky on the side. Irish whisky was the main ingredient in the blend called scotch. Irish barley made the best base in the world for blending whiskies.

Listening to the band sing the song about lost and unrequited love, Frank caught a rear glimpse of someone he thought looked alarmingly familiar. The hair was in a bun, but the woman's long neck, the way the hair blossomed upward at the nape, the way he'd seen it that day in her health club and the vital bounce in the step . . . ?

Ridiculous, he thought, as he lifted his glass to the lips Sarah Cross had once kissed, and the band played a song called "Isn't It Grand Boys, to Be Bloody Well Dead?"

43

Zoe dug the hole deeper in the sand.

"Where are you trying to reach," the man asked her, "China?"

"No, Coney Island," Zoe said. She remembered a big Ferris wheel and kiddie rides and a giant loud roller coaster that Daddy said she could not ride until she was grown up.

"Jesus Christ, Pol," the man said to Zoe's mommy.

"This place is prettier than Coney Island," Zoe's mommy said. "Coney Island is dirty."

"No," Zoe said. "Daddy takes me to Coney Island. I like Coney Island. I want to go to Coney Island with my daddy."

"Sometimes this makes me sick," the man said to Zoe's mommy.

"If you're sick, go to bed," Zoe said. "That's what Daddy always says."

"Dig your hole, baby," Zoe's mommy said.

"I'm gonna dig to Coney Island to find Daddy," Zoe said, as the waves splashed on the clean and pretty beach.

"Let's go home and have dinner," Zoe's mommy said to her friend.

"I'm not very hungry," he said.

"Daddy says you have to eat if you want to be strong like him," Zoe said.

44

"What do you mean she isn't coming in?" Kevin asked the man behind Gail's desk. His name was Dave Lawlor.

"She took a sick day," Dave said.

"But she'll be back?"

"She didn't quit, if that's what you mean."

"Are you implying I did?"

"Drinking? I hope so," Dave said with a smile.

Kevin assessed him. Dave was about forty, ginger-haired, five foot eight, suety from too many calories and fats and not enough protein, fiber, and exercise.

"You should change your diet," Kevin said, figuring if this guy could be a ball buster, he could be one right back.

"You should worry about you."

"You're right. I do," Kevin said. "That's why I'm concerned about Gail."

"Your recovery comes from you, not any one other person," Dave said. "We counselors are just here to guide you. We aren't doctors. We're flagmen who've been down the bumpy road, still on it."

"What's wrong with her?"

"Jesus, I don't know," Dave said. "She's a woman. It's probably just a personal day."

Kevin had been looking forward to Gail's reaction to what he'd written and had imagined their tête-à-tête all through morning group therapy, during which he did not participate.

Now he had to deal with a different counselor, one who didn't know anything about him.

"Gail was reading my Fifth Step," Kevin told Dave.

"She did leave word that your autobiography was inadequate," Dave said. "That you had to start it over."

"There are no second drafts to a life that started three weeks ago," Kevin said.

"Huh?"

"You hadda be there," Kevin said.

"Like I said, I've been to the mountaintop and under the volcano, man," Dave said. "So let's talk. You want to give me an oral Fifth Step?"

"I don't know you."

"That makes it better."

"For you, not me," Kevin said. "Look, Dave, I'm not trying to be a smart-ass. I thought I had it going good with Gail. If she's out today, maybe we should just postpone my one-on-one Fifth Step until she comes back. Tomorrow."

"Okay," Dave said. "But what if she's out a week? You'll be due for release."

"She'll be back," Kevin assured him.

"It's good to see you have so much confidence in someone," Dave said. "If you have as much in yourself when you pack your bag here, you'll be heading in the right direction."

Kevin got up from his chair and reached out to take Dave's outstretched hand.

"Did you ever doubt your manhood?" Kevin asked.

"When I was using, no," Dave said. "Beer balls got in the way. Sober, being a man is harder. But more fulfilling because of the challenge. You face the doubt instead of drowning it. That's basic 'being a man' stuff. Even for a fat guy."

"Were you ever afraid to tell a woman how you felt about her?"

"Only sober," Dave said.

"Thanks," Kevin said, and made for the door.

"But if you do something stupid sober, it doesn't mean it's right just because you're sober," Dave warned.

"I'm sorry about the diet remark," Kevin said.

"No problem," Dave said. "Maybe next time you can give me a few pointers on how to get in your kind of shape."

"I wouldn't wish that on anyone."

"I meant physical shape," Dave said, smiling.

"Be glad to," Kevin said.

Kevin nodded and left for the gym. He felt the need to hit the bag again.

45

Frank was in the hotel lobby at seven in the morning, reading the *Boston Herald* and watching the elevators. At 7:22 A.M., Clive Morton, hair perfectly sculpted, face freshly shaved, carrying a briefcase, dressed in a dark blue suit with blue-and-red striped tie, stepped off an elevator escorted by a large man in his early thirties, dressed in a gray sports jacket, white shirt, and black tie, who looked muscular and fit.

Bodyguard, Frank thought.

Frank donned the Irish walking hat and sunglasses on the slight chance he would be recognized from his photographs in the New York papers. He followed Morton and bodyguard across the lobby to the back entrance where a taxi rank was formed. A bunch of drivers stood around the first cab, gabbing about the Red Sox, when Morton approached. Four drivers dispersed and the lead driver opened the back door for Morton and the bodyguard, who both got in.

"The Sheraton," the bodyguard said, taking no notice of Frank in his touristy disguise.

"You got it," the driver said.

Frank got in the second taxi on line and took it to the Sheraton, which Frank remembered Barker saying was a convention hotel.

Frank hadn't slept very well, tossing and wrestling with the pillow. He'd gotten maybe three hours of nod, in the half-frozen spirit state between consciousness and true sleep.

And he had awakened thoroughly surprised to find himself with an erection, even though he had no need to urinate.

Frank's cab followed Morton's into the dock of the Sheraton. Morton and the bodyguard took no notice of Frank getting out behind them. Frank gave the cabbie ten dollars on a four-dollar ride, overtipping as he had the bartender and the band in the Black Rose the night before, when he'd asked them to play Peggy Gordon a second and then a third time before closing.

Now he moved through the revolving door, tapping the *Boston Globe* against his leg, folded open to Mike Barnicle's column. The lobby was a hive of activity, as conventioneers in suits and ties and name tags milled around in squadrons of chatter. The Pharmaceutical Researchers of America Convention was a mix of people from all over the country who were associated with medical research from institutes involved in cancer, tuberculosis, AIDS, heart disease, Parkinson's, Alzheimer's, even alcoholism.

Frank looked at the name tags and their affiliations and realized that the various pills he took to stay alive each day came out of research done by these people, many of them doctors, some chemists, others lab technicians, quacks, charlatans, middlemen, and banking hustlers like Clive Morton, who spliced together networks of investors looking to turn their seed money into mega-millions.

Frank followed Morton at a safe distance as he moved across the carpeted lobby with his bodyguard, past the conventioneers, carrying his briefcase like a man on a mission.

The conventioneers were all part of the biggest industry in America, health care and its profits. They were the twenty-first century. The future. God help us, Frank thought. He thanked God he had no kids who someday might need a doctor.

It gave Frank a shudder when he saw the state of some of them. Overweight, emaciated, rumpled, plain, young, old. Some with so many face-lifts their cheeks looked like bongo drums. Others had so much plastic eye, ear, and nose surgery their faces were puzzles of age. Some were as boozy as he was but not clever enough to hide it.

Just folks. Wearing buttons that read THE PULSE OF THE NATION, they were not unlike hardware conventioneers who called themselves THE NUTS AND BOLTS OF AMERICA. Except that the future of life and health was in their hands and they were here in Boston, the medical capital of America, to swap medical, scientific, and financial ideas and get in on the ground floor of new breakthroughs that could save and prolong lives and make billions.

The conventioneers had just come from the buffet breakfast in the main ballroom, and they talked with toothpicks bobbing in their lips. Most made for the elevators to go to seminars in the various convention rooms.

Frank watched Morton and the bodyguard stop near the front desk, where he was greeted by the platinum-haired man he had seen him with earlier in Osbourne's restaurant in the Wall Street area.

Frank noted the platinum man's name tag: LYLE QUINCY, M.D., ST. JOSEPH'S HOSP.

Could be anywhere, Frank thought.

Morton introduced a third man, silver-haired and in his fifties, to Quincy. They shook hands and Quincy remained silent after that. Frank casually strolled toward the desk, looking at his newspaper, and caught a glimpse of the name tag on the lapel of the silver-haired man: ALISTER EDGEWORTH.

Pay dirt, Frank thought.

Edgeworth was Polly's maiden name. This was her dad. They'd never met because Polly's parents had boycotted her wedding to the Brooklyn fireman. But Frank remembered seeing a photo of him while going through Polly's belongings at the new house. He wasn't so silver in the photo. The silver could have come in the 1987 crash. Sarah said it lost him millions. But it was Alister Edgeworth, all right.

Frank walked to the desk, playing the baffled tourist. "Where do I pick up the Freedom Trail?" he asked the receptionist.

"I'll get you some brochures," she said, as Frank eavesdropped on Morton and Edgeworth.

"I thought I would get to see my daughter here," Edgeworth said.

"She won't be coming this trip," Morton said, "but she did want us to meet."

"It's a lot of money to invest, frankly, and I'd like to speak with her about it," Edgeworth said. 'I don't know if she's in the States or in London or Timbuktu. I'd like to see her before—"

"I thought you had the letter of credit with you," Morton said, irritated. "I thought you had already spoken to Polly."

"Just briefly," Edgeworth said, wiping perspiration from his forehead. "On the phone. She was vague about her whereabouts. I wanted to hear more about it before I transferred my letter of credit. I'm afraid these days it doesn't go higher than five hundred thousand."

"I see."

Edgeworth belched into a linen hankie and pounded his breast softly. "American bacon, I'll never get used to it," Edgeworth said. "As I was saying, that's dollars, not pounds, of course. I didn't want to do a wire transfer until I came here personally. Spoke to Polly."

"Of course," said Morton. "Well, clearly she's not here. But all the other potential investors are. Come up to the seminar. I'll be speaking to the other ten investors, doctors from ten of the biggest strategically located cities in the country, kicking in fifty thousand apiece. Your five hundred and Polly's one hundred will keep the controlling fifty-one percent of the product in our court."

"Spread three ways," Edgeworth said. "I know Polly supplies one hundred; her mystery genius provides the formula; I supply my money. What exactly, Mr. Morton, do you supply?"

"Everyone else," Morton said. "And the marketing. And the press. And, of course, the plan."

"Yes . . . yes, of course . . . just wish Polly were here," Edgeworth said. "I took a beating in 'eighty-seven on Wall Street. Then in 'ninety-one came the BCCI fiasco in London. I can't afford another disaster."

"Come upstairs to the seminar and you'll get an idea of what's involved," Morton said. "If you get in on this now, your credit line will be unlimited by next year."

"Yes, that's what Polly said. But still, I'd like to speak with her myself."

"She's in a transitional period now," Morton said. "She's relocating, sorting out her marital problems, as you know."

The receptionist handed the brochures across the countertop to Frank.

"Leaving your husband without notice is bit more than transitional, I'd say," Edgeworth said.

Frank glanced at the brochures and took them from the receptionist and looked at Edgeworth. He was starting to like the poor old mark.

"Will those do, sir?" the receptionist asked Frank.

"Yes, thank you," Frank said. "You've been a great help."

"Come up to the seminar," Morton said to Edgeworth. "You'll feel better."

Edgeworth walked across the busy lobby with Morton and Quincy, who remained silent and reserved. But Frank noticed a fidgety tic in Quincy's nose and remembered the platinum-haired guy had gotten a look at him in the restaurant near Wall Street. Frank averted his face when Quincy looked his way. The bodyguard trailed several feet behind as the trio made for the elevators. Frank followed on the right flank, pretending to go through his brochures.

"I'd feel a lot better if my daughter and this so-called genius friend of hers were here," Edgeworth said.

"Polly is safe and sound, never out of touch, believe me," Morton said. "As for her genius, remember that without investors the genius is a ninny. Without financing, Columbus would never have found this great continent."

"And my daughter might never have married a bloody American fireman," Edgeworth said, annoyed.

Just when I was starting to like him, Frank thought, he reveals himself as an asshole. Now Frank hoped Edgeworth did get fleeced, as he followed him and the other three men into a waiting elevator. The bodyguard pushed floor two so Frank pressed three. Morton, Edgeworth, Quincy, and the bodyguard got off on the second floor and Frank rode to the next.

He stepped off on three, walked directly to the fire door exit and entered the stairwell, where a fire hose was stack-mounted against the cinder-block wall. Frank removed the Irish walking hat and the sunglasses and stuffed them in his trench coat pockets. He combed his hair, took two big gulps from his Gatorade bottle, removed the trench coat, and smoothed his sports jacket. He jammed the folded trench coat behind the fire hose and walked down one flight to the second floor.

The bodyguard was sitting in a chair outside of a seminar room.

"This the Morton Syndicate Investors Group?" Frank asked.

"The one and only," the bodyguard said with slow deliberate speech. Frank made him for sports-scholarship educated. "You got a voucher?"

"No, no voucher."

"Then sit in the back with the public," the bodyguard said. "Investors with vouchers sit up front. Public, back of the bus."

Frank nodded and walked into the room and took a seat in the rear. Morton was already speaking. There were only half a dozen people in the public seating area. The ten doctors sat in red swivel chairs in the front of the room, waiters serving them coffee and tea and snacks from trays.

". . . so the beauty of this new amazing drug, which we call Q-Twenty-one-hundred, is that we will not have to wait the standard seven years for FDA approval because all the ingredients are already FDA-approved and available over the counter. It is the *formula* and *method* of application, in conjunction with *supervision* of dermatologists such as yourselves, that will retard the aging process. Not reverse it, but slow it down so that a woman in her thirties can still look like a woman in her thirties well into her late forties. By the next century, with modifications, we think this might take twenty years off the aging process. You as physicians will reap twofold benefits. You will get a reputation for prescribing it first in your region. And, as investors, you will get a percentage of the profits of the drug you prescribe. All very legal, ethical, and moral. Once the press gets hold of this in an organized national print and electronic media public relations campaign, there will be a stampede for Q-Twenty-one-hundred. Each of you will be eligible for franchises of the special Q-Twenty-one-hundred clinics that will be set up in storefronts in your areas because you will be years ahead of anyone else on the expertise."

"Will it mean people will live longer?" asked a doctor from Palm Beach, Florida.

"Not right away," Morton admitted. "There will be only a cosmetic effect at first. But the mastermind of this drug is convinced that what slows down the free-radical aging process of the skin will also eventually work in slowing down the deterioration of vital organs and muscles. So, yes and no to that question. But Q-Twenty-one-hundred is the magic wand of the future. Invest now, and you'll be in on the ground floor."

"Where will Q-Twenty-one-hundred be developed?" asked another doctor, from Dallas.

"We've finalized negotiation with a major research facility right now, but I'd rather not say where," Morton said. "Espionage is rampant, as you might expect."

"Won't the research facility own it?" asked another potential investor, a doctor from Chicago.

"No," Morton said. "You will. They'll get a fee for lab space and prestige. And of course the father of the drug will own a sizable interest."

"So it's a man," said a doctor from San Francisco.

"Yes, it's a man," Morton said. "But behind every great man—"

"—is another great man," said the same doctor.

"Men," corrected Morton.

The men in the room all laughed in jocular unison. Frank realized there were no women among the investors.

Morton spoke like a snake oil salesman for another twenty minutes and then ran a slide show on how Q-2100 would retard aging by combating the enzymes called free radicals in the body. Frank thought that if he were still in Bunco he would have raided the place for fraud. A few of the doctors were concerned with whether Q-2100 was effective, but most didn't seem overly converned with whether or not the drug was the miracle that had eluded Ponce de Leon in his quest for the fountain of youth. They wondered more about whether it would sell and how soon they'd get a return on their investment.

This was simply a consortium of investors in a new get-rich-quick medical gimmick. No different from cures for baldness or last-chance-diet scams. Morton the finagler was using Polly to get her dad to provide the bulk of the so-called research funding with what little credit-line money the poor old fool had left. Polly would rip off anyone, Frank thought. She'd already robbed Kevin of his dignity, his baby, almost his mind. She had duped countless European suitors over the years and had even conned her best friend Sarah out of her life's savings. And now, on the lam, she was ripping off her own father.

Near the end of the seminar, Alister Edgeworth signed his letter of credit over to Morton. This caused a stir among the potential investors. Foreign money, especially the pound, the yen, and the deutsche mark, always made Americans itch to jump in with both feet. As if their patriotism were at stake in letting something this big and universal slip away from American soil.

Frank couldn't care less who got burned. All he was concerned with was where Polly had taken Zoe. And at least now it was clear that if she was in Britain she wasn't with her folks. The father, who also was being fleeced, didn't even know where she was.

Frank's guess was that if Polly was involved with Morton in this get-rich-quick scam, he had to know where she was.

And Frank was determined to get it out of Morton, one way or another.

Before the meeting broke, Morton told the potential investors he would be available in his hotel room for private consultations all day. He added that he would like to have them as his guests for dinner at Bobby's Pier Three that night at eight.

"For those of you who didn't bring sand to the beach," Morton said, pausing as if for a drumroll, "there will be a few unattached ladies from my staff with me. When Q-Twenty-one-hundred is available, they'll be able to look the way they look tonight for twenty more years. I hope you can slip away and join me to see what a benefit that will be for *man*kind."

There was great mumbling in the room and smiling and handshaking. Frank Dempsey was the first one out the door. He made for the bar to figure out how to isolate Morton. He already knew there was no better way to do that than in a crowd.

46

Margie Dempsey had agreed to meet Gail Levy for lunch in the diner near the school where Margie taught. It was a place called George's Diner, a greasy spoon on East Eighteenth Street near Washington Irving High. Margie ordered a gyro platter of chopped spit-roasted lamb over a bed of romaine lettuce and fresh beefsteak tomatoes and french fries. Gail picked at a piece of feta cheese and toyed with the straw of a Diet Coke.

The night before, Margie had read Kevin's new story, "The Week of the Worm of Jealousy." If it had a basis in reality, Kevin believed he had been sterile since the day he got mumps after the high school championship game, sharing champagne from the same bottle as a rival player.

In the story, the cheerleader was clearly based on Kevin's old girlfriend, Lucy Carbone. The main character was certainly Kevin. And the story suggested that the aborted baby in question could not have been Kevin's because he had since learned that the mumps had made him sterile *before* he had ever slept with the girl.

If this was true in real life, it was something Kevin had not told her. Margie thought all along that Kevin was confused. Now he was being very specific. He thinks he was sterile before he ever had sex with Lucy Carbone, she thought.

If this was correct, Kevin had been hauling some awful cargo all these years. And it explained why he wanted the family to call off the search for Zoe, who could not be his baby either.

But Margie knew she would have to talk more to Kevin about this, confront him. Or, better still, do a little investigating on her own. Kevin had asked her not to let anyone else read the story.

Now, here was Gail Levy, distraught, telling Margie about another of Kevin's stories, one called "Lifesaver," a story Gail said was about her.

"Not only do I think it's about me," Gail said, "it's about him too. About him and me. As in *us*. *Us* as in an *item*. And it disturbs the hell out of me."

"Why?" Margie asked. "Is it violent?"

Gail shook her head and moistened her lips with the soda. "Anything but," she said. "It's wonderfully romantic, and . . ."

"And what?"

"I don't know how to say this without sounding like a buffoon, so I'll just say it," Gail said. "It's flattering as hell. The part about me. And, well, knowing it's about me and him, it's one of the sexiest things I've ever read."

"Oh, Christ," Margie said. "I *thought* he had a thing for you."

"Really?" Gail said, brightening and then sinking sullenly back into the booth, as high school kids made a ruckus with George, the diner owner, in the front of the store.

"It be true Greeks love butt fuckin'?" one kid was asking George. "And that's why so many Greeks are assholes?"

Margie shouted past Gail at the kid. "Hey, ladies here, Howard."

"Oh, shit . . . I mean damn. I'm sorry, Miss Dempsey, I didn't know you was there," the kid said, pulling off his hat in deference to Margie before George chased him out the door with two laughing friends.

George let a stream of Greek curses follow them into the lunch-hour street, where a beat cop's uniformed presence kept a fragile semblance of order.

"And *he's* one of my better students." Margie shook her head. "So you called in sick?"

"I can't continue to be his counselor," Gail said. "When emotional attachment begins between a client and a counselor, the entire relationship must be severed."

"Is it just client slash counselor?" Margie asked. "Or do I detect that the counselor also is attracted to the client?"

Gail looked up at Margie and held her cautious gaze. "It's never happened to me before."

"Like you said," Margie said, "you're a professional, not dead. It's understandable."

"I wanted you to know why I'm taking the next two weeks off," Gail said. "I'm putting in for a vacation. By the time I go back, Kevin will be finished and home. I worry that after being abandoned by his wife and losing his child, he'll do something drastic if he feels I've deserted him too. But I have to avoid him. Ethics really suck sometimes."

"That sounds like Greek-diner Plato," Margie said.

"I'm confused," Gail said. "Guys like Kevin aren't easy to find."

Margie sipped her Diet Coke. "Well, I appreciate your telling me," she said.

"You might be the only woman he ever trusts again," Gail said.

"I'll talk to him," Margie said. "I'll explain. Kevin is pretty good at separating emotion from intellect. He won't like what you're doing, but he'll understand."

"I hope so," Gail said. "I'm afraid he'll hate me."

"Can you tell me what he says about Zoe and Polly?"

"That would be unethical," Gail said.

"At least you're consistent."

"This is not easy for me," Gail said. "Like I told you, good guys aren't that easy to find."

"Tell me about it," Margie said, and they laughed.

"Anyway," Gail said. "Now I have two weeks to get over him and relax."

"If you're no longer his counselor, is it still unethical . . . ?"

"This soon?" Gail said. "Yeah. Maybe if we ran into each other later. . . . See, people in recovery get together all the time. It's natural because they have their addiction in common. Misery needs company. They can understand and empathize and forgive the failings of the fellow addict easier than those who were never addicted. But we don't recommend it in the first year. That first year you're supposed to focus on yourself. Your recovery should be your primary relationship. So it's better that we—Kevin and I—just go our separate ways. It's life, it's human . . . and it's so goddam sad I feel like crying, so I better go."

Gail tried to leave money on the table but Margie waved her cash away.

"I think you're a great kid," Margie said, suddenly making herself feel spinster old. "Go be happy. And thanks."

"Take good care of Kevin," Gail said, and Margie could hear the fracture in her voice before Gail kissed her cheek and quickly hurried out the door into the boisterous street.

Margie looked on the table and saw that Gail had left her a Xerox of "Lifesaver," which meant she had kept the original for herself.

She checked her watch. It was almost time to get back to school, where she would try to prepare adolescents for life as adults.

47

Earlier in the afternoon, Frank had placed a call to Buzzy Furie at the China Moon restaurant in Manhattan. Furie said his contact in the British embassy had confirmed that one Polly Edgeworth had renewed her own passport and had been issued a British passport for her child Zoe Edgeworth a month ago.

Now, at 7:45 P.M., Frank sat at the bar of Bobby's Pier Three with a Stolichnaya martini dotted with a black olive and twisted with orange rind, waiting for another bearer of a British passport named Clive Morton.

Also at the bar having drinks were all ten conventioneers he'd seen at the seminar, talking and checking out the Red Sox on the high-mounted television, awaiting Morton and the promise of girls.

"I hear that the women Morton is bringing are so young that if they used this Q-Twenty-one-hundred they'd become embryonic," said the doctor from Dallas to the medicine man from Chicago.

"Morton's annual dinner is usually worth the trip," said the man from San Francisco to the good doctor from Atlanta.

"I wonder if this Q-Twenty-one-hundred really works," said the skeptic from Palm Beach.

"Who cares?" said the doctor from Baltimore. "As long as it sells."

"I just hope the women are clean," said the doctor who hung his shingle in Phoenix.

Frank smiled. None of them recognized him, because he had sat in the back of the seminar. Most came to the convention without their wives, knowing full well that 90 percent of the trip was pleasure and 10 percent business. This dinner was both. The business of getting laid, Frank thought.

The bar looked out over Boston Harbor, where, off to the left, past the tugs and the freighters, Old Ironsides was moored as a tourist attraction. Directly ahead, the planes took off and landed at Logan. The faint gamey smell of the water blew in every time the front door opened.

Frank had taken time in the afternoon to get a haircut and buy a new off-the-rack set of clothes: jeans, Polo T-shirt, soft-soled shoes, and a dark waist-length hooded jacket with two inside pockets and two deep outside pockets and two side pockets. It was the kind of rain-resistant fabric that could come in handy in a place like London. His pockets were filled with cash and his various bottles and assorted paraphernalia, including the can of NYPD-issue Mace, which would look like a breath spray in the airport security X-ray machine when he sent his jacket through.

He'd taken his Dristan and Dilantin and vitamin C pills and once more had forgone the Valium, because he knew he needed the energy if he was to confront Morton.

Frank sat with his back to the bar, listening to the doctors talk like horny adolescents as he watched the front door. The hostess's station was located there, a small pulpit with a reservation book spread before her and a telephone with various flashing buttons. Twice Frank had watched the hostess answer calls, after which she would walk into the dining room and page the customers.

Just as the sun set, Frank ordered another martini and watched the first limousine pull up outside in the parking lot of Bobby's Pier Three. Two more identical limos followed. The bodyguard stepped out first and stood there as Morton climbed out behind him. Now three beautiful young models, whippet-thin and dressed in suggestive evening gear, followed. The next two limos pulled up and seven more models stepped out. It looked like a movie premiere. Frank figured with airfare, hotels, limos, and food, so far Morton had sprung for fifteen grand. Maybe twenty, tops. Considering the potential return, a mere bag of shells, Frank thought, conjuring the Ralph Kramden line. He had more than that in his pockets.

But the glitter made Morton look important, like a man who could get things done. The models would be paid runway scale and get to spend a weekend in Boston and meet very successful doctors. Some liaisons might even end in marriage and lucrative divorce settlements, Frank thought. Some might ignite true love. But the whole setup sickened him. It reeked of whoredom. Morton was the pimp and the doctors were the johns.

Too bad I'm not working vice, Frank thought.

The doctors at the bar all fell momentarily still as they saw the beautiful young women strutting toward the front door, hair and boas and open jackets flapping in the harbor breeze.

"Holy mother of Jesus!" Baltimore finally said.

"Ah, what a grueling subject anatomy is, no?" said Seattle.

"Can you imagine looking like that twenty years longer than you're supposed to?" asked Las Vegas.

"Good God," said San Francisco. "Talk about saving the best for last!"

"She's the knockout of them all," said Baltimore. "A perfect ten."

Frank craned to look at the last one, the Ten, and when he did he almost dropped his glass. His heart sank, his feet stung with pins and needles, and his stomach fell like it does on a fast-moving elevator. He spun on his stool, away from the great beauty dressed in the peasant blouse and the clinging brightly colored skirt and high boots, facing the window and Logan Airport beyond so he wouldn't have to look at her. He felt like swimming for it, catching the last shuttle home to New York. Straight home to his single bed in his dark room to wait for booze or justice, whichever came first, to take him.

But he watched her anyway, in the reflection of the window. Frank saw the hostess go instantly to work as the doctors flocked around Morton, who began introducing the women to them: Doris, Kim, Cathy, Barb, Jackie, Vivian, Connie, Elaine, Alice, Sue, and finally—the word Frank did not want to hear, the name he cherished and revered, the most beautiful word in the English language.

"And this, everyone, is *Sarah,*" said Morton.

From his lips, *Sarah* sounded like something vulgar, Frank thought, as he sat with his back to the lascivious doctors and Morton's props, Morton's bimbos, the women who would help make him millions.

"I hope you all like fish," Morton said loudly, laughing, as the hostess led the parade of tits and ass, legs and hips, gleaming hair and expensive clothing, jewelry and perfume, high heels, and lipstick into the big dining room, decorated in a nautical motif, where a table for twenty-two was arranged.

The bodyguard took a seat at the far end of the bar, with a clear view of the Red Sox game on the TV set. He ordered club soda and ate Goldfish crackers from a bar basket, his back to Frank as he alternately watched the television and kept Morton's table in his line of sight.

Frank, from his spot at the bar, could see the dinner party through the ship netting and anchor chains. Sarah sat next to Morton. It was beyond Frank's comprehension how she could be there. With Morton! What the hell did he have that attracted such beautiful women? Polly and now Sarah too? Did she need money that badly? Sarah turned away from Morton and began talking to a beautiful young red-haired woman with oversized gold earrings. Morton kept interrupting Sarah's conversation, waving a finger at the intimidated redhead. Sarah turned to Morton and grabbed his finger and firmly guided it down, waving a finger of her own at him. Morton straightened in his seat, annoyed, and the redhead turned and chatted with her appointed date.

Frank felt a nervous rumbling in his stomach as he assessed the situation. The dinner would be a long one and he knew he had to get Morton alone. He had to time the confrontation just right, or he would never get the information he needed to locate Zoe. He didn't care, if Sarah saw him, that it would mean the death of his fantasy of her. Frank could see what she would do for a dollar.

Now he had family business to take care of.

Frank watched the waitress deliver a tray of piña coladas and white wine spritzers for the women. The men had ordered martinis and scotch. Everyone drank, and waves of laughter rolled out across the big dining room. Morton sat near the top of the table, whispering into Sarah's ear, and she whispered back into his and shook her head. She lifted a beer and took a sip, undulating exquisite bare shoulders.

The others had paired off into murmuring conversations while glasses clinked and busboys brought fresh bread, celery sticks, and olives.

"To Q-Twenty-one-hundred," Morton said as he stood and raised his glass.

The other doctors stood and raised their glasses in a toast. The women remained seated and smiled in a baffled way.

"To Q-Twenty-one-hundred," the men said in unison.

The women clapped hollowly as the men sipped their drinks. Then Morton sat down and the men followed his lead and there was a rush of food and more drink orders to the diligent waitresses, maître 'd, and wine steward.

Frank watched Sarah and Morton more closely now, as they spoke seriously in hushed tones, almost detached from the rest of the table. Sarah looked stern and determined while Morton's bright facade continued to cover some annoyance.

Frank saw the redhead get up and walk toward the ladies' room. Then Sarah stood and picked up her pocketbook and followed her. An agitated Morton got up and trailed Sarah for several yards. Morton and Sarah stopped and talked in an archway, halfway between the dinner table and the rest rooms. Frank averted his face again because Sarah was passing by the other side of the bar to get to the ladies' room, and his heart started pounding as he watched her from the back, in all her elegance.

Frank drained his drink, placed a book of Bobby's Pier Three matches in his jacket pocket, and left a ten-dollar tip on the bar. He then walked into the vestibule of the big restaurant, where two pay phones were mounted on the wall, plastered with the names and phone numbers of cab companies. Frank jammed a quarter into the phone and dialed the number on the matchbook.

He heard the phone ring and through the glass-paneled door he saw the hostess answer the phone.

Frank asked her to page a customer named Clive Morton. He watched the hostess place the phone on the pulpit by the door and walk to Morton's table. Morton got up from the table, placing his napkin on his chair, excusing himself to the guests. He followed the hostess from the table past the bar. The bodyguard was immediately on his feet. Morton signaled for him to sit down and walked to the hostess's station by the door, where she handed him the phone.

"Hello," Frank heard Morton say. He could see Morton turning sideways through the glass. "Clive Morton here."

"Cheers, Clive," Frank said with his best British accent. "This is Alister, Alister Edgeworth, heah."

There was a silence and then Morton said, "Is something wrong? You don't sound so well."

"An unforeseen problem with the letter of credit," Frank said, and saw Morton switch the phone to his other hand and swivel on his feet with angst.

"My God, Edgeworth, you said it was solid!"

"I'm outside, calling from my car," Frank said. "I think we might clear this up, but I need some details. My bank is awaiting an immediate fax."

"I have a table filled with investors," Morton said.

"My people are waiting in London even as we speak," Frank said.

"What are you driving?"

"A Lincoln town car, silver," Frank said. "And come alone. Leave that big unpleasant gentleman behind. I can't afford anyone's knowing the intimate details of my business."

"You can trust my bodyguard."

"Alone or I'm on the morning flight home," Frank said in the mock British accent.

"I'll be right there, but this better be quick."

Frank watched Morton hang up the phone and check his watch, run his hand through his hair, and try to gather his shaken composure. Then he walked to the bodyguard and whispered in his ear. The bodyguard nodded and checked his watch too. Frank saw Morton walk his way and he turned toward the door leading to the parking lot. As he did, he saw Sarah leave the ladies' room. It might be the last time he ever saw her. He held her in his eyes another second and then went out and flattened himself against the wall.

Morton stepped outside and looked both ways for Edgeworth's car. Frank took the slender Mace can from his pocket and rammed the small round base against Morton's back like a gun barrel. Morton froze. Now Frank stood closer to him, the Mace can against his ribs, holding him by an elbow.

"Walk to the left, nice and calm, palsie-walsie like," Frank whispered. "And don't look at me or I'll do it here."

Morton moved left, panicking, looking for the bodyguard. Frank smiled and nodded to the limo drivers in the distance, standing together, chatting.

"Wave to them," Frank whispered.

Morton waved, and the limo drivers waved back.

"Now let's walk down near the water," Frank said. "Behind the restaurant."

Morton did as he was told. When they got to the rear they were in total darkness except for a light spill from a high greasy kitchen window. The sounds of tugs and buoys from the harbor mixed with the noise of pots and plates and Asian and Spanish voices from the kitchen. The pungent reek of the water and the garlicky smell of frying fish were overpowering.

Frank stopped and in a single hissing motion thoroughly sprayed the Mace in Morton's eyes.

"Ahhhhhh," Morton squealed, his body bucking.

"Quiet," Frank said as he grabbed him around the neck with one arm and pushed his face against the rough cement wall. He hated himself for enjoying Morton's pain. But Morton had recruited Sarah into this scheme that involved Polly who had lammed with Zoe. Zoe Dempsey. So he allowed himself the small pleasure.

"Now, where's Polly?" Frank whispered with hot heavy breath into Morton's ear. "And I want you to be very fucking specific, pal, or else this time I am going to cut off the head of your cock."

"You . . . you . . . who are you? New York, now Boston—"

"Where's Polly?"

"Right this minute I'm not sure," he said.

"I'll slice off your knob and feed it to the birds," Frank warned, unbuttoning Morton's top pants button and zipper and letting his trousers fall around his knees.

"My God, no!"

"In Asian, scorned wives feed their husbands' cocks to the ducks all the time. Now, where's Polly?"

"Give me an hour. I'll cut you into the deal. Millions . . . are you working for Edgeworth?"

Frank started pulling down Morton's underwear. "Where's Polly?" he whispered.

"Okay, okay—" Morton began to answer.

Suddenly, Frank felt a flashbulb pop inside his head. Pinwheels spun in front of his eyes, and a second tremendous thud landed against the back of his neck. He pitched forward and let go of the blinded Morton. The Mace can rattled away from Frank, who tried to get up from the ground. But he felt a large hand yank his hair and twist him around to a seated position.

"You fucking piece of shit!" the bodyguard yelled, his face a smear of teeth and wet hair. He drove two punches into Frank's ribs, smashed him in the nose, and then steadied himself to do it again.

Through the pink blur of pain, Frank waited for the final shot. It would be a relief. But then the bodyguard screamed in agony, so loud that three prep cooks flung open the kitchen door, shouting excitedly in Chinese and Spanish. They saw the bodyguard running in crazy circles, tearing at his eyes, swinging his fists wildly. The already blinded Morton lay on the ground in a fetal position, moaning and rocking.

Frank looked up blearily, and saw Sarah holding the Mace can, bending over, grabbing his hand.

"Come on, dummy," she whispered.

Frank took her hand, got to his feet, and was led to the front of the restaurant, where a taxi waited at the curb.

"You're a little out of shape for this line of work, no?" Sarah said, dabbing at his blood with a perfumed handkerchief in the back seat, as the cab rattled away from the pier.

"Maybe so, but you sure know how to use your body to get what you want," Frank said, with a sneer in his voice.

"It's not nice to be an asshole to someone who just saved said ass," Sarah said.

"Go back to Morton," Frank said. "He has all the money you want . . . like Polly."

"I think I might wash out your mind with a little soap," Sarah said. "I don't like being called a whore. Especially by a thief. But if I *were* a whore, at least I would have *earned* my money. Truth is, I don't want Morton's money. I want *my* money. If I wanted to whore myself for money, baby, I could have done that a long time ago. But right now I'd say you need a little help finding who you're looking for. We're both looking for the same person. But while you were busy getting the shit kicked out of you, I was busy getting some answers. So *I* might know where to start looking."

"Sorry."

She looked him up and down and shook her head. "You're not kidding."

48

Sarah Cross looked from the soft white pillows of clouds outside the airplane window to the bruised and battered man who sat next to her, finishing his second double vodka. Frank waved for the stewardess and rattled the ice in his glass, signaling for another.

They had caught an early morning flight to Tucson and Frank insisted on upgrading to first class. She figured this was because in first class he could drink all he wanted. Even so, he made four trips to the men's room. She figured he must also have a flask on him.

The stewardess came with a new drink, her unfazed smile like a tattoo of first class flying experience.

"I still think Arizona is a mistake," Frank said. "Everything points the other way, across the Atlantic Ocean: the inclement-weather clothes she bought and the British passport for the kid."

"All I know," Sarah said, "is that the redhead at the table in Bobby's Pier Three, her name is Alice, told me she'd seen Polly in Tucson three days ago. At a place Polly and I visited together in the past, a spa called the Mesquite Ranch. It's where fading Hollywood actresses, rising models, and cokey businessmen go to shed a few pounds and kick-start another useless health regime. My friend Alice said Polly had a man and a child with her, stashed at a motel near the spa. She said Polly was afraid she was being followed in a matrimonial case. Alice didn't press her. Models are often stalked by crazy ex-husbands, boyfriends, and fans. It comes with the bone structure."

"That what you and Morton were arguing about in the restaurant?" Frank asked.

"Yeah," Sarah said. "Every time Alice tried to tell me more, he kept interrupting, saying Polly was none of my business. I told him Polly *was* my business. That she was my friend and no one knew where she was. He said she'd be okay. I was going to ask him more after I picked Alice's brains in the ladies' room, but you got to him—or his goon got to you—first."

A kid wearing a cowboy hat and cowboy boots and a vest with a sheriff's star ran down the aisle and pointed a cap pistol at Frank and pulled the trigger. There were no caps in the gun.

"You got me," Frank said. "I'm dead."

Sarah nudged him and said, "Don't say that."

Frank grimaced from the nudge.

"Wow, mister, you really do look dead," the kid said to Frank, pointing at his injured face and shouting down the aisle for his mother. "Mom, the guy I just killed really looks dead."

Frank laughed, touching his swollen nose, bruises, and blackened eyes. The laughter hurt his aching ribs. He smiled at the kid and thought immediately about Zoe, wondering if she had any kids her age to play with, wherever she was. The little cowboy's mother hurried down the aisle and led him back to his seat, apologizing to Frank.

"So did you tell Morton that Polly had your money?"

"Yeah," she said. "He said that soon Polly'd be able to double my money. I said I needed it now, before my opportunity for the health club fell through. He scoffed. I felt like choking him. That's when I walked to the ladies' room and saw you had left the bar. Then I saw you in the vestibule wearing the silly Woody Allen hat."

"You knew I was there all along?"

"I followed you to Boston Sunday night," Sarah said. "Barker told me you went there to look for Morton. I called Morton to say I was available to work the convention, as long as there was no sex involved. He hired me as his beard, his prop. I saw you at the shuttle waiting room at La Guardia. We were on the same plane. I followed you from the minute you checked into the Bostonian."

"Some cop I am."

"And I saw you at the Irish pub," Sarah said.

"So that *was* you at the Black Rose?"

"Yup."

"Why didn't you say hello to me?"

"I wanted to see what you were up to," Sarah said. "That's all. I didn't know if you already knew where Polly was or not. At least you led me in the right direction."

"I'm not so sure about that," Frank said. "Somehow I can't imagine London Fog trench coats as being big in the desert."

He raised his empty glass toward the stewardess again.

"Polly is no dummy," Sarah said, sipping an Evian. "If she wanted to leave a trail, she would have thought of some red herrings. She can always use the passports in the future."

"But what if Polly isn't at this Mesquite spa place when we get there?" Frank asked, ignoring her remark.

"You're the cop," she said. "Why else do you think I'm with you, just to count your drinks?"

Frank looked past her, out at the clouds that rushed by the window. He took a deep swallow of the liquor and turned back to her. Sarah looked him in his lost, swollen, blackened, almost pleading eyes. She wanted to thread her fingers through his tousled hair. Here was a man, a doomed wreck, physically haggard, jammed up with the law, risking what was left of his life for the love of his brother. Sarah wished she could have a man who loved so selflessly.

"I have a confession to make," Frank said.

"What?" She hooked a small tanned pinkie under his whiskey-pale thumb. He stared down at the touch, the fragile connection. She watched him swallow dryly.

"I've thought of you when I was alone at night," Frank said.

"I've thought of you too," she said histrionically. And then said: "On a Stairmaster."

"I have another confession to make," he said.

"Save it for later," she said and kissed Frank Dempsey's lips again, a soft lingering kiss, and then she felt his lips press firmly against hers, and then the tip of her tongue darted into his mouth, somewhere over America.

49

Kevin Dempsey leaned over the desk with angry eyes, his lips pulled taut over his bared teeth. Dave Lawlor sat calmly behind the desk.

"Sit down, Kevin," Dave said. "No need for dramatics."

"How the fuck can she bail out on me in midstream? What kind of fucking head games do you people play here? You put your trust in someone at the crossroads of your life and she takes a fucking *vacation?*"

"It's more complicated than that," Dave said. "And sit down! Remember, there are no bars here."

"No bars? Then how come I feel like I just got hit over the fucking head with one? Huh? I got three days left here, and they have a stranger check me out? How could Gail do this to me?"

"Poor me, poor me, *pour* me a fucking drink," Dave said, his voice dripping with sarcasm.

"Fuck you and your infantile slogans," Kevin said. "I *poured* my heart and soul out to that broad—"

"There you go," Dave said. "To you she's a someone to flirt with. You looked at her and saw a piece of ass instead of a counselor. That's why she's not here. That's why you got fat little ol' me."

Kevin sat down heavily in his chair. "Is that what she said?" he asked, trying to regain his composure.

"She said the client-counselor relationship was in danger of being blurred," Dave said. "So before any improprieties occurred, she asked to take vacation time. She's doing this for you, more than for herself."

"Maybe you think so," Kevin said.

"Look, you got three days left," Dave said. "I can't check you out of here until you do your Fifth Step. If you check yourself out, that negative report goes back to the city, to the Fire Department. Hey, I don't want any part of your losing your job, so you gotta do this by the rules. Understand?"

"She say anything else?" Kevin asked quietly.

"No," Dave said. "Nor should she."

Kevin looked up at Dave and held his stare for a long moment.

"Give me a new notebook," Kevin said. "I'll do my autobiography for my Fifth Step."

50

"Two separate rooms or one double?" asked the tanned, blond, bright-eyed receptionist. She was about fifty with drum-taut skin.

"One double," said Sarah. "King-size bed."

Frank knew he would remember that exchange for the rest of his days, no matter how few.

"We don't get that many from Brooklyn," the receptionist said, counting thirty hundred-dollar bills for five nights and reading the registration card Frank had filled out, "and you're the second one in a week. She paid cash too. Like you."

"No kidding," Sarah said. "I just bet that was my friend Polly Dempsey. His sister-in-law. She said she was coming here. She and I came together three or four times."

Frank took a picture of Polly from his wallet and handed it to Sarah, who showed it to the receptionist. The receptionist looked at it and smiled.

"If you've been here before, you know we pride ourselves at the Mesquite on our confidentiality," the receptionist said. "The gossips and the tabloid shows and private detectives are always sniffing around, trying to dig up dirt on our famous clients."

"You can check my file, to see if I'm legit," Sarah said.

"I'll do that," said the receptionist. She ran Sarah's name through the computer and cross-referenced it with Polly's. She smiled again.

"You'll see we came here together at least twice," Sarah said.

"Yes, you certainly did come here with a Polly Dempsey," the receptionist said. "Three years ago was the last time. Post-maternity. But she used the name Edgeworth this time. She checked out yesterday. In a hurry too, as I remember."

"She leave a forwarding address?"

The receptionist zapped the screen blank and smiled. "Sorry, I've already said way too much." The receptionist dangled a pair of keys. "Cottage number one is open. The honeymoon suite. By the way, Frank, those lacerations on your face will heal in no time here in the dry desert. Drink lots of water, apply plenty of vitamin E oil, eat lots of veggies."

"Thanks," Frank said and lifted his plastic airline bag filled with underwear, dirty shirts, and socks and his various medicines. Sarah grabbed her canvas bag, the one she'd brought to Boston.

"I owe you half the money," Sarah said, leading him out of the office.

"No, I owe you my life," Frank said.

"Well, then, let's go show me some of what I saved."

Frank gazed blearily around the grounds as they walked toward the building behind the Olympic-sized swimming pool. A mild panic began to beat in his breast. He couldn't let this woman see him naked, learn his secrets, know his fears. I'm not worthy of this woman, Frank thought, as Sarah dangled the room key, swung her shoulder bag. He looked at the tanned men and the beautiful women who sat poolside, glistening with the varnish of the rich. Through the bare windows of the gymnasium he could see a group of women and a few men doing a step class with an aerobics teacher who looked too perfect to be human.

Frank felt ridiculous and embarrassed in his dark, bulky eastern clothes, his bashed-in face. He was tired, sweaty, and pale. His mouth tasted like bile.

"I feel like a member of a different species here," Frank said.

"Believe me," Sarah said, "you are. Take me to your leader."

"Just like that?" Frank said. "You want me to go to your room?"

"Our room."

"But I . . . isn't there something we have to do first? Something else? Flowers? Dinner? A movie? Shouldn't it be night? What do I do, here, Sarah? Tell me what to say."

"Your prayers," Sarah said and walked toward the cabana with Frank drifting nervously behind her.

51

Kevin Dempsey was going home.

He had finished his autobiography, telling as much of the truth as possible but omitting the part about his sterility. He did not want that in there for strangers to see.

Now he stood on line with nine other graduates. From the stage of the Burning Bush rehab, he looked out at the audience of about one hundred other clients, some new arrivals, some semipermanent residents, others with three or two weeks or less before graduating.

He was searching for Gail Levy's face, but she was not there.

As the names were called, each client advanced and shook hands with the president, a man named Hunt, whom Kevin had only met once in the month he was there.

After shaking Hunt's hand, Kevin walked across the stage to the stairs leading down to the main floor of the auditorium. The first row was filled with counselors and trustees. Kevin searched again for Gail but didn't find her.

Kevin left the stage with the other graduates. He was proud that he'd gone almost a full month without alcohol, the longest he could remember since he started drinking as an altar boy.

But even this was a kind of fraud, his pride an act of arrogance. He'd done his Fifth Step, all right, but it was scarred by a gigantic omission. Kevin knew he was still in partial denial.

Still, if he was ever to get on with his life, he had to get out of here. Kevin Dempsey was going home. Even if there was no such thing anymore.

He shook hands with some of the people there, including Walter, the crackhead who had been his roomie for a month. He had grown fond of Walter, a sad, harmless fella who longed to see his children but didn't want them to see him until he was sure they would never see him stoned again. He was still too afraid to go back to "the world" and relapse. He walked to Kevin, his yellowed teeth in a wide grin, and extended his open brown hand. Kevin took it and they hugged.

"You be careful of everyone out there, heah, including the girl next door, now, heah?" Walter warned.

"Be good to yourself," Kevin said. "That's who you sleep with at night."

Then Kevin shook hands with Dave Lawlor.

"You never did put me on that diet," Lawlor said. "Under other circumstances I'd say 'Next time.' But I hope to hell I never see your sorry ass here again."

"Thanks, Dave," Kevin said.

Kevin had told his family that he wanted to travel home alone because he needed more time to concentrate on himself. So he picked up his suitcase by the front door and walked out of the big main house. He stopped and looked at Gail's office window but the lights were out.

He imagined her home, making coffee for the artist named Richard Smith, preparing for his big party.

Gail hadn't had this kind of time on her hands in over a year. She had made no vacation plans, so all the airfares were too expensive for her on such short notice. Instead, she decided to stay in the city.

She found herself leisurely strolling along Lexington Avenue, popping into boutiques, looking for something to wear to Richard Smith's party, an affair that offered contact with people whose problems were not hers. Fun. Company in the big city. *Men* would be there. Maybe even a few single, straight, nonalcoholic, un-fucked-up, gainfully employed *men.* She wanted to look nice but her heart wasn't in it. Every time she saw herself in a tight skirt or a clingy dress, it looked like it belonged on someone else.

She had done everything she could think of to get Kevin Dempsey out of her mind in the past few days. She went and saw the new Woody Allen movie, ate French food at La Giraffe and saw Henry Kissinger at a corner table with his wife, read half of Sara Paretsky's new V. I. Warshawski thriller on the lawn of Bryant Park, took her cat to the Feline Finesse beauty parlor for a wash and set.

She was still shopping for something to wear and was determined that this new hot place called Vanessa on Lexington Avenue and Sixty-fourth Street would be her very last boutique. She was willing to spend $250, since this was coming out of vacation money. The salesman, histrionically gay, was getting a bit miffed by the time Gail tried on the fifth dress.

Then she heard it: the siren and the loud honking. The sounds of distress, danger, fire. As the salesman held out a new Versace, she hurried past him to the front door.

"Madame, this is absolutely *you,*" the salesman said.

But Gail was too busy watching the big red fire engine racing along Lexington Avenue.

From the vestibule of the boutique, she watched the men in the rugged raincoats and big rubber boots racing by in the blinding-red truck, men with big strong arms, ready to wrap them around the frightened people of the big scary city. She imagined Kevin Dempsey carrying her from a flaming building, her arms around his neck, as he took her from the smoke to sweet fresh air and gave her mouth-to-mouth.

It was macho fascination, but it thrilled her in spite of herself.

"Madame," the salesman said, shattering her reverie. "This dress will be perfect on you, no?"

"You have any tight jeans?" Gail Levy asked.

52

As he lay there in post-coital drowse, beside the Sarah Cross of his fantasies, both of them naked, spent, and sweaty, Frank Dempsey did not even think of booze.

"I'm so sorry," Frank said.

"Jesus, you really are Catholic, aren't you?" she said and laughed her marvelous belly laugh.

Frank said, "It's been a long time waiting for such a quick result."

"I'm not asking for a refund," she said.

He laughed. He actually laughed, felt himself rumble with a guffaw, let himself open his eyes in bed in the daylight and look over at her on the big bed, through his swollen, blackened eyes. She climbed on top of him and held herself up with strong-toned arms and looked down at him, careful of his sore ribs. Her face was like a glowing light. Her eyes smiled and her teeth sparkled, every pore in her skin an endless fascination, filled with possibility and promise and excitement. He could find no flaws in her at all. Except that she was here with him. With booze leaking from his skin, reeking from his breath, his stomach bloated from abuse and his liver manufacturing bile as he lay with her. He thought of his insides as a Bosch painting, a landscape of sins of indulgence and corruption.

"I won't say what I'm thinking," Frank said.

"I will," she said. "I have wanted you since I first laid eyes on you. Now I'm not letting you out of my sight."

Frank Dempsey blinked several times. He had to take a pressure piss and felt it wringing in his bladder. He held it in and looked up at her beautiful breasts, ran his hands over her back and behind, and felt her lean down and kiss him again as desert sun lanced through the shuttered windows.

"I'm dying, Sarah," he said.

"Well, postpone it until after we find Polly, will ya?" she said. "You want to find Zoe and I want my money back. No time for funerals right now."

"I have all the money you need," Frank said.

"I don't want your hijacked money. Mine came from my daddy, and I know he'd want me to see that I got to spend it. Some of it I worked for. And it's not the money alone. Polly was supposed to be my friend, and she ripped me off. I don't like anyone ripping me off, especially a friend."

"Don't you ever get tired?"

"Not during the day," she said.

"We'll find her," Frank said. "I need some sleep. I forgot what sex does to a man."

And now suddenly he felt the numbness in the feet and the hollow craving in his limbs and the clawing in his chest cavity. He hacked the empty cough of the addict, the desperate cawing demand for booze.

"Tell me what you were going to tell me on the airplane," she said.

Frank swallowed, ached for a drink, tapped her to indicate he needed to get up. He hurried to the bathroom and closed the door. He flushed the toilet as he vomited, hoping the noise of rushing water would drown out the barf. He rinsed his mouth with Listerine she had packed and when he opened the door she stood there, leaning against the doorframe, in all her gorgeous naked beauty, her body everything a man could ever want, her face a mask of dread.

"How sick are you?" she said.

He stepped past her, straight for his suit jacket, where he fumbled for his Dilantin pills and his Gatorade bottle. He washed down a pill with the booze. He dropped the empty Gatorade bottle in the trash and took out another prepared with the lethal mix. He took two more maintenance gulps.

"I wasn't kidding, Sarah," Frank said, peeking through the blinds at the swimmers in the pool and the oiled bodies on the sun chairs. "I really am dying."

The words floated around the room, but she didn't move a muscle.

"I'm not gonna let that happen," she said.

She walked to him and took his face in her hands, looked him in the eyes. Frank just blinked, relieved he had told her the truth.

"We got a lot of work to do," Sarah said.

53

Gail Levy wore her new prefaded tight jeans with the fancy stitching and the slightly flared bell-bottoms. She hadn't worn bell-bottoms since she was seven or eight years old, back in the seventies. But she loved the snug way they fit, so snug she could not wear panties underneath. She'd also bought a matching vest and a pair of high-heeled cowboy boots and wore a bandanna around her neck, seventies style.

The gallery on Fifty-seventh Street was jammed with people from the art world: critics and collectors, dealers and curators, students and journalists, patrons and groupies and artists. And there were celebrities and accountants and lawyers and male and female models and agents and friends. Most openings were wine-and-cheese affairs, but this was a full buffet of caviar, shrimp, lobster, roast beef, teriyaki, and designer vegetables along with two full bars and a five-piece band.

This was, after all, Richard Smith, the painter phenom out of Connecticut, the one the critics were calling the "hero of zero," meaning the first decade of the twenty-first century, the "0" decade. This was still the nineties of the twentieth century, Gail thought. But the critics were saying that the big, tall, macho Smith had seen the future and it was him.

She found his work, consisting of oversized canvases with aggressive clashing colors, filled with masculine themes and phallic symbolism, sort of compelling, certainly worth gawking at and talking about and showing up for. She would never buy any of it, though. Smith liked to talk about his working-class background, Gail thought, but you'd need to be rich just to have the wall space to hang his work, even if you received one of his canvases as a gift. Which he hadn't offered to Gail anyway.

But then again, she hadn't offered him anything but dinner companionship and phone chat so far. And she hadn't returned his last several calls, being too preoccupied with Kevin Dempsey and his stories and his life.

Gail didn't see her relationship with Richard Smith going any further than what it already was, either. She saw a different twenty-first century, a stable one—a home, a career of her own, a family. The cat.

She didn't see Richard Smith and his high-profile celebrity parties and press junkets fitting into her family portrait.

She had told Smith what Kevin had said about his postcard painting looking like "dicks in a crayon box." She never mentioned his name, just said it was a client. This had infuriated Smith, whose ego was as fragile as his criticisms of others were savage.

"The Bowery Critics Corner," he had remarked in response to Kevin's critique.

Gail moved through the room, gazing at the large paintings, trying to avoid Smith, who kept arching his eyebrows at her through the blurred, animated faces, his whiskey glass at various levels of depletion. Smith drank too much for Gail's comfort, and he was gulping pretty good tonight. His unfortunate privilege, she thought. But his drinking was another reason she hadn't answered any of his recent calls. And why she'd decided she was going home early tonight. Unless she met someone else, sober and interesting, with whom to go share a late decaf.

She looked at the massive canvases, reflecting the size of Smith himself, who was six two, over two hundred pounds, broad-shouldered, and an outdoorsman. It was hard to miss him, even peripherally, as he approached her, his head bobbing above most others in the crowd.

"What do you think?" Smith asked. He had managed to isolate Gail from the crowd, as she studied one big yellow painting.

"It's powerful stuff," Gail said, glancing from the painting to his drink to his half-lit eyes. "You should be very proud."

"I would be prouder if you answered my calls," he said, in a cloud of scotch.

"I've been busy, Richard," she said, fanning his breath away.

He smiled, corraling her in a corner between a velvet rope and the wall next to the big yellow painting, which was called "Sunrise for Señorita." Gail thought it looked an awful lot like a huge banana.

"Busy with what?" he asked, his voice a slurry cross-examination. "The goddam alkies upstate? Christ sakes, why don't you get a job with the ASPCA here in the city?"

"You're not insulting me," Gail said. "But you're insulting yourself. Maybe you could use a few weeks up there yourself."

"Care for a club soda, ma'am?" she heard a voice say from the side.

"No, thanks, I was just leav—"

Kevin Dempsey stood there staring at her, his eyes soft, waiting for an answer. He held out a glass of sparkling soda water and she took it. He had another one for himself. He raised it to her and they both sipped. She looked from Kevin to Richard Smith and then back to Kevin. Both men were staring at her.

Smith was still oblivious of Kevin. "I've left four messages for you in three days," Smith said.

"Hello, Kevin," Gail said.

Smith turned to Kevin and eyed him from head to toe. Kevin was dressed in jeans and Timberland boots and an FDNY sweatshirt under a tan zipper jacket. Smith held his glass to Kevin as if he were a waiter.

"Chivas, rocks," Richard Smith said.

"I didn't get a chance to read you my Fifth Step," Kevin said to Gail, ignoring Richard Smith.

"Who is this person?" Smith asked Gail.

"He's a . . . someone I know."

"You have an invitation, person?"

"I gave you the story instead because I thought maybe it would make sense to you," Kevin told Gail, again ignoring Richard Smith.

"The story was beautiful, Kevin. But that's why—"

"Who the fuck *are* you and what the *fuck* are you doin' at *my* show?" Richard Smith demanded.

Kevin turned to him and then pointed to the painting. "Is it circumcised or uncircumcised?" Kevin asked.

Gail could not help herself as she let loose with a burst of laughter. But a crowd had gathered and they were watching the famous artist jab his finger into Kevin's chest.

"You some kind of a smart-ass?" Smith growled. "You're talking about my work. If you weren't invited here, I don't need to hear your infantile criticism."

"It wasn't criticism," Kevin said, backing up. "It was a question. I admire your work. But all your paintings look like penises, which means you must be obsessed with them, your own or other people's. In fact, this place looks like a bunch of dicks in a crayon box—"

Richard Smith turned to Gail who, horrified, grasped Richard Smith's left arm as he poked Kevin with his right index finger.

"This is one of your dipsos from upstate, isn't it?" Richard Smith said to Gail, as he jabbed Kevin. "Because you already told me that crude line! How dare you bring one of your rehab winos to my opening!"

"I came alone," Kevin said.

"Well then, I'll help you leave alone," Smith said, dropping his glass and grabbing Kevin's jacket. Kevin handed his glass to a startled Gail and grabbed Smith by the wrists, slowly pushing the painter's hands in a downward motion with his superior strength. Their eyeballs locked. Smith was infuriated at being outmatched. The fabric of Kevin's jacket tore in Smith's hands as Kevin pushed him away, his triceps straining, and finally freed himself. Smith reacted to Kevin's strength with a badly thrown right hand that hit Kevin high on the head. Kevin took the punch, staggered, but didn't return it.

Gail knew Kevin would not fight, for the same reason he had not moved to save his friend Carmine in the fire that night. Kevin Dempsey, when he found out his child was not his, had lost a crucial part of himself, and it left him vulnerable.

Gail was horrified. She saw Kevin standing pillar still, his face a mask of pent-up violent rage.

"Kevin, let's get out of here!" she shouted.

Kevin stood with balled fists, glaring at Richard Smith, as the guests stood galvanized by the spectacle.

"You impudent skid-row scum," Richard Smith said as he took off his jacket, assessing Kevin, who stood with his ripped jacket in the midst of the party.

A security guard moved in through the crowd. Smith charged Kevin, but Kevin didn't move. Smith threw another amateurish, cocked-arm punch that busted Kevin's mouth open and sent him reeling into the crowd as gasps and screams echoed. Kevin didn't go down.

"Richard, for Christ sakes, he's not fighting back!" Gail screamed. "He won't fight back!"

"He's a coward," Smith said. "What does he know about the work of a man?"

"You think hitting a defenseless man is manly?" Gail demanded, standing in front of him, placing herself between the bleeding, tattered Kevin and Richard Smith as the crowd gaped in silence.

Smith didn't answer. He shoved Gail aside, strode to Kevin Dempsey, and backhanded him. A welter of blood flew from Kevin's mouth, across "Sunrise for Señorita," red on yellow, and now a security guard rushed up to Kevin's blind side and gave him a belt on the edge of the forehead with his baton, drawing more arterial blood.

Then the guard put his baton around Kevin's neck and half dragged him in a baton choke hold toward the exit and into the stairwell.

"Stop it, stop it, stop it!" Gail shouted. "What's wrong with you people? *Stop* it!"

Gail rushed past a panting, hulking Richard Smith, down the steps from the gallery to Fifty-seventh Street, where the security guard released Kevin onto the hood of a limousine and cautiously backpedaled away from him.

"You fucking asshole!" Gail shouted at the guard.

Now Smith came rushing into the street, looking drunk and haggard, filled with remorse and confusion.

"Jesus, Gail, I'm sorry," he said. "I lost it there for a minute."

Kevin looked at Smith and nodded and turned and walked toward Sixth Avenue in the gathering twilight, blood leaking from his mouth and nose and head, his jacket torn and spotted.

"You *are* a dick!" Gail shouted at Richard Smith. "A worthless, pathetic dick!"

She ran after Kevin and tried to hand him a tissue from her pocket, but Kevin was too consumed with his own guilt.

"No, he was right," Kevin said. "I had no right to ruin his party."

Gail pressed the tissue to his head gash and dabbed the other bleeding wounds. Then she hurried into the street, waving for a taxi.

54

Sarah Cross came into the bungalow from a five-mile walk through the foothills surrounding the Mesquite Ranch. She was invigorated, with a healthy lather of sweat gleaming on her face and body. On the walk with a group of ten clients, past the private homes of rock royalty, movie stars, and Texas oilmen with respiratory problems sent here for the desert air, Sarah had fallen into step with a woman trainer named Nancy who had worked with Polly during her recent stay. Sarah was able to glean from Nancy that Polly had driven here in a car, a Mercedes. She remembered because it had been the only one in the lot with a baby seat. And after the first few days a man came in an airport taxi with a young child and collected the car—the same man who picked Polly up the week before.

Sarah had asked what the man looked like, and Nancy was vague, saying he was tall, thin, dark hair, thirties. "He wasn't Kevin Costner," Nancy said, and they both laughed. Then the two women began talking about physical fitness, and Sarah listed her credentials and told of her plans to open a health club in Manhattan. Sarah had said she'd love to teach a few aerobics classes while staying at the Mesquite. Nancy had said she'd ask her supervisor, because she thought they might be a little short-staffed right now.

When she walked into the bungalow, Frank awakened again in a cold sweat, his body trembling, clutching his stomach. Sarah walked to the bureau top, opened the Valium jar, and placed one blue ten-gram pill on Frank's whitened tongue. Foul-smelling toxins oozed from his breath and pores. She handed him a glass of apple juice to wash down the pill.

In the middle of the night she'd given him a Dilantin pill, to control his veer toward grand mal seizure, and now the Valium would calm the shakes.

"I gotta have a drink," Frank said.

"You have three sober days under your belt," Sarah said. "You fought too hard for them."

"I haven't been out of this bungalow."

"I'm not letting you out until I know you're ready," she said.

"How will you know?"

"I went through this with my dad a dozen times."

"What happened after the last one?"

"Well, his liver was too far gone," she said.

"My doctor said mine is too," Frank said. "This is useless."

"I'll take what I can get," she said. "I've been checking your skin color. It hasn't yellowed."

"You keep feeding me all that shrubbery and I'll turn green," he said. "Lettuce, endive, watercress, broccoli, asparagus . . ."

"Two more days and you can start walking," Sarah said.

"Jesus Christ," Frank said. "Polly's trail will be colder than an archbishop's prick."

"After that you start the physical workouts," she said.

"I could bench-press a vat of Absolut right now," he said.

"After the walk, I went by the hotel where the mystery man stayed with Zoe, like you suggested," Sarah said. "He made all his calls from the pay phone, except the ones to here. Slick. They remembered he was tall, thin, dark-haired, thirties. Nancy, the physical therapist, gave me the same description."

"Well that eliminates half the US of A," he said. "The blondes. What name did he use?"

"Get this," she said. "Kevin Dempsey."

Frank looked up at her and shook his head. "Cunt," he said. "Forgive me."

"My sentiments exactly."

Frank took another sip of apple juice and made a face. "Why would Eve have risked God's wrath for an apple?" he said. "I can think of plenty of other things I'd rather go to hell for. Come to think of it, I'd even settle for hard cider."

Sarah peeled a banana and handed it to him.

"Now I feel like Cheetah," Frank said, taking a bite.

"Who?"

"Tarzan's buddy," he said. "Man, do I hate bananas!"

"You need the potassium and calcium. I bought you some magnesium tablets and some more vitamin C and B-Twelve and a potent multivitamin, Theragran."

"From alkie to pill-head chimp," Frank said. 'Did you buy the Vital K?"

"Yes," she said. "The stuff Imus in the Morning says puts a pup tent in your pants."

"That's the stuff," Frank said. "I never tried it because I never had anyone to share the tent with."

"I'll take all you got," she said, and smiled and kissed him softly on his dry lips.

Sarah applied vitamin E oil to his mouth and under his swollen eyes. She gave him a small collection of vitamins, and he washed them down one at a time with the apple juice. Then she gave him two spoonfuls of the Vital K.

"Panther piss," Frank said, grimacing.

"I've been trying to see if Polly made any phone calls from here," Sarah said.

"Who'd you ask?"

"The woman who checked us in," she said. "She's afraid of getting fired."

"Wait until there's a guy on," Frank said. "A straight guy. Wear a bikini."

"You called me a whore for similar behavior in Boston," she said.

"That was before you were my girl," Frank said, loving the way that sounded—"my girl"—and silently mouthing the words again.

"If I get access to the office, I'll work on getting Polly's phone records," Sarah said.

"How about working on a dry martini for me?" Frank joked.

"You can't mix the booze with the Valium even if you sneaked it. It can kill you."

"I've done it a million times," he said.

"Not on my watch."

"What if I have a seizure from the withdrawal?"

"The Dilantin will prevent that," Sarah said.

"Sarah," Frank said, almost pleading, "instead of now, I think I should dry out *after* we find Polly."

"No," Sarah said. "I want you sober. And I want your face and ribs to heal."

"The hell with my face and ribs!"

"Is this our first fight?" she asked. "Because if it is, I'll kick your ass."

"Promise?"

Sarah walked to him and sat at the edge of the bed, brushed his hair from his forehead with her fingers, looked him in the damaged eyes.

"I don't take that word *promise* lightly," she said. "Because one thing I am is devoted. I am devoted to finding Polly. But I am even more devoted to making you well again. When I promise you something, I mean it."

"I'm a dying man," Frank told her again.

"We'll see about that."

"I'm a crook."

"So was Robin Hood, and you're gonna tell me all about that too," she said.

"I love you, Sarah Cross."

"If you do," she said, "you'll stay alive and let me love you back."

Frank Dempsey said nothing more. He started to tremble with chills, and Sarah slid under the sheets once again beside him, to keep him warm.

In the morning, after a fitful sleep, she gave him more tranquilizers and vitamins and Dilantin. And food: oatmeal and bananas and soft-boiled eggs.

"Tell me again about the corrective shoes," she said.

Frank ran through it once more. He told her about how Polly had left in such a rush that she left Zoe's shoe brace behind at Jelly Beans School in Park Slope, Brooklyn. He said he'd tracked it down to a Gutter's Shoes on Fifth Avenue in Brooklyn. He knew if Polly had any mothering instinct left she would have to get a new brace for the child. So he had asked Gutter to see if he could get a list of all new corrective shoes issued by the Achilles Heels Company. He'd told Gutter there was a few dollars in it for him if he could get the information.

"Ingenious," Sarah said.

She thought he sounded clear-headed and bright; even his mouth smelled clean. When he pushed himself to a sitting position on the bed, he looked strong. He stretched and yawned. Then Sarah saw him smile. She could tell he was nearing complete detoxification. She would start breaking the Valium pills in half, cutting the dosage to wean him off them too. He'd have to stay on the Dilantin for another week; then he could gradually get off them too. He needed a shave, a shower, a hike, some aerobics, and a swim. Sarah couldn't wait to get him some sun and a haircut and some muscle tone. He'll be one gorgeous son of a bitch, she thought.

"Not really ingenious," Frank said. "You can usually track someone by medical connections. This is a little odd, but not too odd. Lots of kids wear these corrective shoes. Especially nationwide. But that makes the search a little hard."

She didn't tell him about the Pepper Face Doll because she wanted to keep it as a hole card in case she wound up separated from him. Besides, that lead was so remote.

"When did you last check to see if Gutter the shoe guy called?" Sarah asked.

"How the hell would I know if anyone called?" Frank asked. "I'm not home. Besides, ever since I heard about Zoe's British passport, I sort of gave up on the corrective shoes lead."

"You told me you had a machine, as if it were a rocket ship or something," Sarah said.

"Yeah, but you have to be home to get your messages," Frank said.

"Not in this century," she said. "What make is it?"

"Japanese," Frank said.

"Jesus," she said. "That narrows it down. I bet it's a one-digit code. Most are now. Mine is. I have a Panasonic—"

"That's it," he said. "Kevin bought it for me for Christmas. It's the TV that's a Sony."

"I'll do a little trial-and-error to get the messages for you," she said.

"I'll see if Kevin is out. And I'll call Gutter's Shoes on the phone. I've been asking everyone here about Polly, but no one remembers much about her. There's a dozen things to do. I'll take the cell phone out of the car and sit poolside—"

"I need a triple cellular gimlet," Frank said.

"Which reminds me. Time for half a Valium and some sleep." She handed him a pill with a glass of water. "Salad, baked potato, granola bread, and vegetable broth for din-dins. Tomorrow will be day four."

"Four. Four Roses and ginger," Frank said. "Big Paulie used to drink that. And Three Feathers and Seagram's Seven, Johnnie Walker Ten, Double Diamond beer. Some people paint by the numbers; my old man drank by them. Sarah, I gotta get out of here."

"We're staying till you're better," she said. "As long as it takes. Complete alcohol detox usually takes ninety-six hours."

She looked at him suddenly falling back on the bed, clutching his left side, unfurling to a prone position again.

"Sarah, I'm scared," Frank said, his eyes suddenly like shattered glass. "I wasn't, before I met you, because I had nothing to lose. But now I have everything to lose and it scares the hell out of me."

"We're in this together," she said, and kissed his forehead.

Sarah sat with him and listened to his half-conscious disjointed mumbling for another fifteen minutes until the pill took hold and Frank was fast asleep. She watched him in the half peace. So he wasn't a trophy catch, she thought. But he was a truly noble man.

55

"No hospitals," Kevin Dempsey had said when they wandered down Fifty-seventh Street after no taxi would take him because of his bleeding. "They'll put me back in a psycho ward."

"Then you'll have to come home with me," Gail said. Immediately, he knew she regretted it. A counselor is never supposed to take a client home. He knew that too, but he wasn't concerned with ethics now. Tonight, on this street, with blood drooling down his face, they were not counselor and client, they were man and woman. Need and demand. Here and now.

Once in the kitchen of her apartment on Fifty-sixth Street, Gail kept up the counselor facade as she cleaned and irrigated his wounds with peroxide and put a Band-Aid on the shallow cut on his forehead. Suddenly, Kevin Dempsey, who had been so docile with Richard Smith only half an hour before, urgently grabbed Gail Levy by the back of the neck, twisting a hank of hair in his right hand. He kissed her. She was startled. He wanted her to be. He wanted her to be as frightened as he was. To share his fear—and everything else.

"I cannot do this," she said, moving into the living room, as he continued to hold her. Their eyes met in the reflection in the big blackened windows. She pressed herself closer to him. Kevin sensed that Gail was excited by the image of him gruffly holding her. It certainly excited him.

"You mean you will not," he said.

"I can't, I won't," she insisted. "I'm your counselor."

"No. No, you're not," he said, one hand on her hair, the other wrapped around her waist, his eyes boring into hers, his bloody teeth bared. "You never read my real secrets. You never told me yours. We're strangers."

"Your mouth is still bleeding," Gail said, staring at his crimson lips.

"Good," he said.

He pressed his mouth on her mouth, felt her resist, but he kept his bloodied lips against hers, rolled his tongue over hers, until he was sure his blood was in her mouth. They parted lips and she licked hers, swallowing his blood. He stepped back, held her at arm's length, and saw the blood on her mouth and chin and her eyes wide with fear and desire.

"You scare me," she whispered. "I haven't been with a man in eight months."

"I'm already inside you."

"It's too soon," she said, trembling.

"Life is too short for anything to ever be too soon," he said.

She swallowed again, touched the back of her hand to her lips, looked at the blood. Brought it slowly back to her mouth. Placed her lips over the blood smear on her hand, closed her eyes. Took a deep breath.

"I want the man I saw in the gym," she said.

"I want the woman who watched," he said.

"Promise not to hurt me?"

"No."

He carried her to the bedroom and laid her down on the bed. The cat fled for the living room with a meow. Kevin quickly pulled away his clothes and stood naked and damaged in front of her. Then he knelt on the bed and deftly undid her belt and slid her out of her new tight faded denim jeans.

"You know Billy Joel?" Sarah asked.

"Huh?"

"Someone named the Piano Man left a message on your machine."

"That would be Pinebox," Frank said, laughing, as he walked from the bed and looked out the window through the blinds at the brilliant desert morning sky, magenta red against the mountains. Already, by 7 A.M., the tanned and sober people lay poolside in the sun. "My old man called him the Librarian."

"Who the hell is Pinebox?" Sarah asked.

Frank looked up at the perfect azure sky, dotted with tiny white marshmallow clouds.

"Why do you ask?"

"His message was weird," Sarah said, reading from a note pad, feigning a gravelly gangster's voice. "He said, 'This is the Piano Man. You know that piano we talked about? Talk to me about it. Pay phone.' He sounded like he was calling from Central Casting."

Frank turned and stretched his arms over his head, his ribs aching but clearly mending. He let out a loud grunt as he rotated his body from the waist, arching his back, snapping his head back and forth, and listening to his neck crack.

"Central Booking is more like it," Frank said, taking a deep breath, bending at the waist and touching his toes. "I used to drink in a bar down near Central Booking on Gold Street called the Alibi."

"Who is Pinebox?" she asked, cutting off his drink-related meandering.

"He's a gangster who's going to give back the money for me," Frank said, walking briskly to the bathroom.

Sarah followed him to the door of the bathroom and watched him turn on the water taps. He looked at her, dressed in cutoff white shorts, a halter top, and sandals, gold earrings glinting against gleaming tanned skin.

"You are amazingly beautiful," Frank said, kissed her, reached for a toothbrush, and squeezed the Colgate onto the bristles. He began to brush vigorously, scouring his gums and tongue and the roof of his mouth. He stopped brushing suddenly, stood up straight, looked in the mirror.

"Well, I'll be damned!" he said.

"What?"

"First time in years I remember brushing my teeth without getting sick," Frank said, grinning a foamy smile.

"Congratulations. Welcome to the human race," Sarah said. "But the money, is it the money you took from the evidence room?"

"Yes," Frank said, gleefully brushing his teeth with wild abandon now, indulging in the simple ritual, the lather foaming at his mouth like a rabid dog's.

"The million and a half dollars?"

"What's left of it when we're through," he mumbled with the brush working on the back molars.

"Give it back to who?"

"Botero," Frank said, taking the brush from his mouth and inspecting it for blood from the gums. There was none. His eyes widened in delight.

"Who's Botero?"

"Botero? Oh, he's a Dominican coke dealer. My father was involved in the bust of a guy who was working for Botero."

"So, wasn't that his job?" Sarah said.

"Yeah," Frank said, and then scooped a mouthful of water and swished it around his mouth and spit it out. "Only my dad was also on Botero's payroll. I didn't know about that until it was too late. Big Paulie—that was my dad—was a heavy gambler. He owed a bundle to Pinebox, who is one of your old-fashioned Mafioso-bookmaker slash loan-shark hoods from Brooklyn."

"Yeah, so?"

"So to pay him, my dad rented his badge to Botero," Frank said, flashing his teeth in the mirror, darting out his pink, healthy-looking tongue. "He was supposed to look the other way in a money-laundering scheme. Only in comes a new administration at City Hall and a new police commissioner, who puts in new guys in suits in my dad's dirty crew uptown. They nail Botero's main bagman with the million and a half dollars in coke cash. But the Dominicans have a rule. If you double-cross the dealer you work for, he takes out your family. Especially if you're a dirty cop. It sends out a warning to other dirty cops."

"Oh, Jesus!"

Frank splashed handfuls of steaming hot water on his face until he could feel his five-day growth begin to soften. Then he squirted Edge shaving cream into his right hand and worked it into a Santa's beard of foam. He took a Gillette disposable razor from the medicine cabinet and ran it under the hot water. He waited to let the shaving cream marinate his face before he started to shave.

"Internal Affairs had suspicions about my father, so they never warned him about the bust," Frank said. "And they made him go along on it, blind. And clerk it. On paper, and therefore on the street, it looked like he'd double-crossed Botero. Which meant my family—father, brothers, sister, nieces, nephews—all had bull's-eyes on their backs. And IAB was watching my father like a hawk. But I still had clearance to the evidence room. So one day I took the million and a half and went to lunch. They've interrogated me, harassed me, and eventually they'll indict me. But they can't find the money."

"Why you, Frank?" Sarah asked in a sad whisper.

Frank began to shave, very slowly at first, listening to the scraping of the sharpened steel on his heavy whiskers, remembering standing at Big Paulie's side when he was a child, wanting so much to shave like him that he shaved his own eyebrows, which grew back cockeyed.

As Sarah watched, he took two strokes of his beard with a steady hand on the razor. He turned to Sarah, who stood watching him, her eyes sad and reflective. He held his hands straight out to see just how steady he was. He was amazed that they didn't tremble. He placed a strip of toilet paper on his outstretched right hand to see if that trembled. It did, but only ever so slightly.

"My God, Sarah," Frank said. "I'm sober and I'm not shaking. Like normal people. Like the normal people in their science-fiction normal lives."

"Why you, Frank?" Sarah asked again. "Why'd you have to risk everything for your dad? The family?"

He took two slow shaving strokes and then turned to her. "Because he was my daddy," Frank said, looking clear-eyed at Sarah for the very first time. "And I was his firstborn son. Because I loved him. Because I have no kids."

"That doesn't mean you climb up on the cross, Frank," Sarah said.

"Funny you should say that," Frank said. "Ten years ago, on a Palm Sunday morning when I was working crime scene, I was the first to arrive at a call of shots-fired out on New Lots Avenue in East New York. I walked in, and the whole family was sitting around in front of a television set. *Face the Nation* was on. It was an idyllic scene. The father was in his recliner, his glasses on the tip of his nose, the newspaper spread on his lap. The mother had knitting needles in her hands, in the process of making a sweater for her eighteen-month-old daughter, who sat in the high chair with a bowl of Fruit Loops in front of her. The two boys, fifteen and ten, sat on the couch with Campbell's tomato soup and bologna sandwiches on the coffee table. There were pictures of Jesus and Mary on the walls and a crucifix over the front door."

"Frank, this is all very interesting—"

He put a dab of shaving cream on her nose and laid a finger on her lips.

"It was a lovely family scene," Frank said. "Only thing wrong with the picture was that every one of them had a .25-caliber bullet in the back of the skull."

"Not the baby!" Sarah said.

"Including the baby," Frank said. "The oldest son, who was not there, had double-crossed the local dealer and committed suicide when he couldn't make amends. In those circles suicide does not end a double cross. So the dealer killed his family. This was the dealer's message to the entire community. Cross him, and the whole family dies. He set the bodies up like figures in a wax museum because he knew it would get maximum media attention. It was page one of all the English and Spanish-language papers the next day."

"Did they ever catch the dealer?" Sarah asked.

"We knew whose crew it was," Frank said, "but we could never prove it was Botero."

"Same guy?"

"Yeah," Frank said. "I took Botero's money out of the evidence room because I figured I could get it back to him before he whacked my sister and brothers and their kids for what he thought my father did to him. The alternative was for me to go kill him first. But he has, like, nine brothers and two hundred cousins and nephews, all in his crew. There was no way for me to fight the whole Botero family. The police could never protect my clan. So I did what I had to do to save the Dempsey family."

Sarah looked at Frank, who told his story in a slow monotone, devoid of emotion, like a man reading his lease aloud.

"So you took the weight for your father," Sarah said. "Made it look like you were the one on Botero's payroll. Why?"

"Well, he was the father of my *family,*" Frank said. "It's hard to explain if you don't have one. But it comes down to me, Big Paulie's firstborn son, to see that the Dempsey name, the family line, continues. I never had kids, so I have to protect my brothers' and sister's kids, the ones with the Dempsey name. That's one of the reasons I have to find Zoe. She's part of the chain. I can't let a family that spans the centuries die so ignobly because of the sins of my father."

"But why do you have to do this alone?" Sarah said.

"There's no need to destroy the image the others have of their father," Frank said. "Their grandfather. The family needs a role model. Big Paulie might not have been much of one, but he was the best we had. He never took a dime from an honest man. He had some principles. He had pride. They need Big Paulie more in death now than they did in life. And it's my job to see they don't get slaughtered, that the family name isn't obliterated by a single madman's crew."

"And so you went to another gangster?" Sarah said, incredulous.

"I got word to Botero that I wanted to give him his money back in exchange for him lifting the hit on the Dempseys," Frank said. "He said okay. I sent word about how hot I was and that I couldn't move the money right away. I told him I needed six months to cool off. He gave me four. Three months are already gone. But I can't trust him, so I went to Pinebox to act as middleman, for a fee. As a guarantor of the deal. If he delivers the money, he can get a better promise out of Botero to call off the whack than I ever could. Botero doesn't want a war with the Italian mob."

"Will you ever tell your family the truth?" Sarah asked.

"My father left a note, saying it was all his fault, blah, blah, blah," Frank said. "But that would only have hurt his family more, to know he died dirty. I know what it did to me to learn he might be crooked. A year before this all happened, I heard from a source in IAB that Big Paulie might be on the pad. When I found out, I started drinking real hard instead of approaching him, confronting him, doing something about it. I should have stopped him. But I couldn't ask my daddy if he was dirty. I just couldn't challenge his immense pride. He was Big Paulie, self-made man. Instead I drank to blur the pain. Which was a cop-out. Excuse the pun. I know what it did to me, so I can't let the rest of the Dempseys know they come from dirty stock. Simple as that."

Frank finished shaving, rinsed his face, ran his hands over the smooth skin, toweled his face dry. He looked around the medicine cabinet.

"I had aftershave," he said.

"I threw it out."

"Why?"

"I thought you might drink it."

Frank chuckled. "That's true love."

"Now you're throwing away your life, Frank," Sarah said. "Why don't you just tell the truth?"

"Because Botero doesn't care what the truth is," Frank said. "Just how it looks on the street. The Dempsey family is responsible. I'll get him his money back. As far as my family is concerned, let my father's disgrace stay buried with him."

"And so after you give all this money back to Botero," Sarah said, "you go to jail?"

"Well . . . if they can prove it."

"That's unacceptable," Sarah said. "You only did what you thought was best for the family."

"Yeah, but it's still illegal."

"Maybe your brothers can help."

"No, I'm helping *them,"* he said. "Get it straight. This is one of those things you do outside the law. Like finding Zoe."

"I can't let you go to jail."

"That's down the road," Frank said and walked past her toward the front door.

"Where do you think you're going?" Sarah asked. "Tomorrow is day five, and I'm gonna start you on an exercise regime. Start you running. Right now, you need rest."

Frank pulled open the front door and sunlight exploded into the darkened room. Frank squinted into the morning glare, aware of his pale gray skin, of his protruding belly that was seventy-five-percent liver, his sagging pectorals.

"You'll burn to a crisp," Sarah said.

"Make the devil's job easier," Frank said with a wink.

He stepped out with bare feet onto the hot flagstone and began walking, with the tanned, toned, and smiling Sarah following a step behind him.

"What the hell are you doing, Frank?"

"What else was on my answering machine?" he asked as he walked, suddenly realizing there was no numbness in his feet, no pins and needles, just the hot stone sending warmth up into his pulsating blood.

"Kevin is out, nobody knows where," she said.

"Great," Frank said, walking a step ahead of Sarah. "Just fucking great. If he's drinking and I'm not I'll drown him."

"And I spoke to Gutter; he's nervous and cute," she said. "Said he's expecting news for you any day now. He wouldn't be specific. I gave him this number and the fax line number."

"Sarah," Frank said as he walked straight for the pool, past the curious sunbathers who sat up to gaze at this white apparition in the shimmering desert haze.

"Yeah?"

"Will you stand for me?"

"I told you I was devoted, Frank," Sarah said, quickening her pace to keep stride with Frank, who took long confident strides toward the pool. "I'll always stand by you."

Frank held his face aloft, directly into the sun, as he neared the edge of the pool.

"With this water—" Frank never broke stride as he took a step off the edge of the pool, face to the heavens, and plunged into the deep end, fully submerging himself.

Underwater, he held his breath and began a silent Act of Contrition: *O my God, I am heartily sorry for having offended thee . . .*

When his lungs could hold air no more, he popped to the surface and saw the blue celestial sky and the many smiling healthy faces all around the edge of the pool in the brilliant morning sun. There were rainbows in the droplets on his eyelashes, and through them he saw Sarah Cross beaming at him as she dived into the water after him.

Frank Dempsey had never felt more alive.

Gail Levy awoke in pleasant surprise. She felt the rippling arms around her, hot breath on her neck, and Kevin Dempsey deep inside her again, penetrating her from behind as she lay on her side, his powerful legs straining, hard belly grinding. His probe was slow and gentle at first but now the thrusts came, rapid and urgent, and she arched her back and pushed herself to him, joining the rhythm. She felt his large left hand slide under her blouse and gather both her breasts in his grip, flattening and then individually kneading each breast, rolling her nipples between his fingers.

"Kevin—"

"Tell me you're mine."

"All yours," she said.

He flipped her on her back and mounted her, her arms looping around his neck, as he slid between her legs and back inside, her legs scissoring him.

"How come you can make love but you won't defend yourself?"

"Because you are as scared as me."

"You're right," she said. "You don't have to be gentle."

And so he wasn't, and neither was she.

Later, when it was too late, lying still, breathing heavily, she said, "I didn't use any protection."

She detected secret irony in his smile.

"We have lots to talk about," Gail said.

"I'm here."

"What about your baby? Zoe?"

Kevin looked Gail in the eyes and said, "You're my baby."

She shuddered and abandoned all common sense and reason and lost herself in his arms again, climbed atop him and straddled him.

"I have all the time in the world and nowhere to go," Kevin Dempsey said.

"You ain't going nowhere," Gail Levy said.

Part III

56

Gail Levy looked at Dr. Linda Hartnett with her eyes wide open in query. She had been with Kevin now for just over a week.

"So who's the lucky daddy?" asked Dr. Hartnett, a folksy middle-aged woman.

"Oh, God, no," Gail said.

"Yes, your home kit was apparently correct, babe," Dr. Hartnett said. "Your HCG test is positive and you're ready for mamaland."

"There's no mistake?" Gail said. "I do feel different. Like there's something new and *alive* inside me. You're *sure?* It's not just wishful thinking?"

"I don't do brain surgery," the doctor said. "But I think I know a positive pregnancy test from a negative. They're very sophisticated now in detecting even the very earliest pregnancy. Which in your case means there's still plenty of time if you want to change your mind. How long you been seeing this guy?"

"He's been living with me a little over a week," she said. "I know that doesn't sound so good, but I *know* him much longer and it just happened. I guess I half wanted it to."

"A week! Jesus Christ, where's the fire?"

"How'd you know he was a fireman?"

"Ask a stupid question . . ."

"Maybe this is more than I bargained for."

"You better talk it over with him, no? What's he like?"

Gail smiled so broadly there was no need for words.

"Jesus, what I wouldn't do to be in my twenties again," the doctor said.

"Everything else is okay?"

"You are in perfect health," Dr. Hartnett said. "You should carry a very healthy child. But I detect nicotine on your teeth. Better stop smoking."

"He tortured me into stopping already," Gail said.

"Good, he must care about you," the doctor said.

Gail loved the way that sounded. He cares about *you.* She quickly wrote the doctor a personal check and said, "I'll let you know, okay?"

"Personally," the doctor said, "I'd like to be there eight or nine months from now. But only if it's right. Otherwise, I'll be here when you need me. Make up your mind, the sooner the better. For everyone concerned. Having a baby is not like picking out clothes. You choose and it's a lifer, kiddo."

"Thank you, doctor."

Gail left the doctor's office with her mind a swirl of newborn images. She stepped out of the building on Fifty-seventh Street and caught a glimpse of herself in the window of Henri Bendel and imagined herself with a proud swollen belly, ready to impose on the world an unbridled colt of a child, exploding with the genes of Kevin Dempsey and Gail Levy. Jesus, she hoped it would be a boy! And that it would look like him. Big and strong like Kevin, filled with ideas and smart and eager to learn. A kid who would have the best schools and see the world, a kid who would be proud to say, This is my mom and this is my dad and . . .

And of course all that is preposterous, she thought. Gail Levy, yuppie career woman, wasn't going to have a baby. She'd only known Kevin for five weeks, half of them as his counselor and one of them as his mad, horny, affection-crazed, and rebellious lover.

In that time he'd knocked her up and made her quit smoking, two things she'd wanted since she had gotten clean and sober.

Now her vacation was over. She had to go back to work on Monday. Kevin would have to deal with the Fire Department and get his annulment and find out what he would do to live. Would he go back to school, become a writer? Or would he find some peace and go back to fighting fires and saving lives? Both? What would it be?

Certainly he would be in no rush to walk down the aisle and tie the knot again and raise another baby after what happened the first time.

Kevin Dempsey was in early recovery, and the burden would be too much for him. He wasn't even supposed to get involved in a serious relationship for at least a year after starting his recovery. But there are exceptions. And right now he was going to his AA meetings every day, determined to make ninety meetings in ninety days, as prescribed by the program.

Gail, of course, never went to the same meetings as Kevin. He needed a place to go and air out his feelings without her, just as she needed a place to go shed her own burdens. She even encouraged him to go to men's-only meetings at least once a week.

The truth was she didn't go to many meetings anymore, being so close to the program in her work. But when she did need one, she chose one far away, sometimes in New Jersey or Connecticut or Long Island, where no one knew her.

But right now Gail wasn't in need of a meeting. Instead she found herself drawn to the windows of Bloomingdale's down on Lexington Avenue. She entered the great store in a mood she'd never felt before. She had experienced all the bogus euphoric sensations of cocaine, marijuana, pills, and alcohol in her life. But this was different; this was sheer and utter joy. A swelling crest of promise and hope and fulfillment, a rush of true and honest happiness. She felt giddily proud to be a *woman*.

Over the years she had bought everything in Bloomingdale's, from underwear to leather coats, shoes to earrings, perfume to men's shirts for Father's Day or forgotten boyfriends.

But today would be a different day at Bloomie's. Today she would journey to the third floor to indulge in that sacred club no man would ever have the privilege of joining: the maternity clothes section, the club for women with life growing inside their bellies. Here the clear-skinned women with the dreamy eyes poked through uncomfortable days, touching the fabrics of clothing that would be part of a brand-new experience called motherhood.

Grandmothers and sisters and nieces and aunts and women friends all shopped here too. Even a brave man or two, looking totally baffled.

Gail had always wanted to go to the third floor as a member of the club and see what it felt like to browse for an unborn child. Her own unborn child. In the newborn infant section, she saw a ballerina dress and a sailor suit and a big print dress for herself. She touched them all and then fingered cute and funny hats and big preggie underwear and baby shoes and infant snugglers and down-filled blankets. Yellows and pinks and baby blues and frills and satins and wools and cottons. All the colors and fabrics of a brand-new life that would be the product of Kevin Dempsey and Gail Levy.

Preposterous, she thought.

But, oh, how clean and pure it made her feel inside! She shivered and smiled and bought the sailor suit just because she had never spent money as a member of this special club before.

But as she paid she felt a chilly whisper: No child of hers and Kevin's would ever get to wear it.

57

Zoe Dempsey's mommy tied the shoes too tight. They made Zoe cry. Only her daddy knew how to tie them so they wouldn't hurt so much. Now mommy called the man she called Zoe's new daddy to fix them. He undid the laces on the corrective shoes and pulled all the wrinkles from Zoe's socks and smoothed her soles and gently slid the left foot in.

"Is that okay?" the man asked.

Zoe nodded and wiped a tear. "My daddy says this will make my leg better," Zoe said.

"Your daddy is right."

"What is wrong with you?" Zoe's mommy whispered to the man. "Past tense, use the past tense when you speak about him."

Zoe's mommy walked to Zoe and kissed her mouth. The child made a face and waved her hand.

"Yuk," Zoe said. "Wine tastes like medicine."

The man slipped Zoe's other foot into the shoe and tied the laces snugly but not too tight.

"How does that feel?" the man asked.

"It doesn't hurt like when Mommy does it," Zoe said. "You do it like Daddy does it."

"Daddy's gone," Polly said.

"No, he's coming back," Zoe said, her voice splintering into alarm. "I want my Pepper."

Polly walked to the toy chest and took the Pepper Face Doll from the top of twenty others and brought it to Zoe. The child took the doll in her arms, hugging it tightly, as she lay there motionless in the leg brace.

"Auntie Sarah gave me her," she said to the man. "Her name is Mint. Pepper Mint, like the candy."

"She's beautiful," the man said.

"Her birthday is soon," Zoe said. "It comes a week before mine. She'll be one years old."

"That's great," the man said.

"And she gets a birthday card in the mail," she said.

"No kidding?"

"Right, Mommy?" Zoe said.

"Well . . . we moved, so I—"

"I'm sure they'll find her and send one," the man said quickly.

"Of course they will, honey," said Polly. "They promise they'll send her birthday card anywhere in the world. So they'll know where to find Mint. Everyone knows where to find Miss Pepper Mint."

Polly walked to Zoe and kissed her.

"Go to sleep, darling," Polly said, and closed the bedroom door.

58

Kevin Dempsey put his name up on the bulletin board on the list of new Alcoholics Anonymous members looking for a sponsor. He was ready now to take his *real* Fifth Step, but he could hardly give it to Gail Levy. She could know some of his secrets, and already did, but he was not yet ready to tell her about his sterility. For that, he needed the ear and heart of a stranger. A man. A man who wouldn't judge him on his virility.

His relationship with Gail was too new, too fresh, too important to endanger. She was everything Kevin had ever wanted in a woman—starting with good-looking. That always came first with all honest men, and he was not ashamed to admit it. But Gail was also smart, independent, apparently loyal. And *secure.* Maybe that was most important. If she was secure in her own life, she could eventually accept his. Even the limitations. But if, when he told her of his sterility, she found that she could not live without having a child, he would understand. That would be a pain he could tolerate so long as she was honest and forthright.

"I'm sorry, Kevin, but this will not work out because I want to carry and give birth to a baby."

If Gail ever said that, Kevin could roll with that punch, stagger, but wouldn't fall. Again. It would break his heart but would not steal his soul. The way Polly had.

Now, in the church basement on the Upper West Side of Manhattan, the AA meeting was breaking up. He'd been living with Gail for over a week now, and this morning the phone company came and installed a separate line for him, to which he had hooked up his answering machine. All his calls from Brooklyn were now call-forwarded here. Kevin wanted his own line because he was tired of listening to Richard Smith's messages on Gail's tape, begging her forgiveness, pleading to see her. Twice when Kevin had answered Gail's phone, the caller on the other end—probably Smith—had hung up. He needed his own line.

So now he could take calls and get messages from his family and the Fire Department, who were still determining what to do with him after giving him a battery of new physical and psychological tests.

He took the advice Carmine gave him when he visited him upstate and put in his papers for a three-quarters medical retirement disability. He was certain he could never run into a burning building again. If he couldn't bring himself to throw a punch at Richard Smith, how the hell could he run into a wall of flame? If they did send him to another fire, he might endanger the lives of his fellow firefighters the way he'd almost killed Carmine. The way he'd forced Carmine into an early retirement.

He hadn't called Carmine since he got out. He was afraid to. He was afraid that if he saw him, the first thing he'd want to do was head for a saloon and laugh and drink beer and rap to girls and go nuts, the way they did in the old days. Before he married Polly. Kevin did not want to drink, he already was nuts, and the only girl he wanted to talk to was Gail.

Those wacky days were gone. Like elementary school. Probie school. Polly. And Zoe.

Kevin erased Zoe's face with thoughts of Gail and wrote his new number on the sponsor list. He left the church basement behind a group of men, recovering alcoholics who needed the company of men and their privileged secrets. Kevin had not shared with the all-men's Fifth Step group that night but listened instead to others who had taken their honest Fifth Step, guys brave enough to admit to strangers what they could never tell their wives—that they were bisexual, bigamists, or fugitives. Scared, sick, broke. Out of love, out of time, out of luck.

Kevin couldn't wait to get home to play with some of these stories. Gail had let him use her home computer, and he was getting the hang of it. He was also getting the hang of life with Gail. He might not be able to drink or brawl or fight fires anymore, but he knew there was one part of his manhood that hadn't changed: the part that could fall in love with a woman.

Frank Dempsey knew he had to get out of the spa soon and back on the road to find Zoe. Time was running out on his deals with Pinebox and Botero. He felt better than he had in years, clear of eye and sound of mind, strong of limb and sure of foot. Sarah had brought him back from the ninth circle of hell. But he had stayed here in limbo too long. He couldn't afford to wait much longer. He had a family to salvage.

He stood in the pool in the aquarobics class, pushing his arms through the resistance of the water in time to the rock-and-roll dance music the instructor played from the boom box. But he was not watching the instructor. He had taken this class twice a day now for over a week, this and the indoor weight training and resistance classes. And the brisk five-mile nature walks through the mountains, past the million-dollar homes of the chronic rich.

He'd smiled when Sarah had told him the million and a half he had stashed would only be a down payment on most of these houses. In

Brooklyn a mil and a half was all the money in the world. Here near the Mesquite Ranch it furnished a living room. And yet the money stood between the life of Frank Dempsey's family and their deaths at the hands of a drug gangster.

Now, as Frank did his aquarobics, he watched Sarah through the window of the big gymnasium as she finished leading a step class. After a week in which Sarah showed up the instructors here with her gymnastic ability, Nancy, the personal trainer, had helped arrange with management to barter Sarah's teaching a few classes for room and board for her and Frank at the spa. This dovetailed nicely, as one regular instructor had been lucky enough to get three scenes in an episode of a weekly television series in LA and was away on leave.

Sarah Cross, wearing a yellow leotard under a tonged orange outerwear bikini that split her butt in half, was the talk of the Mesquite Ranch spa. The men gaped at her and the women stared at the men gaping at her. And then the women took her classes in hopes of looking like her, so the men would start looking at them again instead of Sarah.

After three days of angling, Sarah had also finally started working behind the reception desk. The day before, they had showed her how to log on to the main computer, but she had not yet been left alone long enough to check Polly Edgeworth's telephone calls.

Now Frank was watching Sarah walk from her step class, towel around her sweaty shoulders, across the grounds and past the pool. All eyes followed her. Frank continued to push the water, enjoying the strength returning to his arms, feeling the pain in his shoulders and the swell in his chest and lungs. As he watched Sarah Cross walk, knowing that only he got to explore her naked body, he found the strength to pick up the pace with the tempo of the song.

The instructor, half-Indian, half-white, was a perfect-looking, tanned, long-haired Adonis who called himself Thunder, a name Frank laughed at when he was introduced. Thunder had high cheekbones, rippling muscles, long straight jet-black hair, green eyes, perfect teeth. Frank simply couldn't understand why Sarah wouldn't want *him,* a perfect male specimen, over a busted-out dirty cop with a liver the size of a weather balloon. Neither could the instructor, who had tried to chat her up and gotten nowhere.

"I'd never get to use the bathroom," Sarah had said when Frank asked why she didn't go after a guy like Thunder. "After finishing with himself, how much love could he have for anyone else? But mostly because he isn't you."

"I think your only flaw is your taste in men," Frank had said, shaking his head.

"And I do not detect an iota of nobility in him," she said. "He might be nimble but you're noble. The noblest man I ever met—after my father."

And now both the nimble instructor and the noble Frank and almost everyone else watched Sarah stride across the quadrangle of the spa and enter the front office in search of some clue to Polly's whereabouts.

Frank knew this. No one else did. He saw her walk behind the desk and close the counter flap. She was in, he thought.

Frank stayed in the water after his class ended and the music was shut off, gasping for breath under the blazing desert sun. He was naturally high with the endorphins set loose by the exertion. He felt stronger than he had in years. After almost two weeks without drink, he had gone through withdrawal and lost ten pounds of booze bloat, had tanned his body to a golden brown, had his hair clipped short to camouflage the thinning caused by the Dilantin, had regained a healthy appetite for healthful food, could see and hear and smell more sharply, had escaped the pollen in the desert wind, and fallen so deeply in love with Sarah that life should have presented itself as a promise again.

But Frank knew something darker.

Anthony Scala had told him the damage he had already caused his liver was probably irreversible. He could have this last run, but it was a *final* run.

He dared not talk negatively in front of Sarah any longer because such pessimism saddened her and made her cry, because it brought up her own father's death of liver failure. Frank did not want any of the time they had left together to be spent unhappily.

Despite how well he looked and felt, Frank had seen his jaundiced future in his eyes that morning. Saw the orange and yellow poison of the cirrhosis. And it ripped him apart inside, knowing that he would soon have to leave.

He could not let Sarah watch him die the same way as her father.

As soon as he got the information he needed, Frank Dempsey would be gone.

Alone.

59

Margie Dempsey watched the thin, sickly looking woman rake the leaves from her big lawn into small manageable piles. More leaves continued to fall around her in the thin fall wind. Margie climbed out of her car slowly and walked to the front gate of the large estate on Ditmas Avenue. Lucy looked up from her raking and smiled politely and continued to gather the golden and brown leaves of the dead season. Then she looked up again and saw that Margie was still standing by the gate.

"I'm sorry," Lucy said, in her level monotone. "Can I help you?"

"Maybe," Margie said. "Lucy? Lucy Carbone?"

"Bronsky now," Lucy said. "Sorry. You look familiar, but—"

"You were a friend of my brother's."

"Oh?"

"Kevin," Margie said, turning to the private security car that honked hello as it passed, the driver, who sat with a dog, waving at Lucy. She waved back.

"Kevin Dempsey," Lucy said. "Yeah, I remember you now. You're his sister, Marie."

"Margie."

"Sorry," Lucy said, walking toward the gate, dragging the rake behind her across the yellowing lawn.

"It's okay," Margie said. "It's been some time."

"Yeah," Lucy said. "Lot of leaves off the tree since then. I do this because I need the exercise. I'm not too cheap to hire a kid. But the doctors say I should get some outdoor exercise, and I hate jogging."

"Tell me about it," Margie said and laughed.

Lucy bent and scooped up big handfuls of leaves and began stuffing them into a large green plastic bag. Margie pushed open the gate, put down her pocketbook, and crouched down to help. Margie was wearing a navy-blue dress skirt, medium heels, and a blue blazer. She gathered the leaves in her hands and pushed them into the bag. Both women were squatting now, looking at each other eye to eye, their hands filled with the fallen leaves.

"Kevin was here not long ago," Lucy said, without changing inflection. "It wasn't what you'd call a social visit."

"He's been going through a tough time," Margie said.

"Yeah? Well, I can sympathize with that."

"I'm here to ask you something important," Margie said.

"What's important to me is my family," Lucy said. "My husband isn't well, physically or otherwise. I'm no health resort myself. But I have a kid to try and raise with some normal structure. Kevin came to disrupt what little peace we have."

"I'm talking about something that happened fourteen years ago," Margie said.

"Look, Marie—"

"Margie."

"Margie," Lucy said. "What happened when Kevin and I were kids—well, it's best forgotten."

"I need to know about something that hasn't been forgotten," Margie said, trying to get a change of tone out of this woman. "I need to know about the abortion."

Lucy looked at Margie and nodded, her face twitching slightly behind the pacific eyes, flickering with the painful emotions of the past.

She pushed herself to a standing position with the help of the rake. Margie rose after her, dusting off her hands and brushing off her skirt and jacket.

"Bobby—that's my husband—he looks out at the leaves and it drives him crazy that he can't come out and rake them himself," Lucy said, looking across the lawn to Bobby Bronsky's face in a ground-floor window, staring out. "The same when he can't mow the lawn when it gets overgrown in the summer or when the snow needs shoveling. When you have wheels for legs, the changes in the seasons get to you. Each season keeps reminding you of the different ways you're . . . limited. That's why I've been thinking of moving to the desert. New Mexico, maybe. One climate, one set of problems."

"Jesus, I'm sorry," Margie said, now remembering that Kevin's story said the cheerleader's husband wound up in a wheelchair after a construction accident. "I didn't know."

"Yeah," she said, continuing to rake the wayward leaves. "Well. We all have our crosses to bear. Kevin always was high-strung. What's wrong with him now? Exactly what do you want to know about an incident I'd rather forget?"

"It's very complicated," Margie said, feeling even more clumsy now, "but I need to know if that abortion you had back then . . . if it was really Kevin's baby."

Lucy combed the pile of leaves together as if it were a hairdo, smoothing the edges into symmetrical perfection. She stared at the leaves for a long moment and then looked up and glared into Margie's eyes, real emotion agitating the flat demeanor for the first time.

"Was it *his* baby?" Lucy asked rhetorically. Her eyes were incredulous, then outraged. "You're asking me if my dead baby was also Kevin Dempsey's baby? How can you walk out of the past, out of the blue, into my life, and ask me something like that?"

"I'm sorry."

"*You're* sorry?" Lucy said, swallowing and digging the teeth of the rake into the soft earth. She shut her eyes tight and turned her face away from Margie. "You stand there, a face from the awful past, and ask me about a baby I had to kill when I was a kid and you tell me *you're* sorry? If I had every candle I ever lit for that baby of ours over the years, I could set the world on fire. You don't understand. I loved Kevin Dempsey. I adored him."

Margie felt suddenly small next to this woman of daily struggle and sad memories.

"I didn't mean to open old wounds," Margie said, persisting in spite of her awkwardness. "But are you saying it *was* Kevin's baby?"

"I lost my virginity and a baby and the first guy I loved all in that one afternoon, lady," Lucy said. "You figure it out."

"It wasn't Bobby Bronsky's baby?"

"Bobby and me only had the chance to make one baby together," she said. "She'll be home from school any minute now. So if you'll excuse me?"

Margie swallowed and shrugged as Lucy went back to raking the leaves.

"I'm really sorry for bringing all this up," Margie said.

"Of *course* it was Kevin's baby," Lucy whispered, with her back to Margie.

Margie nodded, turned, and left Lucy standing alone in the yard as the leaves continued to fall around her.

60

"I'm dying for a cigarette," Gail said as she stepped out of the bathroom, her face flushed, her eyes watery. She hoped he didn't smell the morning sickness on her breath.

"You okay?" Kevin asked. "Something you ate didn't sit right? What?"

"Just nicotine withdrawal," she said. "It's the last and hardest hurdle of the addict."

"I told you whenever you get the oral fixation . . ."

She punched his arm as she walked toward the kitchen, dressed in a clingy full-length satin robe. Kevin followed, bare-chested, wearing a pair of red house shorts.

"But I'm really glad I gave them up," Gail said, opening the refrigerator door. "Especially now—"

She caught herself as she reached for the container of skim milk in the refrigerator.

"Especially now what?" Kevin asked, reaching past her for the ice-water jug. They each drank while standing in front of the refrigerator, and their eyes met while gulping.

Gail burst out laughing, and milk ran down her face and neck. This caused Kevin to laugh and grab her. They kissed, milk smearing their faces.

"I keep waiting for the adults to come home," Gail said. "I never lived with a man sober before."

"How many did you sleep—"

"Don't start with that," Gail said, waving a finger. "It leads to resentment. The program tells you not to beat yourself up over the past."

"I like that part," Kevin said, carrying the water jug with him as Gail carried the milk carton to the living room. Kevin plopped on a soft chair and draped a leg over the arm.

Gail walked to the bare windows and looked out at the cityscape of Manhattan. "It didn't scare you to raise a kid in New York?"

"No," Kevin said. "Teaches them to know ten seconds before the rest of the world when the light's gonna turn green."

She had her back to him now, placed a hand on her belly and stared out at the city.

"Think you'll ever have another baby?"

She felt the silence behind her as it thickened by the second into a wall of division.

"I haven't thought about that," Kevin said quietly.

"Would you?"

"Why do you ask?"

Kevin's telephone rang, and Gail turned and saw him walk to the bedroom to answer it. Maybe it would be better if she just went back to Dr. Hartnett and asked her to solve the problem. Give the sailor suit to a woman's shelter for some poor kid. Go back to work. Enjoy a kid-free relationship with Kevin Dempsey and see where it went. It was the only thing that made sense.

Kevin returned from the bedroom, looking perplexed.

"That was Margie," he said. "She said she had to see me about something important. She's meeting me here tomorrow. She wants me and her to go out for coffee. To talk. Alone."

"Good idea," Gail said, just a trace of rejection in her voice.

"It's family stuff."

"Of course," Gail said, knowing that a tiny Dempsey was coiled inside her. "For Dempseys only."

"Hey, wait a minute," Kevin said. "Margie likes you, likes you a lot. You two could be like sisters."

"That's a stretch, isn't it?"

"I guess," he said. "Sorry. What were we talking about?"

"Doesn't matter," she said. "Boy, could I use a smoke!"

★ ★ ★

Frank Dempsey dialed the first number on the computer printout sheet that Sarah had easily called up on the Mesquite main computer, once she gained access. The printout had a short list of calls Polly Edgeworth had made during her recent stay there.

"Edgeworth and Associates," he heard the female voice with the British accent say.

Frank hung up the phone.

"The London calls she made were to her dad," he told Sarah, who sat next to him on the bed. He dialed the New York number and hung up again when a receptionist answered: "Morton Associates."

"I thought that number was familiar," Sarah said, when Frank told her.

She checked her watch.

"I have to go teach a two-hour noon step class," she said. "Let me call the last number."

She dialed the number and cupped the receiver.

"It's a Saint Joseph's Hospital," she said to Frank.

Frank told her to ask where it was located and she did. She cupped the phone again. "Santa Monica," she said.

"Ask for Polly or Zoe Dempsey or Edgeworth," Frank said.

Sarah asked if there were any patients registered there by those names. As the operator checked, Sarah held the phone to her ear, glanced at her watch, and said to Frank, "I have to get to my noon class. The rich don't like to wait. . . ."

"No?" she said into the phone. "You have no patients by that name? Thank you, operator."

Sarah hung up the phone and looked at Frank, who shrugged.

"I have to run," she said, and kissed Frank on the lips, and turned to rush out of the room. He held her a few seconds longer, kissed her harder.

Frank had not told Sarah about the name tag he'd seen on the platinum-haired man with Morton in Boston: LYLE QUINCY M.D., ST. JOSEPH'S HOSP.

"Maybe we should go up to LA anyway," Sarah had said, pointing to the television set that showed footage of raging brush fires twisting through the hills surrounding Los Angeles.

"Another wild goose chase," Frank told her. "And dangerous. Besides, I have to get the money to Pinebox back in New York before it's too late."

"We'll talk later," Sarah said. "Gotta get to my class."

During that class, Frank received a call from Gutter, the shoe salesman from Brooklyn. He had a printout from Achilles Heels for every pair of corrective shoes ordered in the last month from all thirty-six of the United States they served. Frank promised to send him the other twenty-five hundred dollars in the mail and asked Gutter to fax the printout to him at the Mesquite.

After receiving the fax, Frank was disappointed. There were no Dempseys or Edgeworths on the list of patients fitted for Achilles Heels corrective shoes.

Then Frank thought of St. Joseph's Hospital and started looking at the names of people associated with hospital clinics on the Achilles Heels list.

He scanned one long page, distractedly tracing his finger down the columns, when suddenly his finger stopped and an icy shock ran through the fingertip, up his arm, into his shoulder, and through his whole body. The cold current shot through his head like the brain freeze of a migraine, and he felt himself shiver.

He had touched a name he had not considered.

Frank Dempsey knew something was wrong.

Terribly wrong.

And he had to go make it right. While there was time. Alone.

61

Kevin sat across from Gail at the dining room table. She looked more beautiful than ever, bathed in the diffuse light that fell through the Tiffany lampshade onto both of their faces. Kevin was devouring the garden salad she had made and had his plate piled high with steaming baked ziti.

"You're awfully quiet tonight," Kevin said, taking a sip of ice water.

"Am I?" Gail asked.

"Yeah," he said. "You look like there's a moving truck rolling around inside your head. What's up?"

He looked at her, smiled, tore a piece of Italian bread, bit into it, and forked some ziti.

"Where we headed, Kevin?"

"Uh-oh," Kevin said. "Is this a relationship conversation?"

"There're a few things I need to know," Gail said.

"Richard Smith called again," Kevin said, letting that drop into the middle of whatever would follow.

"That bother you?"

"It does if you're still serious about him."

"Who says I ever was?"

"Come on," Kevin said. "No guy is that obsessed with a woman without having bedded her first."

Gail placed her fork gently on the side of her plate and sat up straighter in her chair.

"You said you were . . . before you bedded me."

"I'm different," Kevin said.

"How?"

"You helped pull me out of the water, so to speak. You helped save me. My lifesaver."

"Bullshit," Gail said. "I was there, but you were treading water yourself."

"I never got a chance to speak to a woman, think about a woman, dream about a woman, write about a woman before I slept with her, the way I did with you," Kevin said. "You were in my mind every day because of the logistics. That's what makes it different."

"Okay," Gail said. "Maybe there is some truth to that. We met through exploration. One kind of intimacy leading to another. But where do we go now?"

"This is a scary question."

"I have what might be considered scary or wonderful news," Gail said, "depending on how you take it. I could choose not to tell you and you'd never know. But I couldn't do that to you. Not after what you've been through."

"What news? What scary or wonderful news?"

Gail took a sip of club soda and cranberry juice and cleared her throat.

"I'm pregnant," she said.

The words were like sniper fire. *Bing. Bing.* I'm pregnant. Kevin placed his fork gently on the tabletop and sat back in his chair. He swallowed the rest of what was in his mouth without further chewing. He took a sip of water, his eyes never leaving Gail's. His body quickly grew warm, and he could feel perspiration forming on his chest and under his arms.

"That a fact," he said. His insides were combusting, but he was determined not to unleash the murderer who was stirring within.

"That's it?" Gail said. "I tell you I'm having your baby and all you say is, 'That a fact'? Jesus!"

"Funny you should mention him, because right now I feel a little like St. Joseph," Kevin said. "The most celebrated cuckold in history."

"That supposed to be a joke?"

"No," Kevin said, in a low deliberate tone that could not be mistaken for anything but sincerity. "But unless there's a little divine intervention involved here, you're carrying someone else's baby, Gail. Not mine."

He got up and walked quickly across the living room, his head swirling with a rage he was determined to control. Never again will you allow yourself to be manipulated by a woman, Kevin thought. Pack your bags, hit the road, *now.*

A white glare formed in the back of his eyes as he shut them tight. He heard traffic from the street but also a loud rushing noise like a snowy television that has lost its signal. He walked into the bedroom, yanked on jeans, sneakers, and a sweatshirt. He began stuffing his clothes into a duffel bag, emptying the bottom drawer of Gail's dresser and wrenching shirts, trousers, and sweaters from wire hangers in the closet.

Gail appeared at the bedroom door, her arms folded over her breasts, astonished.

"What is *wrong* with you?" she asked softly.

"What's wrong with *me* is physical," Kevin said, his back to her. "*You're* sick in the soul."

"Hold on here," she said. "I'll have an abortion, if that's what you want. I understand. Maybe it *is* too soon—"

"No, go have your baby," Kevin said, as he shoved his unplugged answering machine into the duffel bag. "I'm sure Richard Smith will be a very good father."

"Richard? Is that what you think?" she asked, aghast. "I never even slept—"

"Bullshit," Kevin said, as he carried the duffel bag into the bathroom and gathered his shaving gear and toothbrush. "You're just like her," he said, low and tight-lipped. "Like Polly. And Lucy. Another lying, conniving cunt looking to destroy me."

"Hey, who the hell is Lucy? I'm carrying *your* baby: *yours, mine, ours*. You don't want it, fine. You have a right as a man to have your say in the matter. But stop acting like a madman. And I am not a cunt."

"You don't get it, do you?" Kevin Dempsey told her, taking several hundred-dollar bills from his pants pocket and slapping them on her bureau with a bang, like a john for a whore.

"No, Kevin," she said, a mascara-blackened tear bulging in the corner of her right eye. "I *don't* get it!"

He turned his back on her and hefted the duffel bag onto his shoulder.

"You aren't carrying my baby," he said, turning with a snarl. "Because I can't make babies, Gail. I'm fucking sterile. I had a test. Polly was telling the truth. Zoe isn't mine, couldn't be mine. I can't make babies."

"Kevin, I swear to you—"

"Oaths, vows, promises—lies," he said. "With women, the same thing."

He shook his head and looked at Gail, standing in the doorway between the bedroom and the living room. She dabbed her eye with her shirtsleeve as he walked to the door and unlocked it.

"This is madness," Gail said.

"I truly loved you," Kevin Dempsey said, and pulled open the door and stepped outside.

He closed the door gently behind him.

"Can we go get the mail now?" Zoe asked her mommy for the third time since lunch. "I want to see if Mint's birthday card came."

"It won't be here until tomorrow," Zoe's mommy said.

"Do you think they really sent it?" asked the man who Zoe's mommy said was her new daddy.

"Americans never miss a chance at a vulgarity like this," Zoe's mommy said. "They'll send it all right. I FedExed the change of address yesterday. They'll send it. If they don't, boy, will they hear from me!"

"I want Daddy to be here for Mint's birthday," Zoe said.

"Your new daddy is here, honey," Zoe's mommy said.

"And I want Auntie Sarah to be here too," said Zoe. "She bought me Pepper Mint."

"Auntie Sarah is busy," Zoe's mommy said.

"I bet she is," said the man. "Looking for you."

"Can we check the mail tomorrow?" asked Zoe.

"Yes," Zoe's mommy said. "The card should be there tomorrow."

"And can we buy a cake with candles?" Zoe asked.

"Yes, Zoe," Zoe's mommy said.

"Can we get candles you can't blow out, like the ones you bought for Daddy's birthday?" Zoe asked.

Zoe's mommy didn't answer.

62

Sarah found the envelope on the bed when she got back to the bungalow. She opened it and removed a wad of cash, a key on a small ring, and a note:

> *My Dearest Sarah:*
>
> *I am sorry. You will probably hate me for this but I had to leave without you. I cannot allow you to get any more involved with the problems and danger my family faces. Enclosed please find $5,000*

traveling money, to pay any debts incurred here and for your trip back to New York. Forget about finding Polly. I'm off to London to look for Polly on a new lead. When I find her, I will get your money, and in the meantime I have arranged with my friend Pinebox to give you the $100,000 Polly borrowed from you out of the money I have stashed. When Polly borrowed it from you her name was Dempsey, and that money was meant to clean up the Dempsey name, so I want you to have it. The name and address of the bar where Pinebox can be found is listed below. He will be expecting you. Give him this key and tell him the money is in Greenwood. He'll understand. He will give you your money and you will never see him again.

Same goes here.

It was fun, kid, but it's time to move on. Go open your gym. Thanks for everything. Have a good life. Raise a glass for me.

Best,
Frank

Sarah Cross shook her head sadly. What a terrible liar Frank Dempsey was, she thought. That morning, she had seen his yellow eyes too and said nothing.

Of course he'd left without her. Left without any big farewell speeches, no *I love you*s in his letter. Just gone, with one last noble gesture about the money.

What a special man! Someone else might call him an asshole for running off that way, she thought. But she knew he left because he didn't want her to see him die the same way as her father.

She checked the telephone computer log and found he'd made another call to the hospital in Santa Monica. Which meant that was where he went, not London. She had to decide whether to drive up to Santa Monica after him or head back to New York to collect the money from this Pinebox character. She had only started this chase for her money for her health club anyway.

Bullshit, she thought. You chased the guy. You chased Frank. The question now is, Do you chase him again?

It was too late to get a night flight out of Tucson, so Sarah decided to wait until morning to place one last phone call before making up her mind.

* * *

Frank Dempsey watched the ambulances bringing in the fire victims. Homeowners, campers, firefighters, and other rescue workers were being rushed through the emergency ambulance port, masks over their faces for smoke inhalation and gauze wrapping them for burns. The ambulance port was visible through the side windows of the lobby of the hospital, and Frank watched as a receptionist checked some information for him at her computer terminal behind the main inquiry desk.

The receptionist motioned to Frank. She was a black woman in her fifties wearing a tag that read AMBER. "Sir," she said, "Dr. Quincy won't be back in his office until Wednesday."

"Did you check the other name?" Frank asked.

"Yes, I did," Amber said. "He's also scheduled to head a research project at the hospital starting next week. That team is still being formed. Dr. Quincy oversees all dermatology research projects. Are you part of the team, sir?"

Frank had struck pay dirt, but he showed no surprise or excitement. A good cop never does. Or even a bad one, he thought.

"Yes," Frank said with confidence, and then remembered Morton's seminar in the hotel in Boston. "Yes, I was told to see one or the other. About the Q-Twenty-one-hundred project."

"Yes, that's the one, all right, but I'm afraid you'll have to wait until Wednesday," Amber said. "Do you want to leave a note? Or I can E-mail them a message if you like."

"No, that's okay," Frank said. "Do you have a home address?"

"We couldn't give out that information, sir," Amber said.

"I'd hate to think of him trapped in one of those canyons," Frank said.

"Sorry, sir, but as you can see we're extremely busy today. Because of the fires."

"Yes, of course," Frank said. "I'll just come back Wednesday."

"Have a nice day," Amber said.

Frank hailed a taxi from a rank formed outside the hospital and had the driver take him to the mailing address he'd found on the Achilles Heels fax he'd gotten from Gutter. The address was on Santa Monica Boulevard. Frank discovered that it was a private mail depot, not a residence.

He checked inside, showing a photograph of Polly and Zoe to a middle-aged sandy-haired man who sat behind a Plexiglas partition. The clerk was reading *Daily Variety*.

"Friend, I see more people come in and out of here than I can keep track of," the clerk said. "Transients use the place. Actors, writers, lam artists. The woman looks familiar. Beautiful. But then, this is Los Angeles. Beautiful women fall from the palm trees."

"She has a little girl, three years old," Frank said.

"Kids, I never notice," the clerk said. "Look, it's five o'clock. The mail comes in the morning, about eleven A.M. Come back then, that's when everyone comes around."

"What if I gave you some names?"

"What if I don't feel like getting fired, huh? You nuts?"

Frank nodded at the clerk and flashed some bills.

"Sorry," the clerk said with a sigh. "But at my age, I think I'd rather keep the steady work."

Frank admired his ethics, integrity, and middle-aged caution. He didn't press him any further. He walked back out into the street. The early evening sun was having a tough time penetrating the smoky skies, and the ever-changing winds blew new and multicolored smoke from the canyons in crisscross patterns.

Polly and Little Zoe are here in Los Angeles somewhere, and I'm gonna find them, Frank thought. Because I'm still good at this shit.

He stood on Santa Monica Boulevard, gazing into the sooty sky, wondering how his brother Kevin would react when he found Zoe. He prayed that he would still care enough to come and get her.

Frank checked into an oceanfront room in the Shangri-La Hotel on Ocean Boulevard. He stared out at the Pacific, where helicopters with big buckets scooped thousands of gallons of water to dump on the fire. The television reported about the fires raging through the mountains and canyons and foothills circling the city.

He left the hotel and walked through Santa Monica, past a dozen Irish and British-style pubs, and his mouth began to salivate for the taste of alcohol. His body felt strong and he was clear-sighted and clean-shaven and sober, and his muscles ached with new vibrancy—under skin the color yellow.

Without booze, he did not know what to do with his hands.

He thought about the yellow jaundice that was spreading from his liver, making his eyes look like butterscotch, even yellowing the flesh under his fingernails and below the tanned skin. And he thought about drink. How much more damage could it possibly do to him now?

He thought of the hours, days, nights Sarah had spent nursing him, trying to save his life. But still he walked through the doors of a pub called Robert Burns's directly across from the Santa Monica mail depot.

"Wot ya 'avin', mate?" asked the bartender, with the flattened nose of an ex-pug, as Frank took a seat at the bar, where he could see the mail depot across the boulevard.

Frank thought of all the work Sarah had put into getting him sober and looked from the vodka bottles gleaming on the shelf to the bartender's face.

"What the hell, gimme a club soda," Frank said. "With a twist."

Frank showed a photograph of Polly to the bartender, on the odd chance that Polly had stopped in for a drink some day after picking up her mail. "You ever see this woman?"

"Lovely lookin' bird, mate," the bartender said. "I 'aven't seen 'er, though."

On a television set stacked high behind the bar, CNN was broadcasting more footage of the wind fires caused by the Santa Ana.

"The fires ever come this close?" Frank asked the bartender.

"Few years back they jumped into Pacific Palisades and Malibu," said the bartender. "It depends on which way the wind decides to blow. Terrifying."

"Anybody dead yet?"

"I think they said one," the bartender said. "A homeless guy in a shack. But there'll be more. Always is. We're still recovering from that goddamned earthquake and now more of this. Dirty old Manchester is looking better and better, tell you that, mate."

Frank played with a quarter in his change and thought about calling his brother Kevin. But he would wait until he was certain that Polly and Zoe were here.

He opened a copy of the *LA Times* that was on the bar, filled with stories about the wildfire. Frank took a sip of the club soda and let the sparkling bubbles rasp down his throat. He felt an ache in his heart as he thought of Sarah. Lovely Sarah, the love of his whole entire life. Sarah, who loved him back. Sarah, whom he'd never see again.

* * *

Kevin Dempsey went like a homing pigeon back to Brooklyn, on the subway, out to the Shamrock on Flatbush Avenue.

In the bar a live loud Irish band played a traditional Irish drinking song called "Whisky in the Jar." Kevin took a place alone at the bar and ordered a double shot of John Jameson and a pint of Guinness. The silent television behind the bar was tuned to CNN, showing footage of the Santa Ana blazes out in Los Angeles. Looking at the fires made him shiver and think of how he'd almost killed Carmine. When the bartender placed the drinks in front of him, Kevin caught a sickening whiff of the alcohol and felt his stomach sour. He left a twenty-dollar bill on the bar without touching the drinks and walked out into the night.

Never took sip one.

He walked a mile and a half to Sheepshead Bay and then another two miles down to Coney Island. He sat on the sand for several hours, listening to the drunken homeless men under the boardwalk shouting at each other as they stood around trash fires. Far off he could see the sparse lights on the darkened smudge of Breezy Point, where his mother used to take him to visit some distant aunt years ago, on a stretch of the most beautiful unspoiled beach left in New York. He vaguely remembered breaking the back of a toilet tank, which caused an uproar and the family was never invited back. Breezy Point was populated by lots of cops and firefighters and was still 90 percent Irish.

He tried to remember more about his mother, but memories of her were flimsy and vague: a sweet woman who always smiled, but nothing more.

And so, as the waves crashed, he thought of the first line of the Myth of Sisyphus, "There is but one truly philosophical question and that is suicide."

He understood now how his father, Big Paulie, had come to answer that question. No more. Enough. Goodbye.

For Kevin, that possibility loomed.

He thought of young Zoe and his body tingled with goodness. With a spirit of life and purpose for living. Even though she was not his child, he adored her. But he could not live for the love of another man's child, a child he would never see again.

He tried to erase her face with other thoughts. But he couldn't put Gail's face there any longer to chase Zoe's face away. So Kevin Dempsey stood, and as the stars blazed and the moon glared and an incessant wind blew in off the black roiled sea, he started to run along the surf with no particular destination in mind. Just the face of Zoe stenciled in his head as he tried to outdistance his own life.

63

In the morning, Frank Dempsey sat for three hours in the back of a taxi parked down the street from the Santa Monica mail depot. The taxi driver was asleep in the front seat. Frank had made a deal with him. Hired him for the day. All the driver had to do was read, sleep, and listen to the radio until Frank needed him. Frank simply told him he was waiting for someone. The driver, a Pepperdine student pushing a hack, was more than willing to sit there earning two hundred bucks. He'd done some homework in the first two hours and then decided to get a little shut-eye.

At 11:20 A.M., Frank was popping a Tic Tac into his mouth when a silver Mercedes pulled up in front of the mail depot. There was a man driving and a woman in the passenger seat and a kid in a child seat in the back.

Frank's heart began to thud, and he sat up straight when the passenger door opened and Polly Edgeworth Dempsey stepped out onto the sidewalk.

Polly, in a tight long-sleeved midriff blouse and cutoff jeans, opened the back door and reached in and busied herself with the child. A group of men in front of the mail depot ogled her as she bent over.

And then suddenly Zoe Dempsey was standing on the sidewalk beside Polly, clutching her Pepper Face Doll.

Now Frank watched the driver's door of the Mercedes open.

Dr. Anthony Scala stepped out, dressed in shorts and a tank top, and walked to Polly, who hooked her arm through his as she clutched Zoe by the hand.

"The bastards," Frank said.

"My feelings exactly," said Sarah Cross, as she pulled open the back door opposite Frank with a flourish and climbed into the back seat of the taxi.

The driver awakened with a start, turned, and looked at them both. Frank stared at Sarah in astonishment.

"Sarah!"

"You're not getting away from me that fast," she said matter-of-factly. "I've been parked behind you for almost an hour, trying to decide whether to kiss you or smack you."

She grabbed his face and tried to give him a kiss on the lips, but he offered his cheek.

"Sarah . . ."

"You said that already," she said. "Recognize the skinny guy with Polly? He looks familiar."

"Yes," Frank said, clearing his throat. "It's Kevin's best friend, Anthony Scala."

"Cozy, *my* best friend and *his* best friend," Sarah said. "He was at the housewarming too, wasn't he?"

"Yeah," Frank said. "He's my doctor too."

"Is something going on?" the driver asked.

"Something sure is," Frank said.

"We don't need you anymore, driver," Sarah said. "Do we, Frank?"

"Sarah, I have to do this alone," Frank said.

"I know what you're trying to do, Frank," Sarah said. "Galahad alone on his horse again. Sorry, we're in this together. We'll use my car."

They watched Anthony Scala and Polly and Zoe enter the mail depot a hundred yards down the street.

Frank gave the driver two hundred-dollar bills, got out, and followed Sarah to the Toyota. Sarah got behind the wheel and Frank climbed into the passenger seat.

"How'd you find me?" he asked.

"Put on your seat belt," she said.

"I was hoping you wouldn't follow me," he said, buckling the seat belt. "It's a losing proposition."

"No," Sarah said. "She stole my money. You stole my heart. Hadda get one or the other back. There's nothing left to lose."

"I'm yellow."

"I'm green. Tell me what we're doing next."

"I have to find out where they're staying so I can tell Kevin. He has to confront them. It's his kid."

"Okay. One promise."

"What?"

"No more running from me."

"I'm just about outa road anyway," he said.

Their eyes met and then they fell silent as they watched Polly and Anthony emerge from the mail depot holding hands. Zoe trailed behind them, opening an envelope.

"That's little Zoe's Pepper Face birthday card," Sarah finally said, nodding toward Zoe from behind the tinted windshield. "Holton, the guy at the toy company in New York, told me Polly sent a prepaid self-addressed Federal Express voucher and envelope."

"You found her through the doll?" Frank asked incredulously.

"I had to keep my lead secret in case you ran out on me," she said. "Which you did. Albeit with noble motives."

Frank said, "You should be a cop. No. No, you shouldn't. You'd have an ass as wide as a handball court inside a year."

Frank nodded toward Anthony and Polly as they eased into their Mercedes.

"Class act, huh?"

"Your sister-in-law," Sarah said, "and your doctor."

"At least his prescriptions helped get me sober," Frank said. "Wouldn't want to show up in hell drunk."

"Have a devil of a time," Sarah said.

They looked at each other and smiled. She leaned over to kiss him, and he pulled his lips away again. She pulled his face back toward her and kissed his lips.

"You're not contagious," she said.

"You are," he said.

As the Mercedes slid away from the curb, Sarah followed it down the California Incline to Pacific Coast Highway and then north toward Malibu.

"Jesus, they're living in the hills," Frank said.

"News says the fire is spreading like crazy," Sarah said, staying two car lengths behind the Mercedes. "A place called Chatsworth, where they have horses, is a stampede. Pasadena, Laguna Beach—all in flames."

"And the winds can make it leap any which way," Frank said. "The drought has the whole southland like a tinderbox. One conflagration after another."

As they followed the Mercedes, Frank noticed the helicopter he had watched from his hotel window flying in off the Pacific. The morning *Times* said it was a Boeing 234 (CH47) Chinook with a 150-foot suspended bucket carrying three thousand gallons of seawater from the ocean to the wildfire.

"The environmentalists are complaining that the salt water is bad for vegetation," Frank said, watching the Mercedes change lanes, overtaking a Porsche. Sarah followed discreetly.

"Save the burning planet, eh?"

They shared a small smile as the helicopter chugged with twin rotary blades over Pacific Coast Highway, up over the Santa Monica Mountains, into the smoky heavens. Now Frank saw a pair of C130 fixed-wing aircraft carrying a cargo of fire retardant called Phos-Chek.

"The main ingredient in the fire retardant is fertilizer," Frank said, pointing to the C130s.

"I didn't think there was enough room in this town for any more horseshit," she said.

She smiled as she glanced over at him, then followed the Mercedes up Old Topanga Road into the foothills above Malibu.

The Mercedes wound along the serpentine road into Topanga Canyon, past the swimming pools behind the massive, ivy-covered wrought-iron gates, adorned with video security cameras. A steady but not urgent stream of families were evacuating the hills, carting belongings on roof racks and in U-Hauls. Horse vans and station wagons filled with pets headed down toward Pacific Coast Highway.

Sarah tailed the Mercedes past the high hedges and the barking attack dogs and the foreign cars and the Mexican gardeners and the lashing sprinklers and the brown foliage of blazing autumn. The Santa Ana wind was moving at forty miles an hour, whistling through the thirsty trees and lifting dust from the topsoil. The sky was a mixture of black smoke, red fire retardant, dirty automobile pollution, and brown dust, all backlit by the scorching sun. Police, news, and rescue helicopters also buzzed through the ominous sky. The wails of a thousand police, fire, and ambulance sirens screeched through the mountainsides. The heat beat down on the roof of the car, and now a blizzard of ash blew over the mountaintop on the shifting wind and Sarah put on the windshield wipers to clear her line of sight.

Sarah watched the Mercedes slow and looked over at Frank, who sat in pensive silence.

"It looks like she spent your money well," Frank finally said.

"We should live so high," she agreed.

They saw the Mercedes turn right and roll up a long tree-lined roadway to a circular driveway outside a big wooden split-level house that rested on stilts on the mountain side and faced the sparkling Pacific on the other.

Sarah parked on Topanga Canyon Road, concealed by the white metal gates that held back the hedges. They could see Polly and Anthony and Zoe getting out of the car and entering the house. Polly climbed the steps and unlocked the front door with a key.

Frank lifted the cellular car phone and dialed a number.

"Hello, Margie," Frank said, after waiting for the connection to go through to New York City, "this is Frank. Do you know where to find Kevin? I have some news for him."

Gail was leaving her apartment building when she heard her name called. She turned and saw Margie Dempsey hurrying her way.

"Gail," Margie said. "I've been calling. Didn't you get any of my messages?"

"I got them," Gail Levy said.

"What's wrong?" Margie said. "Why didn't you answer them?"

"Look, Margie, I'm sorry I can't talk, I'm sort of in a hurry," Gail said walking toward the corner, looking for a cab. "I have a doctor's appointment."

"Hope everything's okay," Margie said.

"Actually, everything isn't okay," Gail said. "That's why I have a doctor's appointment."

"Is it Kevin?"

"The question might be, 'Is it Kevin's?' " she said.

"Talk to me!"

"All right. I told him I was pregnant, and he packed and left. But it's my fault. I should never have gotten involved with a goddam client."

Gail turned away again but Margie took her by the arm and spun her around.

"Did he tell you he was incapable of having kids? That he was sterile?"

"That's what he said," Gail said. "But I haven't been with another man in eight months. Kevin thinks I'm lying to him, trying to trick him."

Gail waved for a taxi but Margie pulled her arm down.

"We have some talking to do," she said. "First of all, do you want to have this baby?"

"Not now."

"But you want it, don't you?"

"I even bought it a goddam sailor suit," Gail said, throwing an arm up for a taxi and letting it drop like a weight as one passed. "Blue and white, little sailor hat, short pants. . . . I need my head examined."

"That's the first thing I bought when I learned I was pregnant," Margie said, and laughed. Gail smiled too.

"Really?" Gail said. "And you had a boy, right?"

"Yup."

"That's what I want . . . wanted."

Now Margie hailed a passing taxi and it pulled to the curb and Margie opened the door.

"You're coming with me," Margie said.

"Where we going?"

"We're going to find your baby's father before he does something stupid," Margie said. "I have lots of news for both of you. When I couldn't reach Kevin, I called Mike and he's out looking for him too. I think I know where to start."

Gail climbed into the back seat of the taxi and Margie piled in after her and leaned forward to the Arab driver.

"We're going to Brooklyn, driver," Margie said. "No arguments."

64

As Polly showered, Anthony Scala stood on the back porch looking out at the fires burning in the hills. An orange hue tinged the smoky night sky as the Santa Ana wind swirled. He wore only a pair of denim shorts and slippers, careful not to get splinters in his feet from the wooden planks of the porch.

Zoe was upstairs fast asleep, delighted with her birthday card but saddened because her daddy had not been there to share the party with her.

Every time he thought of Kevin, Anthony grew nervous. He knew if Kevin were ever to find out that he had lied to him about his sperm count, about his sterility, about Zoe not being his child, that Kevin would kill him. He might live to regret it, but he couldn't live without exacting full revenge. He knew Kevin, knew the rage Kevin carried inside.

He knew it well enough that he certainly didn't want Kevin Dempsey finding him, his best friend, with his wife and child.

That's why Anthony and Polly were using the depot mailing address and separate mailboxes. They didn't want anyone to know where they lived or that they lived together. They were not breaking any laws, but according to Clive Morton, someone, a crazy man, was tracking Polly. Maybe it was Kevin, Anthony thought.

But Polly had said she'd convinced Kevin that Zoe wasn't his. And Anthony was certain Kevin had believed him about the lab reports. So why would a man chase after a woman who'd done him so wrong except for sheer revenge? He knew Kevin better than that. First, Kevin was too much of a macho chauvinist to chase *any* woman. And second, he had too much dignity to ever hit one.

Maybe Sarah had hired a private investigator to track her money, Anthony thought.

The radio in the living room was squawking about the increasing Santa Ana fires again. The winds made Anthony mildly anxious. They were continuously shifting, the fires leaping to new pockets of forest. A crazed arsonist was suspected of joining the madness, and police feared that copycats would join him.

Anthony glanced back into the house, worried about the baby's safety in case the fires ever reached this far. Zoe was a beautiful baby. A baby *by* Kevin Dempsey, as these movie people out here might say. Everything you ever touched, Kevin, has been beautiful, Anthony thought.

Don't you remember, Kevin? Anthony imagined himself saying to his lifelong friend.

If he ever had to explain all this to him, he had prepared a mental monologue that he had played over and over in his head. He'd rehearsed it a thousand times, whenever he imagined himself trying to justify stealing Kevin's wife and kid.

It was always you, Kevin. When we were kids, it was always you who had the best-looking broads. You who didn't even have to study to make the honor roll the way I did. You who were the handsomest. You who had the muscles. You who scored the touchdowns. You who fought in the Golden Gloves.

I was the skinny guinea you patronized.

Later, when I struggled through med school and internship, riding the fucking subways, you could get credit by having the city job. So you leased the Cadillac. You furnished the nicest pads. You married the best-looking wife from the magazine covers and the billboards. You had the most beautiful baby.

Even when we both got mumps from Bobby Bronsky, it was you who came out all right and me who became sterile and couldn't have kids. You, you, you!

Well, fuck you!

When Zoe was born into your life, it only underlined my impotence in my wife's eyes. Zoe being born helped Gloria walk out my door in search of someone who could give her a child as beautiful as the one you had given Polly.

And so now, me, Anthony Scala, the skinny little guinea, has taken Fightin' Irish Kevin Dempsey's wife and baby. For me.

Even-fuckin'-Steven, as we said growing up.

Anthony took a sip of his vodka gimlet and stared out at the orange pockets of flame in the night, a pang of guilt gutting him. And he wondered how Kevin was, how he was taking the loss of his wife and baby. Part of him felt sorry for the poor son of a bitch. Still, it was done. He was here. Involved with Polly. Just like I helped in her burn recovery, Anthony thought. Free of charge. Because it was for Kevin Fucking Dempsey's wife. Well, the wife fell for me this time, asshole. For me and my work. Working on Polly led me to stumble onto Q-2100. The research on how to repair Polly's burn scarring helped produce the formula.

Anthony knew it might prove to be just another flash-in-the-pan concoction, with temporary cosmetic effects. Polly knew it too. But they both knew it would make big money, something Polly was sure Kevin would never make in civil service. So she chose the doctor. And Anthony was going to stay for the money, put together a pile, and then run with the girl and the baby. The baby who now slept in this house, leased for him under Morton's bogus corporation name, paid for, like the Mercedes, with money borrowed by Polly from her best friend Sarah.

Two best friends double-crossed.

Ah, well, he thought. What are friends for?

Then, sipping a gimlet in the smoky night, three thousand miles from Brooklyn, he realized that a part of himself also hated everything he had done. He hated himself for making anyone, especially Kevin, feel so much pain. It was the antithesis of what a doctor was supposed to do in life.

And yet he knew, now that he had her, he could never part with Polly. She made him feel whole again and said she was happy they could have no more babies. She was a wife-mother-daughter package all rolled into one. A family.

Polly walked down the stairs in a mini-robe, her hair up in a towel turban. He gaped at her long tanned legs, as had the men outside the mail depot earlier in the day. They had nudged each other to take a look at Polly as she walked by. Anthony loved watching other men hunger for his Polly. The way he once hungered for her when she was Kevin's. The way everyone had always drooled for Kevin Dempsey's broads. That was powerful medicine.

Polly picked up a stack of envelopes from the tabletop, walked to him on the back deck, her face shining pink from the shower, took the gimlet from his hand, and sipped it, handed it back.

She leafed through the envelopes.

"Bills, bills, more bloody bills," she said. "Morton better come through with this money soon. Even Achilles Heels wants three hundred dollars for those blasted corrective shoes. The money I got from Sarah is running out. Car, house, gardener, pool service, bottled water, gas, electric, cable, phone, furniture, clothes, the gym, your seed money to join the conglomerate. When will it show a return?"

"The lab is all set up and waiting," Anthony said, reaching behind her to pull her to him. "The contracts and checks should clear this week."

"What the hell would you have done without me?" Polly asked, as she tore open a telephone bill.

"What's *that* supposed to mean?"

"I mean you were dead broke," Polly said, breaking gently away from him and leaning back against the railing, taking another sip of his gimlet. "Sunk every dime you had into research with no parachute."

"I was trying to find a treatment for your goddamned burns, Polly dearest," he said testily. "I stumbled upon Q-Twenty-one-hundred, didn't I?"

"You mean *I* realized the potential in it and brought it to the right people," she said. "I had to arrange the whole setup to get rid of Kevin."

"I wanted you to go the divorce route," Anthony said. "If you remember. You seduced me. You wanted to dump Kevin. I was for a nice, clean, legal divorce."

"How many times are we going to go over this, luv? He would have anchored me in those bloody New York courts for years, contesting it until I was a wrinkled mid-thirties hen."

Exasperated, she put a Dunhill cigarette in her mouth and lit it with a disposable lighter.

"He'd have fought for custody," she continued. "Made it impossible for me to move more than fifty miles from the marital home with Zoe. He would have been a part of my life forever, just by being her father. I was suffocating in bloody Brooklyn. I needed out. I needed *you,* luv. Divorce is too slow and sloppy. I will never live my life in a place like Brooklyn according to the rules of some decrepit old judge."

"Maybe it would have been better than this," Anthony said. "I feel like a damn fugitive."

"You're forgetting the main reason why we opted against divorce," she said.

Anthony went silent and turned from her, looking out at the fires in the hills.

"Kevin would have killed you," Polly said.

Anthony remained silent a long moment, took a sip of the gimlet, swallowed, pockets of flame reflected in his eyes.

"You have no idea how obsessed he was with Zoe," she said. "This way, instead of killing you or me, he might kill himself. I know him. I know how fragile his macho ego is."

"He would kill us both now if he ever found out we lied to him about Zoe not being his," Anthony said. "I could get in trouble for falsifying lab tests. My license would be yanked permanently. Conspiracy charges—"

"But you didn't falsify lab tests, honey," Polly said. "You substituted your own semen for his and it came up blank. You could explain that away as a lab mixup. Say you wanted to see if your status had changed since the mumps rendered you sterile. That could get you off the hook."

"Not with Kevin," Anthony said.

"I didn't know you were flat broke," she said. "Or else—"

"Or else what?"

"Never mind."

"Did you want me or the M.D. at the end of my name?" he asked.

She turned to a nervous Anthony and smiled reassuringly. "I wanted you, luv," she said. "And now I've got you. Where I want you. Here with me. Relax. We're going to be rich. We'll cash in and run away, anywhere we want. This is all going to work out."

Anthony gripped the wooden railing of the porch and looked up at a helicopter that swooped through the hills, its searchlight piercing the gloom.

"I feel sort of sorry for Kevin," Anthony said. "And the baby. I feel sorry for her most. She loves him."

"She'll grow out of it," Polly said. "She'll love you. She already likes you."

"You really think so?"

Polly moved closer to Anthony, kissed him, and slid one hand between his legs.

"Let's go inside," she said, smiling seductively. "Everything is going to come out just fine."

Anthony looked at her hungrily, as Polly Edgeworth Dempsey smiled at him with her dazzling blue eyes and perfect teeth and full moist lips. Here she was, the magazine cover girl, the kind of girl the skinny little Brooklyn kid dreamed he'd have someday when he grew up. Here with him in Southern California, her hand between his legs, smiling at him.

They walked into the house as the fires burned in the hills and smoke blew across the sky on the Santa Ana.

65

Frank lay beside Sarah in the big bed in the hotel room listening to the roar of the ocean coming through the opened window. In the distance he could hear the sirens wailing down from the hills and the helicopters chugging through the fierce Santa Ana winds that were hurtling up to fifty miles an hour now, spinning the wildfire from canyon to mountaintop to valley, up and down the coast of Southern California.

The TV was on, turned to local Channel 13, with the volume turned off, and the orange hue of the flames bathed the room and flickered on Sarah's face.

"What time does Kevin land?"

"He'll arrive at LAX at four this afternoon," Frank said.

"He's coming straight here?"

"Mike'll be driving," Frank said. "It's all arranged."

"How are you going to do this?"

"The only way is to knock on the front door and go in and take Zoe out," Frank said. "Get her back to New York and let the courts settle it. At least back there Kevin can prove conspiracy and fraud on their part and try to get temporary custody in the New York jurisdiction."

"Yeah," Sarah said. "Where the authorities are waiting to indict you, too."

"They can have what's left of me. Damaged goods."

"I've made some inquiries about a liver transplant."

"They're not big on giving them to alkies," Frank said. "There're people with cancer who deserve them more than self-inflicted cases like me."

"We're gonna try. And then I figure we can go live in Ireland," she said. "Your father was born there, so you could get citizenship. They don't have an extradition treaty for crimes like yours, do they?"

"Sarah, this is crazy talk," Frank said. "Why I wanted to do this alone."

"Promise me you'll at least give me that hope."

"Sarah . . ."

"It's all I ask."

"A liver transplant isn't like getting fitted for a suit, ya know."

"Just say yes."

"Okay, yes, if all goes well we'll go liver shopping. Liberty Meat Market, where I worked as a kid. On sale. Forty-nine cents a pound. Then we'll go live on a farm in Galway—"

"It isn't funny."

"I think it is," Frank said. "A guy out shopping for a new liver. Wearing his Irish wool sweater, tam-o'-shanter, carrying his black thorn stick, color coordinating the liver, having it altered to fit, hemmed, taken in."

"You know why they call it a liver?" she asked.

"Never thought about it."

"Because you need one to live."

He looked at her and they lay there silently staring into each other's eyes as the flaming images played on the television and the emergency sounds of the wounded city roared around them.

The 747 circled LAX, and from the window seat Kevin Dempsey looked down on the smoky sprawling city of Los Angeles. He felt a hollow, pulsating void deep in his gut. In the middle seat next to him was his brother Mike. On the aisle was Carmine.

Kevin had told them both he wanted to go alone. But Carmine had insisted on coming to make sure Kevin didn't drink. "Remember, I'm in the line of fire for you," Carmine kept joking. Then, more seriously, he'd said, "Hey, I really have nothing better to do."

Mike insisted on coming because he said it was family business. Period. Shut up. Let's go. And you couldn't argue with him. It was like trying to reason with a brick.

Kevin was still thanking God or fate or good fortune, take your pick, that Margie had arrived through the side door of Farrell's when she did. Margie had always avoided Farrell's and its men's club atmosphere and the smoke and noise and incessant ball games on the three loud television sets. But mostly she avoided it because this was Big Paulie's place, his saloon, and he'd never wanted his daughter in there where the men would ogle her and speak dirty about her under their breath.

Kevin was surprised to see Margie walking through the back door with his brother Mike, just as he contemplated lifting the beer and shot of whiskey he'd ordered. Carmine had already downed two rounds when Kevin ordered for himself. Carmine tried to dissuade Kevin from drinking. But Kevin was adamant in ordering.

"I'm gonna keep standing in the line of fire of those shots intended for you until they kill me," Carmine said.

But then Kevin saw Gail Levy walk in behind Margie and Mike. Half the bar stopped to stare at this fresh female face.

"Chee-sus Christ! It's the gorgeous Jewish girl," Carmine shouted, and everyone else groped over each other at the three-deep bar for a lascivious gape.

Margie motioned Kevin outside onto the sidewalk where Gail

stood with her hands in her jacket pockets, as Mike spoke to Carmine in the doorway of the bar. Margie walked Kevin to the side a dozen feet.

Margie told Kevin about Lucy Bronsky and how the baby she had aborted was truly his. And she told him the teenage mumps had not caused any sterility. And neither did anything else.

"Think about who told you that you were sterile," Margie said.

"Anthony," he said. "Anthony showed me the lab tests."

"Guess who's playing poppa to Zoe right now?"

"No," Kevin had said in astonishment, blood draining from his face, a knot tightening in his stomach, a million regrets ricocheting around his mind. "No! No, Margie, no! Please tell me you're kidding. Please, Margie, don't kid with me."

"Polly is living with Anthony," Margie said in a flat, even, serious tone. "They're involved in some cockamamy get-rich medical scheme together. Frank tracked them to Los Angeles. Zoe is your baby, Kevin. And so is the one Gail is carrying. You're the father. So, goddammit, act like one!"

Kevin walked to Gail, who stood there on the corner, hands in her pockets, eyes softly watching him. Right then, standing there, his baby in her belly, she had never looked more beautiful.

"Gail . . . I . . . am . . . so . . . sorry," Kevin whispered, his limbs trembling as he approached her. "Can you forgive me?"

"Not unless you take the next plane to LA and get your daughter back," she said. "Our son could use a big sister like you have."

Kevin embraced her and wanted to elaborate but Gail smiled and shook her head.

"Go," she said. "I'll be waiting."

So Kevin Dempsey kissed Gail Levy, mother-to-be of his child, there on the street, in his neighborhood, in front of everyone.

"There's a plane leaving in an hour and a half," Mike said.

"We can still make it if you stop the coochy-coo shit with the gorgeous Jewish girl right now," Carmine shouted, half lit, smiling.

Margie said she and Gail would share a cab back to Manhattan, and Kevin, Mike, and Carmine raced for JFK in Carmine's car.

The flight was smooth and quiet and Kevin spent most of it staring out the window thinking about Anthony. My best friend, Kevin thought. I introduced him to a hundred girls over the years. Gave him his first rubber. I hit big guys who picked on him. I forced the coach to keep him on the football team. I taught him how to swim. How to drive! I even wrote his book reports for him. Helped him study for the SATs. And the bastard, lowlife, selfish, backstabbing, fucking punk steals my wife! Fuck her. He can have her. But he also stole my kid, my beautiful precious Zoe. For that he will pay. He tried to steal my manhood and my child and I have to hurt him for that.

Not even out of revenge, he thought. Out of duty. Some things in life just have to be settled the old-fashioned way. Neighborhood style.

He was trying to project violent images of Anthony begging for mercy as he bashed his face. But the visual images wouldn't form in his mind's eye. He knew he was supposed to beat Anthony to an inch of his life, but he didn't know if he could. Even if he wanted to.

Instead, he thought about Frank. Frank who never gave up the hunt, even with his own life caving in. Big brother Frank, the kindest, most generous man alive. And he thought about Gail, who had not betrayed him, who was now carrying a baby for him and waiting.

And, of course, he thought mostly of Zoe, his little girl, his reason for living, suddenly there in his life again. In a life the way it used to be. Life with a real past, present, and future, instead of life with a make-believe history.

Life as a man.

He felt no real anger. No, he wanted to celebrate.

But now, as the plane made its final descent into LAX and the stewardess awakened Carmine and Mike to put their seats upright, Kevin looked out at the smoke and flames of the city. Somewhere in the middle of that mayhem is my little girl, he thought. He had to get her out, get her to safety, get her home.

And although he had run through flames and smoke most of his adult life, as he looked down at the billowing smog, he felt an inexplicable premonition of doom. And it brought on the only too familiar and acrid taste of fear.

But he could not get the image of young Zoe's face out of his head.

Anthony Scala lifted himself out of the swimming pool at five minutes to four in the afternoon. The winds were twisting through the mountains now, but the civil defense reports on the radio said their area was safe, not to panic, to hold their ground, not to join the hysterical exodus. Fire lines had been drawn to protect them.

He dried himself with a towel. Polly lay on her belly sunning her back, her bikini top unfastened to tan the white lines, her butt cheeks split by the thong bathing suit. Anthony had earlier applied heavy layers of sunblock to the scarred areas of her arms that had been burned in the Halloween fire. Putting the lotion on her had gotten him excited but she wasn't in the mood, so he'd jumped in the pool.

Now he dried his hair briskly as he looked up at the smoky sky and saw that the winds were blowing inland, giving him a sense of security.

Zoe was inside sleeping, so Anthony drizzled cool water on Polly's back to make her bolt up straight, revealing her bare breasts, the tops of which were scarred with burns. The scars had ended her modeling career but did not diminish her beauty in Anthony's eyes. Or Kevin's, he thought. Poor Kevin, who always had the best-looking broads. . . .

"Arsehole," Polly snapped at Anthony as she sat up and fastened her suit top.

"Leave it off," Anthony said. "We're alone. You never let me see your breasts."

"A million wankers in those helicopters," she said, self-consciously. "They've probably been taking aerial shots of my bum as it is."

"Can't say I blame them."

"I wish I could charge them," she said. "We could use the money."

Anthony sighed. "Again with the money. The project will get started next week."

"It better," Polly said. "It took all my persuasion to get Daddy to secure one last fucking letter of credit."

"Morton knows I won't start without an advance."

"I still think you should have made copies of the Q-Twenty-one-hundred formula notes."

"No," Anthony said. "The only existing notes are in the basement safe, right here, eighteen inches below the floor of the house, surrounded by concrete. Without them there's no project. I don't want any Xeroxes. This way without me—us—the project is dead."

"A safe deposit box would have been safer. And cheaper. Installing that safe cost five thousand alone."

"I feel safer sleeping in the same house with them at night. If they go missing, it will be over my dead body."

Polly walked to Anthony and put her arms around his neck, boosted herself on tiptoes, darted her tongue into his mouth. He put one hand on her breast and reached around with the other and grabbed her by the bare behind.

"And mine?" she purred.

"Yours they would kill for."

"Do you really want to put on a show for the helicopter boys?" she asked.

"Why not?" Anthony said, his hair already dry in the hot wind.

Polly stepped back and threw her hands over her head and tossed her hair in the wind in a model's pose. Then she slid her bathing suit bottom off and turned and bent over at the waist and grabbed her ankles and stared at Anthony through her parted legs.

A helicopter circled twice and hovered, as Polly stood and walked dramatically to Anthony and bent and peeled off his bathing suit.

"For the boys upstairs," she said.

Polly lay back on the lounge chair, pulling Anthony on top of her, spreading her legs to take him.

As he mounted her, she looked up and over his shoulder and saw the first ball of fire explode across the mountaintop like an orange asterisk.

"Jesus Christ!" she shouted, digging her nails into Anthony and pushing him off. The helicopter groaned loudly and made a lurching sweep away from the flame ball.

"I heard it but I didn't see it," Anthony shouted, leaping up, his back scratched blood-raw by Polly's painted nails. "Should we pack?"

He was trembling. The fireball retreated back to the other side of the mountain, as if a great dragon had sucked it back into its mouth.

Polly stood, staring at the mountaintop, pulling a towel modestly over her nakedness in the presence of the great power she'd witnessed.

"It was only a flash," she said. "Don't panic."

"As soon as we can afford it, I want out of this city too," he said. "It has four seasons: earthquakes, riots, mud slides, fires."

"You forgot the fifth and most important," Polly said. "The one we came for."

"What's that?"

"My favorite season of all," she said. "Money."

Anthony Scala looked at her and narrowed his eyes. Then he listened to the winds that were as unpredictable as Polly Edgeworth Dempsey.

66

Kevin Dempsey rented a Jeep Cherokee, with a car phone, as Frank had suggested. Mike drove, with Kevin up front and Carmine in the back seat. Traffic on the San Diego freeway was at a crawl. Kevin was anxious, trying to figure out how to use the car phone, which kept going dead after he dialed Frank's hotel.

"Thought they had the fucking roads down to a science here," Kevin said. "And this phone is from the school for the deaf."

"Did you press SEND after dialing?" Mike asked.

The radio news was playing, saying the fire was spreading to Calabasas and Sherman Oaks and was threatening the Malibu area. Traffic was bumper-to-bumper leading away from the city.

"Malibu is where Zoe is," Kevin said, punching numbers on the car phone.

"Relax," Mike said. "We'll get there. Press SEND."

Mike beeped his horn at a motorcyclist who was weaving in and out of the heavy but steadily moving city-bound traffic.

"Relax? My kid might be in that fire and you're saying relax," Kevin said. "And I did press SEND. It keeps saying 'Try again.' "

"Get off at the next exit and take Lincoln Boulevard," Carmine said.

Kevin turned in his seat and looked at Carmine. "What do you know about LA?"

"I'm older than you," Carmine said. "I was stationed in San Diego in the navy. We used to come up here on weekends. I know Lincoln Boulevard goes to Santa Monica."

Kevin continued to punch digits on the car phone. A fender bender had brought outbound traffic to a total standstill, and the rubberneckers in Mike's lane slowed to gape.

"The city is burning to the ground and rubberneckers stop to stare at a fucking fender bender," Mike said.

"Get off at the next exit," Carmine shouted.

Kevin was still toying with the phone. "The power lines must be overloaded," Kevin said. He tried dialing Frank's hotel again but to no avail.

Mike took the exit and headed for Lincoln Boulevard. All at once the winds started blowing past them on the surface streets: hot, suffocating, loud, smoky. Kevin looked over his shoulder at Carmine. The two firemen exchanged knowing stares.

"You could broil cattle in this, Kev," Carmine said. "Reminds me of the liquid petroleum gas tanks fire that night in Queens."

"Or the Domino sugar factory fire on the Brooklyn docks," Kevin said.

"Christ," Carmine said, their mood no longer comic. "The winds are spreading these fires and then the fires are heating the winds."

"Just how bad is that?" Mike asked.

"Perfect conditions for hell on earth," Kevin said.

"Let's get the baby and get the fuck out of this town," Carmine said.

In the hotel room, Sarah watched Frank check his watch again and continue pacing. Kevin was late. The television was saying Pacific Coast Highway was beginning to crowd with evacuees, and police, fire, and other rescue workers were trying to remove citizens from the threatened hills. Fire officials were saying arsonists were lighting blazes in the hills surrounding Malibu and the fickle Santa Ana winds were expected to reach sixty miles an hour.

"I better get up there," Frank said. "If Polly and Zoe and Anthony evacuate, I can follow them."

"Is this another ploy to dump me?"

"No," Frank said. "But I gave Kevin and Mike this hotel number. When they call, you call me on the car phone and I can keep you apprised of what's up."

Frank Dempsey held out his hand for the car keys. Sarah reached into her jeans for them and then looked into his yellow eyes. She saw a sweet bliss lost in the irises. Frank Dempsey showed no fear, not for himself, not for the situation.

Sarah handed him the keys, and he lifted her off her feet and sat her on top of the bureau. Sarah was surprised at his strength. She kept looking in his eyes.

"I want you to know that, no matter what happens, you have made me a very happy and complete man," Frank said.

"Frank, don't—"

He put his finger to her lips.

"This is not a death rattle or a farewell speech because I'm not ready to die just yet," he said. "But I want you to know that I love you. Now I gotta go help get my brother's kid back safe and sound. Later we can talk more about us, okay?"

Sarah shook her head but said nothing, afraid of getting sloppy, which she knew Frank would hate.

Frank kissed her forehead but she pulled his face to hers and kissed his lips again and then he walked to the front door and left.

Even with the Santa Ana blowing in through the open windows, Sarah Cross felt suddenly cold.

Anthony threw the last bag into the trunk of the Mercedes. He came around to the driver's door and found Polly behind the wheel.

"I'll drive," she said.

"No, I'll—"

His words were cut off by what sounded like a gas explosion way above them. A huge fist of flame shot out across the sky, like a wildly thrown punch, a blazing streak in its wake. Zoe screamed.

"Mommy, Mommy . . . I want my daddy!"

Anthony didn't argue anymore. He hurried around to the other side of the car and climbed in. The sagebrush on the hills and the deep forest below his back cliffside porch was starting to crackle with flame. In the morning, Anthony had soaked the house and the woods surrounding the house with the garden hose, but the wind had come as if from a giant blow-dryer throughout the day, tossing and parching everything in its path.

"Get us out of here," Anthony said, and Polly spun down the roadway toward Topanga Canyon Road, leading down to the Coast Highway. Zoe sat in the child's seat, squirming against the heavy Velcro straps.

"I want my real daddy," she said. "He's a *fireman.*"

Anthony turned to her as Polly drove from the house. Then he looked at Polly and anxiously ran his fingers through his hair.

Frank Dempsey crawled in heavy traffic along Pacific Coast Highway, trying to reach Topanga Canyon Road. He scrutinized the traffic inching south into the city in the opposite lane, searching for Anthony Scala's silver Mercedes. There were so many Mercedes-Benzes amid the evacuating Saabs, BMWs, Rolls-Royces, Lexuses, and Ferraris that Frank had a hard time keeping his eye on the Bentley bumper in front of him.

Helicopters and planes buzzed overhead and sweaty, animated cops stood at every corner, preventing cars from trying to get up into the sizzling hills and directing those coming down into the growing southbound traffic.

Frank was impressed with the way the cops kept the traffic going at a steady crawl.

Smoke swirled over the southland, even here by the sea. The radio was saying that arsonists had lit at least six more fires in the hills and that butane canisters from barbecues and trailers were exploding, their flames being blow-torched by the Santa Ana winds to devour the sagebrush and trees and parched shrubs of the hillsides. Fires were swallowing trailer parks and million-dollar homes alike.

"It looks like it's only a matter of minutes before a total evacuation of the Malibu, Topanga Canyon, and Sherman Oaks regions is called," said the radio announcer. "Rescue workers are forming firebreak lines in those areas as I speak. Traffic is beginning to build on PCH. Motorists are advised to avoid PCH at all costs. Repeat: Avoid Pacific Coast Highway if you can."

There, Frank thought. There it is! There they are! He recognized the Mercedes because of the child's seat in the back, which made it stand out among the similar cars holding blond young childless couples and lone occupants.

A police officer was waving madly at the woman driver, whom Frank recognized as Polly. She was trying to make a U-turn.

Frank picked up the car phone and called Sarah. He watched the commotion between the cop and Polly as horns honked all around them.

"Have you heard from Kevin?" Frank asked Sarah over the phone.

"He's in the lobby," Sarah said. "I was just going down."

"Come straight to Topanga Canyon Road," Frank said. "This crazy bitch Polly is on the highway trying to go back up to the house when everyone else is coming down."

Sarah gave Frank the car phone number of Kevin's rented Jeep and then said, "Frank?"

"Yes?" he said.

"No heroics, huh?"

"My other child is up there!" Polly screamed.

"Lady, I can't let you up there," the California Highway Patrol cop said.

"Polly, forget it," Anthony urged her.

She whirled on him in a fury. "Forget it?" she said. "That's our baby up there."

Anthony made a stunned face and glanced at Zoe, who sat in the back seat.

"Pepper Mint is up there too," Zoe said, for the fifth time in two minutes.

Polly threw the car in reverse in a fit of rage, banged into another Mercedes behind her, spun the wheel and drilled the car, almost hitting the CHP cop, and roared back up Topanga Canyon Road while a steel snake of cars crawled down. A man wearing Ray-Ban sunglasses in the damaged Mercedes leaped out to examine his car, hurling an obscenity at Polly's fleeing automobile.

"Are you out of your mind altogether?" Anthony shouted.

"I'm not worried about the doll. The formula notes are in the bag with Pepper Mint," Polly shouted. "You were supposed to take it, asshole. Our future is in that bag with the kid's doll."

"I don't remember you giving the bag to me," Anthony snapped back. "And the formula isn't worth dying for. And I'm not an asshole."

"It isn't worth living without those notes," she said. "It's all I have."

"All *you* have?"

"They'll burn to a crisp, and bang goes the Q-Twenty-one-hundred project up in smoke," she said. "What do I do then, go back to bloody England? Become a hooker? Ask Kevin for alimony? Go on the dole while you scrounge for a new practicc? You don't even have money for fucking office furniture."

"I want Pepper Mint," Zoe said. "Daddy can save Mint from the fire because he's a fireman."

Anthony turned to Zoe, who sat fretting, her eyes reflecting the flaring foliage as Polly climbed the hill. And as they drove higher, Anthony could see flames from the mountaintop reflected in Zoe's eyes.

Polly turned into the roadway leading up to the house, which was not yet threatened with fire.

"You panic too soon," Polly said, leaping out and unstrapping Zoe.

"Why don't you leave her here?"

"The gas tank in the car is a time bomb if anything happens," Polly said, leading Zoe from the car. "Where did you leave the bag?"

"I don't know," Anthony said. "I thought you had it."

"Christ almighty," Polly said.

All three entered the house. Anthony went into the kitchen while Polly searched the living room.

Zoe climbed the stairs to the second floor.

67

Kevin Dempsey had never seen anything like Pacific Coast Highway. Before him was a scene reminiscent of an old Japanese horror movie, where the citizens flee the city from the wrath of some giant monster.

On foot in front of them, weaving through the vehicular traffic, came platoons of seaside residents. Grown men with gray ponytails carted armloads of movie scripts; young people with rock-and-roll T-shirts roller-bladed along, carrying stacks of rope-bound CDs; musicians lugged guitars and amps, and one tall skinny guy pushed a dolly lashed with a full rock-band drum set; children carried birds in cages and men lurched along with sloshing fish tanks. Women cradled small lapdogs and pedigreed cats; men walked pigs on leashes, and a toothless man led two goats on a rope; a balding fat guy in boxer-style swim trunks clung to an Oscar, clutching the coveted golden statuette to his sagging breasts for dear life; a few elderly people were pushed in wheelchairs; and two topless women sold ice cream from push bikes. Radios blared news accounts of the firestorm, and rock and heavy metal and rap music exploded from honking cars. Helicopters roared overhead and planes sped into the mountains, dropping red streams of fire retardant. Sirens pierced the dying day and thousands of headlights ignited.

The hot wind kept shifting and howling, and Kevin saw cars coming down from the firebreak at Old Malibu Road. He noticed three cars in a row with their colored plastic turn-signal caps melted into yellow and red and orange stalactites, baring the bulbs underneath.

"Carmine," Kevin said, pointing to that illustration of the unseen fire's intensity.

"I see it, Kev," Carmine said. "It's some fuckin' clambake, all right."

"If Zoe's up there, we don't have a lot of time to get her out," Kevin said.

"Just one more stoplight, we need to make a right," Sarah said, sitting next to Carmine in the back. "But they won't let us up."

" 'Let' has nothing to do with it," Mike said. "These cops are gonna try to stop us, but they don't have time to chase anyone."

The phone rang.

Frank sat on Topanga Canyon Road looking from his car into the roadway leading to Polly and Anthony's rented house. He saw flames shooting up from a stand of trees a hundred feet below the cliff porch that rested on stilts at the rear of the house. The fire had not yet touched the knotty pine of the home, but Frank held the phone he'd just dialed, watching firefighters in shiny white space suits battling blazes on different ridges all around him. They looked like astronauts invading some hostile fiery asteroid as they wielded streaming hoses like weapons against alien enemies.

Bulldozers flattened a line of trees in the distance, and teenage inmates from a nearby reform school were digging a firebreak near Old Malibu Road.

As the phone rang, Frank saw a streak of red fire retardant stain the heavens to his left, heard it cascading down onto the sagebrush and the thick shrubs that had flourished in the spring rains and turned to parchment in the Santa Ana winds of fall.

Way off in the distance, as the first rumor of twilight came, Frank saw the wild winds fan brilliant orange flames through the giant palms surrounding a sprawling research laboratory. The fire slashed across the hillside behind the lab buildings like paint from an angry artist's brush.

Frank then saw a tree behind and above Polly's rented home *poof!* into flame, the crackling of the blazing papery leaves here and gone in a flash.

Frank heard Kevin's voice finally answer the phone.

"Kevin," Frank said into the car phone, "get up here no matter what. Now."

★ ★ ★

"Where the fuck are they?" Polly shouted.

"Forget the goddam papers," Anthony shouted, sweat leaking from his spongy face. "Where is Zoe?"

Polly spun, looked in the living room, the kitchen, the dining room. "Zoe," she called, as smoke curled around the windows of the house. "Zoe, where are you, honey?"

"Zoe! *Zoooo-eeee!*" Anthony was in a panic.

"Zoe, baby," Polly said, as she climbed the stairs to the bedrooms. "Come to Mommy."

Frank Dempsey could wait no longer. Night would soon own the hills and he saw the first big flaming tree splinter into giant embers, the largest section lurching toward the rented wood-frame house. A glowing section of branch landed on the roof, like a groping neon hand. Frank saw an instant puff of flame dance on a smoldering roof shingle.

He got out of his car and felt the heat, immense and loud and disorienting. The winds blew in circles and whistled through the trees and wailed from the valley below, driving into the ravine behind the house, where they fed the fire and pushed the flames upward in a shower of sparks. Hundreds of sirens screeched and the roar of planes and helicopter engines echoed from the sky.

Frank Dempsey walked briskly toward the side of the house. Oddly at peace, he picked up the outdoor garden hose, turned on a spigot, and began to soak the flames on the roof of the house.

Kevin Dempsey saw a tree limb fall across the rear of the roof of the wooden house that was surrounded by advancing fire. Mike pulled the Jeep to a lurching halt on Old Topanga Road outside the front gates, then spun it into a U-turn, facing downhill, for a quick escape. He had almost run a California Highway patrolman over with his Jeep rushing up past a barricade.

Carmine and Kevin and Mike leaped from the Cherokee, followed by Sarah.

"How many inside?" Carmine yelled to Frank, who was spraying the house with the garden hose.

"Just the three of them, I think," Frank said, watching Kevin drift by him, oblivious to everything but the fire.

Mike and Frank exchanged warm nods and watched Kevin drift across the front lawn, trancelike, his eyes widening as he examined the doomed house.

Zoe is inside, Kevin thought. You must go in and get her. He felt the fear rising from the void inside. The high white siren started to build in his inner ear and then died just as quickly as it began. There was no room for fear here, he told himself. All the steps you have taken in your life lead to here. Inside, your child is in danger. You must get her out. Nothing else matters. The past is finished. Tomorrow might never come. Forget the betrayal of Polly and Anthony. Get your kid and get her now. You are Kevin Dempsey. You are Zoe's father.

He saw flames hopscotching across the roof shingles and rippling up the edges of the window frames and the posts of the front porch.

And he started to run, directly into the house.

Kevin Dempsey felt absolutely no fear.

68

"Zooo-eeeee!" came the shouts of Polly Edgeworth Dempsey as she searched the upstairs master bedroom.

"Polly," shouted Anthony. "I think you better come down here."

Polly hurried to the stairs. "Did you find her?"

She was halfway down when she saw Kevin Dempsey standing just inside the splintered front door. She swallowed and glanced instantly at Anthony, who looked as if he was coming unhinged, eyes popping, hands dancing, shoulders rolling, tongue licking his dry lips.

"Where is my baby?" Kevin said.

Anthony shook his head, fluttered his hands, his face a decal of sweaty panic, his eyes darting toward the top of the stairs. Polly began to rattle, shaking her fist in anger at Kevin.

"She's *my* baby," Polly said. "Stay away from her."

"Shut up, Polly," Anthony said. "Do as I say. I'm in control here."

Kevin hurried toward the stairs, and Polly held up her hands as if to defend herself. Anthony trailed after Kevin.

"You always had everything, Kevin," Anthony said, grabbing Kevin firmly by the arm. Kevin turned to him with incredulous eyes. "I had nothing."

Anthony began to recite as if from a prepared script.

"You had everything," Anthony continued. "You had the girls, you had the trophies, you had the glory—"

Kevin yanked his arm free from Anthony's grip. "You . . . you don't even exist," Kevin whispered, turning to head back upstairs. Then he felt the punch, hitting him loud and hot in the left ear, a lifetime of betrayal in the shrill ringing. Kevin spun and caught Anthony's second punch in midair and squeezed the doctor's smaller fist in his big hand.

"Oh, I exist all right," Anthony said. "Ever since I made those phone calls. About Bronsky and Lucy. I crawled in your brain and I poisoned you. Made you lose your scholarship. Lose the game. Lose your girl. And I wound up in med school while you went civil service. Where you belonged. Beneath me. So, Kev, I exist all right."

Anthony smiled as Kevin stared into his old friend's eyes, saw all the buried jealousies, slights, inadequacies.

"I told you about Bronsky and Lucy, even though it wasn't true. That way, I took her away from you even if I never had her myself. And now I've taken your wife, your wife and your precious kid. Took them from the big shot, Kevin Fucking Dempsey."

Kevin squeezed Anthony's hand tighter, felt the bones crush together like soft wet sticks, and heard him yelp in pain as fire now licked up one of the four support columns of the living room.

"Where's Zoe?" Kevin asked again, then turned to face Polly.

The heat in the house was reaching flash point. "Kev, this whole place is gonna go right up!" Carmine shouted. "Get the kid and get the fuck *out!*"

Kevin was distracted by Carmine and felt a second punch from Anthony thud against his temple.

"I fucked her. I made your wife face China and I fucked her and fucked her and fucked her until it was like fucking *you,*" Anthony said, with a taunting cackle. "Then I stole your precious kid. I outdid you, Kev. Me, Anthony Scala, I scored. Kevin Dempsey fumbles again. I got the beautiful broad *and* the baby. Because I am a better man than you—"

Kevin unleashed a right hand that caught his old friend between the right cheekbone and the jaw, sending him reeling back, slamming him against the support column that lapped with flame. The pillar shifted in a hissing shower of sparks.

Suddenly a great thundering crash hit the high section of the A-frame roof covering the big living room and kitchen area. The other half of the house was split level, with the stairs leading to the bedrooms.

The whole house seemed to shift five feet toward the stilted cliffside, where the balcony overlooked the sheer bluff drop.

A hole opened in the A-frame roof and flames from the fallen tree exploded in the living room with a crash of blinding, sparkling light. Now several flaming roof beams fell into the living room.

Anthony was hit across the temple with a falling roof timber as Polly raced up the stairs, clawing at the steps, gasping for air, her hair a mop of soot and ash.

Mike was thrown against the dining room wall in a bleating thud and sank, momentarily winded, to the floor.

The house pulsated, like a living creature in a death rattle. Chandeliers shook and molding slid from the walls in flame. Paintings on the walls ignited from the heat. Flames devoured the red velvet window drapes from bottom to top in a wolfish gobble. The leather couches burst into fire, the hide peeling back in ashen coils.

Carmine saw three more roof beams fall on top of Anthony, pinning him in the middle of the burning room. He tried to lift the fallen timbers from Anthony's body but it was more than one man could do. He checked for a pulse under Anthony's watch band. There wasn't one. He began mouth-to-mouth resuscitation.

Kevin crashed against the burning banister, as the house began to lick with a thousand forked tongues of fire. He felt the house shift another foot toward the cliffside. Kevin yelled to Carmine, trying to revive the lifeless Anthony.

"Carm, fuck him, find Mike and Zoe."

Carmine left Anthony in the middle of the floor. He ran inside and checked on Mike, who sat up in a half daze. Carmine helped him to his feet.

Frank entered the front door with a hankie over his face, forcefully shoving Sarah outside, sending her tumbling down the stoop. She tried to get back up but fell again on a badly twisted knee.

"You dumb bastard, Frank."

Frank slammed the door shut.

Kevin raced up the stairs after Polly, with the fire climbing one step at a time behind him as if in a deadly game of chase. At the top of the stairs, Polly turned to Kevin, holding up her hands.

"You gonna beat me to death? That it? Kill our baby's mommy?" Polly ranted, defying him.

"Where's Zoe?"

Polly backed away from Kevin, who was oblivious to the fire that ran around his feet. Polly fell and Kevin bent and picked her up and looked her in the eyes. Then he tossed her back down again and kicked open the master bedroom door.

"Zoe deserved better," Polly shrieked. "I deserve better!"

"Zoe!" Kevin shouted, stepping away from Polly, jerking open a closet door. He searched amid the clothes and boxes. He looked under the bed and in the wicker chest at the foot of the bed.

"Zoe!" Kevin shouted again. "Zoooo-eeeee! It's Daddy!"

Kevin crawled under the smoke, out the bedroom door.

"She ain't down here, Kev!" Carmine shouted from downstairs.

Then Kevin Dempsey heard his daughter's voice. Sweet and thin and beautiful.

"Daddy!" Zoe shouted. "Daddy!"

Kevin ran to the child's bedroom door, but it was locked.

He kicked it open.

Polly was on the windowsill of the opened window, half in, half out, looking determined and demented. Holding Zoe and the canvas bag, the bag containing the Q-2100 research notes and the Pepper Face Doll.

"Give me my baby," Kevin said, his arms outstretched. Disney characters melted from the wallpaper. Mickey Mouse sheets danced with flame.

"No," Polly said. "I'm leaving here with her. Alone."

"Daddy! *Daddy,"* Zoe said. "Daddy's here, Mommy."

"You are not getting her," Polly said.

"Give me my baby," Kevin said, feinting a move toward her.

Polly wrapped both arms around Zoe, leaned backward like a parachutist exiting a plane, and fell from the window.

Kevin's heart pounded as he heard Zoe's trailing voice, "Da-a-a-addy!" He ran for the stairs.

Downstairs in the living room, Frank looked suddenly through the glass porch door as Polly landed heavily on the wooden deck. Zoe was motionless in Polly's arms. The porch joints squealed from the impact and sagged under the weight of Polly and the child.

Much of the railing was already in flames. Frank hurried to the sliding door and saw that the porch was dangling now above the hundred-foot drop from the cliff to the scorching forest.

Zoe was unconscious but her eyelids fluttered with life.

Beyond the drop, the hills were smoking, spotted with helicopter searchlights and a hundred orange pockets of flame and dozens of squares and triangles and circles of roaring wildfire.

It looks like Halloween in hell, Frank thought.

Polly clutched Zoe and the canvas bag with the Pepper Face Doll and the Q-2100 research notes, as she lay near the edge of the creaking porch.

"Frank, I have Zoe," Polly said weakly, when she saw Frank appear at the glass door leading to the porch.

Frank saw the deck swaying and creaking above the flaming void.

"Give her to me, Polly," Frank said.

"No, get us both inside, Frank," she said.

"Just hold on," Frank said, and he took a step onto the porch. Suddenly, a panting Kevin was behind Frank and about to step out.

"No!" Frank shouted. "No more weight. It'll go."

Kevin grabbed Frank's left hand as Frank reached his right hand out toward the precariously positioned Polly. Mike and Carmine grabbed Kevin around the waist.

As Frank took a long, gentle step onto the wooden porch, the sound of the joists creaking underfoot was louder in his ears than all the sirens and helicopters and winds and flames in the night.

"Frank, let me go out there!" Kevin shouted.

"No!" Polly shouted. "Not Kevin."

Kevin stood braced against the doorframe, grasping Frank's hand as he inched closer to Zoe, out on the swaying porch. He could see flames coming from the trees covering the cliff below.

Kevin clutched Frank's left hand as Frank reached toward Polly with his right hand. Mike and Carmine held on to Kevin.

"Give me the baby," Frank said to Polly.

"Not unless you save me too," Polly said, her voice a cold negotiation.

"Okay," Frank said. "But if you're any kind of mother, give me the baby first so I can hand her in."

"Give me your foot and I'll give you the baby," Polly said.

Kevin Dempsey felt his grip on Frank moisten and squeezed tighter.

Frank held out his foot to Polly. She looped the straps of her canvas bag securely over Frank's foot and up around the ankle. Polly now held onto the bag with her left hand for her life. And with her right hand she offered the limp Zoe to Frank.

Frank looked at the handle of the bag around his ankle and the determination in Polly's wild eyes and suddenly knew the final score.

Frank grabbed Zoe by the jacket front and dragged her toward him and then took a deep breath as the porch made an urgent tilt downward.

"If I go, you go, Frank!" Polly shouted.

Kevin squeezed Frank's hand tighter, every muscle in his body contracting. Mike and Carmine held Kevin by the waist as the weight began to drag them all.

After several deep breaths, Frank finally managed to lift Zoe to his chest, thankful to Sarah for the last gasp of health that gave him the strength. He held her tightly, taking deep breaths. Kevin looked into the face of his little girl, angelic in unconsciousness. Then he looked at Frank, sweaty, sooty, yellow.

Polly held on to Frank's ankle with the loops of the canvas bag. The wooden railing gave way and Polly started to slant off the ledge of the creaking, flaming porch. Flames rose higher and more intensely from the inferno below. Kevin's grip on Frank was beginning to slip.

Kevin stared frantically at his big brother, his eyes wide and shattered.

"Frank!" he shouted.

"Lookin' good, kid," Frank said with a custard-colored wink. He tried to show no fear but his eyes skitted back and forth from Kevin to Mike, knowing it would be the last he ever saw of his brothers.

"Please don't let me die," Polly screamed, finally realizing the end was near.

"Ready or not, lady," Frank said.

Polly twisted the bag handle tighter in her hands, her eyes popping in terror.

"Frank, Frank, please hold on," Kevin shouted as he felt himself being dragged into the fall.

"Be seein' you guys," Frank said.

And with all that was left in him, Frank Dempsey swung little Zoe toward Kevin, slamming her firmly to his chest. Kevin grabbed Zoe with his free hand but the impact broke his hold on Frank and sent him reeling into the dubious safety of the living room floor. Carmine and Mike fell to the floor around him.

The recoil of the action sent Frank toward the abyss. Polly clutched the bag that was looped to Frank's ankle as the whole flaming porch disappeared.

The only sound was the trailing scream of Polly Edgeworth Dempsey.

On the lawn, Sarah Cross saw three figures staggering through the smoke from the roaring inferno. In the brilliant light she saw that none of them was Frank.

Then she heard a child crying, "Daddy!"

Epilogue

The last of the guests were finally gone.

Gail Levy Dempsey was upstairs breast-feeding Francis Xavier Dempsey II, after the infant had been manhandled by Margie and Sarah and Mike's wife Bridie and Carmine and the rest of the guests at the christening party.

Zoe was sleeping in her upstairs bedroom.

Kevin walked through the new house on Langston Place alone, picking up discarded beer bottles and soda cups and collecting dirty plates stained with Italian food.

He was feeling good. His papers had been approved for disability retirement, which meant he could go back to school, write stories, and spend plenty of time with his family. Mike was back at work, having lost just a month's pay. Sarah had her health club in Manhattan. She had told the Dempsey family the truth about Big Paulie and Botero and how Frank got Pinebox to sort everything out, even giving her the hundred thousand dollars Polly had borrowed, out of the stolen money, which had been buried all along with Big Paulie in the family mausoleum in Greenwood Cemetery.

There wasn't much to say about Frank Dempsey except that at least he died in love. Kevin knew that meant he died happy. If there was a heaven, Frank had a stool by the Pearly Gates.

Now Kevin heard screaming coming from upstairs and a loud wail from the back yard. Suddenly Gail was thundering down the stairs, as the sounds of the baby shrieking in his crib pierced the quiet house. The noise awakened Zoe, who came scurrying down the stairs in her pajamas.

This is what I was born for, Kevin thought. To raise my family, loud and nuts, here in this house.

Kevin grinned when he saw Gail run into the kitchen, grab a broom like a club, and reach for the backyard door. He caught her in his arms.

"What the hell's going on?"

"In the yard, the cat—"

Gail couldn't get the words out fast enough so Kevin looked through the window. There in the yard, wailing for the sky, was the one-eyed orange cat he called the Pirate, in the middle of romancing Mimi, Gail's pet parlor cat.

Zoe ran into the kitchen, having unlaced her foot brace herself, wiping sleep from her eyes, startled by the noise, her arms outstretched. Kevin scooped his daughter into his arms and placed the broom against the refrigerator and put his free arm around Gail's waist.

"You have to stop him!" Gail shouted, pointing at the Pirate, who was keeping an appointment with fate.

"Gail," Kevin said, carrying Zoe in one arm and leading his wife to the stairs with the other, as little Frank screamed from upstairs. "Sometimes, you just got to let a man be."